The Irregular at Magic High School

3

Tsutomu Sato

Illustration **Kana Ishida**

Illustration assistants **Jimmy Stone, Yasuko Suenaga**

Design **BEE-PEE**

Mayumi Saegusa

Magic High School's student council president. The eldest daughter of the Saegusa family, one of the Ten Master Clans. Petite but glamorous. Said to be a once-in-a-decade genius of ranged precision magic. Has an impish personality.

"Then let's head for the Nine School Competition stadium. Let's all have fun and win!"

"All of First High's official staff is here."

Suzune Ichihara

Magic High School's student council treasurer. More suitable to be called a "beauty" than a "pretty girl." Has a composed appearance. Her nickname is Rin, but only Mayumi calls her that.

"Does
this
suit me
well?"

Miyuki Shiba

The younger sister of the Shiba siblings.
Part of Class 1-A. An elite who entered
Magic High School as the top student. A
Course 1 student, called a "Bloom," whose
specialty is cooling magic. Her lovable only
flaw is a severe case of a brother complex.

"Can I have a peek?"

"Shizuku, help me!"

"It's fine. You have a big chest."

The Nine School Competition.

Officially known as the National Magic High School Goodwill Magic Competition Tournament.

Every year, excellent magic high school students gather here from around the nation and stake their youthful pride on ever-expanding stories of glory and failure.

The biggest competition for magic high schools, which draws not only those related to the magical arts but also a large turnout of spectators.

And this year, once again, the curtains on the competition are about to rise.

The Ten Master Clans

A group of the most powerful magicians in Japan.

In exchange for renouncing their public rights, they maintain a near-sacred presence behind the government, wielding power and influence from the shadows. The ten families in this group are chosen from twenty-eight families once every four years at the Ten Master Clans Selection Conference. Each family name contains a kanji character that corresponds with a number from one to ten. They are: (families that incorporate the number 1) the Ichijou, the Ichinokura, the Isshiki; (number 2) the Futatsugi, the Nikaidou, the Nihei; (3) the Mitsuya, the Mikazuki; (4) the Yotsuba; (5) the Itsuwa, the Gotou, the Itsumi; (6) the Mutsuzuka, the Rokkaku, the Rokugou, the Roppongi; (7) the Saegusa, the Shippou, the Tanabata, the Nanase; (8) the Yatsushiro, the Hassaku, the Hachiman; (9) the Kudou, the Kuki, the Kuzumi; (10) the Juumonji, and the Tooyama.

The eighteen families not selected are referred to as the Eighteen Support Clans, and they take up a support position for the Ten. The Ten Master Clans currently consist of the Ichijou, the Futatsugi, the Mitsuya, the Yotsuba, the Itsuwa, the Mutsuzuka, the Saegusa, the Yatsushiro, the Kudou, and the Juumonji. These names coincidentally use the numbers one through ten once each, but this is the first time such a thing has occurred since the inception of the Ten Master Clans; until now, there had always been two or three multiples and absences.

The Numbers

Just as the surnames of the Ten Master Clans all include a kanji character corresponding with a number from one through ten, the surnames of the prominent members of the Hundred Families also use numbers, starting from eleven and higher, such as the Chiyoda (1,000), the Isori (50), and the Chiba (1,000). How high or low the number is doesn't express strength or weakness, while the presence or absence of a number in a magician's surname is a common way to gauge their latent power, by understanding their bloodline's history. Families of magicians with numbers in their surnames are referred to on the whole—that is, the Ten Master Clans and the Hundred Families—as the Numbers.

The Extras

The Extras—also called the Extra Numbers—are families that had their "numbers" revoked from their names. Long ago, when magicians were treated as weapons and experimental samples, "exemplary" magicians would be granted a number in their name for their achievements. But if they ever failed or could not continue to deliver results to match their elevated status, they would be stripped of their number and stamped with the label of "Extra." Nowadays, it is prohibited to use the term "Extras" or "Extra Numbers" publicly in this way. Discriminatory behavior based on the fact that a family is one of the Extras is seen as a grave crime in the magic community.

The
Irregular at
Magic High
School

The Irregular at Magic High School

NINE SCHOOL COMPETITION
PART I

3

Tsutomu Sato

Illustration Kana Ishida

YEN ON
NEW YORK

THE IRREGULAR AT MAGIC HIGH SCHOOL
TSUTOMU SATO

Translation by Andrew Prowse
Cover art by Kana Ishida

© TSUTOMU SATO 2011
All rights reserved.
Edited by ASCII MEDIA WORKS
First published in Japan in 2011 by KADOKAWA CORPORATION,Tokyo.
English translation rights arranged with KADOKAWA CORPORATION, Tokyo, through Tuttle-Mori Agency, Inc., Tokyo.

English translation © 2016 by Yen Press, LLC

Yen On
1290 Avenue of the Americas
New York, NY 10104

Visit us at yenpress.com
facebook.com/yenpress
twitter.com/yenpress
yenpress.tumblr.com
instagram.com/yenpress

First Yen On Edition: December 2016

Yen On is an imprint of Yen Press, LLC.
The Yen On name and logo are trademarks of Yen Press, LLC.

Library of Congress Cataloging-in-Publication Data

Names: Satou, Tsutomu, author. | Ishida, Kana, illustrator. | Prowse, Andrew (Andrew R.), translator.
Title: The irregular at magic high school. Volume 3, Nine school competition, part I / Tsutomu Satou ; illustration, Kana Ishida ; translation by Andrew Prowse.
Other titles: Mahōka kōkō no rettosei. English
Description: New York, NY : Yen On, 2016.
Identifiers: LCCN 2016043293 | ISBN 9780316390309 (paperback)
Subjects: | CYAC: Magic—Fiction. | High schools—Fiction. | Schools--Fiction. | Science fiction. | Japan—Fiction.
Classification: LCC PZ7.1.S265 Iu 2016 | DDC [Fic]—dc23
LC record available at https://lccn.loc.gov/2016043293

ISBN: 978-0-316-39030-9

10 9 8 7 6 5 4 3 2 1

LSC-C

Printed in the United States of America

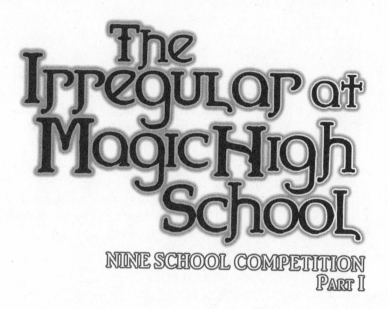

The Irregular at MagicHigh School

NINE SCHOOL COMPETITION
PART I

An irregular older brother with a certain flaw.
An honor roll younger sister who is perfectly flawless.

When the two siblings enrolled in Magic High School,
a dramatic life unfolded—

Character

Tatsuya Shiba

Class 1-E. One of the Course 2 (irregular) students, who are mockingly called Weeds.

Miyuki Shiba

Class 1-A.
Tatsuya's younger sister; enrolled as the top student. Specializes in freezing magic.

Leonhard Saijou

Class 1-E.
Tatsuya's classmate.
Specializes in hardening magic.

Erika Chiba

Class 1-E.
Tatsuya's classmate.
Specializes in *kenjutsu*.

Mizuki Shibata

Class 1-E.
Tatsuya's classmate.
Has pushion radiation sensitivity.

Mikihiko Yoshida

Class 1-E. Tatsuya's classmate. From a famous family that uses ancient magic.

Honoka Mitsui

Class 1-A. Miyuki's classmate. Specializes in light-wave vibration magic.

Shizuku Kitayama

Class 1-A. Miyuki's classmate. Specializes in vibration and acceleration magic.

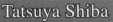

Shun Morisaki
Class 1-A. Miyuki's classmate. Specializes in CAD quick draw.

Subaru Satomi
Class 1-D. Frequently mistaken for a pretty boy.

Eimi Akechi
Class 1-B. A quarter-blood. Full name is Amelia Eimi Akechi Goldie.

Mayumi Saegusa
A senior. Student council president.

Azusa Nakajou
A junior. Student council secretary.

Suzune Ichihara
A senior. Student council accountant.

Hanzou Gyoubu-Shoujou Hattori
A junior. Student council vice president.

Mari Watanabe
A senior. Chairwoman of the disciplinary committee.

Koutarou Tatsumi
A senior. Member of the disciplinary committee.

Katsuto Juumonji
A senior. Head of the club committee, the unified organization overseeing all club activities.

Midori Sawaki
A junior. Member of the disciplinary committee.

Kei Isori
A junior. Top grades in his class in magical theory. Engaged to Kanon Chiyoda.

Kanon Chiyoda
A junior. An energetic, vivid girl. Engaged to Kei Isori.

Takeaki Kirihara

A junior. Member of the *kenjutsu* club. Junior High Kanto *kenjutsu* tournament champion.

Sayaka Mibu

A junior. Member of the kendo club. Placed second in the nation at the girls' junior high kendo tournament.

Yakumo Kokonoe

A user of an ancient magic called *ninjutsu*. Tatsuya's martial arts master.

Haruka Ono

A general counselor of Class 1-E.

Masaki Ichijou

A freshman at Third High. Participates in the Nine School Competition. Direct heir to the Ichijou family, one of the Ten Master Clans.

Shinkurou Kichijouji

A freshman at Third High. Participates in the Nine School Competition. Also known as Cardinal George.

Retsu Kudou

Renowned as the strongest magician in the world. Given the honorary title of Sage.

Harunobu Kazama

Captain of the 101st Brigade of the Independent Magic Battalion. Ranked major.

Shigeru Sanada

Executive officer of the 101st Brigade of the Independent Magic Battalion. Ranked captain.

Muraji Yanagi

Executive officer of the 101st Brigade of the Independent Magic Battalion. Ranked captain.

Kousuke Yamanaka

Executive officer of the 101st Brigade of the Independent Magic Battalion. Medical major. First-rate healing magician.

Kyouko Fujibayashi

Female officer serving as Kazama's aide. Ranked second lieutenant.

Glossary

Magic High School
A nickname for the high schools affiliated with the National Magic University. There are nine schools throughout the nation. Of them, First High through Third High each adopt a system of Course 1 and Course 2 students to split up its two hundred incoming freshmen.

Blooms, Weeds
Slang terms used at First High to display the gap between Course 1 and Course 2 students. Course 1 student uniforms feature an eight-petaled emblem embroidered on the left breast, but Course 2 student uniforms do not.

CAD (Casting Assistant Device)
A device that simplifies magic casting. Magical programming is recorded within. There are many types and forms, some specialized and others multipurpose.

Course 1 student emblem

Tatsuya Shiba's CAD

Miyuki Shiba's CAD

Four Leaves Technology (FLT)
A domestic CAD manufacturer. Originally more famous for magic engineering products than for finished products, the development of the Silver model has made them much more widely known as a maker of CADs.

Taurus Silver
A genius engineer said to have advanced specialized CAD software by a decade in just a single year.

Eidos (individual information bodies)
Originally a term from Greek philosophy. In modern magic, *eidos* refers to the information bodies accompanying events. They are a record of those events existing in the world, and they can be called the footprints that events leave on the world. The definition of *magic* as it applies to its modern form is that of a technology that alters these events themselves by altering the eidos composing them.

Idea (information body dimension)
Originally a term from Greek philosophy; pronounced "ee-dee-ah." In modern magic, *Idea* refers to the platform upon which eidos are recorded. Magic is primarily a technology that outputs a magic program onto the Idea and rewrites the eidos composing them.

Activation program
The blueprints of magic and the programming that constructs it. Activation programs are stored in a compressed format in CADs. The magician sends a psionic wave into the CAD, which then expands the data and uses it to convert the activation program into a signal, then returns it to the magician.

Psions (thought particles)
Massless particles belonging to the dimension of spirit phenomena. The information particles that record awareness and thought results. Eidos are considered the theoretical basis for modern magic, while activation programs and magic programs are the technology forming its practical basis—these are all bodies of information that are made up of psions.

Pushions (spirit particles)
Massless particles belonging to the dimension of spirit phenomena. Their existence has been confirmed, but their true form and function have yet to be elucidated. In general, magicians are able to only "sense" energized pushions.

The Nine School Competition

Officially dubbed the National Magic High School Goodwill Competitive Magic Tournament. As its name suggests, magic high school students from First High through Ninth High gather from all over the country to compete as groups in heated magical competitions.

There are six events: Speed Shooting, Cloudball, Battle Board, Ice Pillars Break, Mirage Bat, and Monolith Code.
* Monolith Code is a men's event, and Mirage Bat is a women's one.

Each school can enter three people in a single event, and a single person can compete in up to only two events. Teams of athletes generally consist of ten male and ten female students, with twenty athletes for the main events and twenty for the rookie events.

The competition takes place over the course of ten days, and it includes a rookie competition where only freshmen compete (the main competition has no class restriction). The rookie competition is held from day four to day eight.

Victory in the Nine School Competition and rankings are based on the total number of points earned from each event. First place gains fifty points, second gains thirty, and third twenty. For Speed Shooting, Battle Board, and Mirage Bat, fourth place gains ten points. In Cloudball and Ice Pillars Break, there is no fourth through sixth place; the three teams that lose in the third round are granted five points each. The most popular event of the Nine School Competition, Monolith Code, grants one hundred points to the winning team, sixty points to second place, and forty to third place, making it the most heavily weighted event. (Points in the rookie competition are halved and added on to the total scores.)

Date	Category	Events
Day 1 August 3 (W)	Main (All classes)	Speed Shooting: men's and women's qualifiers to finals tournament Battle Board: men's and women's qualifiers
Day 2 August 4 (R)	Main (All classes)	Cloudball: men's and women's qualifiers to finals Ice Pillars Break: men's and women's qualifiers
Day 3 August 5 (F)	Main (All classes)	Battle Board: men's and women's semifinals and finals Ice Pillars Break: men's and women's qualifiers to finals round-robin
Day 4 August 6 (S)	Rookie (Freshman)	Speed Shooting: men's and women's qualifiers to finals tournament Battle Board: men's and women's qualifiers
Day 5 August 7 (S)	Rookie (Freshman)	Cloudball: men's and women's qualifiers to finals Ice Pillars Break: men's and women's qualifiers
Day 6 August 8 (M)	Rookie (Freshman)	Battle Board: men's and women's semifinals and finals Ice Pillars Break: men's and women's qualifiers to finals round-robin
Day 7 August 9 (T)	Rookie (Freshman)	Mirage Bat: women's qualifiers to finals Monolith Code: men's qualifiers round-robin
Day 8 August 10 (W)	Rookie (Freshman)	Monolith Code: men's finals tournament
Day 9 August 11 (R)	Main (All classes)	Mirage Bat: women's qualifiers to finals Monolith Code: men's qualifiers round-robin
Day 10 August 12 (F)	Main (All classes)	Monolith Code: men's finals tournament

Event

Speed Shooting

Sometimes called "quick-draw" by competitors.

Competitors use magic to destroy targets fired into the air, like in skeet shooting. One hundred targets each of red and white are prepared, and competitors try to destroy more of their own color targets than their opponent. During the qualifiers, a single competitor will aim to destroy as many targets as possible within five minutes, and each is scored individually. From the quarterfinals onward, the matches are one-on-one.

Cloudball

Sometimes shortened to "cloud" by competitors.

A compressed-air shooter fires bouncy balls two inches across onto a court inside a transparent box where two players use either a racket or magic to keep as many balls as they can on the opposing player's side. Each set lasts three minutes. An additional ball is fired onto the court every twenty seconds, and in the end, the players chase nine balls around. Girls play three-set matches, while boys play five-set matches.

Event

Battle Board

Sometimes referred to simply as "surfing."

Originally an activity conceptualized for magic training in the navy, competitors ride a flat surfboard-like sheet and make three laps around an artificial waterway two miles in length, utilizing things like acceleration magic to make them go faster. As a rule of Battle Board, directly interfering with another competitor using magic is forbidden. The qualifiers consist of six races of four players each; the semifinals are two races of three players each; third place is decided between the four losers from the semifinals; and the finals is a one-on-one competition.

Ice Pillars Break

Each player stands on a thirteen-foot-tall tower on their own side and aims to knock over or destroy the twelve ice pillars on the opposing side, forty feet square, while defending his or her own twelve ice pillars on his or her own side. Players compete only with distance magic, with no need to use physical means. Because of this, competitors don't have a set uniform; they're free to wear what they want to within the bounds of public decency. As a result, the girls' Ice Pillars Break event is sometimes called the "fashion show" of the Nine School Competition.

Mirage Bat

A women-only event sometimes abbreviated to "mirage" by the competitors.

The players set their eyes on holographic balls projected into the air and use magic to leap up and hit them with sticks. It has the least number of matches of all the events in the competition, but it lasts the longest. Because the players have to continuously use magic to keep leaping into the air throughout the match, some say the event rivals a full marathon in how difficult it is.

In the Nine School Competition, since only girls participate, some call the competitors flitting about in elaborate outfits "faeries."

Monolith Code

A men-only event sometimes abbreviated to "monolith" by the competitors.

On the match field, called a "stage," each three-man team fights using magic to protect their monoliths. Victory is decided either when one team is no longer able to fight or when one team splits the other's monolith in half and transmits a code to it. Direct attacks made against the opposing team that use anything other than magic are strictly forbidden. In order to split a monolith and read the code inside, a player needs to fire a special typeless magic sequence at it. Because of the exciting combat, it is the most popular event in the competition, always resulting in white-hot matches.

ATTACK: MAGIC ONLY!

VS

[0]

Presently, there are nine magic high schools affiliated with the National Magic University across the nation.

First High in Tokyo, Kanto. Second High in Hyogo, Kinki. Third High in Ishikawa, Hokuriku. Fourth High in Shizuoka, Tokai. Fifth high in Miyagi, Tohoku. Sixth High in Shimane, San'in. Seventh High in Koichi, Shikoku. Eighth High in Hokkaido. Ninth High in Kumamoto, Kyushu.

These nine are the only magic high schools in the country. These are not the only nine schools affiliated with the National Magic University, but they *are* the only nine schools to teach magic formally.

In truth, the government wishes to increase the number of magic high schools. It cannot, however, because of an inability to secure more magicians that become teachers.

First High, Second High, and Third High have two hundred freshmen each. The other six have one hundred, bringing the nationwide total to twelve hundred. This is the upper limit on how many new magicians can be supplied to the country each year. This is thought to be roughly equal to the number of boys and girls in the entire population who possess enough magical talent to be useful. That being said, it is also believed that there is a nontrivial chance of discovering late-blooming children with latent magical potential if they were given the appropriate educational opportunities.

The reality, however, is that this country's human resources are strained to the limit just managing these nine magic high schools. Therefore, it has no choice but to train these twelve hundred magic high school students as much as possible and raise the standard of their abilities to satisfy the important and precious manpower needs for trained magicians. With this method, the nation expects a positive feedback loop to resolve the lack of teachers, who can in turn go on to raise a greater number of magicians.

One of the policies created for this purpose is to have the nine magic high schools compete for points and rank in order to strengthen student aspirations. The greatest stage they have for this is the summer's Nine School Competition.

The National Magic High School Goodwill Competitive Magic Tournament.

Every year, excellent magic high school students gather here from around the nation and stake their youthful pride on ever-expanding stories of glory and failure.

It is the biggest event in these students' high school lives, drawing not only government officials and members of the magic community, but also common corporations, huge audiences, and those scouting future magical researchers, sometimes even coming from overseas.

And this year, once again, the curtains on the competition are about to rise.

[1]

2095 AD, mid-July.

The students of the National Magic University Affiliated First High School had just finished with their first semester exams last week; they were now devoting their energy to prepare for summer's Nine School Competition. Tatsuya Shiba, though, found himself unable to go along with the enthusiasm filling the school grounds. Part of it was, certainly, that he had a sober personality. But today, the main reason was that a teacher had called him to the office about his exam scores.

"Tatsuya!"

"Leo... What's wrong? What are you all doing here?"

After Tatsuya was finally released from the student guidance office, his classmates—Leonhard Saijou, Erika Chiba, and Mizuki Shibata—confronted him.

Circumstances dictated that his younger sister, Miyuki, wasn't here; she couldn't get out of her competition preparations and had to go to the student council room without seeing him first.

Still, as though implying they were here in Miyuki's place, her classmates Honoka Mitsui and Shizuku Kitayama were present, both with worried looks.

The guidance office was on the faculty floor; the classrooms for students weren't on the same story nor were they even in the same building. That didn't mean students never came by here, though. Fellow freshmen and upperclassmen alike passed by, giving furtive, scrutinizing, or otherwise nonchalant glances to the group of five in front of Tatsuya.

There was no helping that, either; they stood out.

Of course, that wasn't something limited to just *today*—this was par for the course.

Despite being a Course 2 student, he was chosen to be a disciplinary officer and went on to display exceptional martial aptitude during the new student club recruitment week. Tatsuya had become famous at school.

The fact that he'd also crushed a terrorist group was a secret, but his efforts during that recruitment week alone were more than enough reason for freshmen, as well as upperclassmen, to pay attention to him.

Erika was a positive, beautiful young girl, and ten out of ten people would agree.

Mizuki seemed rather plain—perhaps because she was usually caught between Miyuki and Erika—but she had a mature, refreshing sort of beauty and she was garnering popularity mainly among upperclassmen.

Leo always found himself on the receiving end of Erika's disparaging criticism (although roughly 100 percent of that was simply abusive language), but with his strong German features and his excellent motor skills, he'd earned a place among female students as "a boy they were a little curious about." (To Leo, "pure Japanese" apparently meant having pale skin and dark eyes.)

In addition, Honoka and Shizuku, both of whom were considered to excel in studies even among their fellow Course 1 freshmen, had looks that most would place in the "cute" category. (All said and done, Tatsuya's face and figure were the most average of the bunch.)

With this many people gathered around, Course 1 and Course 2 mingling without regard to the class boundaries, they were bound to draw prying eyes whether they liked it or not.

Even so, Miyuki, the matchless beauty who was not only the top seat upon enrollment and the year's new student representative but also a member of the student council, was absent from the group. That was the only reason they could still tolerate how many looks they were getting.

Of course, *certain people*, including one closer to him, didn't mind the stares at all—this man here, for example.

"What do you mean what's wrong? That's my damn line! Why in the world did they call you down to the guidance office?"

Tatsuya nodded to himself at Leo's response. His friends appeared to have all gathered out of worrying about him. The thought of dodging the issue crossed his mind for a moment, but he thought better of it. He knew it would be dishonest.

"They were interrogating me about my scores on the practical portion of the exam."

Leo narrowed his eyes, displeased at that. "...Interrogate? That doesn't sound very good. What did they ask you?"

"In summary, they thought maybe I didn't try very hard on it."

Erika was the first to get indignant. "What's *that* supposed to mean? You wouldn't get anything out of doing that! What are they, idiots?"

Tatsuya was in complete agreement with the sentiment, so he just gave her a pained grin in reply. If he was doing something unfair to raise his grades, that would be one thing. But what would be the point of actively trying to get fewer points? It was, as she said, an idiotic suspicion.

"But I think I understand how the teachers feel," remarked Shizuku.

"What do you mean?" answered Mizuki, looking at her sideways.

"Tatsuya's grades were really shocking, you know," replied Honoka.

That gave Tatsuya pause. He considered what facial expression that comment warranted—he couldn't puff out his chest with pride, but being modest about it would come off as sarcastic. So he made another wry smile.

At First High—actually, at all magic high schools—periodic exams were separated into a written portion on magical theory and a practical portion.

On the other hand, general subjects like language, math, science, and social studies were usually graded based on just homework assignments. This was a high school to foster magicians, so it was believed to be unnecessary for the students to compete in anything but magic. (Tatsuya and the others knew the difference between magicians and magic engineers, but only because it was the main thing separating their paths in the future. For the rest of society, "magic engineers" just looked like a type of magician. They didn't refer to those that worked on magical engineering but couldn't use magic as "magic engineers.")

The written portion on magical theory included fundamental magic science and magic engineering as requirements. There were then two electives selected from magic geometry, magic linguistics, magic pharmaceutics, and magic architecture, and one additional elective selected from either magic history or magic phylogenetics. This all brought the total to five subjects.

Magical practice looked at one's magical throughput (the speed at which one could construct magic sequences), capacity (the scale one could achieve when constructing magic sequences), and interference (the strength with which one's magic sequences could overwrite eidos, the information bodies accompanying events). All three of these constituted an individual's "magic power," meaning the practical portion measured four areas in total.

The best grades in the school were announced on the school network, full names included. Of course, freshmen student marks were no exception.

The students with the highest combined theoretical and practical scores were as expected.

First place was Miyuki Shiba.

Second place was Honoka Mitsui.

Third place, by a slim margin, was Shizuku Kitayama.

The entire top three were from Class A, with the first Class B student being a boy named Hagane Tomitsuka at fourth place. Other familiar names included Shun Morisaki at ninth. Of the announced top twenty scores, all were Course 1 students.

The scores for just the practical portion saw a somewhat different ordering than the overall rankings, but once again, Course 1 students were the only ones on the list. Specifically, Miyuki was first, Shizuku was second, Morisaki was third, and Honoka was fourth. The top spots were all taken up by Class A, giving the teachers a little something to worry about. (Classes A through D had been split up so that each class had an equal average score on the entrance exam. The issue here was that Class A displayed a clearly higher degree of proficiency than the other three.)

But when it came to the grades on purely the theoretical portion, the results were a stunning upset.

First place was Class E's Tatsuya Shiba.

Second place was Class A's Miyuki Shiba.

Third place was Class E's Mikihiko Yoshida.

Honoka was fourth, Shizuku was tenth, Mizuki was seventeenth, Erika was twentieth, while Leo and Morisaki were both lower than that, so they were unranked.

While practical exam scores were a big part of the Course 1/ Course 2 separation, normally, people couldn't understand theory well enough if they couldn't do the practical part of it. If they didn't have an intuitive grasp of magic, they would have trouble understanding several difficult concepts from a theoretical viewpoint.

And yet, of the top three scores, two were from Course 2 students.

That in and of itself was completely unprecedented, but in average points—not total points—Tatsuya's score was *over ten points* above second place. His score was far and away the best.

"Theory and practice might be separate, but not *this* separate," said Shizuku, offering an objective viewpoint.

"But to say that Tatsuya was slacking, I don't think it's possible," argued Mizuki, a little angry.

"Shizuku knows that, too," soothed Honoka.

"But the teachers don't know Tatsuya personally like we do," added Erika.

"Yeah. They only know us from over a terminal screen..."

As Leo said, this could be called a glaring deficiency in their modern educational system. That said, even teachers from the last century didn't necessarily understand what their students were really like on the inside.

Plus, with schools these days, there were replacement positions that supplanted the old homeroom teacher system to deal with this very problem.

"...Right," continued Leo. "Why not go talk to Haru?"

The role of responding to student dissatisfaction and consulting them on school-related trouble belonged to the class counselors. Leaving aside whether it was proper to call Haruka "Haru," Leo's suggestion itself was appropriate.

Tatsuya shook his head anyway. "I talked to the teacher Miss Ono about it yesterday. She actually told me why I would be called down today."

"You can't rely on her for anything, can you?" blurted out Erika, not mincing words.

"Now, don't say that," chided Tatsuya, grinning. "Novice counselors don't have the power to do much of anything in the first place."

"...Tatsuya, that sounded a lot worse than what I said."

Erika was right, though—Tatsuya had a way of talking that managed to be even more unreserved than most things she said.

"Ohhh?" Leo grunted at the accurate retort.

Erika gave him a narrow-eyed glare. "What?"

"So you can say normal things, too," he explained, as though talking to himself, eyes wide.

"Shut up." Erika hit him with a rolled-up notebook.

Incidentally, the demand for paper notebooks hadn't gone away even in this advanced age of information systems. With magic high schools in particular, the act of writing characters by hand was very important in subjects like magic linguistics. And it was simply easier to physically draw diagrams and charts in classes like magic geometry than use a terminal. There were probably more students walking around with paper notebooks here than in regular high schools. Although it *was* a little suspicious how she was carrying a notebook in the hallway without a class to go to.

"Oww..." Leo, unable to avoid the swinging notebook, clutched his head and squatted low. It wasn't as though he let her beat him without offering any resistance—it was just that Erika, for the moment, was more skilled than him, and Leo's reaction time was too slow to evade the hit. Because of that (?), he always ended up saying the wrong thing and experiencing pain for it.

"...This girl's crazy! My head isn't a drum!"

Erika turned her face away, not listening to Leo's perfectly reasonable protest.

Even Mizuki, who would always fidget around, unsure at first, seemed to have gotten used to the same sequence of events that have occurred over and over again for the past three months. She gave a perplexed sort of smile but didn't say anything about their peculiar form of communication. Instead, she prevented further escalation of the conflict by steering the conversation back to where it was before.

"Anyway, Tatsuya," she said, "did you clear up the teachers' misunderstanding?"

"Yeah. Well, more or less."

"More or less?" repeated Mizuki.

Tatsuya explained further, his tone and expression both reluctant. "I got them to understand it wasn't that I wasn't trying. But then they recommended that I transfer to a different school."

"Transfer?"

"What? But why?"

Mizuki and Honoka both cried out, their faces changing color. The other three gave him similar looks.

"They suggested Fourth High was more suited for my talents because of its focus on magic engineering among the Nine Schools. I turned them down, of course."

Two of them breathed sighs of relief, but two others displayed clear indignation.

The former were Mizuki and Honoka, while the latter were Leo and Erika.

Furthermore, the last remaining one maintained her impenetrable poker face.

"...Doesn't it seem sort of contradictory for a *school* to tell you to go to a different school where your practical skills don't need to be that good? It'd be one thing if it was like your grades are bad and you can't keep up, but even your scores on the practical portion were *passing*."

"I think the teachers just don't wanna see him. Tatsuya might know even more about magic than they do!"

"I think the two of you should calm down," said Tatsuya, shifting into firefighting mode—who knew how much Leo and Erika would have flared up if left alone? "Leo's right. Even if my scores were just barely in the red, I'm under no obligation to drop out, so there's no real harm done. It might really have been an act of goodwill on their part. Though, if it is, it was a pretty insensitive one... Self-righteousness, I guess you could call it."

Tatsuya's smooth, calm, and stinging assessment caused their noble fury to subside as their anger faltered. If he'd actually been trying to cool them off, it would seem like he had a deep and complex plan. But the reality was it just happened to look that way. Everyone seemed hesitant to answer after that.

"I think you've failed as a teacher if you mistake your basic premise," said Shizuku in her unique monotone, her words possibly supporting theirs, and possibly not. It did thin the bite from Tatsuya's statement, though, so once again, it happened as an unintended result; but he thought to himself that might have been what she was going for.

"It's not as if Fourth High actually treats practical skills lightly. They just emphasize more complex, layered, technical magic instead of the combat-oriented magic reflected in Nine School Competition scoring."

"Really? Shizuku, you're very well-informed," noted Mizuki.

"My cousin goes there."

Everyone but Honoka nodded, now understanding. If she'd heard this from someone who actually attended Fourth High, then it must have been accurate information.

But, as the group nodded along with Shizuku, that only strengthened the sense of distrust they felt toward the teacher who had called him down here.

Of course, the topic of someone not actually present (in other words, the teacher) wasn't enough to hold the attention of their young minds for long.

"Come to think of it, Nine School Competition season's here soon, isn't it?" mentioned Leo, reminded by what Shizuku had said.

Tatsuya nodded back to him. "Miyuki's been grumbling about how many things there are to prepare, like work vehicles, tools, and uniforms."

"Miyuki is going to participate herself, isn't she? It must be hard on her." Mizuki's words of worry for Miyuki were no false pretense.

"She seems like she'd totally kill the rookie competition, though. The prep work'll probably be harder for her," replied Erika, half-argumentative and half-sympathetic.

"She can't go in unprepared. The noble son of the Ichijou from Third High will be there this year as well."

Shizuku's objection seemed a little strange. Both the main games and rookie games in the Nine School Competition were separated by gender, so Miyuki wouldn't be facing the noble **son** of the Ichijou.

Still, nobody in the group went so far as to point that out.

"Huh..."

"Ichijou—from the Ten Master Clans?"

Erika and Leo both seemed unaware that there were direct relations to the Ten Master Clans in the same year as them, and their surprise at the fact seemed pretty genuine. Mizuki wasn't thrown off as much, though. Maybe she already knew about this "noble son of the Ichijou."

"He might be tough to beat," agreed Erika. "You seem like you know a lot about this, Shizuku."

Honoka answered the question for her; she knew Shizuku almost as well as she knew herself. "Shizuku's crazy about Monolith Code. That's why you go to the Nine School Competition every year, isn't it?"

"...Mmhmm, well..." Shizuku nodded at the proxy answer—and while the changes in her expressions were as minute as ever, she seemed a little bashful. Unlike Honoka, who had a debt to repay to Tatsuya—well, more like she felt an interest in him—he and Shizuku had only become acquaintances indirectly through Miyuki, since the two of them were good friends. Shizuku had begun to show this sort of frank emotion around him lately, though.

"I see," nodded Tatsuya, convinced, to Shizuku diagonally opposite him; she gave him an awkward look. "You don't get to see Monolith Code matches outside the Nine School Competition, save for the All-Japan Championship and the international goodwill matches that the National Magic University plays."

The Nine School Competition hosted games between the high schools affiliated with the National Magic University—intramural matches, as it were—but the event was open to public spectators. It was, after all, one of the few places you could see magic competitions.

There were 1,200 freshmen total among all nine magic high schools. Given all the fifteen-year-old boys and girls in the nation, the total number who possessed a practical level of magic power ranged from 1,200 to 1,500 each year. In other words, nearly 100 percent of children with magical talent who wanted to be a magician or magic engineer enrolled at one of the nine schools. Because of that, the nine schools monopolized high school magic competition, save for certain sports like the sword-based matches of *kenjutsu* and *kenpo*.

The Nine School Competition was one of the few places to stimulate interest and deepen understanding of competing with magic, as well as raising public awareness of magic itself.

"Third High is going to be strong again this year, then?"

"Probably."

Shizuku nodded and replied concisely, a little happy. Erika realized the event was her area of expertise so she tried to capture her interest with a leading question.

"This year you won't be in the audience, but onstage, right?" remarked Mizuki, joining Erika.

Shizuku's practical abilities were second in their class. The official announcement of which students would be participating in the rookie competition had yet to be made, but like Miyuki, Shizuku was practically guaranteed a spot.

"Yep…" Shizuku nodded, reserved, but her face showed the beginnings of determination.

◇ ◇ ◇

Tatsuya spent his after-school hours in the disciplinary committee headquarters nearly every day since exams ended.

The student council elections would be right after summer break. After a new president was chosen, he or she would appoint a new disciplinary chairperson. Traditionally—though not a very nice tradition—there was no real test for inheriting the disciplinary chairperson's post. Most of the time, it was left entirely up to their unorganized records of activity.

Still, Mari had been on the committee since she was a freshman, so she wasn't that worried about whether or not there was someone to inherit the post. However, the junior she had her eye on for the chairperson position didn't have any experience at leading the committee, so Mari wanted to ease her into the position as smoothly as possible.

——And to do that, she'd left all the paperwork to Tatsuya.

"I've started to feel like I'm a lot more softhearted than I ever thought I was…"

"Softhearted *and* nefarious, eh? Quite the dual nature you have going on."

"……"

The retort was so on-point that Tatsuya couldn't find anything to say back.

"But this time, I'm grateful for that softhearted side of you," added Mari. Even *she* couldn't help but feel guilty at watching him silently do the paperwork. "Without your help, I'd have been in the same rut as always."

Tatsuya, however, didn't have a split personality. Nor was he merely "helping"—he was *creating* all these documents from scratch.

Her semi-apology fell flat.

"You are preparing for this considerably in advance, though," said Tatsuya with an inadvertent dubiousness, still working. He'd complete the control-transfer paperwork he was drawing up within a week. As long as he didn't have to draft anything more detailed after this, there would be over two months before it came into effect. There was no guarantee nobody better would appear for the position, either, or some other important matter wouldn't arise. It wasn't always best to get these sorts of documents done early.

"Once our preparations for the Nine School Competition really start getting under way, I won't have any time to draw up the paperwork. Practice will start as soon as we've gotten the members together, and then I'll have to get tools ready, collect and analyze information, think up strategies and plans… I'll be swamped."

Now that he'd heard the circumstances, he reflected on the fact that none of her reasons had anything to do with him. Still, he suddenly felt that he didn't want to let this conversation expire. "…When was the competition again?" he asked to maintain momentum, returning most of his focus to the paperwork.

"It'll be ten days, starting on August third and ending on the twelfth."

"That sounds like a long stretch."

"Hm? Haven't you ever watched it before?"

"No, I'm always busy with minor business during summer break."

Mari looked at him with even more confusion. "According to Mayumi, your little sister goes to watch every year, and even seems to remember matches the two of us were in..."

Tatsuya nearly burst into laughter. "Well, it's not like we're together three hundred sixty-five days a year... We do different things once in a while, you know."

"Hmm? ...Well, I suppose you do. It's just whenever I look at the two of you, it seems like you're never apart even for a moment."

"When we're not at school, we're usually off doing our own thing."

Mari looked uncertain confronting the objective truth offered to her, but she seemed to accept it for the moment. "I suppose that's why you don't understand how much preparation there is for it."

"Exactly. I actually don't even know what sorts of sports are played. I do know about Monolith Code and Mirage Bat, though." He was talking while creating documents, but Tatsuya pretty much had to split his thoughts like this to prevent himself from falling asleep. And without anything to do—or rather, not being allowed to do anything—Mari was just killing time, so she was more talkative than necessary.

"Well, those are the two famous ones..." She tilted her head, wondering how to explain it. Then she put a loose fist to her mouth seemingly clearing her throat. (He didn't actually hear her do it, though.) "The events at the Nine School Competition all need a lot of magic power, even compared to other magic sporting events."

"Right, I know that," agreed Tatsuya without stopping.

"They used to change the events every year, but for a few years it's been the same six events: Monolith Code, Mirage Bat, Ice Pillars Break,

Speed Shooting, Cloudball, and Battle Board. They have separate tournaments for combative martial arts like *kenjutsu* and magic martial arts, and for ball games like gymnastics and highpost basketball."

"Isn't physical condition fairly important for things like Cloudball and Battle Board?"

"Well, yeah. Magicians are people, too. They can't neglect their physical abilities. There are plenty of cases where a one-on-one fight between magicians comes down to physical abilities in the end, too. I'm sure I don't have to lecture you on that again, though."

"You're right about that," answered Tatsuya; not much else came to mind to say. Mari nodded slowly. He asked, "Isn't Cloudball usually played in doubles, though?"

"That's the unpleasant part of the Nine School Competition. They make all the events individual ones in order to make magic power matter more. I have a pamphlet with a rules summary in it—do you want to see it?"

"Yes, after this," he said, taking a thin booklet from Mari while still typing. "Printed materials? How unusual."

"They're not that unusual when it comes to the Nine School Competition. There's a pretty deep-seated idea that using virtual terminals harms your magic ability. On the other hand, not many non-magicians use the old screen types these days. Even among magicians, more and more are using the virtual kind."

"I see. That's why the Nine School Competition uses printed, paper materials—so that there's no need to use a terminal in the first place, is that it?"

"Oh? Are you one of the people who approves of the virtual kind?"

She must have noticed the criticism in his voice. She had extremely sharp senses, though she misrepresented them with her normal open-minded behavior and charming (?) lack of ability to keep things tidy and in order.

Reminded once again of that fact, Tatsuya chose his words carefully, but without stopping his work. "There *are* grounds for making the statement that virtual terminals can have a negative influence on inexperienced magicians. I, too, believe that teenagers in particular, whose abilities are still developing, should avoid usage of virtual terminals. But I don't think there is any reason to forbid mature magicians, whose magic power has already solidified, from using the virtual kind."

"…I suppose that's one way of looking at it. Yeah, maybe telling adults to renounce their convenience just because they can harm children is going too far."

The conversation settled for a little while. Tatsuya, following the characters on the screen he was inputting, didn't know what kind of expression Mari was making, but she was probably thinking about the implications of what he'd just said.

However impulsive she usually pretended to be, there was no hiding her natural seriousness deep down. It seemed somehow charming to Tatsuya.

"…Anyway, we got off topic." She seemed to have come to her own conclusion, and without warning, she changed the topic back to the Nine School Competition. "Each school takes a total of forty players—twenty men and twenty women, with ten of each for the main competition and the other ten for the rookie competition. The rookie competition is only for freshmen, while the main competition has no grade requirement. Still, one player can enter up to only two different events, so freshmen never appear in the main competition. Well, even without those limiting issues, it wouldn't be a true test of skill for juniors and seniors if they played against freshmen anyway.

"The men and women played together in the rookie competition until last year, but starting this year, they'll be separate like the main one. Plus, there were two events girls couldn't participate in last year, but that looks like it'll change this year."

Mari didn't have to mention the name Miyuki for Tatsuya to know she had her in mind.

With girls' stamina, going through a series of magic competitions would be harsh. No matter how far beyond the norm they trained themselves, many of their bodies were delicate to begin with. Tatsuya resolved himself to support them as much as he could.

"Four of the six events are done by both the men and women. Monolith Code is men only, and Mirage Bat women only… Monolith Code is the only event where direct combat happens, after all. I suppose I can't say I *don't* understand why it's only men."

There was a clear look of disagreement on Mari's face. From what he'd heard around the disciplinary committee, her magic was suited to personal combat, so she must really have been displeased at not being able to participate.

"Each school can enter a maximum of three people in a single event. Men and women entrants are counted separately, even if they are entered into the same event. With a total of five possible events (four unisex events and one male/female-only event) and fifteen possible slots for each sex, the general strategy is for five men and five women to be entered in two events each, while the other five men and women focus on one. The entries for the rookie and main competitions are also considered separate from each other, which is why schools bring twenty athletes (ten men and ten women) for each.

"It's a team-based competition, so it's important to plan who to place in each event. We have to ask things like whether we'll let our strong players devote themselves to a single event and aim for a sure win, whether to have them play in two events to get more points, and where enemy aces will show up as well as who to pit against them."

"I see."

"Also, the Nine School Competition allows an operations staff for planning, composed of four people separate from the players. Though not all schools put together a team. We bring as many as we're allowed every year, but Third High, for example, never brings one. Each of their players operates alone, thinking for him- or herself."

"And they rival us for the championship every year? That's interesting."

"We've only lost to them twice, though—three years ago and seven years ago. The Nine School Competition was first held in its current form as a summer event ten years ago. In those nine years, we've taken first place five times, Third High two times, and Second High and Ninth High once each."

"So we'd be going for a third championship in a row this year?"

"That's right. For the current seniors, winning this year will be the *true* victory."

Many called First High's current graduating class the "strongest generation."

Mayumi Saegusa, Katsuto Juumonji, and Mari Watanabe.

Two of them were straight from the Ten Master Clans, and the other one rivaled them with sheer ability.

Just the fact that they were coincidentally all in the same class at the same school was surprising, but even aside from them were several other skilled students who actually had class-A ratings (they couldn't acquire an official license due to lack of work experience, but they had been judged by international standards to be skilled enough to merit a class-A license).

The participants for this year's Nine School Competition hadn't been announced yet, but First High was seen as the likely winner anyway. They were seen as so powerful nobody thought it was even worth it to set up any betting pools.

"But I heard that if all goes well, our school will win the championship for sure."

"Well, yeah. Nobody doubts the skill of our players. The rookie competition rankings might be added in, but as long as we don't flop too badly there, we'll be able to win with our points in the main competition. If there is one thing we're uneasy about, it's our engineers."

"Engineers? You mean people who adjust CADs?"

"Yeah. The official Nine School Competition lingo calls it a technical staff. The competition specifies a common standard for CADs used in the games; they have to be a type that conforms to that. On the other hand, as long as it fits within the hardware specs, we can do whatever we want on the software end. Whether or not you can tune CADs to bring out the most from the athletes while still staying within the limitations has a lot to do with whether you win or lose."

The expansion speed of activation programs relied on the CAD's hardware, but the performance of a magic sequence construction could vary greatly depending on its software. In sporting events where a single wasted moment could cost a player a victory, the skill with which the software was tuned certainly meant a lot.

Sophistication and versatility on the software end weren't necessarily good things. Software that exceeded the capabilities of the hardware would hamper the hardware from doing its job, and that would only lead to lower performance instead. With a limitation on the hardware specs, choosing the right software and tinkering with it was even more important.

With these conditions, software engineering skills could lead to surprise upsets, thought Tatsuya.

"Compared to the level of this year's seniors, we're lacking in the engineering department. Mayumi and Juumonji are great at adjusting their own CADs, so they'll be comfortable, but…

"……"

Mari must have been bad at tuning hers. Tatsuya accurately predicted what she'd avoided saying, but said nothing in reply because he understood. Her words faded into silence after that, and he immersed himself in his drafting work.

◇ ◇ ◇

Advancements in centralized traffic control technology had caused a fundamental change in trains, yielding the leading roles in intracity transportation facilities to cabinets and server racks. Rail-based vehicle service was all centrally governed by a control room, which established safety, convenience, and high transportable volume at the same time.

On the other hand, traffic control on public roads hadn't advanced as far as people had hoped. An automatic operation system had been introduced into highways connecting cities, but systems to control and self-drive individual cars on regular streets and inner-city highways had only been introduced on an experimental basis in a few larger cities. It hadn't yet reached the stage where it could be called popularized nationwide.

Instead, there had been advancements in the development of onboard AI to assist drivers.

Excepting cases of illegally modified modern self-driving cars, you couldn't cause a traffic accident if you tried. (The reason Katsuto's car had been able to smash into Blanche's hideout was because the car had been modified to be more like a military vehicle.)

Self-driving cars were exported with the same onboard AI systems, giving smaller nations without the money to spare on large-scale traffic control systems the benefits of traffic accident eradication. Because of this, the world tended to rate individual control technology more highly than centralization.

Of course, in exchange for the safety, inexperienced—or, if a more candid expression is permitted, *bad*—drivers caused traffic jams instead of accidents. Instead of one car braking and all the ones behind it crashing into it, the ones behind it would immediately apply their brakes, so maybe the traffic jams were just a natural consequence of this.

So even though there were fewer worries about safety, society stuck to its old driver's license system under the pretense of preventing this sort of societal detriment.

Tatsuya waited in front of his brand-new motorcycle for his sister to come out.

He had bought the bike the moment he received his license in the beginning of April. It was a purely practical purchase, so he'd never taken it on any sort of leisure trip, but he had used it a few times already. He still made sure to tune it up every day, though, so even after two months, its still looked brand-new.

"Sorry for making you wait, Tatsuya!"

Tatsuya looked up at the voice to see his sister's slender body emerging from the light of the gate lamps.

Miyuki had grown out her hair even longer, and she was wearing almost the same exact riding suit as Tatsuya was. The jumpsuit was tight on her body, showing off her graceful, immature yet feminine curves.

She put on the helmet he was holding, then unconsciously lifted her chin up. Seeing his sister treat this so naturally gave him a slight dry grin as he hooked the helmet strap under her chin for her.

Her neck drew back from the ticklish feeling, and a smile came to his face as he put on his own helmet and mounted the bike.

Raising the windshield, he prompted Miyuki, who got into the tandem seat behind him, to hold on tight.

After feeling her body glued to his back and her arms around his waist, he put the shield down and raised the position of the stage-less power selector (equivalent to the throttle on internal combustion engine motorcycles).

The siblings then sped off quietly into the starry night.

◇ ◇ ◇

He set a course for the Yakumo temple.

Tonight's goal was for Miyuki's training, however, not Tatsuya's.

Miyuki had been unofficially offered a Nine School Competition slot, and they were going to prepare for it.

The competition's events had been selected to be sports where magical ability was especially vital even among other magic-based competitions. That didn't mean physical training was unnecessary, though. In Battle Board you had an advantage if you possessed good physical reaction time and balance, and certain strategies in Cloudball called for a high fitness level.

Miyuki specialized in deceleration and cooling magic, meaning the Ice Pillars Break event, which involved destroying pillars made of ice, was practically meant for her. Even if she took part in the main competition instead of the rookie one, there were few doubts that she would probably win.

However, with the increase in events she could participate in now that men and women were being separated in the individual events this year, she would likely take part in the Mirage Bat event as well. For that, she would need to be able to strike virtual orbs of light floating in the air with a baton.

Miyuki had been initiated into martial arts by Yakumo just like Tatsuya had, so she did possess more physical ability than you might imagine by looking at her delicate physique. She hadn't had much time to move her body lately, though, so they decided to get some training in just to be sure.

At this time of night, Yakumo's pupils would all have their lights out as part of their own studies.

As he expected, as they approached the darkened dojo they heard stifled breathing, the occasional step or two that couldn't be completely hidden, and the creaking of floorboards.

Tatsuya quietly opened the old-looking door lest he disturb their training.

Despite not making any noise, a long, straight shuriken came flying at him not a moment later; he swatted it away with his bulletproof, knife-proof glove and in return fired lead balls hidden inside his jumpsuit.

However, he didn't hear the "marbles" (this was a type of skill that launched small, hidden balls of lead with finger strength, a technique akin to slinging a marble) hit anything.

"You don't seem to have progressed very much with marble-flicking. Don't take it easy just because you have magic—you need to practice throwing weapons, too. Still, Tatsuya, it was a good judgment on your part to knock the shuriken away instead of grabbing it."

There was no sign of anyone present. Only a voice.

Tatsuya hadn't heard the voice come from in front of him, but from the wall to his right, and he fired a second lead ball in that direction.

"Whoa!"

At the same time he heard a distracting yell, Tatsuya felt the ripples of someone's presence from where he'd sent a shot. Then he immediately wrapped Miyuki up and sprang back.

It was just in time; only missing by a paper's width away from his sister's back, a black sword-wind swooped down from the ceiling. He took a quick step with one foot, catching the wooden sword that was painted completely black, then stopped it from moving.

When Yakumo tried to pull it away and strike again, it didn't budge an inch. He gave up and let go of it.

"...That was a rather violent welcome, Master."

"...Oh, you know you were aiming to kill with those marbles."

The teacher and student, staring at each other in the darkness, both exchanged wicked smiles at the same time.

Miyuki's face, completely red now that she was buried in Tatsuya's arms, was, thankfully, hidden by the darkness...or so she thought, but by the way her brother's body stiffened up, it was obvious to Yakumo what face she was making.

◇ ◇ ◇

They moved to one corner of the temple grounds, a square that had bonfires burning in iron baskets at each of its four corners. Normally, such a place would be used for firing cedar sticks to ask for blessings. (The temple apparently championed itself as a branch temple of Mount Hiei, but neither Tatsuya nor Miyuki had ever seen Yakumo conduct training in any sort of Buddhist prayers.) There, dimly blue and vaguely red balls of light floated in the air.

The place being what it was, those who didn't know better might look at the lights, think they were disembodied souls, and collapse to their knees in fear. Fortunately, though, there were no outsiders present.

A long, narrow shadow passed through the blue lights, and one of the orbs winked out of existence.

A second one disappeared, and then a third.

A willowy silhouette pursued the scattered, floating orbs with surprisingly swift and forceful movements, cleaving them with the short cane in its hand.

Once the number of light orbs she struck reached thirty, Tatsuya signaled Miyuki to take a little break.

Tatsuya approached Yakumo with a large teacup in hand. His master was inside a simple barrier approximately thirty-six square feet drawn with lime on the temple grounds. The amount of skill needed to construct a barrier with four white lines was astonishing in itself. Yakumo let him in through the barrier with a mudra, and he entered.

His job was to supply Yakumo with drinks and put up with his heavy sighing. Usually that was Miyuki's job, but today he was filling in. Tonight, Miyuki was inside the white lines, also sighing, so he was treating the both of them.

"Thank you very much, Master. Not only did you let us use this space, you're even helping with the training," he said, bowing to the man after handing him his drink.

Yakumo placidly nodded. "Hitting physical objects and hitting illusions is pretty different, after all. Miyuki is one of my cute students, so I would never turn her down if she asked for help."

Tatsuya sensed a strange force behind the word *cute*, but he knew he shouldn't let it bother him. At least until after the Nine School Competition.

Ninjutsu's main field was illusion magic, and the art had a level of polish that exceeded modern magic in every way: projection speed, image realism, and fluidity of movement. Modern magic had made it possible to invoke many kinds of unusual powers with speed and precision, but there were still plenty more limited areas you'd be better off using old magic for.

Tatsuya could only use a limited amount of magic well; he couldn't take Yakumo's place as a human hologram projector as he used his Demonfire illusion technique.

"Miyuki, should we call it quits for tonight?" asked Tatsuya as he handed Miyuki, short of breath, a drink, but she shook her head and took a sip.

"If it's all right with you, Sensei, I would like to get a little more exercise."

"I don't mind. Why don't you join in the Demonfire chasing, Tatsuya?"

"No, I... I'll pass, thank you."

Yakumo smirked, and Tatsuya got the feeling he knew why. He certainly would have liked to topple the man's expectations, but he prudently reminded himself that Miyuki's practice came first today.

"I see. That's too bad," Yakumo replied with a smile he couldn't hide, shaking his head, looking truly disappointed. After seeing his face, Tatsuya was convinced that declining had actually been the right move.

The evil grin suggesting ulterior motives changed to a mild, amiable one as he looked back to Miyuki. "Let's begin, then, shall we?"

"Yes, thank you very much."

At the signal to restart, Miyuki bent down at the waist.

Tatsuya had already collected the cups from both their hands.

She stood in the middle of the four iron basket lanterns at the corners of the square, and just as Yakumo was about to use his skill again—

"Who's there?!"

A sudden and unexpected arrival.

Tatsuya had been the one to ask their identity.

Actually, chronologically, it was backward.

The moment Tatsuya had expanded his senses to the Idea to help coach Miyuki, he turned toward the **presence** caught in the limits of his awareness and demanded who was there in the seemingly empty darkness. Only after that did a person **actually appear**.

"Oh, Haruka."

Yakumo addressed the presence with levity.

Both Tatsuya and Miyuki knew that name. A slightly more adult silhouette than Miyuki's stepped out of the darkness into the flickering lights. It was a counselor of the National Magic University Affiliated First High School—Haruka Ono.

The dark-colored jumpsuit she wore was similar to Miyuki's, and it looked like it highlighted her bust and waist quite a bit.

Miyuki followed Tatsuya's eyes and made an irritated expression, but before she could plant her elbow in her brother's side, she saw the steel color frozen in his eyes and calmed down.

His gaze might have seemed lecherous at first, but it was actually measuring Haruka's physical capabilities.

"Tatsuya, you don't need to be so cautious. Haruka is one of my students, just like you."

"I wasn't taught as intimately as you were, though, Shiba." Haruka's tone was light and jovial in contrast to her current dangerous outfit blending in with the darkness. "Sensei was one thing, but I didn't think Shiba would notice me like that. Could my skills have declined?"

"Now, don't lie to yourself. If you do it too much, you'll lose sight of what you actually think, Haruka."

"Shiba told me the same thing."

"Whoops, guess I didn't need to tell you, then. Well, leaving that aside, your invisibility was close to perfect, so I don't think you need to worry that much. That is, if you really *were* worried about your skills declining."

Haruka shrugged off the gaze Yakumo cast at her with the very definition of a deceptive smile. She probably didn't think she *could* deceive him, and wasn't trying to. Given the man's smirk, Tatsuya figured it was their usual style of communication.

"Tatsuya didn't notice your **presence**. His eyes are a bit different from ours, you see. If you want to fool him, you can't hide your presence—you have to misrepresent it."

"I see... Thank you for the lesson."

"I would like to have my questions answered at some point, too," interrupted Tatsuya, tired of listening to them amusing themselves with their master-student talk at his expense.

"Hmm... It *would* be unfair to only give information to Haruka. Would you mind?" The man made a show of saying "hmm" to insert a pause, but Tatsuya could tell from his attitude that he'd been waiting for Tatsuya to say something, too.

At Yakumo's mention, Haruka shrugged and answered, "If I said I did, you'd just tell them after I left, wouldn't you?" The action was candid, showing her state of mind had already reached the point of resignation.

"Now that I have her consent... Haruka is a Public Safety investigator."

Yakumo's explanation was concise indeed. Tatsuya could fully understand wanting to ask about just that, but in honesty, he would have liked a little more information.

However, Yakumo was the first to ask for an explanation. "Hm? You don't look very surprised." He seemed to have been hoping to astonish the siblings, and now he looked mystified—or rather, unamused—at not only Tatsuya, but Miyuki as well for accepting Haruka's true identity so calmly.

"I do have a meager information network of my own, so I knew Miss Ono wasn't related to the military. The only things left were Public Safety [the Ministry of Police Agency of Public Safety], the COIA [the Cabinet Office Information Administration], and being a foreign spy."

Yakumo frowned. "An information network... Oh, him? Interesting... If word got out that someone in his position was leaking information to a First High student, things wouldn't go well for him." His frown, however, was also aloof, and it didn't look at all like he was seriously concerned.

"His *position* isn't all that different from yours, Master... In any case, am I correct in understanding that you are a Public Safety infiltrator posing as a counselor to scope out anti-governmental activities in First High beginning with Blanche, ma'am?" This time he asked Haruka for confirmation, his question brimming with implications.

"No." Her reply, however, was a relatively firm denial. "It's true that I am a spy from Public Safety, but my counselor position isn't a disguise. If we're speaking chronologically, I got in contact with my current superiors while trying to get my counseling certification, and after I was assigned to First High, I became a secret investigator for Public Safety. I trained with Sensei for one year two years ago, so you're both my senior as his apprentices."

"For a year's worth of training, ma'am, your invisibility was wonderfully done."

"Thanks to my magic traits. I can't use other magic, though. That's why my superiors first approached me."

"...I see—you were a B.S. [Born Specialized] magician, then, ma'am?"

"I don't like that title," said Haruka, turning her cheek sullenly like a girl his age might do, causing an inappropriate chuckle from Tatsuya's lips.

I.S. magicians, or I.S. espers. They were also called innate unique espers or innate unique magic technicians. The terms all referred to those with supernatural abilities specializing in unusual powers that magic found difficult to systematize.

As could be understood by their mean-spirited nickname of "one-trick ponies," I.S. magicians were seen on a level below that of normal magicians. However, many of their unique abilities couldn't be emulated by others, and if there was someone who could, they would have an extremely high level of technical ability. If the unique ability could be matched up to a profession, then often they were valued more highly than normal, jack-of-all-trade magicians.

"I personally consider those who have mastered one trade to be superior to those who have dabbled in all of them. But I suppose that's an issue of your own sense of values, Miss Ono." Saying that made him feel like their student and counselor roles had been reversed, but this wasn't school, and it was too late to be considered after-school hours. He figured he didn't need to worry.

Haruka, seeming displeased, stopped sulking, perhaps feeling the same role reversal as he had. "I didn't have a choice today, Shiba, but my status as an undercover investigator is top secret. Please keep if off the record from others."

Tatsuya immediately wondered if there was any use in doing as she asked. Public Safety spies would be easy for the Ten Master Clans to discover within minutes. Erika might have already figured it out, too, given her family's deep police connections. Even Tatsuya had been convinced for a while that Haruka belonged to an intelligence agency, though he hadn't known which one.

Haruka might have been the only one who thought her true identity was still a secret, but he didn't say that. Instead, he answered her request. "I won't tell a soul, ma'am. This may be slightly rude of me, but in exchange, would you be able to give me some information about what happened in April soon?"

"...All right. Give and take, right?"

The two of them shook hands, each hiding their various intentions.

◇ ◇ ◇

It went without saying that magic high schools included classes on general, nonmagic subjects. One of them was physical education. Classes were set up to play as teams, so the boys were all burning with their usual excessive fighting spirit.

Today's class was legball.

An encyclopedia would describe the sport as derived from *futsal*, an indoor version of soccer played by five on a team. Legball was played in a completely covered arena, a clear box with numerous small holes in it, but unlike *futsal*, players wore headgear to prevent injuries; heading the ball was prohibited as much as using one's hands was. (As an aside, the "ball game played inside a clear box with numerous holes" was one of the particular sport trends of the 2080s.)

It was also played in concert with magic, but normal matches had a no-magic rule, and that went for how they were playing it in class today, too.

Legball used a light ball made for maximum elasticity, with walls and a ceiling that possessed springlike qualities enclosing the field. Players would chase after the ball as it hectically bounced from up to down and left to right like a pinball and kick it into the opposing team's goal. The sport was speedy, powerful, and flashy, making it highly popular as a spectator sport as well.

Right now, the girls of freshman Classes E and F were taking a rest, cheering on their own classes.

"Out of the way!"

Leo rushed toward a rebound. Given how bouncy legballs were, dribbling like in soccer or *futsal* was difficult, so no one did it much. The general strategy was to pass the ball among the team's five players using any surfaces available, including the walls and ceiling, and then try to score a goal. How much momentum the rebounds picked up was pivotal in deciding the outcome.

"Tatsuya!"

Leo, running everywhere he pleased, sent the ball to Tatsuya, who was near the middle, with the force of a shot trying to score a goal. The pass was so hard that if he tried to trap it with his chest or stomach he'd get knocked over, so instead, he kicked it straight up to kill its momentum. After it bounced off the ceiling, he trapped it under his foot.

After receiving the pass with precise ball handling, he aimed for the wall at the side and kicked the ball to it—he was using the wall to pass.

There was a slender boy there to get it once it bounced. His physique could be more appropriately described as toned and compact than thin; even now, he dealt with Tatsuya's fairly fast pass in a single movement, and without turning back.

With the ball at his feet, he aimed for the other team's goal and shot.

The electronic buzzer announcing the goal went off, and cheers erupted from the girls watching.

"He's pretty good!" said Leo, giving honest praise as he ran up to Tatsuya.

"Yeah. He makes good reads, and he's more fit than he looks."

Even Tatsuya had to feel a little surprised at the unexpected level of physical ability. Of course, this wasn't the first time they'd had gym together—they'd been in the same class for three months now. Tatsuya thought he had a handle on his abilities, and he'd made the pass like he had in the expectation that he'd be able to handle it. Still, there was a composed feeling to his—Mikihiko Yoshida's—movements.

With only twenty-five classmates, everyone knew everyone else's names. Tatsuya knew more than that about him, too. Mikihiko Yoshida was a direct descendant of the Yoshida family, which was famous for its old magic. Tatsuya had heard that the family was an old one that passed down outer magic of the spirit magic category, with each child inheriting it through traditional training. And if it was old methods of training, it was probably focused around asceticism. That told him Mikihiko would have been physically trained enough for that.

But as far as he could see, Mikihiko had no vestiges of such training on him. That was the main source of Tatsuya's surprise. *Looks like we had a hawk hiding its claws in a place we wouldn't have thought to look...*

As he ruminated, Tatsuya swung into a high roundhouse kick and slammed the ball coming through the air at him toward the opponent's goal.

The match ended in overwhelming victory, mostly due to the three of them.

After Tatsuya and Leo went back into the spectator's zone, they went up to Mikihiko Yoshida, who had taken a seat a little farther away.

"Nice play," said Tatsuya, who had already regained control of his breathing.

"You, too," answered Mikihiko, also with calm breaths.

Neither Tatsuya nor anyone else had built up equal friendships with everyone in their class. Whether out of an unsocial attitude or some other reason, there were classmates who treated Tatsuya somewhat distantly; he could talk to maybe half of Class E normally. But Mikihiko was even less social than Tatsuya, and he'd never seen him talking amiably to anybody else in the class. He'd even left the classroom by himself at orientation right after they came to school on the first day. Even Leo, who had a bigger relationship network, had only ever exchanged regular greetings with him.

"You're pretty good, Yoshida. This might sound kinda mean, but you surprised me."

But Leo had apparently thought of something after seeing Mikihiko's performance, and invited Tatsuya—well, Tatsuya had been the first to say something to him, but Leo told him to do it in the first place—to take a walk over to where Mikihiko was sitting.

Leo's tone was familiar, perhaps even overly familiar, depending on who he was talking to.

"Mikihiko." Leo's frankness, however, seemed to influence Mikihiko to do the same. "I don't like being called by my last name. Please, call me by my first name." He, too, responded frankly, something they'd never seen him do before.

"Sure. You can call me Leo, then, too."

Despite class activities not being as prominent as the previous century, their conversation still may have sounded weird. It was three months after school started. That's how big a wall Mikihiko had built between himself and everyone else, classmates included. Maybe this was just a flight of fancy brought about by the exhilaration of sweating through a sports game. Whatever the case, it was still an opportunity.

"May I call you Mikihiko as well? You can call me Tatsuya, too, of course."

"Sure thing, Tatsuya," he replied, relaxed, showing a slightly embarrassed expression. "I was actually thinking I wanted to talk to you at some point."

First impressions were a weird thing. Sometimes you could say a thousand words and not change it, and sometimes you could give a short sentence and it would change completely. Tatsuya's impression of Mikihiko changed from "antisocial" to "shy." "What a coincidence—so have I," he replied.

Though they had both enrolled as Course 2 students—substitutes, in other words—they were first and third on the exams among the freshmen. Practical skill was seen as more important, of course, but it wasn't at all strange that they had an interest in one another.

"...Heh, I kind of feel left out." Of course, whatever the case was for Mikihiko, Leo didn't think that Tatsuya would show an interest in someone just because of that. In fact, they seemed to be feeling something more, leaving Leo with a faint smell of alienation.

Mikihiko's next words cut through his gloom, though. "You're imagining things, Leo. I wanted to talk to you, too."

Not by the unexpected consideration he just showed after they thought he was too unfriendly to talk to anyone for real...

"At the very least, there's basically nobody who can keep up with Erika as patiently as you can."

...but by those spoken words of sincere astonishment.

"...Ehh, I don't know."

Leo's face scrunched up at Mikihiko treating him and Erika as a packaged set. Tatsuya and Mikihiko started laughing at the same time. A moment later, though, Tatsuya thought about what Mikihiko just said. He quickly realized what had drawn his attention. "Mikihiko, do you and Erika know each other from before?"

He didn't mean much by the question, so when he saw Mikihiko make a face like he wished he hadn't said anything, Tatsuya decided to change the subject. Unfortunately, his forethought ended before it had a chance to start by the appearance of the girl herself.

"Yeah, sorta. We're what you might call childhood friends, I guess?"

"Erika, why did you phrase that as a question?" asked Mizuki, who was tagging along.

"We met each other when we were only ten. It's like, I'm not sure you can call that childhood friends, you know? And I haven't seen him outside school at all for half a year. He always avoids me when we're in class." Erika, who had suddenly intruded on the conversation, answered Mizuki's question without paying much attention to Tatsuya and the others.

"Hey, Tatsuya, what do you think?"

And suddenly again, she brought Tatsuya back into it. *Going at her own pace as usual.* "I think that makes you childhood friends, doesn't it?"

And Tatsuya's answer, spoken without hesitation or nervousness, might have indicated him going at *his* own pace, too.

Leo and Mikihiko weren't just keeping silent out of mute amazement for Erika's overbearing behavior, of course. Their widened eyes told him that.

The dress code in 2095 AD encouraged people not to show their skin in public spaces. School being a public space, wearing your school uniform's jacket was mandatory even in summer, and female students were required to wear either opaque tights under their skirts or leggings that went down to their ankles.

These rules didn't follow through all the way to sportswear, however. The more physical clubs normally wore uniforms that exposed the arms and legs, and nobody could blame them. Gym class didn't have a dress code, either. Tatsuya and the other male students were all wearing shorts that ended above the knees. Mizuki was wearing leggings that hid only half her thighs, too—essentially normal for girls' gym clothes.

And as for the problem, Erika...

Well, she was showing off.

Everything from her hips down was exposed to the hot midsummer's air. You couldn't measure the length of her bottom clothing, because there was no length—and with her short sleeves that were a strange length, at a glance, it almost looked like she was wearing only underwear.

Her thighs were tight but not the least bit brawny. The slight tan coloring of her body was actually emphasizing her light complexion.

"Erika, what are you wearing?!"

Having finally rebooted, Mikihiko's voice cracked a little and his face grew red for reasons other than the ultraviolet-packed sunlight—it was understandable. There was no lack of opportunities to see a girl's bare legs outside of school, so he should have been used to it, but Erika engendered enough charm to steal the presence of mind away from boys of the same age.

"What do you mean? These are traditional girls' gym clothes."

It was plain to see what mental state Mikihiko was in right now, but Erika didn't make any mention of it. She just answered blankly, her slender neck tilted. She didn't seem to be wearing this just to tease her childhood friend with it.

"Traditional?!" However, Mikihiko didn't agree with that sentiment—he thought he was being teased. His face grew even redder as he lost his temper.

"Really? That seems like a strange design for leggings." Tatsuya, though, by interrupting and deflecting the attack, prevented Erika's unintentionally irritating behavior from angering Mikihiko any further.

"They're not leggings."

In the end, his efforts only resulted in the victim being Tatsuya instead of Mikihiko, but judging by the color of Mikihiko's face, Tatsuya had a lot more resistance to this than he did. Or perhaps he just didn't get ruffled by impish remarks not meant to hurt anyone.

"But it's not just underwear, right?"

"Even I wouldn't just go out in underwear without a skirt or something! These are called bloomers."

"Bloomers? You mean like that really old kind of underwear girls used to wear?"

"Of course not! I just said they're part of a girl's gym outfit!"

Erika actually seemed to be the one on the ropes from Tatsuya's witticism, whether it was intentional or not.

"Oh, I think I've heard of them," said Leo, rejoining the conversation at last. "During the old days of loose morals, female middle school students used to sell them to middle-aged men for pocket change, right?"

…Unfortunately, it would have been better for both him *and* Erika if he'd remained in his frozen state.

"Shut up, you idiot!" cried Erika, her face going bright red, kicking Leo, who was on one knee, in the other shin as hard as she could.

Leo fell over in agony and grabbed his shin as Erika hopped up and down on one foot.

It seemed like the match between verbal violence and physical violence ended in a draw due to injuries on both sides.

The next game was a close one, compared to the one before that Tatsuya and the others were playing in. The score held even for a while. The skills of both teams were equal. At a high school level, of course. Because of that, most of the female audience had left. They had classes, too, so they probably couldn't stay for very long. Unlike other subjects and magic practice, in gym class, there were faculty members certified as personal trainers watching. (It was one of the rare differences between those who could teach magic and those who could instruct students in training.)

The only girls still in the boys' spectating zone were Erika and Mizuki.

"I just can't believe it. Your brain is overflowing with that kind of stuff, isn't it?" asked Erika with a sincerely scornful glare.

"Oh, shut up. It was in a book I read once," answered Leo a little rudely, maybe thinking that the odds were *not* in his favor—this time, at least. Her eyes were already on something completely different anyway.

It would probably be all right to say the fact that Erika didn't press him more thoroughly about it was one of her good points. "What book was *that* in... Actually, now that I think of it, you were looking at me the same way, weren't you, Miki? Are these clothes really that arousing?"

Of course, it was probably just a whim of hers in the first place.

"Erika..." began Mizuki hesitantly. "Maybe you should just go with regular leggings next time." Her difficulty speaking meant that she was in one of those states where she could think it, but not say it out loud.

"Maybe... These aren't as easy to move around in as I thought they'd be. They actually feel a little tight, you know?"

The two boys present immediately turned their faces away, but fortunately (?) Erika didn't notice.

"Hmm... When I dug them out of the dresser, I thought they'd be okay since they were unused and the perfect size. But I guess I'll go back to leggings like you said, Mizuki."

"I think that's a good idea."

This wasn't really a topic for her to get so insistent over, but Mizuki nodded slowly a few times anyway.

"Huh?" And it would be lying to say it wasn't like Mizuki to react a few moments too late. "Erika, who is Miki?"

Mikihiko's shoulders stiffened. He was still looking away. Erika didn't notice it, though, and inconsiderately pointed at his back. (Of course, whether she would have done something else if she *had* noticed it was up for debate.) "His name's Mikihiko, so *Miki*."

As the words came out of her mouth, Mikihiko whipped back around. "What kind of logic is that?!" Apparently this "nickname" wasn't something Mikihiko could ignore even if he tried.

"What do you mean? You shorten *Mikihiko* to get *Miki*."

"How many times have I told you not to call me that girly name?!"

Erika didn't seem fazed in the slightest, though. Maybe she was used to being yelled at. "Huh? Should I have went with *Hiko* instead?" In fact, her face had even grown critical of Mikihiko, as if to say that he should have just said something about it.

"Why that?! Stop shortening people's names without asking first!"

"So you want me to call you *Mikihiko*? Hmm… Mikihiko, Mikihiko, Mikihiko… No, that's too hard to say. I don't wanna."

Mikihiko was certainly not the only one who felt like that was a little unfair.

"Besides, wouldn't it be embarrassing?"

"What do you mean?"

Erika, standing, suddenly leaned over him suggestively and brought her face close to his. "Mikihiko…" she whispered sweetly.

Mikihiko was too agitated to stay mad.

"…Who *is* that?" He wasn't the only one affected; even Leo was disturbed. Erika's provocation was quite destructive.

"That's embarrassing, right?"

Erika's hair seemed to have grown out at an especially fast speed, and within just the three months since starting school, her medium-short hair had gotten down to her shoulders. She brushed the hair up over her ears and grinned.

Mikihiko still hadn't lost his strength, but he couldn't hide his discomposure. "Th-then just—"

"Ow, I bit my lip…" said Mizuki suddenly. Maybe she wasn't as merciful as everyone thought.

Thankfully, Mikihiko didn't have the flexibility at the moment to hear it. "Just call me by my last name, then!"

"Huh? But, Miki, I thought you hated being called by your last name."

It immediately appeared that what she said had been insensitive. Mikihiko's face stiffened tightly. His face was still red, and he still wasn't calm—but at the root of all his anger was embarrassment. Tatsuya, however, felt that a darker sentiment more akin to hatred was mixed into it. "Erika, are you good for time?" Perhaps it wasn't his place to mention it, but Tatsuya's interruption drew Erika's attention. He stuck a thumb over his shoulder. The physical trainer (aka the gym teacher) was looking in their direction with a bitter expression.

"Ack! I'll see you later, Tatsuya!"

"Huh? Erika, wait, not so fast!"

Erika ran off in a hurry with Mizuki frantically following.

Tatsuya waved to them as they left, a dry grin crossing his face.

After an awkward silence, Mikihiko lowered his head and said, "Sorry for causing you trouble." He was aware of it, and yet still lost control anyway; he must have had some deep-rooted family troubles.

"I think you were handling, anyway." That wasn't a lie told to comfort him, but what Tatsuya actually thought. From what it looked like, this wasn't the first time this had happened, and Erika could have been driving Mikihiko up the wall on purpose, too. If he'd come out and said what was on his mind, they might not have had any future troubles.

"No, not at all. I mean, we are in class, after all," said Mikihiko. That was exactly why Tatsuya had butted into it. There was a time and place for everything. Besides, Tatsuya wasn't keen on getting involved in Mikihiko's—or Mikihiko and Erika's—personal issues. "You sure are calm, though, Tatsuya."

Perhaps Mikihiko accurately sensed Tatsuya's feelings and changed the topic. "What do you mean?" Tatsuya had learned from their conversation earlier that Mikihiko, despite his in-class attitude, was fairly sensitive to the feelings of others. Still, the change in topic was too sudden—or, rather, lacking reasonable context.

"What do I..." It seemed like Mikihiko had spoken before getting a very solid image in his head, too, so he had some trouble explaining. Eventually he managed to continue. "Err, I mean, you weren't affected at all when you saw what Erika was wearing."

That was a bit unsuitable to choose for a concrete example. It sounded pretty desperate. "...Well, I didn't see it coming, so I was surprised. She wasn't exposing *that* much skin, though, was she? It covered more than a swimsuit or a leotard, I think."

In his mind, Tatsuya was thinking, *What the heck is he talking about?* His relationship with Mikihiko, which had really just begun today, would worsen if he said that, though. His decision to offer a harmless, inoffensive response might have made their conversation come off as a little dull to a third party.

"It was more plain than a swimsuit or leotard, but I don't know if that quite made it all right..." noted Leo, understandable from a teenage boy's perspective.

"...You're pretty mature, Tatsuya." Now even Mikihiko was saying something rude with a sigh, mentioning him again. At some point, maybe because he and Leo felt a connection in that they were both victims of Erika fooling around (?), they had chosen Tatsuya as a target.

"I don't think he's mature, I just think his rating scale is too harsh. With a beautiful sister like that, it'd make sense he wouldn't be interested in most girls."

"Oh...that's right. Her name's Miyuki, right? When I first saw her at the entrance ceremony, I was more surprised than fascinated. I couldn't believe it was possible for a girl to be that beautiful."

"What's this?" asked Leo with a mean grin. "Hey, Tatsuya, someone's goin' after your sister. How does that make you feel, as her brother?"

Instead of Tatsuya, though, Mikihiko answered the betrayal (?) from his comrade-in-arms using him as an excuse. "Stop it. It's not like that. I could talk to her, maybe, but anything more than that intimidates me just thinking about it. I'd want a girlfriend I could be with a little more comfortably."

Leo nodded deeply—so deeply it looked like he was exaggerating. "Yeah, I hear you. Besides, she has that impregnable brother complex of hers, and to even get to her you'd need to bust through the invincible brother with a sister complex... Talk about high hurdles."

"Leo... I think I need to have a nice, long talk with you at some point."

"Whoa, scary! I'll pass, thanks. It isn't worth risking my life for."

Leo dramatically trembled under Tatsuya's heavy stare. He meant it to be an act, but a nontrivial part of it seemed real, causing Mikihiko to look between them with interest.

Leo was a size bigger than Tatsuya, and his limbs were thicker to suit. From how they were playing earlier, there didn't seem to be much of a difference in agility between the two. The rumors said Tatsuya was trained in classical *ninjutsu* by a renowned master, but was it really so insanely strong? Enough to make up for his lack in magic power?

Mikihiko didn't understand what about him had drawn Tatsuya's interest, but he knew exactly why he was interested in Tatsuya since the beginning.

Mikihiko wanted to know the secret behind Tatsuya's strength. They were both Course 2 students who had just enrolled, and yet he had shown he was powerful enough to make Course 1 upperclassmen yield. Mikihiko wanted to know how. His greatest wish was to find a way to make up for his own gap in magic power.

Something to replace the power he'd lost a year ago. Before then, he had been lauded as a prodigy, the start of hope for the Yoshida family. They said his skill in summoning magic, the central form of magic passed down through the family, had already surpassed that of his brother, the next leader of the family. Until the accident, he'd been one of the strong ones for as long as he could remember; now, he couldn't stand having to be content as one of the weak.

He knew he wasn't thinking calmly about it. That's why he'd unnecessarily isolated himself and why his current mental state, which lacked any relaxation, was causing him to exhaust himself more than he needed to. And he knew all that. But he couldn't help putting himself in this situation anyway.

In the past year, he'd devoted himself to studying more than he ever had. He began taking martial arts seriously, though he'd never been passionate about them in the past. But he still couldn't get rid of the sense of loss.

That's why he couldn't help finding Tatsuya interesting: Despite his real disadvantage in performing magic, he could defeat upperclassmen with far more magic power than him.

Hand-to-hand combat skills that could make up for a difference in magic power?

Mikihiko wanted to have Tatsuya and Leo fight here so that he could see. And, though he didn't realize it himself, *he* wanted to fight Tatsuya.

"Mikihiko?"

"Huh?"

And perhaps because of that, at the sudden mention of his name, he essentially put himself into a fighting stance.

Tatsuya and Leo both saw him and gave pained grins.

"Hey there, settle down, partner."

"What's wrong? First you stopped saying anything at all, and now..."

"Oh, uh... Sorry, it's nothing."

All Mikihiko could do was apologize awkwardly. He wasn't very skilled in communication in the first place. They'd done so much to create a friendly atmosphere, but now it was a strained one. Though Tatsuya and Leo started joking around enthusiastically, the air between them wouldn't be repaired before the end of class.

◇ ◇ ◇

Summer's Nine School Competition was one of the biggest events for the high schools affiliated with the National Magic University, along with the Thesis Competition that took place in autumn. With its appeal as a spectator event, however, it could be called number one, far and away the more entertaining of the two.

The competition involved magical sports. (Magical competitions included more than just sports-type games; there were 3-D puzzles, board games, mazes, and treasure hunts as well.) Each of these games had its own club at First High, as well as the other schools, but the Nine School Competition was all about different schools facing off against each other. So for this competition, promising athletes were selected from the entire school, not only those clubs.

Therefore, the student council, not the club committee, carried out the preparations for it.

"But still, we can't ignore the athletes in the clubs. It's so much work just to decide on who will compete..."

Even Mayumi, who always had an energetic smile to give, seemed a little less lively. For some reason, her chopsticks didn't seem to care much for the contents of her lunch box. Miyuki had been substantially busy lately as well, but the student council president had more to do than just office work. There was an imperceptible hint of anxiety in her normally easygoing bearing.

"Juumonji *did* help me with choosing the competitors, so we got through that, at least."

Today's luncheon meeting had been more of a platform for Mayumi to endlessly vent her complaints, but it was almost over. Tatsuya's stomach was strong enough not to let the anxiety cause him indigestion. He reflected, though, that some nice relaxing mealtime music would have been better for his mental health than her stream of grumbling. He sighed with relief at the prospect of being released from the pessimism.

...Unfortunately, he was too quick to that conclusion. "Still, the engineers were always a bigger problem than the competitors..."

"You still haven't found enough?" asked Mari.

Mayumi nodded tiredly. "Our school has so many who want to be magicians that there's a clear bias in favor of those with excellent practical skills... The seniors this year especially so. There's a critical shortage of the sort of magic engineers that we need. The juniors have

Ah-chan and Isori, as well as a few others, but we still just don't have enough..."

"Isori, huh... He's best at geometry, and his technical skills are pretty much all pure logic. He wasn't very good at adjusting CADs, was he?"

"You're right—but that's the situation we're in."

Mayumi and Mari both sighed; the rare sight gave a vivid account of the gravity of the situation.

——He got the feeling that measuring the gravity using body language alone probably wasn't the best idea, though.

"Juumonji and I can make up for some of it, but not all of it..."

"You two are our best players! If your match results suffered because you were looking after other people's CADs...well, that wouldn't be very funny."

"...It would certainly be easier if you could at least learn to make adjustments to your own CAD, Mari," said Mayumi, directing a nice, friendly gaze to Mari.

"...You're right. This is quite the predicament," she replied, hypocritically looking away—whether out of exhaustion or some other reason, Tatsuya didn't know. The council room was degrading into something that was clearly not psychologically healthy. Thinking that he needed to get back to class—and flee the scene—he waited for an opportunity to give Miyuki a glance and make his intentions known.

"Rin, couldn't you be one of the engineers?" said Mayumi yet again. Suzune had been chained to the student council room even for lunch break during this precompetition crunch time.

"I cannot. With my skill, I believe I would only get in the way of Nakajou and the others," came the curt refusal yet again.

Mayumi looked quite disheartened. Tatsuya hesitated, but this would probably be his best chance. He made eye contact with Miyuki, then began to rise from his seat...

"Umm, would it be possible to have Shiba with us?"

…when suddenly he was struck with an unexpected attack from Azusa that caused his launch to fail.

Mayumi, facedown on the table now, looked up without moving and gave a strange answer in an unknown language: "Whaa?"

Azusa had been groaning in front of a large tablet the whole time—likely struggling with her course work. She sighed a little, turned it off, and looked up. "I think Shiba does the adjustments for Miyuki's CAD. She let me see it once. It was done so well you'd think it was the work of a craftsman from a top manufacturer!"

Mayumi immediately shot upright. Life returned to her face as though she'd never been tired at all. "Have we been blind this whole time…?!" She turned a predatory, hawklike gaze on Tatsuya. Just that caused him to give up almost completely.

"I see… How did I never see it? I even work with the guy!" And with Mari added into the equation, there was really no getting out of here anymore. "He tuned up all the CADs in the disciplinary committee room, too, didn't he? He's the only one using them, so I never actually noticed."

I don't think anything will change their minds now, thought Tatsuya, 99 percent giving up. Still, he hated losing by default, so he offered a modest—but likely useless—argument. "The chairwoman told me yesterday how important the CAD engineers are, but there is no precedent for a freshman being part of the team, is there?"

"There's a first time for everything!"

"Rules are meant to be broken."

Mayumi and Mari both answered without skipping a beat, their viewpoints radical.

"Progressive people such as yourselves may think so, but will the other competitors appreciate it? I'm a freshman, *and* I'm a Course 2 student, *and* I haven't exactly earned the best reputation in my time here." Actually coming out and saying that was a little disheartening, but he couldn't avert his eyes from the truth. "The most important part of CAD adjustment is to have a relationship of trust with its user. The CAD capabilities that the magician can actually make full use of depend a lot on their mental state, after all. If the competitors would rather me not be there, then I don't think I'd be a good choice..."

Tatsuya's opinion seemed understandable at first, and Mayumi and Mari exchanged glances. But no matter what he said, the girls knew how he really felt. They made eye contact with him in turn, attacking him one by one, to give the final word to their difficulty-averse, slothful underclassman. Before they could speak, however, Tatsuya found himself on the receiving end of some unexpected support fire.

"I would very much like to have my brother adjusting my CAD during the competition... Is that at all possible?"

Miyuki's stunning betrayal (?) caused Tatsuya to freeze in place. A good classical expression for his state of mind would be *"Et tu, Brute...?!"*

Mayumi wasted no time in delivering a follow-up attack. "You're right! Miyuki, you'd be much more relaxed while competing if you had the trustworthy engineer always adjusting your CAD there, wouldn't you?"

"Yes. If my brother was added to the engineer team, then I believe Mitsui and Kitayama could go into their matches with some more peace of mind as well."

This was the first concrete statement he'd heard that those two had been chosen for the rookie competition. *They were expected, and right for the job,* thought Tatsuya...trying to take his mind off the reality before him: This was checkmate, no doubt about it.

The final decision of whether to add Tatsuya to the team would be made during a prep meeting held in the club committee headquarters after school. That meant there was still a ray of hope, but he'd already given up on it as impossible.

As soon as Miyuki said she wanted it, he had no recourse. He knew that even if he expressed disapproval, he'd need to make an impassioned argument to defend it.

It was a lose-lose situation. And in times like these, people generally reached for what they were good at. He was incredibly low on the priority list here, but for now, he got his grip back on his self-worth. He thought about what he was capable of, what he was used to, and what he was good at. It was a sort of compensation mechanism to help him calm down. He almost never needed to use it—maybe it was the stress—but right now, Tatsuya was falling into the same subtle trap as anyone else: the desire for self-compensation.

Two-thirds of lunch break had passed, but Tatsuya was trapped in boredom because of the piles of desk work Miyuki was burdened with. To keep himself occupied, he removed the silver CAD from his shoulder holster and began to check on all the physical moving parts, like the cartridge drive and the activation program selector switch.

"Oh, you brought your Silver Horn today?"

Azusa, who had been groaning over her course work a moment ago, spotted him with her sharp eyes and came over. He glanced away, and his eyes found Suzune this time instead of Mayumi or Mari. She correctly understood what Tatsuya wanted to say, and skillfully gave the facial equivalent of a shrug by using only her eyebrows. In other words, Azusa probably couldn't concentrate on her work with the distraction.

"Yes. I bought a new holster, so I wanted to get myself used to it," he answered, friendly enough on the surface—though to himself, he was thinking some objectively cruel things, like how birdbrained the girl was for being so distracted by the Silver Horn she wouldn't be able to continue her course work until her curiosity was sated.

"Really? Can you show it to me, please?" she asked, her eyes glittering, drawing even closer. She seemed to be more interested in the accessory than the CAD itself. Tatsuya was unable to suppress a dry grin, given that she always avoided him—probably out of fear. Still, when the girl hopped over to him like a small animal, he found it impossible to act coldly.

Figuring it would be an act of kindness, Tatsuya removed his jacket, which he wore properly even in the middle of summer—and was, of course, made of high-tech heat-protection fabric—removed his shoulder holster, and gave it to Azusa.

"Wow! This is a genuine Silver model. Such a nice shape…and perfect curves to make the CAD easy to draw. It takes usability into consideration without going overboard with technology. Ahh, I want one so bad…"

Azusa was happy enough to take it, and she seemed about ready to rub her cheek against it in affection. Tatsuya was finding it difficult to keep a straight face. She turned the holster over and over again in her hands for a while, feeling it all over, until finally she returned it to him with a fully satisfied smile. "Are you a fan of the Silver model, too?" she asked. "They seem a little bit on the high end in terms of price if you just compare the value and specs to things like Maximillian's Shooting model, Rosen's F-class, and the Sagittarius series that FLT also creates—but the customization brings that kind of satisfying feeling that makes the price not matter as much!"

Mari had informed him some time ago that Azusa was a "device nerd." Back then, he sympathized with Azusa, thinking it was a mean thing to call her—but now he was pretty sure she'd earned the name herself.

Tatsuya was also of the opinion that the holster had poor abilities for the cost, but he thought it lacked a certain "satisfying feeling," too. Sometimes, though, the specs didn't match the data in the catalog. It was often a matter of how much you could rate things about it that couldn't be expressed in numbers; saying something was satisfying without doing that kind of analysis was essentially a simple act of an almost religious belief in it.

Still, satisfaction was a largely subjective issue, so if she said it was satisfying, then who was he to throw cold water on her?

"Actually, I have a minor connection to them, so I get the Silver models for cheaper in exchange for being a product tester."

As soon as the words left his mouth, Miyuki's shoulders gave a jolt as she sat facing the terminal at the wall, but nobody noticed.

"What?! Is that true?" Azusa's face was positively shining with admiration.

Even Tatsuya had to make a pained expression at that. "...If I get another opportunity to test a new product, would you like me to give the set to you?"

"Huh?! Is that okay?! You would do that for me?! Thank you so much!"

There was no room to interrupt her reply. He managed to eke out a nod as Azusa grabbed Tatsuya's free left hand in both of hers and started shaking it up and down.

Understandably unable to let this keep going, Mayumi paused her progress on her piles of paperwork and said, "...Ah-chan, why don't you calm down a little?"

Azusa abruptly stopped moving. Slowly, she looked down at her hands...became aware of the fact that her hands were tightly gripping Tatsuya's (visually now, rather than just in a tactile sense)...quietly looked up at Tatsuya's face, lowered her gaze back to her hands trying to avoid his expressionless face...and then, as though she'd just put her hands into a fire, not only took her hands away but jumped back.

"I'm sorry, I'm sorry, I'm sorry...!"

There was a metaphor about people getting red all the way up to their ears, but this was no analogy—Azusa's ears were actually red as she bowed vigorously in apology, over and over again. Tatsuya started to actually worry about her making herself dizzy because of it, so he made eye contact with Mayumi for help.

"...Let's leave it at that, okay, Ah-chan? I think you might be troubling Tatsuya."

With the same concern in mind, Mayumi chided Azusa, not trying to stir things up with her usual mischief.

Azusa took a deep breath as she was told, and seemed to regain some calm. With a sigh and a shake of her head, Mayumi got back to work.

Azusa smiled bashfully at Tatsuya, then became suddenly serious and asked, "Then would you happen to know what kind of person Taurus Silver is?"

——She was obviously trying to hide her embarrassment by asking something else.

Unfortunately, this particular question was extremely difficult for Tatsuya to answer.

"...No, I don't know much at all."

There was a beep sound from near the wall. It was the electronic tone accompanying a mistaken input for the workstation Miyuki was using. Everyone mistyped things every once in a while, but Miyuki making enough of a sound for that tone to go off was rare.

Mayumi and Suzune looked in her direction, surprised, but Miyuki simply continued her database work as though nothing had happened. They got back to their own jobs without a word.

"...Miyuki doesn't make mistakes often."

"Well, everyone does sometimes," he said, explaining the situation to smooth it out.

Azusa didn't seem to care at all about it, and went back to the original topic—or, the one she had just begun, anyway. "He may hide his true identity, but other scientists there would know who he was, right? Or does he make everything all by himself?"

"...No, I don't think even he would be able to do that."

"Yeah, you're right. Oh, Shiba, couldn't you ask that connection of yours?"

"...Well, it doesn't quite work like that... Besides, there's probably some internal reason Four Leaves has for keeping it secret, so I don't think I'd be able to ask any of the scientists there, either."

"Hmm, I guess you're right..."

"...I'm sure I don't need to tell you that using mental interference magic to gain access to secret information is a serious crime."

"Huh? O-oh, no, the thought had never even...occurred to me..."

Tatsuya gave her a narrow-eyed stare and Azusa's already-small body shrank even further. "...Well, just as long as you really understand. I was just saying it to make sure, that's all."

"I-it's all right. I know that much, at least. Aha, aha-ha-ha..."

One drop, two drops—after seeing the physical, not metaphorical, cold sweat start to run down her cheek, he let up the pressure. "In any case, you really seem to be interested in who Taurus Silver is, aren't you?" The CAD Azusa used wasn't even made by FLT. Was the identity of the designer of the Silver model, one she didn't use, really so interesting? It was a simple question for Tatsuya. The obvious one to ask.

"Huh?" Azusa, though, looked back at him like the question had been completely unexpected. "Well, of course I am. Are you saying you're not, Shiba? I mean, it's Taurus Silver! *The* Taurus Silver, the first one to realize the Loop Cast System, the one to improve the activation program expansion speed for specialized CADs by *twenty percent*, and the one who even brought the recognition error rate for noncontact switches from three percent to below one percent. *The* Taurus Silver who shares all that knowledge freely, who thinks advancement of the whole magic world is more important than personal gain. He's a technical genius; he brought specialized CAD software forward by ten whole years in just one! Anyone who wants to be a magic engineer would be interested in what kind of a person he is."

Azusa spoke with such keen force that it felt like she was criticizing him. Even Tatsuya couldn't help but falter. The public image of Taurus Silver had grown far greater than he'd imagined. "I didn't understand. As a user, it wasn't like I didn't have my share of gripes with the model, so I didn't think he would be praised so highly..."

"Oh...I get it. You test their products, so the Silver model is pretty

カタ CLACK
カタ
CLACK
カタ
CLACK
カタ CLACK
カタ CLACK
CLACK
カタ
CLACK

familiar to you... I guess that's why you feel differently." Though her face seemed a little noncommittal, he seemed to have gotten through to her.

"Hey, Shiba, what kind of person do *you* think Taurus Silver is?"

Eyes of pure inquisitiveness. Thinking he needed to change the topic soon at this point, Tatsuya answered in such a way as to buy himself time. "Let's see... Perhaps he's actually a Japanese man, and young like us, too."

There was another beep from near the wall. Miyuki continued her work, not breaking her proper sitting posture.

——She never showed them what sort of expression was on her face.

"By the way, Ah-chan..."

"Yes, what is it, President?"

In the end, as Tatsuya was beginning to find Azusa unmanageable, Mayumi was the one to throw him a life jacket. It may have been out of self-interest, but this was the first time he felt like she was dependable. He was sure she just wanted to get Azusa back to working on student council things as soon as possible, of course.

"Weren't you going to finish that assignment by the end of lunch break?"

But though it may have been a life jacket for Tatsuya, it was essentially a merciless trumpet blast in Azusa's ear... Well, that may have been an exaggeration, but her face was so shocked that he could have believed that happened. The conversation about Taurus Silver had been a distraction from reality for her.

"Presideeent..." Azusa, seeming about to cry, looked to Mayumi for help. She must have been in a pretty bad spot with her work.

"Don't sound so pathetic," said Mayumi with a pained smile, looking up from the order requests she'd been observing so carefully and at Azusa. "I can help a little bit if you need. What's your assignment about?"

Mari gave Mayumi a look to tell her she was babying Azusa again, but Mayumi didn't care—in fact she pretended not to notice—and smiled at Azusa instead.

"I'm sorry... It's a report on the Three Great Practical Problems of Weighting Magic," explained Azusa, looking despondent, causing Suzune, Mari, and Tatsuya to look straight at her. "Wh-what is it?" She gave a start and drew back at their collective stares. When she made that expression like she could burst into tears at any moment, it made Tatsuya feel like they were torturing her somehow. He immediately averted his stare for that reason, and perhaps Suzune thought so, too.

Mari was the only one who kept looking at her. "Oh, I see..." she muttered, looking at her—or rather, the tablet she was using—with keen interest. "You've never fallen below the top five in terms of grades, so I was wondering what could have been causing you so much trouble."

"Isn't there always at least one question about that by default?" asked Mayumi, looking baffled, then she followed up. "What is the question exactly, Ah-chan?"

Given the topic's spot as a standard on tests, you could say that they had exhausted every possible question they could possibly ask. The topic was so important that it was all over the entrance exams for the National Magic University. She should have been able to find the answer to any question quite easily if she looked for it.

"It has to do with why the Three Problems are so difficult to solve. I figured two of them out, but I can't quite explain why multipurpose flight magic can't be done..."

Suzune nodded in understanding. "That means you aren't satisfied with the answers to that question that have been posed so far."

"Exactly!" Azusa's head bobbed up and down at Suzune's accurate reading of her thoughts. "Magic that defies gravity and makes your body float has been a thing ever since the eight families of modern magic were systematized, right?"

"Right, and one of the risks is that you could die if you fall," remarked Mayumi.

Azusa looked at her. "Magicians specializing in acceleration and weighting magic can jump dozens of meters with a single spell, and there's one that set a world record of over a hundred meters in the long jump. Actually, landing is even more amazing; some have even successfully jumped twenty meters into the air and landed perfectly."

"So the question is…why hasn't anyone figured out how to actually fly around in the air?"

"To be more precise, it's why hasn't flight magic been formalized so that anyone can use it?" explained Suzune to Mayumi. "There aren't many, but there are a few people who use old magic who can fly very well."

Azusa shook her head slowly, and perhaps unconsciously. "But those are essentially unique skills of I.S. magicians. It can't be called *technology* if they can't share it. Theoretically, you should be able to fly by canceling out gravity using acceleration and weighting magic. And magicians have formulated ways to float or jump. So then why can't they fly…"

"I would think the answer would be in a lot of higher-level reference books…" mused Mayumi, her eyes asking Azusa why those answers weren't convincing enough.

"Magic sequences always have an ending condition described in them, and until that condition is met, its event-altering effects will continue. If there's an object currently under the effects of event-altering magic, then in order to bring about a different event alteration in that object, you need more influence over the event than the previous spell has.

"If an object is currently in flight, then every time you wanted to accelerate, decelerate, raise, or lower it, you would need to overlay a new spell on top of the one already affecting it. Each time the amount of event influence you would need grows. The very most a single magician can regulate his or her event influence is by ten separate degrees. After making ten changes with spells to an object in flight, that would be it... That's the reason everybody says flight magic can't be formalized, right?"

Mayumi assented without a moment's thought to Azusa's long explanation. "See, you get it, Ah-chan. All your points are in order, too. What has you so worried?"

"When you look at it, the issue is overlaying magic on an object already affected by magic, right? I feel like you could just cancel the currently active spell before executing a new one."

Azusa had left her crybaby face far behind her, and now she almost seemed *angry* as she firmly presented the issues.

"Logically, you are correct, but practically, how would you go about canceling a spell?"

"Couldn't you program in an ending condition into the active spell beforehand to respond to a different magic sequence, like a key? In other words, you could use a tiny spell and inject that into one currently active to trigger its ending condition and cancel it out."

Azusa's face was almost red as she passionately debated what was entirely her idea. In contrast, though, Suzune offered a cool and composed counterpoint. "Unfortunately, magic sequences cannot affect other magic sequences. They can only overwrite eidos. If you simultaneously inject two magic sequences into the same eidos, only the one with more influence will affect the eidos; it won't *erase* the weaker magic sequence. That isn't to say there is no anti-magic that can dismantle and erase magic sequences, but they're extremely high-level spells that directly interact with the makeup of information itself. Doing it in a laboratory would be one thing, but I don't know of any magicians that can do such a thing perfectly."

"Oh, I see..."

The things Suzune explained were knowledge related to lessons on anti-magic—spells to counteract an opponent's magic—which were a part of applied magic science, a subject not taught until the second semester of a student's second year, when it took the place of fundamental magic science. The specific topic, in the regular syllabus, was given to seniors in their first semester, so there was no reason Azusa would have known about it. The very fact that she didn't seem at all frazzled by the term *anti-magic* was a sign that she put a lot of effort into her studies.

"It is, however, an interesting idea," said Suzune, smiling gently at Azusa's zeal and depression. "I think you are correct in your thought to cancel a magic sequence's active state."

"Yes," said Mayumi, showing assent to Azusa's idea as well. "The rapid increase in the influence you need is caused by overwriting active spells, after all. I've never thought of it before, but if you stopped the active event alteration, you wouldn't need more influence to overwrite it with the next spell... If you were in the air at the moment, you'd need to make the switch without any lost time, but with a CAD meant for the purpose, you could make it activate the next spell before you started to fall..." After muttering to herself for a while, she seemed to remember something, and cocked her head to the side. "But if all you needed to do was negate the spell's effectiveness, someone would have already tried it, right? You're basically just expanding Area Interference retroactively..."

Mayumi's question prompted Suzune to bring up the search window on her workstation. "One moment, please... There was indeed a large-scale experiment held in England last year. The concept is just as you say—making flight magic practical by applying Area Interference retroactively." Suzune immediately pulled up the relevant article from a database of magic-related news.

"How did it turn out?" she asked, in a rather lively way—Mayumi was still just a normal high school student, and she couldn't hide her anticipation.

"A complete failure. They reported that they saw a sudden and radical increase in the needed influence because of the successive spell casting."

"...Oh." And with just that report from Suzune that betrayed (?) her anticipation, she couldn't conceal her disappointment, either. "Does it say the reason?"

"No, it isn't listed here. What do you think, President?" asked Suzune in return.

Mayumi put her finger on her chin. "Hmm... The previous magic would have stopped being active, though... Tatsuya, what do you think?"

Her question was to buy more time for her to think of an answer. She hadn't actually been expecting it to come from him.

"The experiment in England that Suzune cited was mistaken in its basic premise."

So the conclusive response that he gave took Mayumi completely by surprise.

"...What was wrong with it?" Mayumi managed to ask, her eyes wide.

Tatsuya launched into an indifferent explanation—neither boasting nor condescending. "When magic sequence ending conditions aren't met, they remain on the target eidos until they decay naturally over time. When you use one spell to nullify the effects of another spell, it may *look* like the other spell is destroyed, but that's only on the surface."

Mayumi, Suzune, Azusa, and even Mari were now looking at him eagerly. He kept a straight face and maintained his businesslike tone, as though the pressure they were putting on him didn't exist. "Let's say there's a magic sequence A that was cast first, and a magic sequence B meant to nullify the effects of magic sequence A. By executing sequence B, the event-altering effects of sequence A are negated. However, the only thing it loses is its ability to alter events—the sequence *itself* still remains on the eidos. Sequence A and sequence B will continue to act upon the target eidos at the same time; it's just that sequence B is the only one showing an effect. As Ichihara mentioned, magic sequences only overwrite eidos. They can't act on other magic sequences. It's the same even if we're talking about Area Interference. As long as it isn't a spell that erases the magic sequence directly, even anti-magic doesn't break this basic rule."

"...Does that mean the experiment in England was casting more spells than they needed for flight magic?"

Tatsuya nodded, then added, "What this means is that each time they want to change flight path, they have to use an extra magic sequence to overwrite the old. Those extra writes pile up each time you change your flight state, so it's evident that you would more quickly reach the upper limit of the magician's event influence. The English scholars on the experiment were probably under some illusions regarding the nature of anti-magic."

Just as he finished his explanation, the portable terminal in Tatsuya's breast pocket vibrated. It was a replacement for a school bell, notifying him of the end of lunch break.

"Miyuki, shall we go back?"

"Yes, Tatsuya."

Miyuki, who had her back facing them the entire time, stood at once upon hearing her name. Her voice, expression, and behavior were just as elegant and ladylike as always.

That meant Mayumi, Suzune, Mari, and Azusa didn't notice anything.

They never noticed it—how straight and proud Miyuki's back had been as she sat at the console. How jubilantly her fingers had danced over the keyboard.

◇ ◇ ◇

The air in the club committee headquarters had been tense since before the Nine School Competition assembly began. Those students who performed well in their matches would be given bonuses to their grades to match, but just being chosen as a member for the competition granted them an extended exemption from having to do homework—an A-class privilege by anyone's standards.

This went for the engineers, too, not just the competitors; this competition was extremely important to the school. Even among the students, anyone participating had great status. As this assembly was to finalize the members who would be going, it was no wonder the mood was raw and harsh.

——If Tatsuya had been an unrelated third party, he would have been looking at his fellow freshmen and upperclassmen with some sympathy as he watched their faces, now happy and now sad. Now that he was one of the people on the chopping block, however, he had to resist the urge to give a melancholic sigh—he just wished this farce would end as soon as humanly possible.

It wasn't that he had no interest in the competition.

He, as much as anyone else, had the desire to pit his own skills against other magicians (in training) of the same age, though it was a different sort of hunger from the desire to prove his intellect filled with CAD improvement techniques he'd learned in his father's laboratories.

He had been **created** to have less emotion than those around him, but he was still at the most energetic, vigorous point of his life. No matter what his classmates might have said about him, he wasn't so mature that he wasn't interested in competing with others at all.

But to do that, he would have to get past this ceremony seething with conceit, envy, vainglory, and bitterness. That's why he felt so gloomy.

Ignorant of his current mood—as was only natural—the seats in the conference room filled up steadily. Once every seat had found a person, Mayumi took her seat in the speaker's chair.

"I'd like to begin the Nine School Competition member selection conference."

And thus began the hugely populated conference, including the junior and senior athletes and engineers who had already been unofficially offered the position, the club presidents of each of the relevant athletic clubs, the student council members (except for Miyuki, who was minding the student council room in their absence), and the club committee executives.

Tatsuya had been given an observation seat along with the other unofficially confirmed members. And it could be said that, given a large enough group of people, there would always be some nitpicker whose sharp eyes would discover an outsider among them.

As expected, immediately upon the conference's start, the topic turned to why a Course 2 freshman was present.

That wasn't to say none of the people looking at him were doing so favorably—in fact, much to his surprise, most of the opinions were in his favor.

Unlike his fellow freshmen, the upperclassmen seemed to be aware that despite Tatsuya being a Course 2 student, his achievements as a disciplinary officer set him apart from the rest.

Even so, there were many with opposing viewpoints. Their opposition was not clear nor was it based in logic; it was an emotional, passive opposition. Thanks to that, the debate regarding him ended up going in slow circles, with no conclusion in sight.

"So basically…" Suddenly, a grave voice silenced the conference. It was not a very loud voice, but it quieted the chaotic arguments of everyone present as the speaker turned to look at the one who had originally suggested there was a problem. It was the club committee chairman, Katsuto Juumonji, who had maintained his silence until now, returning all the gazes that had come upon him. "I understand that the problem is that we don't know how high Shiba's skill level is. If I am correct in saying so, then the best way of resolving this would be to see his skills firsthand."

The big room fell silent. It was simple, effective, and nobody would be able to argue the results. Plus, it was a solution to the potentially substantial risks involved that nobody had been willing to mention aloud.

"...That makes sense," said Mari, breaking the silence, "but how should we actually do it?"

"We should have him perform adjustments right now," answered Katsuto, simply and clearly. "If you like, I can be his test subject."

The CADs currently provided for their use would have to be adjusted to suit their users. Ten magicians would need to have ten different setups, even if they all used the same exact machine. Magicians absorbed the activation programs expanded by their CAD straight into their unconscious regions. In other words, the magician's mind was completely exposed to their own CAD. In recent years, they were equipped with tuning functions for accelerating and smoothing out the reading-in of activation programs, and that was more than enough to have quite an effect on the mind of the user.

If this tuning process were done improperly, it would cause not only a decrease in magic efficiency, but also discomfort, headache, dizziness, and nausea—and in the worst cases, mental damage such as hallucinations—so the latest and greatest CADs would need adjustments that were meticulous enough and precise enough for the magician to handle them.

Therefore, leaving one's CAD adjustments in the hands of an unproven magic engineer meant the magician would be shouldering a huge risk. Katsuto's suggestion, while his own, had essentially been a very brave one.

"No, I'm the one who recommended him, so I'll do it." Mayumi immediately made an offer to stand in for him. Her suggestion was probably based on a sense of responsibility, but on the other hand, it meant she didn't completely trust him, and that made Tatsuya rather uncomfortable.

"No, please, allow me."

Kirihara announcing his willingness, however, was unexpected, quite the surprise—and Tatsuya found his masculine eagerness rather comforting.

The school's CAD adjustment facility open to students and faculty was located in the lab building. But they weren't going to use the adjustment devices provided there this time; instead, they brought the onboard adjustment machine they would actually be using in the Nine School Competition into the conference room. They also readied a CAD that was to the competition's specifications for him to adjust.

The preparations for his test, at least on the equipment side, had been finished without a hitch, with skill and efficiency; they also made the lateness of the competitor selection stand out.

Tatsuya sat down in front of the adjustment machine, and Kirihara took a seat on the other side of it, though they couldn't see their faces. The student council members and club presidents all gathered around them.

First he booted up the machine. Obstinate stares had already gathered on Tatsuya's hands at this early stage, but he was used to using far more intricate adjustment devices on a daily basis; he could do this part perfectly in his sleep. He kept a straight face, ignoring the annoying stares, and quickly progressed to the point where he would need to prepare for measurements.

He asked for a confirmation of the test conditions. "Let me confirm: The task is to copy Kirihara's CAD settings to the competition one, then tune it to allow immediate usage, but not to alter the activation programs in any way, correct?"

"Yes, that will be fine," said Mayumi, nodding. Tatsuya, however, shook his head just a little at that. "What's wrong?" she asked.

"I can't say I recommend copying his settings to a CAD with different hardware…but that's the task for now. Safety first, then."

"?"

Mayumi wasn't the only one who looked at him askance. Copying

CAD settings was something done whenever you got a new device, so they didn't know what the issue was. But as expected, the members of the engineering team, beginning with Azusa, seemed to understand what he suggested. Their reactions were all either a slight nod or an eager smirk from those who wanted to see his skills.

Tatsuya didn't engage in any further useless talking and got to work.

First he took the CAD from Kirihara and connected it to the adjustment machine. It semiautomatically extracted the setting data; the process wasn't one that would make any differences in skill clear. However, when he created a workspace on the machine and saved the setting data there, rather than copying it straight to the CAD, several people gave him strange looks.

Next he had to measure the particular characteristics of Kirihara's psionic waves. At Tatsuya's signal, he put on a headset and placed both hands on the measurement panel. This was the normal procedure as well; with machines equipped with auto-adjusters, it would automatically do all the adjustments just by setting up the CAD and doing the measurements. That was where it usually stopped for students who used the school's machines to adjust their personal CADs.

At the same time, an engineer's skills would be highlighted if he or she manually accessed the CAD's operating system and made adjustments that were more precise than the automatic process would have done.

"Thank you. You can take it off now."

With Tatsuya's indication that the measurements had completed, Kirihara removed the headset.

Normally, at this point, the only thing left would be to connect the CAD to do the setup on, then make minor adjustments to whatever the auto-adjuster gave. But to do that, one needed to prepare the CAD that was either already set up, or, in this case, that already had the settings copied to it.

Most of the people observing thought he'd accidentally switched parts of the process around. And as if to substantiate that idea, Tatsuya sat still and stared at the display.

However, from the way he sat, it didn't feel like he had made a mistake and didn't know what to do anymore. No, he seemed far from helpless. His eyes were frightfully serious.

Azusa, unable to suppress her curiosity, leaned forward suddenly and looked at the display from over Tatsuya's shoulder.

"Eh?" she muttered a moment later, a grunt that was a little inappropriate for a young maiden.

Tatsuya didn't flick an eyelash at the sound.

Too hesitant to ask out loud what was the matter, Mayumi and Mari peered at the display from Azusa's sides—and just barely managed to restrain themselves from giving the same kind of grunt.

There was no graph displaying the measurement results, which normally appeared on the screen at this point. Instead, the entire screen was filled with countless letters and numbers flying by very quickly.

The two of them could only make out a few numbers here and there; their eyes couldn't keep up with the strings of characters rushing by.

The parade of letters and numbers stopped soon. It had taken only a few dozen seconds, and not even five minutes since Tatsuya had begun staring at the screen. Immediately after freezing the automatic scrolling, Tatsuya set the competition device on the adjustment machine and began typing fervently.

One after another, windows opened and closed on the screen. Two of the windows were left open; one had the raw data from the measurement results that he'd just been reading, and the other was the raw data copied from the original CAD. Only Azusa could tell all this.

Almost none of the people watching at the moment understood how high-level an operation was being performed. A lot of them were probably just in awe over his keyboard-only input speed, an unusual skill in this day and age. But Azusa knew that the truly astonishing thing was his skill at directly understanding the results of the psionic wave measurement in its raw data form.

Doing it this way meant that he could apply every last bit of the measurements to his adjustments—at least insofar as the device's capacity would allow. It was a fully manual adjustment, not relying on the auto-adjuster feature at all.

She watched as before her eyes the setting data he'd saved to the temporary workspace was overwritten in the blink of an eye. Everything on the screen was still raw data like before, but Azusa was just barely able to understand the settings he had created.

They left a huge safety margin—"safety first" indeed. With these settings, the user would be at less risk than if the auto-adjuster had been used. Not only that, he could now supply the CAD with far more efficient activation programs.

In reality, it didn't even need to be tested. This freshman's skill at doing adjustments was above literally everyone else on the engineering team. Azusa resolved to drag him on to it no matter what it took.

With the condition being not to alter any of the activation programs, he finished doing the adjustments in no time. The performance had felt extremely short to everyone watching.

They tested it right away. The tension on Kirihara's face, so subtle that observers wouldn't notice it, was still in the "entertainment" category. But in reality, there were no accidents, no almost-accidents, and no bugs. The CAD Tatsuya had adjusted worked **exactly the same** as Kirihara's personal device.

"Kirihara, how does it feel?"

"No problems here. It feels just like the one I use."

Kirihara's response to Katsuto's question came immediately.

It was clear to everyone there that he wasn't giving any unfair bias due to personal friendship. Even if someone only **sort of** knew of the connection between Kirihara and Tatsuya—the incident in which Tatsuya slammed Kirihara into the floor after he barged into the kendo club's demonstration during the club recruitment week in April—they would still never believe Kirihara would be trying to make him look good. But even without such a misunderstanding, everyone there understood that the CAD was in perfect working order just by watching him cast a spell with it. However, other than the obvious result of the magic going off smoothly, which was only average, in a way, they couldn't understand just by looking.

"...He seems to have some skill, but it doesn't seem to be at a level to represent our school."

"And the time he took to finish was average. I can't call his performance overly good."

"He does things in a strange way. That might mean something in and of itself, but..."

Sure enough, the first opinions to come from the junior competitors were negative ones, citing a plain and simple result. They were not necessarily out of resistance to selecting someone so singular for the team, though; some of it was just recoil. The student council president directly recommending him, and as an exception, even, had made them unconsciously hope for an eye-popping display of skill.

Azusa, however, opposed them violently. "I strongly support Shiba being on the team!" Her normally timid expression was gone without a trace. "The technique he just showed us is so advanced that I still can't believe a high school student did it. At the very least, doing the adjustments all manually without using the auto-adjuster is something I can't even hope to do."

"...That might be a high-level technique, but if the end result is average, then what would be the point...?"

"It may look average on the outside, but on the inside it's anything but! It's amazing how he maintained its efficiency and still put in such a huge safety margin!"

"Nakajou, calm down… I feel like the time he spent putting in such an unnecessarily large safety margin could have been used to bring its performance up."

"Well, that's…probably because it was so sudden…" Unfortunately, Azusa was never what one could call eloquent, so her enthusiasm tapered off.

When it looked like Azusa was at a loss for words, suddenly, one male student raised his hand and stood up, drawing the attention of everyone in attendance. "The CAD that Kirihara uses isn't so much for competition; it's an extremely high-spec model. The fact that its user didn't feel a difference despite the gap in specifications between his CAD and the competition one is, I believe, evidence of quite a lot of skill."

"Huh? …Hattori?"

Surprisingly enough, Hattori had been the one to come to the rescue. "President, I also support Shiba being on the engineering team."

"Hanzou?" Mayumi's face, too, belied a clear surprise.

But Hattori, whatever his true intentions were, frankly explained his opinion, without (visibly) flinching from the negative impression doing so could make on the student council president he so respected (?). "Our school's dignity will be on the line during the Nine School Competition. I believe we should select students with the most ability, regardless of their title. The job of an engineer is to support the athletes so they have an easier time competing. If Kirihara said it felt the same, then his skill can only be described as extremely advanced, like Nakajou said. We have such a shortage of engineers that we're struggling to even find candidates; this isn't the time to be caught up on him being a freshman or this whole thing being unprecedented."

There were thorns in his voice, making themselves known every now and then—and they spoke to the fact that he was telling the truth. Nevertheless, Hattori having turned coats to support Tatsuya greatly impacted the entire room.

"I think Hattori's explanation is correct. Shiba has displayed enough skill to be a team member and represent our school. I will support him for the team as well."

With Katsuto clearly picking a side amid the silent opposition, most people there made up their minds.

[2]

After the siblings finished up their usual dinner between the two of them, the phone rang as if it knew they were done.

In passing, as you are aware, most telephone instruments came with video these days. There had been silly debates among third-rate cultural circles that they weren't so much telephones as tele-*videos*, but on the whole, even after the practical implementation of three-dimensional images, they were still just called "phones."

Returning to the topic at hand.

Miyuki was currently cleaning up the kitchen after dinner.

One might expect manual labor such as dishwashing to be handed off to HARs, but there were no 3Hs (Humanoid Home Helpers, essentially servant robots) in this house, though they had finally started to become widespread. The two of them had both rejected the idea of annoying ceiling-attached manipulators being installed. Therefore, they needed to wash and dry the tableware themselves—with Miyuki claiming that skimping on such simple labor would make you atrophy.

Once again, returning to the topic at hand.

* * *

Tatsuya was the one to pick up the phone; in short, it was for him, and not a product of coincidence—at least, it shouldn't have been.

"It's good to hear from you again... Did you time this?"

"...I have no idea what you mean... It's been a while, Specialist."

Displayed on the screen was an old friend of his, with an evasive expression on his face.

"Yes, two months since the last real-time conversation. Still... Is this a private channel? You called me by rank. You have some nerve cutting into a civilian residence's private line every time you want to talk."

"It wasn't easy, though, I'll tell you. Specialist, don't you think your security is a little too strict for a *civilian residence?*"

"Hackers these days are indiscriminate. There are plenty of things on our server that I wouldn't want them seeing."

"Seems like it. We almost tripped up the counterhacking just now."

"That is what we call your just desserts. As long as you don't try to access things too deeply, you won't trigger the counterprogram."

"It was a good lesson for our newbie operator, in any case." The face on the screen, leathery as though from sunburn or gunpowder burns, twisted into an evil grin. *Three years and he still hasn't aged a bit,* thought Tatsuya.

Then he briefly considered how despite the exhausting work that would come with his status and station, the man didn't seem tired in the least. Tatsuya was reminded again that this man, Major Harunobu Kazama, commanding officer of the Independent Magic Battalion of the army's 101st Brigade, wasn't the sort of person who would take well to excessive wasting of time with pleasantries such as these.

"Major, what do you need from me today?"

"Yes, let's leave the prefacing aside. First, we have some work for you."

"Yes, sir."

"We overhauled the Third Eye and made upgrades to several of its parts today. We need you to do the software update to match and run some performance tests."

The brigade's number, 101st, was pronounced "one-oh-first," but it didn't actually refer to a one hundred first brigade. It was an experimental group, separate from normal military compositions, that used magic equipment as their main armament. Within that brigade, the Independent Magic Battalion was the group tasked with carrying out tests for newly developed equipment. Its level of confidentiality was five or six stages above normal military secrets. Normally, a mere high school student would never have even known of their existence, let alone be involved in one.

Tatsuya, however, due to circumstances that could really only be chalked up to happenstance, was actually integrated as part of Kazama's unit. "Understood, sir. I will be present first thing in the morning."

"...No, it's not quite pressing enough for you to take a day off from school."

"Actually, sir, I was planning on going to the lab to run tests on the new device on my next day off."

"Given my post, I don't have much place to tell you this...but ever since you became a high school kid, you've been acting less and less **like a student**."

"I don't like to use this phrase, sir—but it can't be helped."

"I see... There's no helping how busy either one of us is, is there? All right, then come to the usual place tomorrow morning. Unfortunately I won't be able to meet you there, but I'll tell Sanada about it."

"Yes, sir." Tatsuya saluted in a businesslike way, and Kazama answered it with his own. They weren't formal military salutes, but he was an irregular member of the unit, so they didn't need to be that strict.

"On to the next topic—from what I hear, you'll be participating in the Nine School Competition this summer, too."

"...Yes, sir." He needed a split second of time to answer that, but from another point of view, *only* needing a split second in this case was worthy of praise. He'd been placed on the engineering team only three hours ago. He knew it would do him no good to ask the man where he got that information, so he suppressed his curiosity.

"It'll take place in the southeastern area of the Fuji Maneuvering Ground. I suppose this applies for every year...but be careful, **Tatsuya**."

The changes in Kazama's conversations were always abrupt, but today they were especially so. The fact that he'd used his real name instead of his rank, his last name, or an alias meant he was giving him a warning as an old friend rather than as a superior officer. It was no trivial matter, however, to warn a civilian—and just a high school student, with no societal status—a piece of advice that came from information from military intelligence and counterintelligence networks. Tatsuya braced himself and waited for him to continue.

"There are some unsettling movements in said area. We've found traces of unlawful intruders there."

"In a military maneuvering area?"

"The whole thing really is pathetic. In addition, East Asians thought to be members of an international crime syndicate have been spotted several times in the vicinity. That didn't happen last year. Given the time, we think they have their sights set on the competition."

Tatsuya was about to say, "For a silly high school competition?" but then thought better of it. They were just high school students, but they were all magical talents at the top of their generation gathering there to test their skills. If they set up explosives during the awards ceremony, for example, it would end up causing great damage to the number of capable people this country possessed.

"An international crime syndicate, sir?"

So it wasn't a terrorist organization in the same vein as Blanche, the group posing as an anti-magic government organization that Tatsuya had gotten aggressively involved with in April. A crime syndicate probably wouldn't take action purely to cause such bloodshed. Still, terrorist organizations were one thing; a military man like Kazama should have been wholly unrelated to international crime groups. How had he figured out the syndicate's identity?

"I had Mibu look into it. I believe you've already met?"

"The father of First High junior Sayaka Mibu, sir?"

"Yeah. After retiring from military service, he transferred to the COIA. He's currently section manager of their foreign affairs department. Specifically, he's assigned to foreign crime organizations."

"That's…surprising." He wasn't just saying that, either—he really was surprised.

For one thing, he was surprised that Kazama had just plainly exposed the true identity of someone working for an intelligence organization over the phone. He was also surprised at the fact that Kazama had leaked this information to ask for help from the Cabinet Office's intelligence agency for what was, in a way, a military oversight—it was rumored that they were not on friendly terms with one another; relations between civil officials and military officers rarely were. But above all that, he was surprised at how the daughter of a foreign intelligence and counterintelligence manager had belonged to—or rather, been subcontracted to—a terrorist organization under the patronage of a foreign spy agency, and that for her father, a manager—though he didn't know how much power he had—to have left it alone was an act of senseless noninterference.

"Separate divisions are responsible for crime syndicates and terrorist organizations, after all. Sectionalism is one of those incurable diseases of the state." Kazama guessed his thoughts correctly, probably more out of his personal powers of insight (and not a small amount of sympathy) than the length of their acquaintanceship. "But you can always trust the information in a field you know well. In Mibu's case, whether they were members of the Hong Kong crime syndicate No-Head Dragon. Its objectives are still unknown, but when we get additional information, I'll contact you."

"Thank you, sir."

"I won't see you tomorrow, but maybe we'll be able to meet at Fuji."

"I'll be looking forward to it, sir."

"Me too... Whoops, looks like we've been talking for too long. The newbie is getting a little restless, so I'm hanging up." The network police must have caught wind of their wiretapping. Tatsuya wasn't sure whether to praise their technical skills or sigh at the *lack* of skills Kazama's subordinates had. "Say hello to Master for me."

"I will, sir."

"Good-bye." Before he could answer, the screen blinked off.

That means he wants me to tell Master, I think... Tatsuya sighed, thinking of their mutual master, for whom, in spite of having an official priesthood license, the term *fake* was quite fitting. How much of what he'd just heard was he supposed to reveal to the man?

◇ ◇ ◇

From the other side of the living room door, which had been closed at some point, he heard Miyuki's voice. "Tatsuya, if it is all right by you, would you like to have some tea...?"

She must have waited in the kitchen until their conversation was over so that she wouldn't hear the details. In reality, Miyuki possessed a much higher position than Tatsuya, to the point where she was able to listen in on military and diplomatic secrets alike without any reservations. She had never made use of that position when around him, though.

Tatsuya went toward the kitchen without saying anything and opened the door before she had to repeat herself. Miyuki froze, her eyes wide. As expected, she carried a tray with a tea set and tea cakes on it. "...Please don't surprise me like that. You could have just answered... You are quite unkind, Tatsuya, concealing your footsteps to get a good laugh out of scaring me."

Miyuki tuned her face to the side sullenly. Tatsuya took the tray from her and apologized. "Sorry, sorry," he said. "I wasn't trying to be mean. I figured your hands were full, so I came right away. I can't let my cute little sister carry something so heavy forever."

"...I am fully and acutely aware that you are lying to me...but I will allow myself to be tricked this time." She tried to keep a displeased face, but her expression was loosening. She felt easily placated—it had only taken a few silly words from his mouth. She didn't particularly mind it, though.

"Black tea today?"

"Yes. I got some good second flush tea leaves and thought it would be nice to have once in a while."

He nodded. As soon as he sat down at the table, he brought the cup to his nose and gave it a smell. "Muscatel? How unusual... Were these hard to find?"

"No, I really did just come across them by chance... But if you're happy, that is the best reward I can have."

He took a slow sip of the tea. When she saw him smile in satisfaction, she smiled sincerely as well.

"The black tea is great, but this shortbread is amazing, too. Did you make this yourself?"

"Yes, well... I do feel they are a bit mismatched."

"No, I don't mind it at all. They really are delicious."

Miyuki looked down in embarrassment, but her brother reached for one piece of shortbread after another. She brought her face back up as if lured by his hands, then finally gave a sparkling smile.

Tatsuya didn't bring up his talk with Kazama, and Miyuki didn't ask him. His mouth was too busy eating the tea cakes his sister had made and tasting the black tea his sister had worked so hard to get anyway, and Miyuki simply spent teatime watching her brother's satisfied expression.

◇ ◇ ◇

Though it doesn't need to be clearly stated again here, Miyuki was widely accepted as an honor student. Not only did she have natural talent; she never gave anything any less than her best. On top of being too helpful to her brother, she made a habit of staying up late every night studying.

It was almost midnight before she finally switched off her electro-fluidic display (otherwise known as e-paper), stowed her desk, and stood.

She wasn't that tired yet tonight. She knew from experience that if she went to bed in her excited state, she wouldn't be able to get to sleep. It would be easier if she used a sound-sleeper (a device that placed you into a peaceful sleep), but her brother, for no clear reason, hated the machine that was now used by 70 percent of the country. Miyuki wasn't about to use any technology that Tatsuya didn't appreciate.

She decided to put on some more tea to take a break. Partly for her brother, who kept late hours, of course. He'd been really happy with the tea today—the rare leaves had been very hard to get, and she'd acquired the best kind, so the work was worth it. Just thinking of his smile would be enough to give her sweet dreams, but if she could see the real thing one more time and maybe get him to pet her head, she'd have no more to say.

As she went toward the kitchen, she spotted herself in a mirror and paused to think for a moment. Then she nodded, an impish smile on her face.

◇ ◇ ◇

"Tatsuya, it's Miyuki. I've brought some tea."

"Oh, good timing. Come in."

It was basically a matter of daily routine for Miyuki to bring him tea at this hour, but she had to stop and wonder for a bit about how his response implied he'd been waiting for her; usually he would just give her an apologetic word of thanks.

Still, if her brother was waiting for her, that made her all the happier. Eager to see what kind of face he'd make when he saw her, she entered the basement room Tatsuya used as a laboratory.

"I was just thinking of coming to get y—" The rest of his sentence was supplanted with silence. Feeling a devilish sort of satisfaction as Tatsuya turned in his chair and stared at her, she pinched the hem of her skirt with one hand—the other still holding the tray with the tea—and curtsied, bringing it up to show off her knees.

"…Oh, right. Is that the Faerie Dance costume?"

"Correct! I am glad you knew, Tatsuya."

She wore a colorful, fluttering miniskirt made of layers of choice silk organdy, leggings of thin make that generously showed off her pretty leg curves, and short, tight boots. Squeezed around her waist was a vest with an open back, made of a glossy material that looked thinner than it was, with her chest blocked securely with a finely detailed object whose material had curves naturally, rather than sewn ones. Under her vest was a shirt that clung to her arms but was loose around the shoulders. It was the same pattern as her leggings. Actually, they might not have been leggings and a shirt, but rather a long-sleeved leotard. Without the vest, she would look like a female figure skater.

And clasping her long hair was a headband, wide as earmuffs, with wings attached to it.

There was no doubt that the clothing, combining air resistance and chest protection with beauty, was the costume for the most famous magical sporting competition ever used as part of the Nine School Competition: Mirage Bat, otherwise known as Faerie Dance.

"How do I look?"

Miyuki placed her tray on a side table, flashed a smile, and spun around. Her skirt floated up, and despite how short it was, it was indescribably elegant when matched with her fluttering, bouncing hair.

She came back around to face him and stopped turning, then took her skirt in both hands and curtsied. Tatsuya openly praised her. "Very cute. It looks really good on you. And punctual, too."

"Thank…you?"

She had been 100 percent certain her brother would compliment her. She had only thought of one thing to say as she curtsied, and that one thing had been enough. But, not understanding the last phrase to come out of Tatsuya's mouth, her planned thanks turned into an unplanned interrogative statement.

She stood up again and looked at Tatsuya; he was still sitting in his chair. As she was about to give him her usual look to ask what *punctual* was supposed to mean, she suddenly felt like something was out of place.

She quickly identified it—Tatsuya was sitting down, but his eyes were as high as they were when he stood next to her. Hastily she looked down, then gasped.

There should have been a chair under him—but there wasn't.

Tatsuya had his right leg over his left, and was leaning forward with his right elbow on his right knee...sitting in midair.

"I wanted you to test out this device, too." He slid through the air over to Miyuki without changing his pose. He stopped within arm's distance, then sat up and uncrossed his legs, putting them to floor as though he were rising from a chair. When he did, his body naturally returned to the floor.

There was a slight pause as she stared at him agape. "...A flight spell... You perfected permanent gravity manipulation magic!" She took her brother's hand with enough force that she was basically embracing it and cheered. "Congratulations!"

Tatsuya had been researching this spell for a long time. It was in the acceleration-weighting family, always the first of the four families and eight types to be named in normal magic. It was the most fundamental family of modern magic, developed out of simple psychokinesis. Permanent gravity manipulation magic—a flight spell—was theoretically possible through acceleration and weighting family magic, but despite modern magic suggesting from an early period that it was possible, it had never been realized, at least publicly, until today.

When they talked about flight magic in the student council room at lunch break today, the consensus, based in modern magic science, was that while it was theoretically possible, it was practically close to impossible.

But here, before Miyuki's eyes, another one of the accepted opinions of modern magic science had been overturned. "You've done the impossible once again! I am so proud to be the sister of the one who accomplished it, and witness to a brilliant historical feat!"

Her grip on his right hand was so tight she might have hugged him at any moment; Tatsuya gently put his left hand on top of their hands. "Thanks, Miyuki. The goal wasn't to actually fly in the sky—old magic already has their own flight spell—but this brings me yet another step closer to my objective."

"Only very few magicians can use flight spells from old magic. It's essentially a superpower. Couldn't anyone use your flight spell if they supplied the required magic power?"

"That's how I tried to make it. That's why I want you to test it."

"I would be glad to!" she replied, eyes glittering, nodding deeply.

After receiving an explanation on the spell, Miyuki looked down to her left hand, at the CAD that had just been adjusted. It was the same portable terminal-shaped CAD that Miyuki always used. It was even smaller than her miniaturized one, though, and it fit snugly in the palm of her little hand.

The shape was the only thing similar about them. This one was a specialized type. She wasn't accustomed to using them, but operating one was exceedingly simple. All it had was an on-off button. Once you turned it on, it would automatically absorb psions from the user and continue to process activation programs until its battery ran out. They were violent things, in a way. However, there was a limit on how many psions they used. The fundamental design concept was to devise ways to minimize the burden on the user.

"Starting," she said, gulping with uncontainable nervousness. Her mouth was too dry to swallow any moisture. She wanted to give herself a pat on the back for not letting her hands shake.

Even if she failed this test, her brother wouldn't blame her. Instead, he would probably redo all the settings for this "flight device" from square one. She would hate herself for making her brother go through that because of her own lacking power.

She switched on the CAD.

She knew it had begun absorbing psions from her body even if she couldn't feel it. Still, it was absorbing such a minuscule amount that she wouldn't notice unless she really paid attention. It was barely enough to use up the flow of excess psions she emitted on a daily basis.

By the time she realized it, the activation program had already been copied into her magic calculation region. Tatsuya had told her beforehand, but she was still surprised at just how tiny the sequence was. She inputted variables into the sequence and constructed a magic sequence.

Normally, magicians were unaware of this process occurring. They would create a clear vision in their mind of the reality-altering effect by using language, numbers, or images, then send it to their unconscious region. The magic calculation region's role was to convert this image into input data for the magic sequence. The variable portion of an activation program indicated what the magician had to envision especially strongly. Magicians could be aware of the activation program read into their bodies, as well as the magic sequence constructed in their minds. The process of creating the magic sequence, however, was a semiautomatic process that took place without the person willing it. If it wasn't, then there was no way a human could create enough information bodies to alter a physical phenomenon with his or her normal data-processing capabilities.

Miyuki envisioned herself floating up to the ceiling.

As soon as she did, gravity freed her from its fetters. Her five senses lost important information and brought about a slight panic as she suddenly felt that her body had disappeared. But there was enough joy in her heart to make up for it.

To think flying in the air could bring such a feeling of liberation! She grew a little jealous of astronauts for being able to experience the same joy before her. At the same time, though, she felt sorry for them—the only way they could feel this was if they were wearing a heavy space suit. Then she realized she wanted to fly through the sky, not this cramped basement room.

"How is it? The activation program chain isn't a burden for you?"

Her brother's voice snapped her back to reality. She felt embarrassed for losing herself in bliss during such an important experiment. But this wasn't the time to be occupied with thoughts of self-hate. *Get it together, Miyuki*, she scolded herself, then answered, "I feel fine. No headaches or fatigue, either."

"That's great. Next, try moving slowly, parallel to the ground. Once you get used to it, could you gradually raise your speed and fly as you'd like?"

"Yes."

She envisioned herself moving slowly and horizontally as her brother said. The super-tiny activation program was automatically expanded and copied, and a magic sequence to alter gravity's vector horizontally was constructed.

The trick to this flight device was that it executed magic from activation programs continuously being processed. It was programmed so that the previous variable values would be carried over as long as the magician didn't read a new mental image into his or her calculation region. Loop Cast worked by adding typeless magic information that would copy *itself* and paste it inside the magic calculation region at the final stages of its compilation into a magic sequence, thus allowing the same activation program to be used again without the magician needing to use his or her CAD; but this flight device constructed the same magic sequence continuously from the same activation program, inputting the same variable automatically. Taurus Silver's famous Loop Cast System and the flight device Tatsuya had created were counterparts.

"Does the magic feel intermittent at all?"

"No. The time recorder is functioning perfectly, as expected from your skill."

Essentially, this system's function was to accurately record the time of the magic's execution while it was active. Digital processing like that was unsuited for humans, and one of the pieces that required a machine's abilities to supplement. This system would have been completely impossible to create if the creator was concerned only with flying through magic ability alone.

Miyuki steadily increased her speed as directed. She made full use of the limited basement space, turning, spinning, and somersaulting freely through the air. Her skirt fluttered, and her hair waved. Her stretching and bending movements exposed her graceful curves.

At some point, Tatsuya forgot he was supposed to be observing; it was as if he was entranced by the unexpected nymph's dance.

◇ ◇ ◇

Four Leaves Technology, or FLT for short, had its CAD development center quite far away from their residence—two hours by public transportation (you could actually get there in one with an electric motorcycle, but it was raining today, so they used public transportation). Tatsuya was familiar with the path there, but the more he got used to it, the more the length of the trip bothered him.

"Miyuki…?"

"Yes? What is it, Tatsuya?"

"…Actually, never mind. It's nothing."

"Yes…?"

Whenever he went to this laboratory, rather than the lab room in the main building, Miyuki was usually with him. She would have been just as used to it, but despite the poor weather, her mood was sunny like they were going for a picnic, and Tatsuya had found himself unable not to ask why.

He hesitated, though, because he realized it was a strange question.

Miyuki looked at him confused, of course, but eventually went back to her radiant mind-set. If they hadn't already been inside the lab building, he wouldn't have been surprised if she had actually started to whistle or sing.

This was the R & D center of the company, for which its technological prowess was its selling point, and, in some ways, the core of all of FLT. The security was strict enough to match, not being left to machine monitoring but stationing an almost excessive number of human personnel policing it.

None of them called out to stop Tatsuya, though. He even bypassed the reception desk, proceeding ever farther down the windowless hallways.

At last, they arrived at a room where one of the walls was glass. On the other side of it was a semibasement atrium, wide enough to be an aircraft hangar. Opposite that was another observation room like this one.

This was the CAD testing block.

The room was filled with over ten scientists and researchers, restlessly moving to and fro, discussing among themselves, and operating measuring instruments.

Despite the busy work everyone was doing, somebody called out a moment after he entered. "Oh, Prince Shiba!"

Unusually—actually, this was probably the only place it would happen—it wasn't Miyuki being welcomed with attention and respect, but Tatsuya. At first, the title *prince* had been meaningless banter aimed to make fun of the fact that he used his position as one of the top director's sons to come and go as he pleased. Now, though, they used it as an honorable title toward the next company head.

Tatsuya would have preferred them to stop using the embarrassing nickname, but he knew they were doing it out of friendliness now. He decided not to say, "Please, stop." Instead, he said, "Excuse me for disturbing you. Where might Foreman Ushiyama be?" Tatsuya asked the white-clothed researcher who had just called to him as Miyuki stood respectfully behind him. She was happy at the reverent eyes on

Tatsuya, as though they were on her, and she gave a charming smile and pulled one set of them after another away from him—there were virtually no men able to ignore her smile—it was close to an obstruction of business, in fact.

His reply came from the back of the crowd of people. "Did you call, monsieur?"

"Excuse me, Foreman. I apologize for asking you to come while you were so busy."

"Oh, don't apologize, monsieur." The scientist named Ushiyama turned to Tatsuya as he gave the man a well-mannered bow. He made a pained face and shook his head. "I'm all for modesty, but we're all your underlings here, y'know? Going overboard like that's gonna cause you some discipline issues."

"No, my father is the one who employs all of you—you aren't *my* subordinates…"

"You're such a card. You, the world-famous Monsieur **Silver**. We all think it an *honor* to work under you." All the scientists and researchers present within earshot nodded.

This was Four Leaves Technology's CAD R & D Section 3—the section that had developed the internationally renowned Silver model, widely known as the product representing FLT's current technological prowess. Section 3 was composed of those pushed out of engineering divisions—it was where the company sent its nuisances. However, it had come to be very influential within the company due to the worldwide popularity of the Silver model.

The scientists and researchers here, therefore, were understandably very loyal and earnest to Tatsuya, the **Silver** part of Taurus Silver, who had been the central figure in the model's development.

"Still, the one in charge here, in both name and reality, is you, Monsieur **Taurus**. You throw a tantrum whenever people want to make you manager. Section 3 hasn't had a manager *or* assistant manager for a long time now."

"Please, stop with the *monsieur* and the *Taurus*—they ain't right for me. I'm just a techie. All I do is mess with products from time to time to make your fantastic, genius ideas a little easier to use. I'm the one most against my name being with yours on this stuff. I'm not *that* shameless. They were just like, *Prince Shiba is a minor and a student; we can't have only his name on the development credits* and everything, so they just tacked on my name to make it look better."

"…If you didn't have engineering skills, Ushiyama, you wouldn't have made loop casting real. I don't know much about the hardware side of things. Besides, skills and theory don't mean anything if someone doesn't put it together as a product."

"Oh, come on, stop it. You're so logical I can barely talk to you." Ushiyama scratched his head and waved the white flag. "Anyway, let's get down to business. You didn't just come here to see my pretty face, did you?"

Tatsuya's super-serious expression broke and an evil grin crossed his face. "Okay, Ushiyama. Here you go—today's prototype."

Consciously modifying his words and actions to be more familiar, he held out the portable terminal-shaped CAD. Ushiyama stared intently at it for about ten seconds. This prototype CAD, T-17, was one Ushiyama had lent to Tatsuya for a certain purpose. If the software insertion was complete for this prototype, then that could only mean…

"Wait… Is this the flight device?" he said, his fingers trembling a little as he plucked the CAD from Tatsuya's hands.

"Yes. I've programmed the activation program for a permanent gravity control spell into the prototype hardware you made for me. It's simple to overwrite things on its system, so it was very easy to do."

"Did you test it?"

"As always, Miyuki and I tested it, but we're not exactly normal magicians."

He could hear gasps—and not just one or two, either. Everyone who had heard what he said was breathlessly staring at the object in Ushiyama's hands.

Finally, with a quiet but smooth tone, Ushiyama asked one of the researchers, "…Tetsu, how many T-17s do we have on hand?"

"Ten," came the reply.

Ushiyama's eyes shot open. "You moron! That's all?! Why didn't you get more of them?! What's that? No, we can order them later. Do a full copy on as many as you can with the prince's system! Hiro, get all the testers in here! What? They're off today?! Who the hell cares?! Tie 'em up with rope and drag them here if you have to! All you other idiots, stop what you're doing and get the precise instruments up and running! Do you understand? A flight spell! This will change the history of modern magic!"

There must have been a phone line connecting the rooms; those in the opposite survey room as well, all working on their day off, began to raise a stir and move at once.

The indoor CAD testing ground was as wide and high as a large gymnasium. Communication cables hung from the ceiling, connecting to the vest each tester wore.

The cables doubled as their lifelines. They already knew this spell would make them fly. Those in this test laboratory had experience testing spells that put them in the air, but all the other workings here were different. This wasn't jumping or falling deceleration—it was unknown territory.

The testers' faces were pale with nervousness. New types of magic were always no more than variations on well-known spells, but they never knew how much of a risk they posed. Magicians had actually ended up dying before because of the slightest bug in a magic sequence. But this was a world-first type of magic (as far as they knew) with an entirely new scheme. There was no being too careful in this case.

With the flooring swapped out for buffered materials and verification that the hanging cables were working, the experiment could finally get under way.

"Let's start the trial!"

At the signal of Ushiyama, who had taken refuge in the observation room—not for the safety of the spectators, but of the testers—the test began.

They couldn't make out the testers' faces from above; they were hidden in the shadows of their helmets. They did, however, see the lead tester—in his twenties, but already with a career long enough to be called a veteran—gritting his teeth.

He didn't hesitate to flip the CAD switch, though.

"Liftoff confirmed."

Before they even visually saw it, those at the measuring devices started throwing status reports back and forth. "No increase in ground pressure due to recoil detected." "Measurement error for upward acceleration within acceptable bounds." "CAD functioning stably."

The testers' bodies slowly rose. They could now distinctly make out that their feet were not on the floor. The cables loosened, indicating they weren't being pulled up. Aside from the sounds of the observation devices and voices giving measurement reports, there wasn't even a rustling of clothes in the observation room. Everyone was frozen in place, their eyes fixed on the scene before them and the values displayed by the measuring devices.

"Upward acceleration decrease...zero. Ascending at uniform velocity."

The testers slowly floated up, their bodies coming to eye level about ten feet up, same as those in the observation room.

"Upward acceleration now slowing... Upward velocity zero. Stopping confirmed."

Up until now, this was all within the realm of possibility for floating spells.

"Horizontal acceleration detected."

Someone, everyone, gasped and caught their breaths.

"Acceleration stopped. Now moving horizontally at three feet per second."

They could see the testers moving through the air at a clear speed before they heard the observation reports.

"He moved..."

"They're flying..."

The incredulous mumbles lent a sense of reality to what they were seeing.

"Tester One to survey room. I'm walking on air... No... I'm flying in the sky. I am free..."

And after the unexpected transmission came in over the speakers, all of the restrained surprise and amazement burst.

"We did it!"

"Success!"

"Congratulations, Prince!"

The survey personnel all started to give cheers of joy. The testers arced along random flight paths. Amid the congratulations of the manic staff, Tatsuya stood, he alone unaffected by the craze, accepting it with a calm, observing face.

"Are all of you morons...?"

Ushiyama looked down at the testers, appalled, as they lay on the ground in heaps, their magic used up.

The test had gone way over the allotted time, and all nine testers had run fresh out of magic power. It wasn't because they couldn't get good measurements—it was because the testers wouldn't stop. By their wish, they switched the wired cables doubling as lifelines for wireless ones, and they ended up starting an unplanned game of tag among themselves; this was the result.

"Of *course* you couldn't use permanent magic for that long!"

Most of modern magic consisted of instantaneous or short-lived spells. Most that were used continuously specified a length of activation time; there were few magicians who habitually used magic that they needed to keep activating over and over again. For example, while the High-Frequency Blade was a permanent spell, it actually had to be reactivated by the user each time he or she struck. Even the very technique of continuously executing a spell had been the sole possession of a select few magicians until recently; it had only gained its citizenship after the creation of the Loop Cast System, which automatically copied activation programs to the magic calculation region in order to continuously construct magic sequences.

"You morons are paying for the damages, got it? And no overtime, either."

Fortunately, none of the testers' magic power stores were dried up so much it would leave lasting effects. It had ended as a harmless joke, so Ushiyama sneered and crushed the voices of opposition. Then he walked over to Tatsuya, who was busy going over the test results.

"Something in particular catch your eye?" he asked.

Tatsuya turned around; his expression was far from satisfied. "Well, there's plenty more that I'd like…but I still think the burden of continuously processing the activation programs is too heavy."

For whatever reason, Ushiyama nodded in understanding, then looked between Tatsuya and Miyuki, who was standing to the back. "Compared to the prince and princess, those magicians barely have any psions."

When measured on a modern scale of magic power, Tatsuya was no more than a dunce magic user. But the scale used for that had been born at the advent of magic, and had changed over the years.

For example, they didn't know as much about activation programs thirty years ago. Constructing magic sequences from them had been incomparably slow compared to today's speeds. Magic sequences were less efficient, and constructing the ones with practical use needed many times more psions than today. At the time, the amount of psions a person's mind-body (referring to both the body and the mind as one) possessed was seen as a more important scale of a magician's power than the speed at which he or she constructed magic sequences. On that scale, Tatsuya and Miyuki had top-class amounts of psions.

Now, with advancements in activation and magic sequences as well as in CADs, lack of psions was seldom a direct problem with executing magic. Aside from spells that released psions themselves, such as ones categorized as typeless, there wasn't usually much point in having a lot of psions, except maybe to brag.

However, nothing changed the fact that both expanding activation programs and constructing magic sequences consumed psions. If you repeated the process a hundred or a thousand times over, magicians would feel the burden even if each individual cost was small.

"We need to optimize the CAD's automatic psion absorption scheme more..."

"...I'll think of something for that. If we deal with it on the hardware end instead of the software end, we can reduce the load a bit." He thought for a moment, then said, "We should probably put the time recorder on its own circuits."

Tatsuya gave a broad grin, as though that was exactly what he had been thinking. "I actually wanted to ask you about that very thing."

"Well, well—what an honor."

They traded knowing smirks.

◇ ◇ ◇

Though they uncovered several aspects of the hardware that could be improved, the actual usage of the spell had borne satisfying results. The biggest takeaway of the day was discovering that it was fully possible for the flight spell to be used with store-bought CADs by average magicians.

Once they got the test results in order, they would announce the flight spell under the name Taurus Silver, which would likely happen by the end of next week. With something of this scale, they wanted to do it as fast as they could, even if it meant cutting corners. The impact between being the first in the world to do something and the second was completely different. The *very first* would have huge publicity just for being the first.

Other than that, they decided on a redesign of the flight spell–specific CAD and slated its production for September (the month they reported half-year accounts).

With those two items decided on, the briefing session ended. Tatsuya rejoined Miyuki, who had been waiting for him in the tea lounge, and they started on their way home.

Ushiyama, now pressed with urgent business, scratched his head apologetically—he had essentially come to kick them out. "Sorry. I put in a word with the department manager, but…" The man was worried over the fact that during the course of the experiment, and even when it succeeded, the siblings' father—the development manager of FLT who supervised all its R & D centers—never showed his face.

"Please, don't worry about it. Today's a holiday, so even if he turned up, he'd be at the main offices."

Inside, though, Tatsuya found it easier not to face him, and Miyuki actively didn't want to see him. Ushiyama wasn't about to say that, though. Not only did their father have an important role at FLT, but he was also their biggest shareholder, and Ushiyama knew that. It wouldn't be good to expose the shame of the owner's family to his employees, even if the technicians did have the true craftsman's spirit at heart.

Once Tatsuya deflected his intent with a publicly acceptable answer, Ushiyama's expression grew increasingly uncomfortable. "…No, actually, the manager is here in this building today…"

Miyuki's eyebrows shot up; Tatsuya could clearly tell even though his back was turned to her. He, however, felt rather relieved. This meant they'd nearly avoided a mishap. "The directory probably doesn't have the kind of time to come on-site. I certainly don't believe he is neglecting the research division," he added, averting the conversation and twisting it into consoling Ushiyama instead.

"Well, I know that… He did practically double our budget."

He felt bad for Ushiyama being overly ashamed, but there were things even Tatsuya would rather not discuss.

Unfortunately, nothing is ever that easy. Upon nearly making it to the laboratory's entrance after leaving Ushiyama, they ran straight into the one they wanted to avoid; they were only a few steps away from the entrance hall, too.

"Oh, hello, Miss Miyuki. It has been quite some time."

First to break the ice was neither parent nor children, who all looked at each other in silence, but the fourth person present among them. He was an old friend of both Tatsuya's and Miyuki's, and though they'd known each other for a long time, they weren't particularly close.

"It's nice to see you, Mr. Aoki. Yes, it has been a rather long time since we last talked. Of course, I am not the only person here at the moment. And you, Father—you're looking well. Thank you for the phone call the other day. However, if you'll permit me to say so, I do not believe it would be a bad thing to speak to your son every once in a while."

The smooth, sweet tone of her voice was thick with rose thorns. Those she was speaking to, however, had thick skin that those thorns couldn't penetrate.

"If I may have a word, miss. As a steward of the Yotsuba family, and one entrusted with managing part of the family assets, asking me to show etiquette toward a mere bodyguard would go against the order of the family."

"He is my brother!" Miyuki did her best to keep her voice calm, but Tatsuya, at least, realized she was quickly approaching her limit.

"With all due respect, Miss Miyuki, you are the one who everyone hopes will take the seat at the head of the Yotsuba. Your position is wholly different from *that* bodyguard."

Just before Miyuki broke into hysterics, Tatsuya cut in with a calm voice. "Oh, Mr. Aoki, I'm aware it would be rude to interrupt, but you are saying some unkind things." His tone was thoroughly level. The blatantly rude words and behavior hadn't affected his mind at all.

That's just how his mind was put together.

Tatsuya was more concerned with avoiding Miyuki getting angry and hurting someone in his place.

"It matters not," said Aoki. "You are Lady Miya's son, after all, if only a lowly bodyguard. A few missteps in terms of courteous conduct are to be expected."

Thus, he didn't have the time to respond to the man's haughty attitude.

"I believe you mentioned all the Yotsuba's servants wishing for Miyuki to be the next leader, but is that not rather unfair toward the other candidates?"

He couldn't have his sister shouldering all the malice directed toward him, so he pressed the man without giving her the opportunity to interrupt. He needed to make the man yield.

"Our aunt has still not named a successor, correct?" Tatsuya noted. "Or have you heard from her that an official decision has been made?"

The steward was sharp and able, and that was plain to see; he was an elegant gentleman in the prime of his life, more suited for the title of lawyer than steward—and yet he wasn't sure how to respond to the points made by this sixteen-year-old boy.

"If our aunt has indeed made that decision already, Miyuki would need to make many preparations, so I would prefer it if you gave her that word at your earliest opportunity."

His unmodulated, monotone voice got an answer from Aoki. "...Lady Maya has yet to say anything," he said with a bitter face.

Tatsuya widened his eyes theatrically. "Well, this is a surprise! Did the steward ranking fourth among the Yotsuba just suggest his personal *speculation* to one of the candidates for the next family head regarding inheritance? I have to wonder which of us is truly causing an issue with *order*."

He sighed, again in an affected way, and Aoki's face reddened as he glared. He didn't have the means to produce a logical argument any longer, judged Tatsuya, and he was about to announce his victory and leave...

...but his judgment had been naive. "...It is not speculation. As I am employed in the same household, I gain insight to her thoughts. I don't need to be a telepath to know when a like-minded person thinks the same way."

It was an evasive, muttered answer, abandoning all logic and reason. However, the man had prepared a poison that shouldn't have been used at the very end of things.

"I don't expect a fake magician without a mind to understand."

A moment after Aoki uttered those words, all of a sudden, the air on the walls condensed into frost. The heating system groaned, trying to return the rapidly lowering temperature to normal. A wave of cold gathered around Miyuki's feet.

However, Tatsuya held out his left index finger, and with the squeal of a magnetic tape quickly rewinding—an auditory illusion only those who could sense magic could hear—it all disappeared.

His sister's hands were white, having gone beyond red or blue, as he took one of them in his, then turned a piercing glare on Aoki. "The one who created that *fake magician without a mind* was my mother, Miya Shiba, the older sister of the current Yotsuba family head, Maya Yotsuba, maiden name Miya Yotsuba. The very one who planned her human magician experiment in which she'd use forbidden outer magic—mental structure interference—to format the sections of my unconscious relating to strong emotions and responsible for the strongest thoughts, then implant an emulator to perform magic calculations—it was Maya Yotsuba just after she became the current leader, and Miya Shiba, after it was revealed her six-year-old son had no magical talent, carried the experiment out. This means that by calling me, the subject of the experiment, a fake, you are slandering the magic experiment conducted by the current family head and her older sister as having produced a counterfeit article. Do I understand you correctly?"

Gently embracing his beloved sister's shoulders as she shed tears in his place, he dug into Aoki, the one who had made her cry, with his words, as deep and as mercilessly as he could.

"......"

"Tatsuya, stop it."

As Aoki stiffened and found himself unable to come up with anything to say, his father, Tatsurou Shiba, who had been silent up until now, stopped him from going any further.

"You will not speak poorly of your mother."

His words, however, were completely and utterly absurd and off the mark. They were likely spoken out of self-preservation, so as not to damage the well-being of the family. This company was invested in and founded by the Yotsuba in secret. Despite being the largest shareholder inheriting his late wife's shares, the Yotsuba still had substantial sovereignty, so Tatsuya could somewhat understand his father feeling subject, but...

Tatsuya unintentionally let out a laugh.

"Tatsuya, I cannot say I don't understand your hatred toward your mother, but..."

And his father didn't even pay attention to his inappropriate laughter.

Tatsuya strongly felt that walking away *now* would be beneficial for the mental health of both sides. Before that, though, he felt the need to get one last word in. "Dad, you're wrong. I don't hate my mother."

"I-I see."

That was all he said.

He didn't need to say the rest of it out loud.

Tatsuya's mind no longer had the ability to *hate*.

Fierce anger, strong sadness, powerful jealousy, grudge, hatred, excessive want of food, excessive sexual desire, the desire to sleep in excess...and feelings of romantic love.

He would never lose himself in anger.

He would never suffer heartache.

He would never burn with envy.

He neither bore grudges nor felt hatred.

He would never have his heart stolen by the opposite sex.

He felt the need to eat, but never in excess.

He felt sexual desires, but never reveled in them.

He felt the need to sleep, but never to lounge in inactivity.

The part of him containing the strongest emotions and desires had been erased from his mind via a special magic that only his mother out of everyone else in the world had the ability to perform.

He didn't hate his mother.

He wasn't angry at her, either.

He couldn't *really* get angry at her, and he couldn't *really* bear a grudge toward her.

The one and only strong emotion left to him was a passion purposely excluded: to abide by the will of the Yotsuba clan to which he had been assigned.

Not, of course, out of familial attachment to his father.

Tatsuya left without saying good-bye, still holding Miyuki's shoulders as she sobbed.

[3]

At school, one of the advantages to assigning fixed classrooms was that it encouraged the students to build and foster personal relationships. As can be understood from the strong human unity brought about by blood relations and geographical proximity throughout the ages, locative affiliations connected to systematic attribution were a tendency shared by formal and informal groupings alike.

The actual point of all this, well...

"Morning. I heard about it, Shiba. That's amazing!"

"Good morning, Shiba! Do your best!"

"Good morning, Shiba. I'll be rooting for you."

"Yo! Knock 'em dead, Shiba!"

...it could result in the creation of friendships at least to the degree where they could add encouragement to their greetings, despite not being people Tatsuya was all that familiar with.

Tatsuya found himself on the receiving end of one cheer after another after arriving at school on Monday. In regards to what—well, having been selected for the Nine School Competition team's staff, of course.

"Man, news sure spreads fast."

"It's true. It was only decided last week; it hasn't even been formally announced yet."

"Seriously! Where do they get their news, anyway?"

Leo, Mizuki, and Erika weren't playing dumb. They really didn't seem to be the ones who told everyone about it. *Well, it's not like there was a gag order on anyone. Only upperclassmen were at the meeting, but they probably heard from their club mates.*

"Wasn't the official announcement going to be today?" asked Erika, wondering. Tatsuya nodded back, his face sullen.

The selections for the Nine School Competition members had finally ended last Friday, including those for the engineering team. It was supposed to be done two weeks ago, so they were running pretty late. Perhaps fortunately, things had been progressing in terms of arranging the apparatus such as competitive CADs and uniforms, which took the most time. Still, given that the engineer lineup hadn't been solidified, the checks and operation testing on the delivered devices was mostly unfinished.

Even Miyuki was completely preoccupied with preparations despite being a competitor herself, so Tatsuya was determined not to let himself get lazy. He couldn't get away from the feeling that he was doing so reluctantly, though.

"They're making fifth period a school-wide assembly, aren't they?" remarked Mizuki.

He checked today's schedule on his classroom terminal. Third period in the morning and second period in the afternoon were shared between all the grade levels. Still, modern schools allowed students to work at their own pace using individually assigned terminals even though there was a concept of "standard progression" (the learning schedule and pacing determined to be standard), except for in the case of labs, practice, and gym class.

This meant the start and end times in such schools weren't observed very strictly. The older you got, the more distinctions between class time and break time were ignored. The fact that the whole school had to gather for its representative team inauguration showed just how important the administration thought the event was.

"You're going to be at the inauguration, too, right, Tatsuya?" asked Mizuki.

"Well, I suppose..." Tatsuya's answer was rather unclear. That point was the main reason he didn't look too happy.

"You're the only freshman who'll be there, aren't you?" As Leo said, Tatsuya was the only first year selected for the technical staff. CAD-adjusting experience was essential, so the upperclassmen's choosing him for the staff was the natural course of events. His level of skill was abnormal.

Of course, given that he was working as a professional at the forefront of CAD software development, being made an engineer for a high school competition might have actually felt below him. However, nobody, neither freshman nor upperclassman, knew about that. Only his little sister, Miyuki, knew.

"All the Course 1 kids seem preeeetty annoyed," remarked Erika, though it was perfectly clear the Course 1 students were fuming from his selection, having had their pride destroyed just the other day in the exams.

"Still, all the competitors were Course 1 students..."

His complaint was correct. Every one of the athletes chosen for the rookie competition were Course 1 students, so it shouldn't have been a big deal for him to be chosen for the tech staff—of course, that was his logic as someone who had already been chosen. It didn't bring any comfort to the Course 1 students who wanted to go into engineering fields.

Tatsuya had seldom been on the envied side. He didn't ever feel much envy himself, either. He still had too little life experience to take a guess at the subtleties involved here.

"I guess there's nothing we can do about it," said Mizuki. "Envy isn't logical anyway."

Her indication was right on the mark, but Tatsuya found himself unable to respond.

"He'll be fine! There won't be any rocks or magic flying onstage this time."

And all he could do was grin drily at Erika's extreme consolation.

◇ ◇ ◇

After fourth period ended, he went backstage at the auditorium at the specified time. Miyuki, who arrived before him, held a blouson of thin make out to him.

"What's this?" he asked, even though he got the feeling it was just what it looked like—he wanted to know what it was for.

"It's the technical staff uniform," answered Mayumi. "You wear it instead of your school uniform for the inauguration."

——That was what he expected. Mayumi was currently wearing a tailored sports jacket; it was probably the competitors' uniform.

Miyuki, still in her school uniform, held the blouson out to Tatsuya with a smile teeming with anticipation. An antagonistic impulse crossed his mind, but he knew there wouldn't be any point in resisting her. He obediently removed his blazer and placed it on a hanger placed nearby for the purpose, then bent down to put his arms through the blouson Miyuki spread out for him. She stretched it out behind him to get it on his shoulders, then came around front to fix up his collar and shirttails. Finally, she took a step back to get a good look at his entire upper body and smiled, satisfied.

Tatsuya was pretty sure he knew why she was in such a good mood: She was happy to see the emblem embroidered on the blouson's left breast.

It was in the design of an eight-petal flower—First High's school insignia.

The mark of a Course 1 student, not a substitute.

"It suits you so very well, Tatsuya…"

There wasn't much variation in the uniforms between schools during interschool competitions, so it was obviously there so that people could tell what school a member was from. Miyuki, though, felt moved—as though something had, at last, been put in its rightful place.

Tatsuya didn't care one way or another, and that's why he didn't feel the need to throw cold water on her excitement. There was a little time left before the inauguration, but he decided to wait for its commencement wearing the engineer blouson.

Miyuki gazed at him and his uniform with rapt attention, never growing tired of it. She did this while still in her own school uniform. Tatsuya glanced around, but he didn't see a tailored jacket for her. They had a bit of time, but wouldn't it be better to put it on early? "Shouldn't you get changed?"

"I'm helping as a presenter for the ceremony," she replied, her delirious face now replaced by her usual smile. That meant she would put her own position as a competitor on hold for the ceremony and play the part of the one sending them off...at least, that's how Tatsuya interpreted it.

"I see. That's a big job."

"Please don't pressure me..."

He knew she'd never actually feel timid about something so simple, but when her eyes wavered forlornly with her fainthearted words, he smiled and placed a hand on her head.

——Earning them cold, piercing glares from others nearby.

◇ ◇ ◇

The introduction of the so-called inauguration ceremony began at the scheduled time and proceeded without incident. Even with Tatsuya on the stage, nobody threw rocks or flung magic at him. *Well, of course not.*

Still, he was extremely uncomfortable here. The competitors and engineers had each formed their own lines. He was the only freshman on the engineering team, so he felt understandably out of place. He had proven his skill at the prep meeting, so fortunately nobody was being strange and acting hostile or disdainful toward him. They still couldn't be said to be friendly and welcoming, though. Thinking highly of someone and being courteous were not the same.

His being placed on the team was an exceptional selection and special treatment in a few different ways. Now he was wearing the eight-petal emblem despite being a Course 2 student. Tatsuya, standing in the dazzling spotlight, thought to himself that some would have to take that as a provocation and oppose it, as if it were someone else's problem.

Meanwhile, each competitor was being individually introduced by Mayumi. Each member, upon being introduced, had a badge embedded with an ID chip to let them enter the competition areas fastened to their uniform collar. Miyuki had been chosen for that job, as it gave her a moment of glory on the stage.

It was quite a process considering there were forty competitors alone (thirty-eight excluding Miyuki and Mayumi), but, perhaps due to her training in proper ladylike mannerisms, she nimbly and earnestly attached the badges to each uniform without breaking her smiling expression.

The male students, when faced with her smile at such a close proximity, could hear her breathing, and mostly turned red and had to work hard to maintain a straight expression. Female students all across the school would probably be making fun of them for it later, but over half of the female competitors were losing their calm—some getting red in the face in embarrassment—upon having the badge fastened to their uniforms as well. That evoked smiles rather than animosity from the audience—mostly the upperclassmen.

The badges were distributed not only to the competitors but to the staff as well. Once the operations staff members were all introduced, it was finally the tech staff's turn.

"I'm getting a little nervous," came the sudden voice from next to him. Tatsuya turned his head inconspicuously to look, and his eyes met a male student's who was doing the same thing. Tatsuya was a little taller than him. If he recalled correctly, he was a junior named Kei Isori, and a Course 1 student, of course. (Indeed, the only Course 2 student on the stage was Tatsuya.)

"Understandable," replied Tatsuya. Kei was one of the few students who showed a clear friendliness toward him. He was a good-looking boy, with gentle, androgynous features; when combined with his naturally delicate build, he could have passed for a slightly taller female student if he switched his slacks out for a skirt. In any case, he was a warrior; not only were his grades in magic theory at the top of the junior class, he was maintaining excellent scores in practical areas as well.

Looking at his **beauty** from up close again, he was convinced: You couldn't judge a book by its cover.

Given the fact that they were onstage, their conversation ended there. However, the casual kindness he'd displayed in the midst of the vague hostility in the room was enough to put his mind more at ease despite how thickheaded he tended to be. It felt like a fog had lifted, giving him the opportunity to look down, off the stage.

As always the seating was freely chosen, and as always the students were split, with Course 1 in the front and Course 2 in the back.

But in those rows of people in the front half were a few outsiders.

They must have noticed Tatsuya looking at them.

Amazingly, in the third row back, in one of the *front rows*, Erika waved at him.

Tatsuya was shocked, as were others. Upon closer inspection, Mizuki sat next to Erika, with Leo on the other side and Mikihiko next to him. Behind them were a few more faces he knew. His classmates from 1-E were lumped up in front, not discouraged by the cold eyes of the Course 1 students.

As he stood captivated at their courage, the wagon Miyuki was pushing along came to him. Forty competitors, four operations staff members, eight technical staff members, minus the two presenters. Out of the fifty onstage, forty-nine had been introduced and conferred with a badge.

It was down to the fiftieth student—Tatsuya's turn.

Mayumi announced his name. Was it just his imagination, or did she put more oomph into it than before? He took a step forward and

bowed. Miyuki gave a bewitched smile—Tatsuya couldn't help but feel concerned about his sister's mental state—and came in front of him.

Just as she finished fastening the badge to his blouson...

...there was a huge round of applause.

He didn't need to look; Erika and Leo had caused it, and his classmates all clapped for him at once.

The presenters, Mayumi and Miyuki, were surprised at the commotion. However, right before the Course 1 freshmen could begin to boo him, as though to ward it off, Mayumi and Miyuki both began clapping from either side of the stage.

The applause happened directly after the final member was introduced, and it smoothly changed into applause for all the chosen members and spread throughout the entire auditorium.

◇ ◇ ◇

After the inauguration ceremony, the school-wide preparations for the Nine School Competition accelerated drastically. Once their events were determined, Miyuki, along with Shizuku and Honoka, practiced right up until school closed every day. With Tatsuya's CAD adjustments and Miyuki's job, they were running around late into the night, every night. Erika and Leo, who belonged to athletic clubs, were doing all kinds of assistant work as well.

Mizuki was the only one in a liberal arts club, so she often found herself waiting alone for everyone else this week. Last week's ceremony had been heart-pounding for her—seating was free, but it took a lot of courage to go against the unspoken rule. She couldn't have done it herself. In fact, if not for Erika, she couldn't have even done it with other classmates. Mizuki knew she was introverted, and that made Erika seem so much more dazzling and enviable.

But I wonder why Erika was going through all that trouble...

Mizuki herself had been pulled into it by Erika. Mizuki greatly wanted to cheer Tatsuya on as much as anyone else, of course, but thinking back on it, she probably would have been satisfied giving him applause from the back.

Erika could be quite a thrill seeker sometimes, so part of her motivation probably arose from a desire to mess with the Course 1 students' sense of elitism. At the same time, though, she was whimsical and capricious. She liked butting into other people's problems, but she never asserted ways to deal with those problems—at least, not that Mizuki had seen. She didn't get the feeling Erika's passion in mobilizing the rest of their classmates in addition to their usual circle could be explained by the amusement factor alone.

Could Erika really... Could she...like...?

The boy that Erika was most friendly with, as far as she could tell, was Leo. She also seemed to have a convoluted past with Yoshida, who had taken third place in the theory portion on the exams. It seemed to Mizuki that she had a different kind of feeling, with a different sort of *weight*, toward Tatsuya. But even in the privacy of her own thoughts, Mizuki, **for some reason**, hesitated to define that feeling clearly.

It still hadn't been five minutes since she started waiting at the entrance; it was too early to get tired and leave. Still, it was more than enough time for her thoughts to lose their inhibitions. She let her mind begin to wander. Essentially, she was vacantly daydreaming. And as her mind remained unfocused on any single thing, as her senses had been opened to the world, she noticed strange waves she wasn't familiar with.

She only took a second to worry before boldly removing her glasses. A moment later, color surged forth. Rays of light of all shades and hues flowed into her vision. The stimulation made her eyes hurt, but she endured it for a little bit.

Mizuki taking her glasses off was like stepping out of a dark room into the bright summer sunlight. Things that once couldn't be seen were now clearly visible. Her sense of sight and her brain groaned, trying to process the overload of information that she felt completely unable to control.

But while normal people would lose consciousness at such an information atrocity, this was the "other world," which had been with her since she was born.

Human eyes grew used to even the brightest sunlight on them given a little while. Some people with dark-colored eyes suited for strong light would grow used it without even needing to wait.

Mizuki's eyes were just as fast; she shut them hard, then blinked a few times, and her eyes got used to seeing many times the psionic light that normal magicians could perceive—as well as pushion light (pushion radiation) that normal magicians could barely even distinguish the colors of.

She put her glasses neatly in their case and focused on the waves that she had noticed earlier that seemed out of place. The light had been visible even blocked by her specially coated lenses, and she easily spotted it right away: pushion signals, wavering but regular, like breathing. She could tell exactly where the light source was now, too.

As though being lured toward it, she made her way to its source—the lab building.

The closer she got to the lab building, the more she thought she could feel chilly air floating. It was currently the middle of summer, and the evening sun was shining not evenly over the horizon, but unevenly from between the ridgelines of hills and mountains, and as the sun approached it, it created additional heat.

It was an illusion: Something was slipping a false cold air into the midsummer blaze.

Whatever it was, it was telling her to turn back. Threatening her, telling her not to get close.

She flinched away in unease toward the unknown *thing*…but she didn't stop walking. Her reason told her to turn back, but her intuition as a user of magic and one preordained to live alongside it told her that she needed to confirm with her eyes what was there.

The entrance to the lab building opened quietly, without any squeaking or loud laughter to speak of. The lighting panels on the ceiling were staying bright enough that one could have read small letters without a problem. Everything was the same as usual.

Well, this was a school that taught magic, so a lot of people used this lab building. There wasn't a real way faculty or upperclassmen wouldn't have noticed something going wrong here.

There was less room for ghost stories in magic high schools than normal ones. If nothing had been reported, then the abnormality Mizuki was feeling had to be a magic-based phenomenon—or else a real supernatural occurrence, one that modern magic was unable to detect.

Though her spine shivered at the hazy, inauspicious thoughts crossing her mind, her feet carried her forward, as if being spurred—or dragged—along, farther and farther in.

Upon reaching the top of the stairs, Mizuki smelled a slight fragrance in the air. It was something she'd smelled before in magic pharmaceutics labs: the smell of various woods blended together to grant calming properties.

The waves she'd been chasing led toward the pharmaceutical lab room. The strange pushion radiation appeared to be a by-product of a student's magical experimentation. Basically aware now that it wasn't some sort of unknown supernatural occurrence, at least, Mizuki sighed in relief.

And then her curiosity, which had been hidden behind her unease, reared its head. One of the first things they learned in experimental magic courses was never to enter a room someone was doing magical experimentation in without being invited; the uninvited intruder's magic calculation region could interfere with the currently active spell, meaning it was possible for magic to unexpectedly go crazy. In particular, inexperienced magicians—freshmen like her, for example—barging into a magic experiment was folly wrought with danger, as they'd repeatedly been warned.

That little warning, however, had completely slipped Mizuki's mind. Her wariness was for the wrong thing as she tiptoed up to the closed lab door and pushed it open a tiny bit so she could peek in. Taking the utmost care not to make a noise, she brought her eye to the slightly open gap.

And the next moment, she very nearly shrieked.

Well, perhaps not so much a shriek as a grunt of surprise, for inside the pharmaceutical lab room, there were glowing orbs of blue, sky blue, and indigo dancing around in the air. Each of those lights had both "power" and a "will."

The distribution of energy in the natural world was not homogeneous, nor did it attempt to be—she knew by "seeing" how the energy was dispersing, gathering, and flowing without end. The sight of a mass of natural phenomenon–causing "power" turning into a bubble-like object and floating around was something she was used to seeing. Her eyes could see the energy of everything in creation, and it looked a lot like the pushion radiance that streamed from the human mind.

But today was the first time she'd felt one of those floating, flitting masses had a *will*.

Spirits...? Is that what they are? she wondered. It was such an impact, such an emotional moment, that all other thoughts fled her brain. And the one calling those spirits, it was...

"Is that Yoshida...?" she muttered, forgetting what little caution she'd come into this with. It was a completely unconscious action, but the one she said the name of didn't let it slip. Especially considering she had witnessed a skill of his, when nobody should have been looking—nobody should have ever come around here.

"Who's there?!" he demanded, essentially on reflex. The "will" of the "lights" reacted to the reflexive anger in his words.

"Ahhh!" yelped Mizuki, closing her eyes as the glowing orbs advanced on her.

A moment later, what felt like a sudden gust of wind hit her from the side and she fell over.

It had been a torrent of psions that neither shook her hair nor fluttered her skirt.

It washed away the glowing orbs descending on her, protecting her, but she didn't realize that since her eyes were closed.

She opened them very slowly to see Mikihiko glaring with a burning animosity toward someone meeting it expressionlessly: Tatsuya.

"...Calm down, Mikihiko. I don't want to fight you—not now, and not here."

Her eyes widened at Tatsuya's sudden appearance. As she sat there frozen in place, she saw him raising his hands; he wasn't holding anything. A sign that he didn't want to fight, known and accepted by both magicians and non-magicians alike.

Mikihiko looked startled, and his own hostility vanished without a trace in that moment. With the tension in the air dissipated, Mizuki found herself able to move and stand up again as Mikihiko looked down dejectedly. "...Sorry, Tatsuya. I didn't mean anything, either."

He looked like a kid who was lost and couldn't get home. Mizuki impulsively wanted to comfort him, but, vexingly, she couldn't seem to find the right words.

Fortunately, she didn't need to endure awkward silence for very long. "I'm not worried, so you shouldn't worry, either. In the first place, it's Mizuki's fault for throwing a magician off while he was executing magic."

"Huh? Who, me?!" she stammered, turning to him. When she saw Tatsuya's mean-spirited smile, she realized he wasn't seriously blaming her, to which she felt relief.

Mikihiko didn't seem to take it that way, though. "No, it's not her fault," he denied a little hastily. Tatsuya's indication had had *some* truth to it, and it had him all the more flustered. "It's my own fault for losing my calm just because I heard my name; I'm still inexperienced... And, sorry, I forgot something important: Thank you, Tatsuya. You're the reason I didn't hurt Shibata."

"I didn't need to intervene; she wouldn't have gotten hurt. That was spirit magic, wasn't it?"

For some reason, Mikihiko hesitated a moment, then nodded.

"We call it deity magic at home, though, following the doctrine of heavenly and earthly *kami*." Still, he couldn't yield on a part of his identity as a magician, so he asserted himself thus.

Spirit magic was a type of old magic. Anything involving altering eidos by using independent bodies of information that most people referred to as spirits was classified as "spirit magic" in the magic sciences. Occasionally the term *spirit* was shortened to *SB*, for *spiritual being*, but they were mostly called *spirits* by scholars.

"I don't have the ability to see spirits, but I could tell you were in control of the spell. And it would certainly be hard to tell you *not* to be surprised if someone came walking in through your warding barrier."

"How did you know about the... I see; you must have studied old magic, too. And you even knew the spell was working... You know, everything about you seems so irratio—er, beyond my comprehension."

"I don't really mind people calling me *irrational*, you know," replied Tatsuya, grinning teasingly, causing a wry smile to come over Mikihiko's face as well—as his clenched teeth loosened up.

"Well, I suppose it's just as *irrational* to spread a barrier over a school lab room just because I didn't want anyone to see, huh?"

"It certainly was."

They both laughed, driving away the tense air once and for all.

"Was that a spell to summon natural spirits? It's the first time I've seen it done."

"...I guess there's no point in hiding it now. Yeah, I was practicing summoning magic using water sprites," answered Mikihiko, cleaning up the burning wood on the tabletop furnace. Mizuki was next to him, wiping the ashen table down with a cloth. Mikihiko had refused her help, of course, but she was too serious about these things to let it go.

"Water sprites... Unfortunately, I didn't know anything more about them other than the fact that they're masses of pushions... How did they look to you, Mizuki?"

"Huh? Oh, they looked the same to me," she replied, smiling dubiously and waving her hands. "All I saw were balls of bluish-colored light." Her swinging hands sent dirty water droplets into Mikihiko's face, but she didn't notice, since she was too preoccupied with the conversation having suddenly turned to her.

As for Mikihiko, splattered with the dirty water…well, he didn't notice it, either.

He opened his eyes wide and his face stiffened. "Color…? You could tell what colors they were…?"

"Umm, well…yes?" said Mizuki, a little nervous about why Mikihiko was making such a scary face (subjectively, anyway). She couldn't look straight at him; instead she glanced over to him every once in a while as she stammered, "Umm…there were blue ones, sky-blue ones, indigo ones… Oh!" Then she realized the water droplets on Mikihiko's face. "I-I-I'm so sorry! Umm, right, my handkerchief! Where did I put that thing?!"

She frantically took her handkerchief out of her bag and went to wipe off Mikihiko's cheek. Before it got there, though, he grabbed her wrist violently. Mizuki's face distorted in surprise as he pulled her in close, catching her before she lost her balance. Then he brought his face close to hers as if to kiss her and looked right into her eyes.

"Umm, I, err…" Mizuki's perplexed, flustered voice failed to convey her thoughts to him. He stared fixedly at her, unmoving, and she, unable to move, was starting to panic.

The unexpected pair locked eyes with each other.

"…If this is consensual, I'll take my leave, but otherwise, won't this be a problem?"

"Wah!" "Eek!"

The two of them were locked in silence as though they forgot breathing was an important function, but at Tatsuya's skeptical words they snapped back to reality and practically bounced away from each other. What followed was a rather odd exchange.

"…Sorry about that."

"N-no...I'm sorry."

Tatsuya understood why Mikihiko apologized—it had almost been sexual harassment, and he would have been lucky to get away with a slap on the cheek—but why did Mizuki? She was probably confused. Tatsuya started to feel like not being here anymore.

"...Mizuki, Erika and Leo are already at the meeting place. We can leave without you two if you want."

"Huh? Oh, Tatsuya, you came all this way to get me... Wait, what?!" Only understanding what Tatsuya's words implied after some time (though she was the only one) she suddenly cried out and stopped talking. She probably had something she wanted to say, but her mouth flapped open and closed without a sound. Her speech center must have broken down under the extreme duress.

Tatsuya, in one of his bouts of "it's not my problem," figured it was only temporary—though unfortunately, he couldn't keep up his straight face—and looked over to Mikihiko. The next topic of interest to him was Mikihiko's sudden outburst. What could have caused it? Mikihiko seemed relieved at the change of topic, but Tatsuya took advantage of it and asked, "What was that all about, anyway, Mikihiko?"

"Sorry, I was just...a little surprised..." came the reply.

"Well, there's no point apologizing to me," remarked Tatsuya, causing Mikihiko to bow in apology to Mizuki again. "What were you surprised about?"

"Well... I'm really sorry. I just didn't think *anyone* could see the colors of spirits... When I thought that she might have Crystalline Eyes, I couldn't help myself... I'm just making excuses, but I definitely didn't mean to be rude! I really just...sort of wanted to make sure, that's all."

Mikihiko's sincere apology evoked a calming effect in Mizuki's panic. As he said, it was just an excuse. It was wholly due to his own curiosity and affairs, and had nothing to do with her.

But as Mizuki watched him frantically make the excuse, she smiled kindly to indicate she wasn't trying to fault him for anything anymore. "It's okay, Yoshida. I was just surprised too," she said, giving a bright smile to put him at ease before saying softly and quickly, "But it was embarrassing, so please don't do that again."

Mikihiko reddened and nodded several times.

With the attempted sexual harassment having been resolved peacefully, and Tatsuya's teasing going indecisive, he didn't feel like bringing it up again. He judged that they had both calmed down, then asked Mikihiko another question. "By the way, Mikihiko, what would be so surprising about it? You said something about seeing the colors of spirits being unusual."

Tatsuya had the capacity to analyze psion information bodies, but he didn't see them as images before his eyes, so he didn't know whether distinguishing the colors of pushion information bodies was unique or not. Well, actually, just being able to perceive pushion information bodies was a rare skill, to be sure, but he didn't know if seeing their colors had some sort of particular meaning. Mizuki empathized with that question, the same doubts in her mind, and looked at Mikihiko.

"And what are Crystalline Eyes, if you don't mind me asking?" Mizuki's eyes indicated that she wanted to ask the same thing.

"...It's fine. It's not really that much of a secret anyway." There was a pause, seeming to indicate it wasn't a light topic at all. Tatsuya realized then that every now and again, Mikihiko would show an irresponsible—no, a desperate—side of his attitude. "Spirits have colors. Those of us who employ spirits can tell their types by their colors." Still, the actual explanation he gave, the words describing magic, weren't irresponsible—they were earnest.

"But we're not actually *seeing* them in the true sense of the word."

Mizuki looked at him askance. Tatsuya didn't know what he meant, either, but he didn't impatiently ask him to continue, only urging him on with his eyes.

"Spirits don't actually possess colors. The practitioner 'sees' different colors depending on the type of the technique and its school of style. For example, in my school, water sprites are blue. But in Europe, there are some schools saying water sprites are purple. Central Asia says they're deep blue, close to black. This isn't because the waves spirits give off are different depending on the location and type of technique being used. People see different colors purely because they perceive the world differently."

"...So you're not visually perceiving the color; you're just interpreting what the waves should look like through your techniques, then?"

"That's correct. We interpret the color of their waves as a matter of convenience to tell them apart. I guess you could say *we* assign the spirits colors. That's why the spirits we're aware of all have the same one. In my school, water sprites are blue, fire sprites are red, earth sprites are golden, and wind sprites are green. They don't have any shades or saturation. We're coloring them in our own minds by type, so they wouldn't each have slight variations in color. Water sprites, no matter what kind, are always pure blue. Given this all happens in the mind, there shouldn't be light blue or dark blue ones."

"...But Mizuki saw them as such."

"I think she's able to perceive the difference in strengths and qualities among water sprites by differences in color. She's **actually** seeing what color they are. In our school, we call such eyes Crystalline Eyes. Other schools seem to use the term to mean something else, but in our school, it refers to eyes that are able to see *kami*, the Shinto nature deities. Those who can see spirits are actually seeing these *divine* spirits, which are the source of these lesser spirits, their gathering place, and the embodiment of the natural phenomenon itself. They are aware of it, and are thus said to have the ability to locate the keys to interfering with this system. For us, those with Crystalline Eyes are shamans, priestesses who can access the system of divine spirits."

"So for all of you, Mizuki is someone you would desperately want to get your hands on?"

"Well, yes, but... You don't need to be that cautious! I don't have the ability to control *kami* at the moment. A year ago I might have been conceited, blinded with ecstasy, and tried to make her mine by force, but now I don't have the desire or the guts to do something like that. I also don't really want to tell other practitioners about someone with the keys to techniques that use *kami*, either. I wouldn't be able to stand twiddling my thumbs while some other divine magic user mastered its esoteric aspects, even if it was an immediate relative to me. I won't tell anyone about your eyes, Shibata."

Mikihiko's eyes were firm, but somewhere in them were lights of madness. Tatsuya perceived them as his transformed desire to monopolize her. Not to make her his own, but not to let her belong to anyone else—that's how he was looking at her.

"...I see. I'll keep this all to myself as well, then," nodded Tatsuya, his own interests aligned with Mikihiko's desire not to let a friend be used by another.

He nodded both to Mikihiko and to Mizuki.

Mizuki returned his gesture with surprise, but quickly forced a smile, not understanding why he nodded to *her*.

[4]

At last, it was August 1st, the day they would set off for the Nine School Competition.

Schools that had farther to go, like Eighth High in Otaru, Hokkaido, and Ninth High in Kumamoto on the island of Kyushu, would be arriving before the others. First High took up its residence on the western edges of Tokyo, though, so every year they usually arrived at their lodging at the last moment before the competition began. This was less of a strategic act and more to prioritize the faraway schools' usage of the site's practice grounds. First High wouldn't be able to enter the grounds until the day of the competition, so they didn't need to get there particularly early...

"...So that's why we don't leave until today."

"Right... I guess the explanation was easy enough to understand, anyway."

The moment Mari finished, Tatsuya had to resist the impulse to make fun of her and ask her who exactly she was lecturing. He shook his head instead and looked away.

The two of them were making conversation out under the midsummer skies, with the sun doing its best to make its presence known. He wondered who on earth would enjoy being out in such extreme heat, but he didn't come up with any answers—he didn't like doing this, either.

"Sorry I'm laaate!"

Mari sighed and grinned as she saw the owner of the voice, whose sandal heels clapped nimbly on the ground; Mari had shrewdly placed only herself under the parasol, leaving Tatsuya to burn up under the sizzling sunlight as he silently checked off an item on the list displayed on his terminal.

One hour thirteen minutes late. They were all finally here.

"Mayumi, you're late."

"Sorry, sorry."

Those were the only words of criticism and apology passed between them. They stepped onto the big bus as though nothing had happened.

A moment later, though, Mayumi came back out empty-handed.

"...Did you forget something?" asked Tatsuya, feeling a little uneasy about whether he was keeping a straight face. The things they'd need for their multiple-night stay, such as extra clothes and makeup (having makeup when lodging away from home was, of course, a necessity taught to him by Miyuki) were already packed into containers and loaded on the bus. The packages were delivered directly from each student's house, so they all would have known by now if they had forgotten something. Even if someone *had* forgotten something, most of what they'd need would be provided by their lodging anyway; there wasn't all that much they'd need to take with them on a bus ride that was two hours long at most.

"No, that's not it... I'm sorry, Tatsuya. I made everyone wait quite a bit."

"Don't worry about it; I heard what was going on."

Mayumi wasn't late for some irresponsible reason like she'd slept in or mistaken the time. Three hours ago, she had called and hurriedly explained that family issues were going to cause her to be late. She had told them to set off without her and she'd meet them there, but every senior present agreed on waiting for her, so Mayumi had ended up in a frantic rush to get here.

She wasn't the next heir to the Saegusa family—she had two older brothers. Not only was she the third child, she was still a high school student; situations where they would need to round her up to do something were seldom at most. It probably would have been more convenient for her if the other students had left ahead of time. She wouldn't have had to hurry in that case. However, they said they would wait—though Tatsuya was quietly against it—which meant they forced her to get here quickly. That was why Tatsuya didn't feel like criticizing her for being one or two hours late.

"Wasn't it hot out, though?"

"I'm fine. It's still morning, and it's not *that* hot outside."

He was given the role of taking attendance for the ride for the allegedly inevitable reason that he was the only freshman noncompetitor going. There were forty competitors, four on the operations staff, and eight on the tech staff. He was the only freshman among the twelve who weren't competing.

Of course, there would be more than just those twelve ready in the wings. Aside from the operations and tech staff, they'd put together twenty volunteers as assistance personnel for outside the venue, but they were taking a different route there. None of the school faculty was here at the moment, either. Their caravan consisted of a single large bus and four work vehicles, and the only ones on them, save for the drivers, were official staff.

"But you must be sweating as... Wait, what? You really *aren't* sweating at all."

"Well, I mean, I'm good enough at magic to be able to prevent myself from sweating... I'm not a lizard or anything—even I'd normally sweat in the middle of summer like this."

He had used a spell that took the moisture and other components from his sweat off of his skin and clothing and dispersed it into the air. In terms of the magic families and types, Tatsuya's characteristic spell, Dismantle, was a compound spell involving convergence, dispersion, absorption, and emission, and was a subset of separation magic. If any part of that held any particular weight, though, it was the dispersion part. Because of that, he specialized (relatively speaking) in the dispersion family.

"A lizard…" He hadn't meant it to sound funny, but she seemed to think it was, and she giggled a little. Probably because of the season—Tatsuya thought to himself then that her smile reminded him of a sunflower. It was probably just an illusion caused by the sunlight, heat, and humidity…and as proof, it only took a moment before her smile changed into her usual mischievous grin.

"By the way, Tatsuya, how does this look on me?"

Yes…the same as always.

She was probably referring to the sundress she was wearing. She held the brim of her wide hat down with both hands and struck a pose. It would have been a little hard to misunderstand *that* even if he'd wanted to.

Today they'd just be checking into their rooms; there were no official events. Because of that, despite it technically being a school event, they weren't required to wear their uniforms. All the freshmen, including Tatsuya, were wearing theirs, but about half the juniors and nearly all the seniors were in normal clothing.

Still, it was best to keep skin exposure in public locations to a minimum. It was the modern-day dress code, so like Mari, many of the students were wearing comfortable, drafty, long-sleeved shirts and thin pants down to their ankles. In terms of exceptions, there was one junior named Chiyoda, who was wearing short shorts and long socks that reached up to her thighs; it was a fashion statement, and one Tatsuya found difficult to decide whether she was exposing a lot of skin or not. A male student named Isori, at her coercing, was in shorts and high socks in a hiking style, and they looked like a matching pair. (Incidentally, the two of them were apparently dating.)

Amid all that, Mayumi's outfit was extremely conspicuous. Strangely conspicuous, in fact. Her sundress exposed both arms all the way to her shoulders, and only reached down to her knees. Her bare feet were clad in high-heeled sandals. The tan tint of her skin was probably because she had put an infrared-reflecting, ultraviolet-proof breathable coating film on it. From that point of view she wasn't exposing any skin at all, but the film's color was like that of a good suntan, giving her skin the troubling illusion of sexiness.

"It looks very good on you." The bold, flowery dress did indeed suit her exquisitely.

"Really...? Thank you." Her silly tone and bashful expression combined for maximum effect as well. "...It would be nice if you were a little more shy about complimenting me."

Two years older than him, and she intertwined her fingers in front of her waist and looked at him with upturned eyes as she approached. Her breasts, of average size for her small height, found themselves caught between her arms, giving him a clear glimpse of her cleavage. At this point, he had no doubt she was doing all this on purpose.

"...You must have had it rough."

"...What?"

Tatsuya had no way of knowing what her sudden errand had been about, but she had obviously built up a lot of stress. "We should get going, President. You should be able to rest a bit on the bus."

...At least, that was what Tatsuya chose to believe.

"Wait, hold on, Tatsuya. Don't get the wrong idea..."

Mayumi found herself surprised and bewildered at his sudden attitude of consideration mixed with a hint of sympathy somewhere in there.

◇ ◇ ◇

"...That was so rude. He was treating me like I was bipolar or something!"

The bus had begun its journey, and Mayumi was inside puffing out her cheeks in anger. Suzune watched her cordially from the next aisle seat over.

"He said he'd be nearby, then just ran away."

Incidentally, Tatsuya was riding in one of the work vehicles as a member of the technical staff. From an objective standpoint—or at least from a visible one—he hadn't done it to avoid Mayumi.

"Just who does he think I am, anyway?"

"It was the appropriate decision," Suzune cut in flatly to Mayumi's excited stream of complaints.

"Hmm? Rin, did you say something or was it just me?"

Her expression was scary: She formed a pleasant smile on her lips, but her eyes weren't smiling at all. She responded in a cheerful voice, once again from a visible standpoint—and *only* the visible standpoint—but it didn't put a dent in Suzune's steely expression. "I did—it was an appropriate decision if he wished to avoid becoming your prey."

"Huh? Hey! That was really mean!" In fact, her own serious assertion put cracks in Mayumi's mask of composure.

"There are few male students who can endure your alluring figure. What I meant is that your beauty has great magical power in and of itself."

"…Umm…"

"……"

Suzune spoke with such a serious face that Mayumi wondered for a moment whether she was being serious or joking. Of course, as soon as a magician heard the words "the magical power of beauty," it was all but assured that it was a joke.

"It's reasonable—I hear Shiba excels at negating his opponent's magic. Perhaps your magic face just doesn't work on him."

"…Rin!" Finally she realized she was being 100 percent teased.

"There, there. Please calm down, President."

"You're one to talk!!"

Mayumi brought her indignant face closer to her friend, who still hadn't broken her serious expression. Upon realizing it still had no effect, she turned her back to her, huddled over, and lay down on the seat, sulking to herself.

But depending on your point of view, her curled-up posture looked...

"Excuse me, President... Are you feeling under the weather...?"

...more like that.

A tense, incredibly worried voice addressed her from the aisle behind Suzune.

"Huh? Oh, no, that's not..." Mayumi hadn't personally expected such a misunderstanding. Still, the misunderstanding—perhaps better called an *assumption*—had caused Hattori to stand up and come see what was the matter as she sulked like that. It marched on ever onward.

"Shiba mentioned that you were tired. I see it wasn't out of the question. If he'd just remember his place once in a while, he'd be...no, I'm sorry, this isn't the time for that."

"Umm, Hanzou? Like I said, I'm not feeling sick..."

"We truly believed your consideration worthy of respect—I mean, you didn't want to make us worry—but if you push yourself too much and get hurt, it won't have made a difference."

Hattori, with a completely serious expression—*this* one earnestly worried for her well-being—watched Mayumi. He was a little red, perhaps of the rather slovenly way she was sitting, or maybe because of her thighs peeking out from under her dress. Her knees were still properly closed, though.

"Vice President Hattori, may I ask what you're looking at?"

To explain the situation again, just to be clear, Hattori was looking at Mayumi's face. He wasn't looking at anything else, but at the same time, he seemed to be clearly avoiding looking at anything else. He had come around the seat, worried, and looked at her, then quickly averted his eyes from what he saw—and with the guilt that came with what he felt, he was unable to conceal his confusion.

...Feeling guilty about it and being flustered by it was, still, proof that he was a serious, pure-hearted young man.

"Ichihara?! I wasn't...looking at... Well, I mean, I thought the president could use a blanket, and..."

In this particular case, unfortunately, his pure-hearted naïveté made him easy prey for the older girl.

"You were going to place a blanket on the president? Oh, then, go ahead." Suzune rose and stood by her seat, her face an understanding one, then prompted Hattori with her eyes to proceed.

Mayumi, for her part, had figured out what was happening. She hid her wide-open chest with both hands and pretended to be embarrassed as she looked up at him.

Hattori froze, the blanket spread in his hands.

Mayumi's eyes were trying to hide a very clear sadistic impulse. She certainly seemed to have less restraint at the moment. *Shiba's analysis was correct*, Suzune thought to herself—putting her own role in this little fracas to the side.

◇ ◇ ◇

"What the heck are they doing...?" sighed Mari softly enough so others couldn't hear the irregular three-way deadlock between the frozen Hattori, the expectant and hopeful Mayumi, and Suzune watching indifferently from the side. After realizing Hattori had been turned into Mayumi's toy as per usual, she sat back down. (She was in the seat opposite Suzune's, across the aisle.)

She could say anything about it, but she was kind of worried about Mayumi's health, and it was making her especially tired. "Well... same as always, I suppose..."

Mari knew it was a vicious cycle; Mayumi would tease him too much, which would stress Hattori out and make him needlessly dismissive of Course 2 students' due, and then his actions as vice president then caused Mayumi, the president, to worry. Mari thought it quite unpleasant. Still, she knew Mayumi led a much more busy and worrisome life than her.

Mari's family was quite an old one, possibly descendants of the samurai Watanabe no Tsuna, though she didn't know whether that was true or not. On the current political map, they were just barely hanging on to a position as a descendant of one of the Hundred.

Whether it was due to a mutation, ancestral reversion, or just a lack of resemblance to her parents, Mari was the only one among all her relatives, blood and otherwise, to have magic abilities that were significant. Because of their position, though, she was almost never bothered by being used as a bargaining chip with another family in the society of magicians.

On the other hand, the Saegusa reigned at the top of the Ten Master Clans along with the Yotsuba. Mayumi may not have been the heiress to the family, but she was still of direct descent—and the oldest daughter. She'd received marriage proposals on many occasions during her time in high school, and some even earlier than that. (This wasn't rumor—it was established fact.) Add that to the fact that even among the Ten Master Clans her magical abilities were amazing, and you had a thoroughbred of the magic world, with many hopes pinned on her future. Of course, she also burdened herself with the unneeded worries of being student council president.

However tough she was at heart, it couldn't be easy. Mari felt she should be allowed some measure of cutting loose from time to time. As her friend. Though she wouldn't even add it in her mind, this side of her might have been more due to shyness than a pretense of evil. Of course, if she said that to her face, she'd end up with a punch to the nose.

——Getting back to the subject.

In any case, she decided (possibly arbitrarily) to let them be until things escalated—and despite everything he said, Hattori seemed happy she was paying attention to him anyway—and looked out the window. She was on the aisle side of a two-seater, so her gaze naturally revealed the person sitting next to her.

"…What is it, Mari?" said another female student seeming to be devoid of energy upon noticing her glance.

"Hm? Oh, I was just looking outside, Kanon." She turned her focus from the scenery to the person next to her, a junior named Kanon Chiyoda, giving the cool grin that made her so popular, mainly with other girls.

She was someone Mari had her eye on in particular, and she had been making secret preparations to place her as the next disciplinary committee chairwoman. The documents to transfer control to her that she'd asked Tatsuya to draw up (though he'd doubtlessly insist he was made to do so whether he liked it or not) were actually for Kanon, too. If she wasn't here, Mari wouldn't have thought to prepare detailed paperwork in the first place.

The Chiyoda family was one of the Hundred Families like the Watanabe—the name contained the character for "thousand"—but they were a main family in them: one of the *true* Hundred turning out great magicians one after another.

The Hundred Families were not called such because there were one hundred families in it. It was sort of a play on numbers: The tenth place is followed by the hundredth place, so the moniker referred to the next families in line after the Ten Master Clans. The Ten Master Clans weren't actually composed of ten families, either. There were a total of twenty-eight families with the qualifications to be called one of the Ten Master Clans. The ones actually chosen for the spots were based on the ones that churned out the most number of powerful magicians at the time (not the *best* ones, however).

The Saegusa family in particular produced many excellent magicians, and the Yotsuba family was host to one of the strongest magicians in the modern world as its leader: Maya Yotsuba, also known as the "Demon of the East" and the "Queen of the Night." The two families were considered the brightest jewels among the Ten Master Clans.

The families currently comprising the Ten were the Ichijou, the Futatsugi, the Mitsuya, the Yotsuba, the Itsuwa, the Mutsuzuka, the

Saegusa, the Yatsushiro, the Kudou, and the Juumonji. These ten happened to have the numbers from one through ten in order, but this was the first time such a thing had happened since the Ten were formed. Before now, having two or three families with the same number in their surname was a natural occurrence.

With the Ten Master Clans and the remaining eighteen, called substitutes by some, the next position down belonged to the Hundred Families. One of them was the Chiyoda family, which Kanon was from. She surpassed Mari in offensive ability against objects, and rivaled or surpassed actual combat magicians of the Ten Master Clans when up against land weapons, having a magical power fitting for one claiming direct descent from the Chiyoda.

Her lack of energy wasn't due to any busy family matters, quite unlike Mayumi's situation. Kanon, after replying to Mari with an "Oh," looked back out the window and sighed lethargically. It was a sigh of futility, and it made Mari a little gloomy.

"Kanon..."

"Yes?"

When she turned around again, she faced a scowl, completely unlike Mari's expression from before. Even that expression, though, with her brows knitted, was charming on her—again, mainly to other girls. "There's only two hours until we get there. Why can't you wait that long?" she asked tiredly.

"What? Hey, that's mean! I'm not a little kid! I can wait two or three hours no problem!" Suddenly she was brimming with energy again, like a different person. Her hair leaped along with her facial movements as she pulled her lips into a frown. "But I thought we were going to be together for the whole bus ride. I'm allowed to be a little disappointed, aren't I?"

"You two are always together, though... I know he's your fiancé, but you two might actually be together even more than the Shiba siblings are."

"Nobody ever travels by bus anymore. It's a novelty, and I was looking forward to it! I was by myself last year, after all. And obviously an engaged couple would spend more time together than siblings!"

"...Really?"

"Of course!" she declared, puffing out her chest—which was, dare she say, a bit lacking in volume.

Mari sighed to herself. Her underclassman was usually a quick thinker, did what she promised, and was tough and positive and the kind of brave, imposing girl Mari liked, but... *It happens every time—when it comes to Isori, she's like a different person...*

"Besides, why does the technical staff have to be in a different car?! They can't do work on the ride, so there's no point in separating us! More people could fit on this bus, and if they couldn't we could just get a double-decker or triple-decker!"

Mari sighed to herself once again as Kanon, who seemed to have found a good outlet to vent her frustration, complained about all sorts of things.

◇ ◇ ◇

There was another girl on the bus with the same frustrations as Kanon—and this one didn't make a fuss about it, instead making her friends oddly scared of her.

"......"

"...Umm, Miyuki? How about some tea...?"

"Thank you, Honoka. But I'm just not that thirsty yet. I'm sorry. I wasn't being forced to stand out under this heat like my brother was."

Her tone was quiet and soft—and like a deep snow burying everything in white, just looking at her made you feel cold.

"Oh. Yeah. Okay," Honoka stammered, flustered. Then she was poked in her side from behind.

Why did you make her think about her brother?

There was nothing I could do about it!

Neither Honoka nor Shizuku possessed telepathy. Still, they clearly knew what the other was thinking just from eye contact, perhaps because they were united in wanting to do something about the ominous intimidation Miyuki was giving off.

"...I swear, they knew someone was going to be late, didn't they? They shouldn't have needed to make him wait outside... Why is it always my brother that suffers..."

Now that Miyuki had begun muttering complaints under her breath, her scariness basically doubled. Honoka wanted to run away. Or at least trade seats with Shizuku. But if she traded seats with her in this situation, what might Miyuki do to her? ...No, Miyuki wouldn't do anything that bad to a friend just for this, but the turbulent mood around the girl was enough to make Honoka think she just might. (Incidentally, the female freshman next to Shizuku was shrinking down in her seat with her gaze fixed on the window.)

"...And making him ride in a cramped work car... I would have at least liked for him to rest during the trip..."

Shizuku looked at how scared Honoka was and sighed. She thought briefly that Miyuki's muttering had left the "next to me" off the end (in other words, she thought Miyuki wanted him to rest next to her), but she said something else. "But, Miyuki, I think that's part of what makes your brother so amazing."

As she addressed Miyuki, she leaned forward to take Honoka's place. Behind her, Honoka placed her hands together in a gesture of gratitude, but neither Shizuku nor Miyuki, facing away, saw it. Miyuki didn't immediately realize her mumbling was being overheard, so she couldn't react immediately.

Shizuku, without wasting a second, pressed her further, her normal taciturn nature nowhere to be found. "I don't think anyone here would complain about waiting *inside* the bus. But your brother was earnest about making sure all the competitors were on board. It may have been just for attendance's sake, but he still didn't take any shortcuts, even when there was unexpected trouble. Not many people can do that. Your brother really is a great person."

Honoka reflected on how Shizuku was able to say those teeth-grating words without blushing—she wasn't one to get flustered easily.

Miyuki's eyes went wide at the excessive praise Shizuku gave with a completely straight face, as though she'd been attacked without realizing it. "...You're right. My brother truly is a softhearted person at the strangest times," she said, barely managing to hide embarrassment.

The air of chilling intimidation went away. Still hidden behind Shizuku, Honoka pumped her fist.

◇ ◇ ◇

Humans, save for a few exceptions, are made in such a way that they can only see what they want to see. More accurately, perhaps, would be to say we have come to pretend we don't see things we don't want to. For living creatures, it is quite often the case that unpleasant information received from the senses is more important than pleasant information. That which is unpleasant is threatening, and locating threats quickly is the key to survival.

Humans, however, avert their eyes from that which they don't wish to see.

For example, even if people knew without a doubt that there was a weapon of mass destruction pointed at them and that it could wipe them all out, they would ignore the truth until the very last moment.

This tendency is especially strong in more advanced nations that have truly grown distant from a struggle for existence. In fact, they don't have to be such bombastic examples—examples of ignoring things we don't want to see happen so often, on a daily basis, that one would be hard-pressed to count them all.

——Take the dangerous pressure emanating from this fair lady, for example.

Miyuki, now back to her usual graceful, ladylike state, was being crowded around by boys—even though they hadn't approached her in the slightest until a moment ago. She was pretty enough to make anyone timid, so nobody tried to get overly familiar with her, but the students, mainly freshmen but with some juniors and seniors mixed in, would address her for whatever reason.

No longer able to let the nonsense pass unnoticed, Mari forced Miyuki, Honoka, and Shizuku to move to the seat behind her. The seating arrangement now had the finally-calmed-down Miyuki and the fully vented, refreshed Kanon at the window seats, the former behind the latter. Kanon sat next to Mari, while they had gotten Katsuto to go behind Miyuki and the others to exert his own authority. With those changes, they managed to lower the tension in the bus. (Also, Mayumi, perhaps satisfied at her incessant teasing of Hattori, was sleeping soundly.)

It was fun to talk among just the girls, but she couldn't escape the feeling that something was missing. The two girls in the window seats felt the same way, lazily watching the scenery go past.

Thanks to that, Miyuki and Kanon were the first two to notice it.

"Watch out!" shouted Kanon. At her voice, almost everyone in the bus looked out the windows toward the opposite lane on the road.

There was a large car approaching—an off-road vehicle meant for leisure, well smaller than the bus—and it was scraping along the road at an angle, sending sparks flying everywhere.

"They've got a flat!" somebody shouted.

"The wheel's not even on!" came another excited voice.

There was no sense of danger in their voices. Opposing lanes on the highway were constructed separately and divided by a sturdy guard wall. It would be impossible for an accident in oncoming traffic to affect them. It was no skin off the young ones' noses—it was an exciting spectacle.

Until a few moments later, anyway.

Somebody screamed.

Maybe it wasn't just the one person.

But that was only natural. By some freak coincidence, the big car began to spin, then collided into the guardrail, flipped over it, and flew straight toward the bus. The driver hit the emergency brakes and all the passengers pitched forward. Some gave cries of pain—probably students who hadn't fastened their seat belts like they'd been told to.

The bus stopped, avoiding a direct hit.

However, after the car fell back to the road, it slid straight toward the bus in flames.

"Blow it away!"

"Get out of here!"

"Stop!"

"!!"

The fact that the bus didn't degrade into panic might have actually been praiseworthy—but unfortunately, in this case, it just made the situation worse. In the span of an instant, the chaotically executed magic spells all chaotically altered the same target of the event. As a result, the spells fought against each other, keeping them from averting the crisis.

Mari realized it right away. "Stop! Idiots!" Thankfully, all the magic that had been used was in an incomplete, still-activating state. If everyone here canceled their unfinished spells, there would still be time to take meaningful action.

Powerful magic could instantly overwrite reality. The magicians here may not have taken flight from their mothers' nests yet, but plenty were able to do it.

…Unfortunately, if they'd still had the good judgment to do what Mari said, they wouldn't have chaotically blasted out all that magic at once. In order to negate the effects of the spells already cast, they'd need enough magic power to overwhelm them all…

"Juumonji!" called Mari, saying the name of one magician who could make that happen. He was already readying a spell. But there was surprise on his face, an emotion not seen very often on him, and it almost made her feel desperate. She knew what was going on: the chaos of magic sequences overlapping one another in the area was similar to the entire bus being under the effects of Cast Jamming. Even Katsuto wouldn't be able to stop *both* the impact and the flames...

"I will take care of the flames!"

A graceful freshman stood up by one of the windows. She had already finished preparing a spell, and when Katsuto saw her, he constructed a defensive magic sequence. Still, she may have had ridiculous talent, but with the storm of psions surrounding them, would a mere freshman's magic have any effect?

A moment later, Mari thought she was hallucinating. She doubted her magic-perceiving magician's senses. Right before Miyuki set off her magic at the approaching clump of metal and fire...

...all the magic sequences that had been activated in the chaos all dissipated.

And *then* Miyuki's spell went off, **as though she'd expected that impossibility to happen**.

Her spell was brilliant, cooling the flames down enough to extinguish them immediately while neither freezing the burning car itself nor cutting off the oxygen to the flames, which would suffocate the driver (though it was pretty unlikely the driver had survived anyway).

Mari's jaw dropped at the performance. But at the same time, understanding that was proof Mari's magical instincts were functioning normally.

As she listened to the remnants of the car being crushed even further by the defensive wall spell Katsuto expanded—a spell of the movement type that put any moving object entering a specified area from a specified direction into a state of rest—her focus wandered away from the threat in front of them. (She had absolutely no doubt Katsuto's spell would hold back the car hurtling toward them.)

What in the world had just happened?

What had just erased all the magic sequences preventing the usage of magic that would let them avoid this disaster?

Was it Mayumi? she thought before immediately shaking her head. She could certainly have dealt with such a chaotic storm of magic sequences. But if she had used anti-magic (magic for going against other magic), she would have fired a psionic bullet and destroyed several of the projected magic sequences at once. She would never have completely smashed every single one of the sequences to smithereens like this. Mayumi's magic was like precisely controlled antiaircraft fire. This spell (if it was magic, anyway) was more like carpet bombing an entire town and reducing it to a burnt wasteland. It wouldn't leave a pillar standing; it would melt all the steel beams and even blow away the concrete foundations of buildings, turning it into a perfectly empty lot. That's how violent it had been.

As Mari and Katsuto had stood petrified at the confused magic power, Miyuki had, without hesitation, cast a spell as though she knew the obstacles would be erased.

Did she know who that "magic" came from?

Could it have been…?

"Is everybody all right?" came Mayumi's calm voice. Mari snapped out of her reverie, staring at the work vehicles following them, now stopped right behind their bus. "That was close, but there's no more need to worry. Juumonji and Miyuki seem to have averted disaster. If you were hurt, then I do hope you will take the time to reflect on how important seat belts are and to put them to good use. Though hopefully there won't *be* a next time," she added in jest, winking, forcing a few laughs.

With everyone's tension and fear gone, she sighed in relief. "Juumonji, thank you. Your skill is always impressive."

"No… It was extinguished immediately, so I could focus on stopping it. Also, was that you who erased the reckless mess of magic sequences?"

Mayumi looked away guiltily at Katsuto's question. "Umm, well, I didn't actually realize what was happening until the bus stopped…"

Come to think of it, she was asleep right before the incident. Katsuto seemed to remember the fact a moment later as well, but he arched an eyebrow and left it at that. He was the number one man of character in the school's leaders without a doubt.

"Oh, and Miyuki! Your magic was beautiful. Even seniors like me would have a hard time striking such a precarious balance with a magic sequence in that short amount of time."

Katsuto and Mari nodded in agreement. The three of them understood how difficult it was not to go overboard in an emergency, to choose an appropriate spell and carefully control its power.

Miyuki blushed faintly at Mayumi's wholehearted praise. "You honor me, President. However, I only had time to choose a magic sequence because Ichihara stopped the bus. Even I would be a little scared to think of what crazy things I might have done if she hadn't. Thank you very much, Ichihara."

Miyuki bowed to her, and Suzune nodded back silently. Kanon turned around in her seat to look at Miyuki with a vacant face. Even Mari couldn't conceal her surprise. Now that she thought about it, the bus's brakes alone wouldn't have slowed them down that fast. It wasn't hard to imagine a deceleration spell at work, assisting the brakes after they were first applied. Mari had been so preoccupied with the spells aimed at the oncoming car that she hadn't noticed Suzune casting a spell to stop the bus.

While everyone else had been focused on the threat, she looked below them and took exactly the right action. Some said her precision surpassed even that of Mari, Katsuto, and Suzune, so it only served to bolster her reputation—and the fact that Miyuki, of all people, had noticed her casting it spoke to how frightening her own talents were.

"Compared to that, you were…" said Mari, suddenly hitting Kanon in the head.

"Ow! Mari, what are you doing?!" Kanon demanded with tears in her eyes.

"Be quiet. No complaining! I can understand Morisaki and Kitayama panicking and using magic to the detriment of the situation, but they're still just freshmen. A junior like you—what were you thinking throwing everything into confusion like that?!"

She groaned. "But I was the fastest! I didn't think other people would start casting, too…"

Her excuse caused Morisaki and Shizuku to look down, embarrassed. There were a few others looking awkward as well.

"Speed isn't always the best answer! You have to read the situation. It's basic logic—you should have talked to everyone else to get them not to cause interference, right? And besides, even after the interference happened, you didn't cancel your spell. You obviously weren't making any calm judgments here."

"…I'm sorry."

Kanon looked down despondently, and Mari didn't pursue it any further.

Though she'd said that, a person normally couldn't maintain calm judgment in a situation like that unless they had some experience with it. And once again, the fact that Miyuki had properly called out that she would handle the flames had been surprising. You couldn't do something like that with just talent. In fact, genius skills tended to place one in front of everyone else, and you usually got worse at that kind of cooperation.

In that sense, Kanon was the archetypal genius.

Miyuki must have been through a lot of fighting or something. And now, as she sat patiently waiting for the bus to get under way again, that sort of experience seemed both to suit her and not.

"By the way, Shiba…"

"Yes?"

Mari had taken to calling Tatsuya by his first name, and Miyuki by their last. She normally referred to others by their last name, reserving first names for those close to her, like Mayumi, Kanon, and some of the disciplinary committee members. One could say she had a particular affinity for Tatsuya.

"That magic sequence... Actually, never mind. It was fantastic."

"Yes? Well, thank you."

She had intended to ask whether Miyuki knew who had used the anti-magic that wiped out all the magic sequences. But as she stood on the precipice of the question, she found herself hesitant to learn the answer. She wasn't sure why, exactly, but she felt like it would conclusively destroy *something* near to her.

Outside the window, the male students on the technical staff had gotten out of the work vehicle and were starting a rescue operation. Of course, the car had been ablaze, and had crashed into the guard wall with enough force to send it flying into the air. Survival of the driver was practically hopeless.

The girls stayed in the vehicle, perhaps because nobody wanted to show them a tragically burnt corpse. Behind the senior trying to cut the car door open was a freshman with a video camera set up, probably to get a record of the incident. He noticed Mari watching him from behind, and she quickly turned away.

◇ ◇ ◇

After the accident they lost about thirty minutes informing the police and getting the road cleared again, and given how late they'd left, they arrived at their lodgings just past noon.

One of the competition's characteristics was that many of the competitors would go on to choose paths in the military. It supported the Nine School Competition on all fronts for the purposes of securing talented combat magicians. To this end, it reserved the stadium hotel for students and school faculty members for the duration of the events instead of for the civil inspectors and high-ranking officers and their aides who came from other countries for conferences.

Still, their support in the matter couldn't be said to be perfect. The hotel was still part of a military facility, so there were no full-time porters or doormen. The base's soldiers on duty usually took on those roles, but given that it was a high school event, the students would be unloading their own luggage. The large devices they loaded into the work cars could be used without taking them out, avoiding no small amount of trouble. The smaller tools and CADs, however, would have minor adjustments done in the students' rooms, so they had to be loaded onto hand trucks and wheeled in.

After quickly finishing that work, Hattori set his eyes on the freshman technical staff who had loaded and pushed the hand trucks and a group of female students walking next to them, laughing and talking, and shook his head gloomily.

Someone casually addressed him from behind. "What's the matter, Hattori? Why the long face?"

"Kirihara... It isn't a long face," said Hattori, turning around to see his friend he recognized from the voice and reflexively denying the statement.

"Really? Well, it certainly isn't a *happy* face you've got."

Hattori knew it. He smiled in a self-torturing way and stopped trying to argue with him. "I'm just...not feeling too confident after that."

"Hey, whoa, the competition starts the day after tomorrow! Now's not the time to develop an inferiority complex."

Kirihara would only be participating in the Cloudball event on the second day, but Hattori was entered in Battle Board on the first and third days, as well as Monolith Code on the ninth and tenth. Unlike Kirihara, who was only entered in one event, Hattori was one of their main competitors, despite being a junior. If he was in bad condition, it would have a pretty big effect on their team's strategy. Kirihara's confusion was understandable.

"What the heck are you so depressed about?"

The Hanzou Gyoubu-Shoujou Hattori that Kirihara knew was a confident, hard worker—or perhaps had confidence because of his hard work. His combat skills were placed right under the so-called three giants of the school, but his talent wasn't the only thing people often talked about behind his back. He had an arrogant attitude—one which even his friends couldn't deny—so he was prone to being mis-understood, but the hard work he put in was just as stunning as his talent. At least, insofar as Kirihara could tell.

With effort, talent, and results all rolled up into one package, he wasn't the kind of person to lose confidence in himself very easily...

"So you didn't feel it? That makes me jealous..."

"What? You calling me a blockhead or something?"

"No, though I do think you're a little dull."

"Hey!"

Hattori gave the mean grin that made other people often mis-understand him. It showed he had gotten a little bit of his usual self back. The fact that he was teasing Kirihara about it made Kirihara feel a little complicated, but it was still obviously a good thing.

"...Moping doesn't suit you, you know. What's the problem?" asked Kirihara, throwing in a bit of revenge.

Hattori wasn't thickheaded; he knew his friend was trying to be considerate in his own awkward way. "About that accident before..."

"Ohhh, right. That was a close one, eh?"

"Yeah. If we didn't do anything, we would have had casualties. Maybe even deaths."

"But the president and everyone got us through it, didn't they? You're worrying about a what-if situation that didn't actually happen. What-ifs normally go the other way, but it's still unhealthy!"

Hattori smirked at the stout remark. "I really am jealous of how you can find such clear solutions, you know. That's not what I was thinking about, though." He paused, then shook his head a little again. "...I couldn't do anything about it."

"Well, if you had tried and screwed it up, they might not have gotten the situation under control. I think the fact that you didn't help meant you were still able to make good decisions."

Kirihara's words were comforting, but didn't give him peace of mind. They were founded in an objective analysis of the event, and Hattori knew he was exactly right. However, his face remained clouded.

"Still… Shiba dealt with it properly. She immediately decided that the problem fell into her realm of expertise, and even remembered to communicate with others. Even if all the magic sequences interfering with each other *hadn't* disappeared, she and Chairman Juumonji would have cooperated and still coped with the situation."

"But not even Chairwoman Watanabe could do anything! That Shiba girl seems to be good at cooling magic, so isn't it just a matter of whether or not your magic was right for the job?"

"Watanabe's specialty lies in personal combat, so her self-restraint in that situation to not try and help was a boon. But I could have done plenty of things… And it's not just a matter of someone's magic power. Watanabe decided right away that she shouldn't try and help, and asked Juumonji to deal with it. And he had already decided he had to do something before she said anything, too, and was in the middle of constructing a magic sequence when she did. He even held back on using it, worried that it would be too difficult for him to avoid the disaster by himself. Then, Shiba, on top of calmly deciding she could do something, communicated with him to help.

"That goes beyond the technical issue of having a lot of magic power, being able to use a wide array of magic, or knowing how to use strong spells. It's whether you can use the proper magic at the right time as a magician—it's not based on the qualities of the **magic**, but on the qualities of the **magician**. I mean, sure, her magic power is through the roof. I probably couldn't beat her in terms of pure strength. But I didn't mind that fact until a little while ago. Because having strong magic doesn't necessarily make you a good magician. Still, to have lost to a younger girl not in terms of magic, but as a *magician*… I can't help but feel unsure of myself."

Now Hattori was dejected again. Kirihara sighed and looked at him. "Right, but that's all based on experience. I think those siblings are special that way."

"The siblings?" repeated Hattori dubiously; he probably hadn't expected him to say "those siblings" instead of "her."

"Her brother... I think he's killed before."

"Killed?" repeated Hattori again, still dubious, but this time surprised as well.

"Yeah. I think he's actually killed people. And not just one or two, either."

"...You're not saying he's a murderer, right? You're saying he has real combat experience?"

"Yeah, maybe it's just the way he acts... You know how my dad is in a navy landing force?"

It may have seemed like a sudden change of topic, but Hattori didn't hesitate to follow up on it. "Right. He has a lot of experience in evenly matched battles on the sea, right?"

"Yeah, but he's a noncommissioned officer. But since he's so low on the ladder, he has a lot of experience on the front lines. He's actually had to get through some seriously life-threatening situations, too. Sometimes his navy buddies will have a party at our house, but they just *seem* different from the rest of us. However much you polish your sword skills, or shooting skills, or whatever kind of combat skill it is, their purpose is to *kill people*. But the soldiers who have actually killed people and the mere athletes who haven't—there's something different between them. Like, there's this *bloodlust* or something. You remember how the thing in April went down?" he asked, changing the subject again.

"You're jumping around here. Apparently it was the work of some anti-magic terrorists. The Juumonji family crushed their organization, but that's all I know." Hattori voiced his discontent at the suddenness this time, but didn't look angry. He had a gut feeling that this all connected somehow.

"Right... So I can't tell you too much... Well, I guess I can say this, since it's you and all. I was there when they were cleaning out the terrorists. And so was her brother."

"...You're not pulling my leash, are you?"

"I know it may seem crazy, but it happened. And I think that I saw his true nature there."

"His true nature?" Hattori repeated out of reflex, noticing the slight tremble in Kirihara's voice as he said it.

"Yeah, what he's really like. Or at least part of it. And it's crazy. He's just like soldiers who have killed people on the front lines and lived to tell the tale. He had this bloodlust, I'm telling you, way more of it than us. He practically wore it like a coat. It was terrifying. Like, I wonder why he's even a high school student."

"...I don't think he would be lying about his age." Hattori wasn't trying to play dumb—it was evident from his expression that he'd been shocked enough to make him say something that was slightly off the mark.

"Well, age and experience don't always match up, right?" Kirihara understood his friend's shock. He'd gone down that road once before himself. He didn't bother to argue Hattori's off-point remark, so he answered normally, with a dry grin.

Hattori asked another question, extremely hesitantly. "...Her, too?"

Obviously most of his hesitation came from not wanting to believe such a thing. Unfortunately for him, his state of mind didn't work on Kirihara—possibly because he'd been affected quite a bit by getting a girlfriend in spring—and he answered his friend flatly. "Well, I didn't see her personally, but her brother took her to the fight scene. She can't just be some normal girl. From what happened today, it's like, pretty roses have thorns—though in her case, she's like a peafowl devouring a poisonous snake with sharp claws and a vicious beak. Making a pass at *her* would probably be life-threatening. Ignorance is bliss, I guess," he added, not to Hattori but to the other boys who had been crowding around her on the bus. As Hattori stood there, unable to hide how disturbed he was, and not quite digesting all the information, Kirihara grinned teasingly. "But wow, I never thought **you** of all people would say something like that!"

"...What do you mean?" he asked, clearly not happy with the meaningful smile Kirihara was making.

Still, his amused expression didn't waver at all. "Having strong magic doesn't necessarily make you a good magician, huh? If the student council president knew you said that, she'd be *so* happy, you know."

"...!" Hattori glared sharply at him. But his friend just kept on smirking—in fact, his smile was deepening at Hattori's extreme reaction—and instead of looking at it, Hattori looked away.

"Well, I guess it's true. Your magic power isn't the only thing that decides if you're strong or not."

Without trying to get a word in edgewise, Hattori began walking away from him. Kirihara didn't seem to care less about it though; he followed and kept talking. "Blooms and Weeds—they're just based on test results from when we enrolled. Even some of the Course 1 students won't progress too much while others do. I mean, Chiyoda is a totally different person. Remember how uppity she was last summer? And if you look at the Course 2 students, there are plenty of them that could get strong if they don't give up on themselves, right? ...Actually, that doesn't just go for the future. There are more than a few of them who can really do it if they need to. Especially in this year's freshmen. Oh, and I'm not just saying that because those siblings got the better of me!"

Hattori's shoulders twitched. Kirihara saw that and decided his friend had realized "that jerk handed this guy's ass to him on a silver platter, too, didn't he?"

"Well, at the moment, he's stronger than I am. I admit it. He may seem like a complete fraud with how strong he is, but I won't stay in the loser's circle forever. I'll keep improving and improving, and when we face each other again I'll beat him. If I give up because I'm not as good as him right now, I'll always be the loser.

"Until this year, the Course 2 kiddies always gave up on the present because they already lost in the past. That's why they couldn't get stronger, and that's why we didn't have to treat them like equals. But if they're *trying* to get stronger, or if they're *already* really strong, there's no reason to be making fun of 'em, right?"

Hattori, again, didn't answer. He headed straight for the room he'd been assigned and kept his mouth shut.

Kirihara shrugged and turned back to look at the siblings they'd been talking about. The younger sister, behind, was staring at her brother's face with a serious expression for whatever reason. He couldn't help but think, *Hope this doesn't turn into any trouble again.*

And then he laughed drily at the thought's lack of logical reasoning.

◇ ◇ ◇

Kirihara's premonition hit the mark in a way that betrayed his own trivial, yet perhaps sincere, wishes.

"Then you say the accident earlier wasn't an accident...?" Tatsuya's sister asked as she walked next to him, frowning.

Tatsuya nodded, pushing his cart along. "The way the car jumped in the air was unnatural. As we expected, we found traces of magic when we looked into it." He spoke in a quiet voice, cautious of the eyes and ears of those around him.

Miyuki followed his example and lowered her own voice. "I didn't see anything, but..." Her statement was an argument, but she didn't doubt her brother's words at all. She'd seen the accident from start to finish, but she hadn't sensed any evidence that magic had been used. But unlike her, who could only see the present, her brother could perceive the past. If he stated there was, then Miyuki knew it was true.

"It was an instantaneous spell of small scope and minimal power. A sophisticated technique; it didn't allow any psionic traces of the magic sequences to be detected. Whoever it was, they're a trained field agent. Skilled enough, you would think, not to be discarded like that."

"Discarded...?" The ominous air behind that term caused Miyuki's voice to go quieter than she wanted it to.

"Magic was used three times. First, to blow out the tire. Second, to spin the vehicle. Third, to add diagonally upward force to the vehicle and have it use the guard wall as a springboard. Each of them was cast from inside the vehicle—likely to hide the fact that magic was used. And it worked. None of the talented magicians, including you, noticed it. I didn't notice it **at the time**, either. They pulled the wool over all our eyes. The driver had to precisely measure the moment of collision while the car was spinning in order to cast the last spell, too. They were no amateur."

"Then it was the driver…"

"Yes, the magician in question was the driver. It was a suicide attack."

Miyuki stopped and looked down. Her shoulders were shaking a little.

"What cowardice…!"

Her trembling was not a product of sadness but of anger. She didn't have any misplaced sympathy toward the criminal; instead, she voiced her indignation toward the one who had ordered such a thing.

Tatsuya nodded with satisfaction at her actions. "Criminals and terrorists are a cowardly sort in the first place. The ones who order others to risk their lives are seldom willing to risk their own. There's no point in getting angry about every single one, you know. I'm more curious about what their stake in this was."

He patted his sister on the back a couple times to soothe her, then resumed pushing his cart.

Miyuki followed shortly after—but then she stopped again before they made it ten steps.

In shorts; high-strapped sandals that exposed her clean, bare feet to the world; and a tank top that let her show her bare shoulders as well, a girl was waving to them from a sofa near the wall.

Tatsuya stopped, too. *What does she think this place is, a beach resort?* he thought, looking at his friend's outfit as she stopped waving and rose from the sofa.

"Hey, haven't seen you all week! How have you been?"

"Well enough… Erika, why are you here?" asked Miyuki dubiously after exchanging a lighthearted greeting.

"I came to cheer you on. What else?" answered Erika readily. Of course, Miyuki had expected that sort of response, so it wasn't enough to convince her.

"The competition starts the day after tomorrow."

"Yeah, I know." Erika seemed to enjoy playing tricks on people like this and seeing them confused. Sometimes it took a while to get to the main subject.

"Miyuki, I have to go. I'll see you later, Erika." Tatsuya, having given it up as hopeless, decided it was more important to get the equipment-laden hand cart over to the room the technical staff had reserved as a work space. He went to the elevator landing, leaving the two of them there.

"Oh, uh, right... You know, it wouldn't hurt to say hello."

"I'm sorry. His upperclassmen on staff are waiting for him," apologized Miyuki in her brother's place, then got back to the subject. "Why are you here two days early?"

"The banquet's tonight, right?"

"......"

"......"

"...And?" She waited for Erika to continue, but she didn't seem willing to conclude her explanation. Without a choice, she decided to get the ball rolling again herself. "I'm sure you know, but they won't let people not part of the event into the party, even if they're students."

"Oh, yeah, that's fine. We're part of the event."

"What? What do you..."

Before she could ask what she meant by that, she was interrupted by the voice of a girl trotting up to them. "Erika, I got the room key... Oh, Miyuki?"

"You're here, too, Mizuki?"

"Hello, Miyuki," said Mizuki, bowing cheerfully in greeting. Miyuki was looking at her intently, though, instead of answering. "What's the matter?" she asked, giving an uncomfortable but cordial smile.

"...Your outfit is quite lovely."

"Oh, umm... Is it?"

Mizuki anxiously looked down at her clothing: a camisole and a skirt that ended well above the knees. Depending on one's point of view, her outfit might have been even more suggestive than Erika's. Miyuki's immediate impression was *Is she mistaking this for a summer resort?*

"Erika told me I shouldn't dress too formally..."

"I see..." Miyuki briefly considered saying something to Erika about that, but the girl in question was looking away and feigning ignorance. She gave up; it probably wouldn't do anything anyway. She thought she understood why her brother sighed a lot whenever he talked to Erika. However, she was a little too serious to play it off with a dry grin like her brother did, and disliked losing more than him. "Mizuki, I won't say anything bad, but I think you should change now. Your clothes are cute and look good on you, but I don't think it's right for the time, place, and occasion."

"Oh...really? ...You think so, too?" asked Mizuki, shooting a glance at Erika.

Miyuki nodded, doing likewise. "Yes, I believe so."

"Huh? I don't know..." argued Erika, dissatisfied, obviously unable to keep up her act.

...This time, Miyuki played dumb. "By the way, you said 'room key.' Are you staying here?"

"Yes," answered Mizuki. Erika looked on in disappointment next to her but didn't make the mistake of getting angry with Miyuki. A pretty girl like her who would never harm a fly—Erika knew from their four months together that she was actually stubborn and merciless at times.

"I'm surprised there was an open room... Actually, I'm more surprised the hotel accepted you. This isn't a place for regular people to be staying."

Erika pulled herself back together. "Yeah, I've got connections," she revealed on the spot, without being shy.

Miyuki couldn't help but giggle. "I should have expected that from the Chiba family." She was smiling, but she hadn't said that to tease her—she was just trying to keep the conversation going.

Just as the Ten Master Clans' surnames consisted of a number from one through ten, the main family of the Hundred Families had numbers above that in their last names, such as Chiyoda, which had *thousand*, and Isori, which had *fifty*. The number didn't signify strength or weakness, but the fact that a number was there at all meant there was a good bloodline involved; it was one of the yardsticks by which to estimate the strength of magicians. Magic families with such surnames were nicknamed Numbers. (Of course, it was only a way to **estimate** that strength; among the student council at First High, the only one for which the term *Numbers* applied was Mayumi, the student council president.)

Erika came from the Chiba family, which also had the character for *thousand* in it, meaning she was one of the main families of the Hundred—one of the Numbers. The Chiba family was renowned for its hand-to-hand combat techniques using self-acceleration and self-weighting. The particularly unique thing about them was not only were they very skilled in the usage of magic, but they had systematized it and almost single-handedly constructed the main style for training hand-to-hand combat magicians. Approximately half of all magicians in the police force and the army's infantry had received either direct or indirect instruction from the Chiba family. Even in the navy and air force, any units who could potentially see hand-to-hand combat situations quite often had instructors dispatched to them from the Chiba.

In terms of their connections to military groups, they might have had even more influence than the Ten Master Clans.

"But are you okay with that? I thought you didn't like using your family as support for things like this."

"What I don't like is people doing things for me because I'm a daughter of the Chiba family. Connections are there to be used, right? They'd be a waste otherwise."

Miyuki's question might have set the person on edge depending on who they were, but Miyuki in particular asking Erika in particular resulted in an extremely indifferent answer.

"Hee-hee, I see," she agreed. "I need to unpack my own things. I don't know how you're related to the event, but let's meet at the party, shall we?"

With Erika waving and Mizuki bowing, Miyuki headed for the elevator landing.

"Hey, Erika. Can't you at least carry your own stuff?"

"Shibata, I brought your things. Not that it matters at this point, but the front desk was really crowded."

As Miyuki walked there, she heard the voices of two boys calling Erika and Mizuki. One of them she recognized, but the other she'd never heard before. The girls hadn't come by themselves; they came in two pairs.

She smiled to herself, not stopping nor turning around.

◇ ◇ ◇

Why, in the first place, had the bus carrying Miyuki and the others planned to arrive two entire days early in the morning even though they didn't need to be there?

The reason: There was a party scheduled for that evening.

As they were high school students, there would, of course, be no alcohol. There would be a buffet meal that brought every competitor together to meet one another before going head-to-head with one another. It was essentially a preopening ceremony with much more tension than harmony.

"And I really didn't want to come, you know..."

Tatsuya politely ignored the student council president's unbecoming remark. The technical staff would always be in the wings here, but as they were official members who would be active during the competition, they needed to attend this party. Tatsuya, for his part, was bad with parties, receptions, and other such events. He concurred with Mayumi in secret.

The dress for the party was each school's student uniform. He was thankful he didn't have to worry about what to wear, but his borrowed blazer didn't fit him perfectly, which only magnified his negativity toward the party.

Miyuki must have caught him shaking himself a little; she frowned and looked up at him. "Perhaps we should have bought them new...?"

"No, this is fine. Sorry for making you worry." Tatsuya was actually embarrassed, too. Who was the older sibling here? This was an official event where everyone participated, so he couldn't be talking about how much he disliked it.

"No, there is no need for apology." Miyuki smiled, knowing her slight change in expression had let Tatsuya get over his foul mood.

"Hey, you there! No getting cozy; you're siblings."

He looked up at the half-teasing voice—strictly speaking, he had to look down after looking back up—and saw Mayumi looking at them, evidently holding back laughter.

"Cozy...? What do you mean by that?"

Tatsuya had read before on a gossip site that some girls were afflicted with a "condition" that made them connect any male-female relationships as romantic, but he wished life would give him a break and not put one such patient so close to him.

Nevertheless, Mayumi probably just wanted to tease him like she always did. He didn't expect an actual answer, but he prompted her to give one anyway. She wasn't looking at him, though; she was looking next to him. And she was about to burst into laughter, too. He followed her gaze to find...

...his sister, looking down, embarrassed. "Miyuki... Why are you blushing at that?"

"Let us sally forth!"

In complete contrast to her earlier backward-looking attitude, Mayumi now, for whatever reason, urged everyone onward with a cheerful expression. Tatsuya couldn't say he was fully satisfied—it seemed like she'd used them to cheer herself up—but he watched how much lighter her step was now and figured it was all right.

◇ ◇ ◇

Even counting only those who would be directly competing in the events, there were three hundred sixty students participating. With all the support staff, the number rose well above four hundred. Although the party was supposed to be mandatory attendance, there was certainly no shortage of people who couldn't make it for whatever reason. Still, the banquet was a very large one, hosting anywhere from three to four hundred people. It was easy to imagine the hotel staff and on-base assistance being unable to cater to all of them, which had to be why there were young people clearly doing this as a part-time job dressed in serving clothes and going around the hall.

Still, seeing someone he actually knew among them surprised even Tatsuya.

After the short opening—he was thankful there were no speeches whose only selling points were their length—Tatsuya had gone straight to get food when someone addressed him from behind.

"Would you like something to drink?" asked the familiar voice. He turned around to see Erika standing there with a drink tray in one hand.

"So this is how you were involved…"

"Oh, you heard from Miyuki? Were you surprised?"

"…Yes." Tatsuya nodded, unable to think of a clever counterattack to Erika's amused smile. "How did you slip in…? Actually, I suppose it wasn't hard."

The place being what it was, high school students wouldn't easily gain employment, even as a part-time job. There was an age requirement, too. Alcohol may have been absent from *this* party, but that didn't mean they could loosen their restrictions. The waiters and hostesses walking around the hall all looked to be in their twenties.

He supposed it would have been an easy feat for the Chiba family, though he felt like maybe she wasn't using her connections properly. "Still, though…"

"Hm? What is it?"

"Nothing…" said Tatsuya, uncharacteristically evasive. Even he found it difficult to come out and say that she looked completely different. Erika probably knew all the mature makeup she had on could cause problems considering her age; she looked as old as the other hostesses present from up close. She was already a sprightly, slender, and pretty girl for her *actual* age, but the grown-up makeup suited her well.

"She"? Singular?

Tatsuya suddenly felt like something was out of place.

Erika wasn't by herself; Mizuki had come with her.

She wasn't exactly a smooth customer in groups of people; would she be able to handle the role of hostess for the party?

In the silence of his thoughts, Miyuki cut into the conversation with just the right timing to compensate. "Oh, hello, Erika. You look very cute! I see this is what you meant by being involved."

"That's right! And thanks, I think so, too! Tatsuya wouldn't say anything, though," she complained, twisting left and right to wave her short Victorian-style dress uniform around, her skirt softly expanding as she did so.

Tatsuya suddenly found himself with the figurative knife at his neck, but he was quick-witted enough to think up a retort in an instant. Unfortunately, Miyuki was just a tad bit faster. "It's pointless to demand such things from my brother, Erika," she said, shaking her head.

Erika seemed more surprised than Tatsuya as she looked back at her. They'd both been caught off guard by Miyuki's clear negative idea about Tatsuya. *That*, however, was a premature conclusion on her part.

"My brother isn't taken with such superficial things as a girl's clothing. He sees us as we are, without indulging in interest in some one-time-only employee uniform."

Tatsuya thought it both an underestimation and overestimation of his nature. In this specific instance, he was just preoccupied with something else—namely Mizuki. He at least knew how to compliment a girl on her outfit, and risqué clothing would cause him to have trouble figuring out where his eyes should go—though perhaps in that case the issue would be less the clothes and more what he could see under them.

"Aha, I see. Tatsuya probably thinks cosplay is stupid, huh?"

"*Is* it cosplay?"

"Not really for me, but I think boys would see it like that."

Unfortunately, their conversation kept on barreling along, with him unable to voice his actual opinion on the matter.

"Boys? Do you mean Saijou?"

"Hah, I can't even say *that* much about him. Miki's the one who brought it up. I made sure to give him a good talking-to for that one, though."

The disturbing phrase at the end caught Tatsuya's ears. Miyuki didn't seem to be worried though. *"Miki"?* The proper noun was unknown to her, and with it sliding so easily off the other's tongue, perhaps it was only natural she would be more interested in that. "…Who?"

Erika made an expression of realization. "Oh, right. Miyuki, you've never met him, have you?" No sooner had she said it than she ran off before they could stop her.

Tatsuya watched Erika dart off with the tray in one hand, without spilling a drop of the drinks on it, and said in admiration, "How nimble. She must have a good sense of balance…"

Miyuki thought perhaps he was a little off point with the comment, but she said something less offensive instead. "I wonder what could have been the matter."

She didn't actually expect an answer; it was just something that slipped out after being left behind so suddenly.

Unexpectedly, though, her brother gave her a clear answer. "She probably went to go get Mikihiko. You know, Mikihiko Yoshida. I'm sure you've heard the name before."

"He is in your class, isn't he?" He'd been famous for his position on the exam grade rankings, so Miyuki remembered it well.

"I think he's known Erika since they were kids. You've never met him, so maybe she wants to introduce the two of you."

Miyuki was convinced; it sounded like the sort of thing she'd do—including the running off without saying anything part.

As the siblings stared off in the direction Erika went for no particular reason, a different two students addressed them.

"There you are, Miyuki."

"And, Tatsuya, you're here, too."

"Shizuku, I'm sorry, were you looking for me?"

"Honoka and Shizuku... You two are together just as much as we are."

Now that he thought about it, he couldn't recall ever seeing the two of them apart. He didn't mean anything in particular by it; it was just a curious observation, but...

"Because we're friends. There's no point in going off on our own," answered Shizuku without any embarrassment.

"That's true." Tatsuya let a pained grin slip at his foolish question. He'd only begun calling the two of them by their first names last month. Honoka had been zealous about asking him, but Shizuku had put her own kind of silent pressure on him to do the same with her, and he'd folded under it.

"Where is everyone else?" asked Miyuki, though not very enthusiastically.

"Over there," said Honoka, pointing to a group of male students who hurriedly looked away. Their female freshman teammates were clustered in the same place.

"Maybe they want to get close to Miyuki, but can't because Tatsuya's here," guessed Shizuku.

"What's that supposed to mean? Am I her guard dog?" sighed Tatsuya. He couldn't laugh it away, though. It was probably true.

"I think they all just don't know how they're supposed to talk to you," said Honoka to soothe him, but he felt like that was also true. He was well aware of his own "weirdo" status. It was probably up to him to approach them first, but...

A new voice cut through the conversation like a knife. "It's so dumb. They're all from First High. Plus, they're your teammates."

"Oh, Chiyoda."

Kanon had joined their circle with a glass in her hand (a soft drink, of course). Behind her was Isori, holding the same glass.

"Sometimes people still can't bring themselves to do anything even though they know that, Kanon."

"But that's only an excuse in certain cases, Kei."

Kanon and Kei called each other by their first names. They were engaged, after all, so nothing could have been more natural.

"I think you're both correct, but there's a simpler way of resolving this." He wondered for a moment whether he was butting in, but he didn't have the energy to get into an argument over what they'd just said—and he couldn't bring himself to worm in between their communication. He had come to a quick conclusion, though. "Miyuki, go over and say hi to everyone. Teamwork is important, after all."

"But, Tatsuya—"

"You can come to my room later. My only roommates are mechanical anyway."

The competitors and staff both generally had twin rooms, but Mayumi had given him a twin room to himself. That way, being the only freshman and Course 2 student on the staff, he wouldn't have to worry about anything. She could put the room down to doubling as an equipment storage room.

"That goes for Honoka and Shizuku as well, if you wish."

Miyuki still seemed unhappy, but she knew the exact reason behind Tatsuya's suggestions.

"...All right. I will see you later on."

"Thanks for inviting us to your room!"

"Later."

Miyuki, Honoka, and Shizuku answered respectively. Tatsuya smiled and waved, then felt a displeased set of eyes on his back and turned around.

"How adult of you. You know you're just postponing the issue, right?"

Tatsuya and Kanon's relationship didn't go beyond the simple knowledge that the other existed. Kanon's interjection about Tatsuya's personal relationships was misplaced, but she was just trying look out for him, so he chose to answer seriously. "I'm okay with that. The problem doesn't have to be resolved right this second. It could take a while to sort out anyway."

"Well, I mean…" stammered Kanon, frustrated. The female upperclassman didn't seem to enjoy losing very much.

"Kanon, he's right. Sometimes hastiness isn't a virtue."

Isori hadn't exactly sided with him; he was just trying to settle things amicably. Unfortunately, an interloper appeared, bringing his efforts to naught.

"I still think he should act more like a kid."

"Hello, Mari," said Tatsuya to the newcomer with a light bow, not arguing her point.

"Isori, Nakajou was looking for you." And just like that, as though she'd expected such a response, she stated what she came here for. She must not have come by just to mess with him.

"I'm sorry. Where is she right now?"

"In work truck number one. The guest introductions are starting soon, so whatever it is, get it done quickly and bring Nakajou back. The other random people might not matter, but being absent during the Old Master's speech would be a blow to his honor."

"All right, I will."

"Excuse us, Mari."

Isori quickly headed outside to follow her directions and Kanon followed in his wake as though it were the natural thing to do.

Mari turned to face Tatsuya. "Looks like it fits," she commented on the blazer he was wearing.

"Well, it's a little cramped under the arms," he replied, looking down at himself.

"Can't be helped—it was a spare. We might have all different sizes, but we can't fit it to your exact body type. Any bigger and it would have been baggy."

"Yes, I suppose you're right," he said, shrugging—inwardly, at least—at Mari's smile and words.

"Should we have gotten it new?" Her voice didn't sound malicious.

"I'll only be wearing it twice anyway, so I think that would be a waste. If it was just a badge, I could take it off and wear it like that, but it's embroidered on, so..." he said, looking down at his left breast a little annoyed. The eight-petal emblem was sewn onto it. He was being forced to wear it to make it easier for the students from other schools at this social gathering to tell which school he was from.

"It might not only be twice, you know. The Thesis Competition is in the fall, and you could always be placed in Course 1." She laughed as she said it, but her eyes were fairly serious.

Tatsuya responded with discouragement. "Even if I *was* chosen for the Thesis Competition, I could just wear my regular uniform, right? And I would never be placed in Course 1. There are no rules or precedents for it."

Mari laughed again, her voice increasing in volume. "Precedent? You being here is unprecedented in the first place! There's no precedent for a Course 2 kid like you, so you saying something is unprecedented obviously doesn't mean anything. You should stop complaining about it and *be* the precedent. For the sake of the other underclassmen."

"......" Tatsuya made a sour face.

Mari laughed again, amused. "Anyway, I'm going to talk to the leaders of the other schools. Want to come?"

"...No, I think Erika is looking for me at the moment."

For just a moment, when he said the name Erika, he saw a flash of agitation in Mari's eyes. He briefly thought about filing it away for later revenge, but he got the feeling things between them were a little too serious to use jokingly. He saw Mari off without a word.

"Huh? Where'd Miyuki go?"

Just as Tatsuya had expected, Erika brought Mikihiko along with her.

"She went over to our classmates. She'll be at my room later, so I can introduce you then."

"Oh. Okay."

Tatsuya's first sentence had been to Erika, while the second had been to Mikihiko. His reaction seemed more relieved than disappointed. "...I'm not going to force you or anything."

"...Huh?" He didn't immediately realize Tatsuya was talking to him, so it took him a moment to reply. "Oh, no, that's not it! I am a little nervous, but..."

"Man, why do boys always want to look cool in front of good-looking girls?"

"Erika, you're pretty good-looking yourself. Especially today."

"Huh? Oh, stop that, you..."

"Anyway, as you were saying?"

After repelling Erika's teasing with some of his own, he prompted Mikihiko to continue.

"Tatsuya, you're..." he began, then shook his head tiredly and answered the question. "Well, I was just a little embarrassed at meeting her for the first time in this outfit."

Tatsuya looked at what the two of them were wearing again. Mikihiko was in a white shirt and black vest, with a black bow tie. Erika wore a black dress with a poofy skirt and a white headdress on her head. Frankly, they looked more like a *servant* and maid instead of a proper butler and maid. "I don't think it's all that strange. That's generally what hotel employees wear, isn't it?"

The waiters walking around the hall were all wearing the same thing as Mikihiko.

"See? I told you you were being too self-conscious, Miki."

"My name is Mikihiko."

Their tones and expressions were the same as they had been for the other million times they'd had the same exchange. Mikihiko didn't seem to like his current outfit very much. Maybe he didn't appreciate dressing like a servant given how far back his family went.

"By the way, where are the other two?" He had to wonder why they were all doing a fake part-time job here, of all places, but he decided not to bring it up.

"What, you think Leo could be on reception?"

"I think he's more than capable of doing something like that..." Tatsuya stood up for his friend in a somewhat reserved way, but Erika still looked like she was about to burst out laughing.

"Mizuki says she hates these clothes, too. Maybe she and Miki would be a nice couple."

"My *name* is Mikihiko!"

"I got it, I got it!"

Mikihiko was getting pretty riled up, but Erika blew it off with a halfhearted response. Then she looked at Tatsuya. "And that's why they're both behind the scenes. Leo's doing some manual labor in the kitchen, and Mizuki's washing dishes."

Tatsuya wasn't absolutely sure *what* was "why," but he felt like he got the picture. "They're both good with machines, after all."

"You're right. Can't judge either of those books by their covers."

These days, moving things to and from storehouses and washing dishes wasn't something usually done by people. Machines could do those jobs just as good as humans, down to the fine details. It meant the two of them must have been using the kitchen automatons to do it.

"I'm good with them, too! So why do I have to wait tables?!"

Mikihiko, however, perhaps because he was actually involved, didn't understand like Tatsuya did—or, at least, wasn't convinced.

"I explained this a hundred times! It was just a little mistake."

"That doesn't explain anything!"

"Okay, okay, stop yelling. It may be just be a part-time gig, but we're still on the job. Look over there, some empty plates!"

"…You better remember this, Erika."

Mikihiko left her with a parting threat and went to a table, though it didn't seem serious to Tatsuya.

"Miki's the one who's gonna forget…" sighed Erika, with no other emotion than that in her voice or in her expression.

It struck Tatsuya, though, that it wasn't *all* she had in mind. "…I don't know what's going on with you two, but can't you go a little easier on him?"

Erika didn't seem to understand what he was talking about for a moment, so she paused before answering. "…It's not that big a deal. But I guess I sort of felt like venting. I know he's bad at stuff like this, it's just…"

"You wanted to make him mad?"

"I dunno. Maybe? He's so uptight sometimes that just looking at him is irritating. I know he can't smile for real yet, but he forgets to be mad sometimes, too… It seems more like delusion to me."

"How nice of you."

"Oh, stop."

Tatsuya hadn't said it as any more than something to keep the conversation going, but the denial he got in reply was unexpectedly violent.

"I told you I was venting, didn't I? Neither of us is here today because we wanted to be. Our parents made us do it. If it looks like I'm being nice, it's only because we feel sorry for each other."

The obstinacy of her spirit showed itself for a moment in her attitude.

"…I'm not gonna ask. It's not like I need to know. I'll forget I heard anything."

Tatsuya didn't try to unravel its mysteries.

"I'm sorry—could you do that?" she said, not telling him off for his lack of sympathy. "...Hey, Tatsuya."

"What?"

"You know, you're...pretty cold."

Despite what she said, she didn't sound criticizing.

"...That came out of nowhere."

"No, I'm thankful for it...I guess. You're not too nice, so I can whine about stuff to you and it's okay. You don't take pity on me, so I don't feel miserable... Anyway, thanks."

The last couple of words were spoken so softly he almost didn't hear them.

As he watched her head to a nearby table as though running away, he thought, *I suppose everyone has their own problems.*

The buffet party hall took up the entire floor of the hotel, and with four hundred strong present, they didn't have the food all on one center table. There were large tables at the right, left, and center of each end wall and in the middle, for a total of nine tables. Food was being resupplied regularly to fill the stomachs of the growing children.

Every year, the students from each school would cluster around their own tables. But while it may have been all right for underlings (?) to sip at their drinks and nibble on their food by themselves, the leaders of each school didn't have that luxury.

Miyuki, having been called away by Mayumi, left her classmates and moved around with the other student council members to exchange greetings with the student council members from the other schools, which doubled as a shrewd ploy to probe the enemy. From behind Mayumi and Suzune, she stole a glance at her brother, who was watching Erika leave.

She sighed. Not audibly, and not in her expression—she did so mentally.

Miyuki thought of Tatsuya more highly than anyone else did

(with "Tatsuya" as the main subject there), but she certainly didn't consider him to be perfect...though she did think of him as kind of superhuman. She knew her brother had no lack of weaknesses. One of those weaknesses was that he couldn't seem to trust the good will others showed him. To a certain extent, he was too thickheaded to actually *understand* that goodwill, but more than that, deep down, he really doubted that others even *had* any goodwill toward him.

In a way, it was natural. Perhaps it was because he was never given love, the highest form of goodwill, by his parents. Instead, they had torn that very love from his heart and mind. Miyuki knew that it was basically a miracle that he responded to her *own* love.

Still, after his cute classmate (Erika, even from Miyuki's point of view, was unarguably pretty) showed him feelings of attachment—perhaps she had already fallen for him—he just watched her go with a disillusioned stare. When she looked at him, she felt more pain than relief.

Miyuki didn't think her brother knew she was looking at him like this, but maybe he noticed her eyes on him. But without a doubt, he wasn't stopping to imagine how she felt right now...and that caused her more anguish.

And it was making her ever more irritated, too.

——She'd need to put in a formal complaint with him before she let this go.

——Being so thickheaded wouldn't do her brother any good in creating harmonious personal relationships.

——Yes, this was for his sake—it was tough love.

Beneath a ladylike, archaic smile, Miyuki made up her mind.
...He had to have picked up on someone staring. He may not have known whence it came, however.

* * *

Mayumi and the rest of the student council were currently smiling (at least outwardly) and having a pleasant chat with the school council from the one that could be their biggest rival—Third High. Behind them, some freshmen from the school were whispering back and forth to each other.

If they had been listening into their upperclassmen's information war and analyzing it for strategies to use later, it would have spoken to how militaristic Third High was. Their seniors might have even choked up with tears over it. Unfortunately...

"Look, Ichijou, isn't that girl super-cute?"

"Super...? What old-timey high school did *you* go to?"

"Oh, shut up. I'm not asking you. Come on, Ichijou, whaddaya think?"

"What are you so excited about...? It'd never work. A girl that pretty is way out of his reach. She'd never even *talk* to you."

"Would you be quiet? Maybe not to *me*, but she might take a shine to Ichijou! He's got good looks, great skills, and he's really smart. Plus he's an heir to one of the Ten Master Clans. And then maybe even I'll have a chance at her."

"You sound so pathetic when you act so proud..."

They were *actually* having a conversation along these lines...and who could fault them? They were high school kids.

"Masaki, what's wrong?"

It was just that the male student in the middle of their circle wasn't answering his excited compatriots. He was busy staring hard at the female student in question.

The boy was gorgeous, though perhaps *dignified* would have been the better word. His features fit right into the old "good-looking young warrior" mold. With his six-foot height, his broad shoulders, and his toned back...the Third High freshman, Masaki Ichijou, was, as his teammates suggested, popular with the ladies.

"...Masaki?"

Masaki turned to look at his dubious classmate. He was smaller, but still well built. "...George, do...do you know anything about her?"

"George" was a nickname. He was completely Asian in appearance, and his real name was purely Japanese: Shinkurou Kichijouji, with "George" coming from the end of his last name. He answered Masaki's question immediately, without pausing to think. "What? Oh. Well, as I'm sure you can tell from her uniform, she's a freshman from First High. Her name is Miyuki Shiba. She's entered into Ice Pillars Break and Faerie Dance. Apparently she's their ace."

"Ack!" muttered Masaki Ichijou, ignoring his teammates' exaggerated surprise. "Brains *and* beauty, huh? Miyuki Shiba, huh…"

The boy called George looked at his friend with a mix of surprise and curiosity. "That's unusual! You don't usually show much interest in girls."

The other students agreed.

"You know, he's right."

"The girls all come to Ichijou first. There's no need for him to be greedy."

"Ah, how indulgent."

The conversation rapidly devolved into unpopular guys venting, but Masaki stayed silent, without responding. He just kept staring at Miyuki, averting his gaze now and again so it wouldn't be *too* obvious. The enthusiasm in his eyes was alarming.

As the guest introductions began, the stars of the day stopped eating and conversing. In a bout of excessive seriousness, as high school students unfamiliar with the world are wont to do, they bent their ears to the voices of the adults.

Tatsuya was fresh out of people to talk to after Erika went back to work, so it was a thankful release from his boredom. It was a good use of his time just getting a look at the faces of the magic world's celebrities, alternating and substituting for one another onstage. Some he was seeing for the first time, and some he'd seen only in images and videos. Of course, there were others he'd seen personally, and some he'd even shared rooms with in attendance at one function or another, despite never having exchanged words with them.

One among them in particular caught his attention: the eldest of the Ten Master Clans and referred to as the "Old Master."

Retsu Kudou.

The creator of the Ten Master Clans hierarchy in this twenty-first-century Japan, and the one man thought to have been the world's strongest magician for twenty years. After leaving the front lines—and taking his title of the strongest with him—he hadn't shown himself in public very often. For some reason, though, he would always attend the Nine School Competition, and he was famous for it.

Tatsuya had never seen the man in person—only in pictures. He found himself excited at seeing such an important historical figure before his own eyes. With encouragement and applause, it was at last the old Kudou's turn on the stage.

He would have been close to ninety years old. Tatsuya wondered how much of his famed magic power still remained. He wondered if he still even had the stamina to use magic. As he thought to himself, the master of ceremonies announced his name.

Tatsuya, along with every other high school student present, held their breaths and waited for the man to step up to the podium. And when he appeared there, Tatsuya forgot to exhale.

Under the softened lights was a young woman with golden locks clad in a formal dress.

There was a stir—Tatsuya wasn't the only one shocked. Countless whispers flew back and forth at the utterly unexpected development. Wasn't the old man Kudou going up to the stage? Why was there a young woman in his place? Had there been some sort of trouble? Had she been sent as his representative?

——*No, that's not it.*

He finally realized what was really going on.

This woman was **not the only one** who had appeared on the stage.

There was one old man standing behind her.

Their attention had simply been diverted to the pretty lady in her showy clothing.

——*Mental interference magic.*

There was probably a huge spell covering the entire hall right now. By preparing something that had stood out, his "alteration" drew their attention away. It was so subtle you could barely even call it event alteration. No, it was a naturally occurring phenomenon. And though the spell acting on everyone present was a huge one, it was so faint and weak that it was quite difficult to detect.

So this is the magic of the man who was once the strongest—the highest, and the trickiest—Retsu Kudou, the "Trickster"...

The old man behind the woman smirked—had he noticed Tatsuya staring at him? It was the smile of a little boy whose prank had gone off without a hitch. At the man's whisper, the lady in the dress quietly moved aside.

The lights illuminated the man, causing a huge commotion. Most people probably just witnessed Kudou appearing out of thin air. The man's eyes once again looked to Tatsuya; he nodded in return so as not to stand out. Kudou's eyes were glittering happily.

"First, I must apologize for the little trick I just played on you." Even bearing in mind that his voice was coming over a microphone, it sounded unbelievably young for a ninety-year-old. "It was just a little sideshow. More a conjuring trick than real magic. And yet I noticed only five people who saw through the trick. Which means..."

He paused. All the high school students waited with bated breath, intensely interested in what the old man was going to say, and what he wanted them to hear.

"If I had secretly been a terrorist bent on massacre, blending in with the rest of the guests and setting up poison gas, or explosives, or what have you, only those five people would have been able to take steps to prevent that."

The old man didn't particularly raise his voice or make it sound more powerful. Still, the hall was now filled with a different sort of silence than before.

"Young scholars of magic, I will say this: Magic is a means, not an end. I played this little trick on you all so that you would remember that. The spell I just used may have affected a very large space, but it was extremely low in intensity. From the viewpoint of magic power, it was no more than a low-ranking spell. But you were all misled by that weak spell. You know who would be appearing here, but you were unable to perceive me.

"Polishing your magical skills is important, of course. You must always be vigilant in your pursuit to strengthen your magic power. However, I want you all to take this to heart: That is not enough by itself. Great magic that is used improperly will always be inferior to lesser magic that is used cleverly. When the Nine School Competition starts the day after tomorrow, it will pit your magic against each other—but more than that, it will compare how you *use* that magic.

"I look forward to what sort of tricks you can devise, young scholars of magic."

The entire audience applauded. Unfortunately, it didn't come all at once. Through the hesitant applause, Tatsuya clapped without ever letting the smile leave his face.

The perspective that the way one used magic was more important than the spell's rank was a stab at the prevailing societal doctrine that power was king. Saying that magic depended on how you used it was, in essence, revealing magic as no more than a tool.

The old magician stood at the pinnacle of magic society, and yet advised them to go against the current trends of that society. Depending on your point of view, his attitude was outright irresponsible. He had enough influence to change magic society, after all.

If Kudou's speech had been insincere, Tatsuya might have disagreed with him, too. But he showed the entire hall in a very easy-to-understand way. He had used magic as a tool in a manner Tatsuya couldn't emulate.

——so this is the Old Master.

Yakumo Kokonoe. Harunobu Kazama. And now Retsu Kudou. There were still magicians in this country he needed to learn from. And there were likely plenty of others he didn't know about, too. This was something he couldn't understand in an FLT laboratory.

At that moment, Tatsuya thought this:

Being a high school student was turning out to be unexpectedly exciting.

◇ ◇ ◇

The banquet was slated for two days before the competition in order to give the students one day to rest. The technical and operations staff would be devoting themselves to the home stretch of their preparations, but each competitor was restoring their energies and spirits for tomorrow's battles in his or her own way.

Still, the freshmen wouldn't be competing until the fourth day of the competition. For them, excitement and adventure won out over nervousness. They were in high spirits despite themselves, as though it were a group field trip with classmates, which was only natural given their age.

Miyuki, Honoka, and Shizuku had come to Tatsuya's room again that night after dinner to hang out, but they left soon after, since he was busy arranging activation programs. The main and rookie competitions had different schedules, so the freshmen were all rooming as pairs together. Honoka and Shizuku were in one room, with Miyuki's roommate being Kazumi Takigawa from Class C. Kazumi had a pretty active disposition, though, and mostly spent her time with her club seniors, so Miyuki spent time in Honoka and Shizuku's room often.

The hour hand on the clock (for some reason, all the clocks in the hotel were three-handed analog clocks) was just about getting to the *X*. Most of the upperclassmen who would be competing tomorrow had probably turned in for the night. In consideration, not only Miyuki, Shizuku, and Honoka, but also their teammates and the freshmen from other schools were discerning enough not to make a huge ruckus outside. Still, the young girls had too much energy to head for the peace of sleep like their seniors.

And when three girls are walking around at night, it generally meant they were talking.

There were exceptions, of course. From her outward appearance one might tend to think Miyuki and Shizuku were those very exceptions, but they were actually pretty normal in this case.

The topic, as it had been for a while now, was the competition. Girls didn't talk just about fashion and romance. Of course, thinking that way bordered on flippancy.

As mentioned before, it was almost ten o'clock, but there was no curfew. So when there was a knock at their door, there was no reason to panic or get confused.

"Oh, I'll get it."

All three of them stood up, but Honoka was closest to the door, so she stopped the other two.

"Good evening—"

"Oh! Hello, Amy. Where's everyone else?"

There was a short girl with impressive lustrous ruby hair peeking in through the open door. She was their teammate, Eimi Akechi. Four other classmates stood behind her, meaning most of the female First High rookie competitors were present.

"Yeah! Well, get this! There's a hot spring here."

She tried to figure out what her excited voice was trying to say, but couldn't. "...Sorry, could you say that in a way I understand?"

Miyuki, though, seemed to understand what she meant. "Yes, isn't there an artificial hot spring in the basement of the hotel?"

"Yeah! Leave it to Miyuki! So smart!"

"...I'm sorry, but I could do without the compliment."

Eimi didn't mean anything malicious or evil by it, but her air-headed praise gave Miyuki a headache for some reason. She pretended to massage her temples. Eimi looked at her and tilted her head, a little confused.

"It's nothing. Don't worry about it. Anyway, as you were saying?" prompted Miyuki.

Eimi grinned innocently. "Right! I'm thinking we should all go to the hot spring."

It sounded crazy—at least to Miyuki—and she exchanged glances with Honoka. She seemed to feel the same way.

The one who answered Eimi's suggestion, though, was Shizuku, all the way from the back. "Are we allowed? This is a military base."

This wasn't your run-of-the-mill hotel. It was a base with a maneuvering ground for national defense forces. Shizuku was worried that they couldn't go into *any* other room without prior permission.

Eimi, clearly not considering any of that, denied it, though. "We decided to ask, and they actually said yes. We can go in until eleven!"

"Good going, Eimi," said Honoka, a little astounded.

"I guess all you need to do is ask!" Eimi's response to what could have been construed as sarcasm actually sounded proud, though, and it had no effect.

"But don't you need a swimsuit for this hot spring? That wasn't exactly on my list of clothes to bring."

"That's okay, too. They said they'll give us some towels and bathrobes."

Eimi had already dealt with the practical problem Miyuki posed. With everything all set for them, none of the three had any reason to refuse. And, in all honestly, they couldn't deny an interest in this hot spring, man-made though it was.

"Then we shall accompany you. We'll get a change of clothes, so please go on ahead."

Eimi nodded happily at Miyuki's answer. "Okay! There's no rush or anything."

Miyuki waved her hand and saw her teammates off.

The big public bath underground had been reserved for First High's freshmen girls. It wasn't just empty—they had gotten it reserved for them especially from ten to eleven. The place was like a group bath, and was originally administrated as such. This was because despite the term *big public bath*, the underground hot spring could fit barely ten people inside at once. The bath was more of a medical facility, constructed to treat muscle pain and joint pain from training. It boiled the cold alkaline springwater that flowed underneath the hotel. Its main users were high-ranking military officials (and only the middle-aged commissioned officers, at that); it wasn't built in the expectation that large numbers of sightseers would use it for recreational purposes. The doctor would specify a time for people to soak in the bath and nothing else, so there were shower booths for washing off with bathing suits or bathrobes inside.

——It didn't look like any other groups besides them had requested permission to use the place, though.

The women's bathing robes were, bluntly, short white *yukata* without the belt. Their loose-fitting designs didn't tighten anywhere so were perfect for using in the bath but also didn't feel anywhere near as good or reliable as swimsuits.

"Wow…"

"W-what?"

The outfit would have been too embarrassing to show someone of the opposite gender, but everyone here was a girl, and a pretty familiar and trusted teammate, at that. Eimi's sigh, however, caused Honoka the sort of embarrassment and caution a man looking would have given her. Without thinking, she covered her chest with her arms, for Eimi's eyes were definitely looking there—straight at her breasts.

"I'm surprised. Honoka, you've got a nice body—" said Eimi, sidling up to her.

Honoka retreated, but soon ran into the wall of the bathtub.

"Honoka..."

"What?!" The impression coming from Eimi was a dangerous one, and Honoka nearly shrieked it.

"Can I undress you?"

"Of course not!"

Eimi's eyes were sparkling. She was obviously just teasing her. The problem was, of course, the joke not having an acceptable punch line for Honoka. She looked around the room searching for help. Her teammates were all either in the tub or sitting with their feet over the edge. With one minor exception, they were grinning in the same joking way as Eimi was.

"Oh, it's fine! I mean, you have big breasts!"

"That's not the problem!!"

Eimi was still grinning, but Honoka clearly caught a glimpse of a dangerous light in her eyes—this wasn't just a joke. "Shizuku, help me!" Unable to endure it, she called out for help from that one minor exception, Shizuku.

Shizuku stood up deliberately. "Well, why not?" she answered, walking out of the tub.

"Why?!" she shouted at her best friend's betrayal.

For a moment, Shizuku looked down at her own chest sorrowfully. "I mean, you have big breasts."

With judgment passed, she left and walked into the private sauna.

Honoka's scream rang out through the bath.

What on earth could be going on in there? wondered Miyuki to the splashes of water coming from the bathing room as she showered to wash herself off again. She had already gotten the dirt and grime off her in her own room's bathroom, but nevertheless she followed the proper procedure, using the fully automatic shower booth, which some called the "human washing machine," to wash her body (from the head down). When she was done, she put her arms through the sleeves of her bathrobe. She wrapped her long hair tightly in a towel, and then finally moved to the bathing room, in which the commotion had finally settled. When she entered, her bathing teammates all locked their eyes on her body at once.

"Wh-what is it?" she stammered in spite of herself, stopping. Nobody answered her, though. Not a single set of eyes peeled from her.

"No, everyone! Miyuki's normal!" Honoka, her expression somewhat heroic, stood up from the bathwater and broke the silence.

"Honoka?" Miyuki would need more than that to understand what Honoka meant.

"No, don't worry. Sorry. We were just a little fascinated." That was the boyish, handsome voice of a girl named Subaru Satomi from Class D, who was sitting nearest to her, legs over the edge of the bathtub.

Miyuki suddenly realized what Honoka meant and why everyone was looking at her. "Wait... What are you talking about? We're all girls," she said hastily, her hand going to her inner thigh to pull down the short hem of the bathrobe. With her action, the room became pregnant with an odd tension again.

The thin bathing robe was clinging to her because of the moisture still on her from her shower and the steam rising from the bathtub, causing her feminine lines, including the pair of mounds on her springy chest, to appear distinctly.

Her pink, slightly flushed breasts tucked inside the front kimono lining.

Her slender, impeccably beautiful legs of dazzling white coming out of her short robe hem.

In Miyuki's case, this bathing robe, while it exposed far less than a swimsuit, had a charm and beauty above even being stark naked.

"...We're all girls... Yeah, I know, but..."

"How should I put it... Looking at you makes me feel like gender doesn't matter."

Before any more utterances could slide out, Miyuki gallantly put her foot down. "Geez! Please give the teasing a rest!"

Amid the hungry stares, she gracefully bent down and submerged herself in the bathwater. She sat with both legs out to one side and went down to her neck. The collar of her bathing robe swayed in the water, giving a momentary but clear glimpse of the nape of her neck.

Everyone present sighed. The current mood was no joke, no prank. If the situation continued on like this, Miyuki's chastity might have been in danger.

That is, if Honoka hadn't sat next to Miyuki with a *sploosh* to block her from the eyes of the spiders with a butterfly caught in their web. "Miyuki, don't worry! I'm on your side! If you all don't quit it, everyone here is going to have a nice cold bath in ice water!"

As soon as they heard that, their teammates turned quiet and they looked away. But even if their eyes were elsewhere, their attentions were still all on Miyuki. Despite so many young girls in one place, nobody spoke.

Miyuki, for her part, wanted to object to what Honoka said, but she felt that if she carelessly told them she'd never do that, it would break the precarious equilibrium they had at the moment, so she said nothing.

"…What's wrong?" Shizuku, who had been holed up in the private sauna and hadn't seen anything, asked simply, cutting into the stiff atmosphere in the bathing room.

The girls finally reacquired their collective sanity, as if the question had snapped them out of it.

Now that they had gone back to normal for the moment, the bathing room quickly filled up with lively voices. Girls' conversational topics aren't restricted to fashion and romance. Still, these girls liked fashion and romance as conversational topics, and their bath talk naturally turned to gossip about guys they'd seen at the party. They mainly talked about boys, but there was some talk about older men as well. Put in a positive light, there was an open-mindedness in the

diversity of their tastes. Of course, as for the actual state of things, it went something like this:

"——And the bartender at the drink bar was such a dreamy guy!"

"Wow... He was clearly in his forties. It's all over if you start getting into old men..."

"I'd prefer it if you called him *handsomely middle-aged*. If you ask me, high school students are all children! Like, you can't rely on them for anything, you know?"

"You think so? I think there are at least a few boys our age you can depend on. Maybe you've just had bad luck with men."

"You're right. Isori is pretty broad-minded, right? More importantly, he seems nice."

"Nothing will come of falling for someone who already has a girlfriend, right? I mean, Isori's girlfriend is actually his fiancée already anyway."

"If we're talking dependable, doesn't Juumonji fit that description?"

"Well, in his case, he's a little *too* dependable. Despite how he looks, he's the heir to one of the Ten Master Clans."

"Speaking of Ten Master Clans heirs, wasn't there one from Third High there named Ichijou?"

"Oh, I saw him! He was pretty good-looking."

"Yeah. I mean looks aren't *everything*, but they sure are nice to have!"

...That was how the conversation was going. Then, suddenly, Eimi referred to Miyuki, who had recovered from her (mental) exhaustion before, now sitting at the end of the bathtub. "Ichijou from Third High? He was getting all googly-eyed at Miyuki, wasn't he?"

Miyuki had been the one Eimi was speaking to, but she found herself unable to answer.

"Wait, really?"

"Could it be love at first sight?"

"It's Miyuki! I'd believe it."

"Wouldn't it be weirder if a guy *didn't* fall for her?"

"Maybe they've met each other before!"

Someone squealed.

"How about it, Miyuki?" asked Shizuku seriously—given her normal monotone, she always sounded really serious even if she didn't mean to—in contrast with the shrill squeak.

Miyuki gave that an answer. "...If you'll allow me to answer seriously, I've only ever seen Ichijou in pictures before. I didn't even know where he was in the party hall." The response, somewhat cruel and somewhat cold, might have brought Third High's fighting forces down into a rut just from hearing it. The other girls waiting in anticipation all looked disappointed.

But there were always those who never got discouraged. "What kind of person *do* you like, Miyuki? People like your brother?"

Honoka reacted to Subaru's question rather than Miyuki. Only Shizuku, who was sitting next to her, saw her whole body freeze up for a moment.

Extremely calmly, and with an expression consisting of both serenity and amazement, Miyuki answered. "I don't know what you want me to say, but... He is my brother by blood, all right? I've never seen him as an object of romantic interest. And I don't think there is anyone else like him anyway."

Subaru and Eimi seemed clearly dismayed at the reply (though Subaru was being melodramatic).

Nobody asked about Miyuki and Tatsuya's relationship after that.

Still, there were two girls in the bathing room that didn't accept her answer at face value—both Honoka and Shizuku felt something more than "not seeing him as an object of romantic interest," as she'd said.

◇ ◇ ◇

After returning Miyuki and the others to their room—unaware that he would be talked about by the three of them and their teammates afterward in the underground artificial hot spring—Tatsuya started to work on arranging activation programs in the work vehicle.

"You should finish up soon, too, Shiba."

He looked up at the voice and saw that there was only one other person still in there. "When did it get this late?"

The clock was about to change the date. Isori nodded with an androgynous smile. (As an aside, Isori's clothing and hairstyle were both unisex, and Tatsuya suspected he might actually be making an effort not to look masculine.)

"The competitors you're in charge of don't compete until the fourth day, so I don't think you should spend all your energy right from the start."

"You're right."

Tatsuya was in charge of the freshmen girls' Speed Shooting, Ice Pillars Break, and Mirage Bat events. This was both at Miyuki and her friends' behest and because the freshmen boys (mainly Morisaki) didn't want him. (Miyuki was entered in Ice Pillars Break and Mirage Bat, Honoka in Battle Board and Mirage Bat, and Shizuku in Speed Shooting and Ice Pillars Break.) He certainly had more legroom than the staff who would be in charge of students competing tomorrow. Kanon was entered only in Ice Pillars Break on the second and third days, but Isori was in charge of some competing tomorrow as well.

"Thanks; I'll go get some rest," he said, leaving the work vehicle behind him, not going so far as to suggest they both call it quits.

The midnight in the middle of the summer still hadn't cooled off very much. It was just warm enough to walk around comfortably in a T-shirt.

Instead of going straight back to his room, as he wandered around the hotel grounds in casual clothing, he sensed a strangely tense presence. Like someone was holding their breath and looking around.

A thief? he thought at first, but he discarded the idea a moment later. Whoever was trying to hide their presence but couldn't quite do it was more violent, more belligerent. Tatsuya opened his senses and accessed the Idea—the giant information body comprised of the information bodies of all things that existed.

Three of them. They're…surrounding the hotel, just outside the fences disguised as hedges.

All three had handguns and small explosives.

Even outside the hotel grounds, they were already inside a military facility. The security at the base was by no means lax. Both man and machine kept watch for intruders and eliminated them. They'd have especially less mercy on those with weapons.

Not only had these intruders squirmed past the security; they also had explosives. Tatsuya didn't have his CAD on hand, but he couldn't just let them run free to do whatever they wanted.

Tatsuya silenced his footsteps and began to run. Then, his senses detected someone he knew approaching the suspicious people just like he was. The person's stealthy movements were as good as his. The trespassers were on the other side of the fence from their starting positions—but Mikihiko would get there faster.

As Tatsuya ran, he assembled a support spell. With his specific spell and specific magic power, he could use that specific spell even without a CAD, and with the same speed and precision others could accomplish by using one—but only with this.

Mikihiko prepared to unleash a spell of his own. He wasn't using a CAD. Tatsuya's perception of the Idea came to him not as images, but as thoughts. Mikihiko had pulled out three long, narrow strips of paper—likely amulets. He wasn't going to use modern magic; instead he would use old magic. As Tatsuya "sensed" him doing it, his psions flowed through his hands and into the amulets, constructing the spell.

Both modern and old magic interfered with the "information" incident to "existence." They were fundamentally the same in that they overwrote events. The method and conditions for doing that overwriting were the only differences.

The magical system Mikihiko had activated didn't form information bodies in his magic calculation region for this interference—in other words, he didn't create a magic sequence. Instead, he appended information to the amulets in his hand, then used that as a medium to place the information bodies, now independent and without mass, which had separated from that "existence" and were now floating around the Idea, under his control. With that, he was constructing a three-layered spell by overwriting the phenomenon.

Compared to modern magic, which directly overwrote the information bodies incident to existence, or Eidos, this process lacked speed and freedom. However, it rarely resulted in resistance to the interference being performed. By limiting the events one alters, one could use magic of a larger scale than modern magic with less power.

With his ability to analyze magic sequences, Tatsuya understood all this in the blink of an eye.

And it made him feel anxious about Mikihiko's spell.

He's not going to make it.

The spell Mikihiko was using was taking too many detours, too many complex and pointless alternate routes. It meant that actually casting the spell was going to take too much longer to ignore.

Tatsuya set the intruders' handguns as the target for his Dismantle.

Mikihiko had sensed the disturbance thanks to his training in magic.

Deep in the hotel courtyard.

He had left the building, gone near the hedges bordering its plot of land, and found a place away from the eyes of others to begin his daily training.

He attuned his senses with the spirits—abstract concepts of things such as wind, water, earth, and fire, which were separate from individual events—in order to practice the fundamentals of deity magic (spirit magic).

By modern magic interpretation, spirits were information bodies floating the sea of information separate from physical objects.

Those concepts themselves moved and changed the world of information, and the energy those concepts manifested combined to move and change the physical world.

It was said they could be measured as massless objects.

But by coming into contact with spirits like this, he felt for sure that they were real and existed in this world.

Not through logic, but by feel.

To him, spirits were always right there, each with its own will. By coming into contact with them, they would grant him many different experiences and observations.

As soon as he began his attuning practice, he "heard" people outside the plot of land the hotel was on.

At first, he put it off as people who had left the hotel on an errand, or soldiers on patrol.

But as the spirits' cycle of informing him of their presence continued, he began to think they might be warning him.

He used his attuning practice to extend the threads of his senses in the direction the spirits were indicating.

And when those threads arrived at their destination, they found malice.

His face stiffened with tension.

He couldn't immediately decide whether to call someone or deal with it himself.

Today, he couldn't say for sure he could deal with **any opponent**. It frustrated him, but he didn't have the confidence. He bit his lip and decided he should go back to the hotel and call for the soldiers on security.

Unfortunately, his emotional response didn't agree with the logical decision.

Something that wasn't logic was telling him it would take too long.

He got the feeling that his disquiet was the spirits telling him to hurry.

He burst into a sprint—not to return to the hotel, but toward the malice.

He was unsure.

If they were armed with handguns, he was unsure he'd be able to deal with them **as he was now**. Not many magicians could beat a handgun being pointed at them from right up close. If there was anything in the way, magic would have the advantage, since physical obstacles didn't affect it. If he couldn't use any cover, then it would be difficult to deal with the speed of a finger pulling a trigger.

But Mikihiko pushed the rational unease from his mind—it was cowardice.

He remembered what happened yesterday.

It was his father who had made him pretend to be a waiter.

Erika said it had been a little mix-up, but he knew the real reason.

——*Go to where you should have been originally.*

That's what his father had said to him the night before last.

His pretending to be a waiter was a means to realize that.

Mikihiko's father probably wanted him to see all those of his generation who were standing in the spotlight, in order to get him back on his feet. Maybe he wanted to inspire him. But those words, and the way he was carrying them out, stuck in Mikihiko's mind as humiliating.

Maybe, at the time, Mikihiko wanted to prove that he wasn't a failure.

The lighting around him was dim, but as part of his family training, Mikihiko had practiced operating in the darkness. Even if starlight was all he had to go by, he felt no inconvenience.

Once he had approached the presence emanating the clear malice, Mikihiko produced a few amulets.

Three of them—one for each of the intruders. They'd probably noticed him, too. The overwhelming malice and hostility allowed Mikihiko to know there were three of them.

He couldn't hesitate. The hostility was changing into bloodlust. If he hesitated, it was over. Shoot first, ask questions later.

Mikihiko filled the paper with magic and let loose a spell.

A light flashed in his hands, and as if to answer it, electricity began to gather above the intruders.

Within a second, the electric attack would hit them. But it wouldn't take them even half a second to pull the trigger.

Tatsuya made a snap judgment and activated the spell he'd been preparing: Dismantle. The three handguns they held, in accordance with the alteration of the eidos, fell apart.

And a moment later...

...the little bolts of lightning created in midair struck the three of them.

"Who's there?!" demanded Mikihiko, not at the three figures collapsed on the other side of the hedges, but at the magician who had supported him, and was now running up.

He already knew what had happened. His magic wouldn't have originally made it in time—it was only thanks to another magician's backup that he hadn't been hurt. He had lost his former speed at magic, and it nearly spelled disaster for him in a real combat situation.

"It's me."

"Tatsuya?"

Tatsuya could see Mikihiko's shock just by looking at him.

He didn't stop after giving his curt reply, though, and leaped over the hedges in front of them.

He applied negative weight to himself with a self-weighting spell and crossed the seven-foot-high line of hedges.

Mikihiko watched him go over, dumbfounded, but then snapped out of it, pulled out a new amulet, and cast a self-weighting spell of his own.

When he landed on the other side of the hedges, Tatsuya was kneeling next to the fallen intruders.

"Tatsuya?"

The simple question was loaded with meaning.

Not even he himself knew what he meant by it.

"They're not dead. That was some good work."

Tatsuya seemed to have taken it as a question about the intruders' condition. Or maybe he'd seen how confused Mikihiko was and chose the least offensive interpretation he could find.

"What?"

Mikihiko didn't understand what Tatsuya was complimenting him for.

I would have been done for originally, he thought, torturing himself.

"A precise ranged attack against multiple targets from a blind position. The attack was made with the intent to capture rather than deal a mortal blow, and you pacified them all in one go. It was the best possible outcome."

Tatsuya's tone was so calm you could call it *hard-boiled*, and it told Mikihiko that his praise wasn't mere flattery or comfort.

What Mikihiko couldn't believe wasn't Tatsuya but himself...

"...But my magic wouldn't have made it in time otherwise. Without your backup, they would have shot me."

...for what came out of his mouth was self-deprecation that beat his self-control.

"Are you an idiot?"

"...What?"

The curt ridicule Tatsuya blasted him with, though, cut any further self-torturing words from leaving his lips.

"If I hadn't backed you up? That's no more than a hypothetical situation. The fact of the matter is that your magic successfully captured these intruders."

"......"

Mikihiko was completely taken aback by Tatsuya's merciless ridicule and exposition.

"In reality, you had my backup, and in reality, your magic made it in time. Originally? Mikihiko, what exactly did you think things were like *originally*?"

"Well, I…"

"You weren't basing this off of some idea like, no matter how many opponents there are, and no matter how well-trained they are, you could win without anyone's backup, right?"

The shock hit Mikihiko so hard it felt like his heart flipped over. He knew just as well as Tatsuya how absurd an idea like that would have been. But deep in his mind, hadn't he been thinking that exact thing?

"I swear… I'll say it again, Mikihiko. You're an idiot."

"Tatsuya…"

"Why do you go to such lengths to reject yourself? What's making you have such a low opinion of yourself? What is the problem, exactly?"

"…You wouldn't understand even if I told you. And it's not something I can change anyway."

"No, you might be able to."

Mikihiko had built a wall and hid behind it with that argument, but Tatsuya had just demolished it with a wrecking ball.

"What…?!"

This time, Mikihiko really couldn't find anything to say. Tatsuya gave him a piercing stare.

"Mikihiko, you're worried about how fast you can activate magic, aren't you?"

"…Did Erika tell you that?"

"No."

"…Then how…?"

"You have a lot of redundancy in your spell casting."

"…What did you say?"

"I'm saying the issue isn't your abilities—it's the spells themselves that you're trying to use. That's why you can't execute magic the way you want to."

"How the hell do you know that?!" shouted Mikihiko.

He was so confused.

He was so enraged.

The spells he used were developed by the Yoshida family over countless years, aggressively implementing the findings of modern magic into their traditions of old magic, heaping improvement upon improvement.

After seeing it only once or twice, Tatsuya treated it like a faulty product, and that made Mikihiko angry.

Tatsuya had presented him with those doubts he'd been trying to ignore for so long, having rejected them as convenient fantasy, and that made Mikihiko confused.

"I can tell with these things. I'm not going to force you to believe me, though."

But then Tatsuya used his calm tone to quell Mikihiko's rage, spouting something that made Mikihiko even more disturbed.

"...What did you say?" he asked once again, though with a different intonation this time.

"I can understand magic composition just by looking at it. I can read and understand the information described in activation programs by looking at them, which allows me to analyze magic sequences."

Tatsuya gave an unbelievable explanation in return.

At that moment, Mikihiko's confusion reached a peak.

He'd never heard of any magician who could do *that*. If that kind of abnormality really existed, it would solve half the issues in modern magic.

"...Like I said, I won't force you to believe me," Tatsuya said again, as if to abandon it.

Mikihiko felt like he was implying that the rest was his own problem to figure out.

"Let's leave it at that for today. We need to deal with these guys. I'll keep watch, so could you go call security? Or do you want me to?"

Frankly speaking, Mikihiko was still unable to even fathom whether Tatsuya's "confession" had been the truth or a lie, so he was thankful for the change in topic.

"Oh, I'll go call them."

"All right. I'll wait here."

Mikihiko activated his jumping spell again and disappeared behind the hedges.

Tatsuya, on the other hand, thought briefly on how to restrain the intruders, and decided to bury them in the ground. If he used Dismantle, it would destroy the dirt he'd need to put back in the holes, so he had to use Dismantle and movement-type magic separately. It was somewhat tiresome work to do without a CAD, but like his jumping from before, he had the magic sequences of simple spells entirely committed to memory, so he could execute them without a problem, as long as he wasn't trying to trigger more than one at once.

Ironically, the virtual magic calculation region artificially created in him had been placed in his conscious mind. The benefit was that he could use the magic sequences easily since he had them right there.

I feel like I'm cheating.

Half of him felt like a victim as the other half of him used it as a convenient tool. He grinned scornfully at his lack of principles and went to activate the spell.

——However, he didn't need to.

Upon sensing the approach of someone he knew, he interrupted his casting. It didn't take long for the person to say something to him.

"Pretty heartless advice, there, Specialist."

"You were watching, Major?"

Tatsuya hadn't realized Kazama was eavesdropping. It wasn't enough to surprise him, though. Kazama had received instruction from Yakumo Kokonoe for far longer than Tatsuya had, and was the man's best student. If Tatsuya wasn't accessing the Idea, he'd have a lot of trouble detecting his presence.

He saluted roughly, and Kazama grinned and saluted in return. "Unusual for a person so apathetic toward others, wasn't it?"

"I take issue with the term *apathetic*, sir."

"Then were you overtaken by sympathy? The boy seems to have the same worries as you do."

"I've already graduated from that level of worry."

"So then it was out of remembering how you were before."

"...Would I be able to leave these people with you, sir?"

Kazama had been grinning more and more evilly—to Tatsuya, *his* was the more heartless attack—and without a means of escape anymore, he tried his best to deflect the conversation.

Kazama, though, knew just as well there wouldn't be any point in pursuing the topic any further. He stopped smiling and grew serious, then nodded at Tatsuya. "We'll take them. I'll inform base command myself."

"I'm sorry to cause you the inconvenience, sir."

"Nothing for you to worry about. You were forced to do extra work here, too."

"Yes, sir. What could their objective have been?"

"Who knows? Shaking down petty criminals isn't in our job description, but... These guys were more aggressive than they had a right to be. They were more skilled than we imagined, too. **Tatsuya.** You should be careful of stray attacks as well."

"Yes, sir. Thank you, sir."

"Let's sit down and have a nice talk. Tomorrow afternoon work for you?"

"That's fine. If you'll excuse me, sir..."

"Yeah, see you."

The two of them parted, but not before their superior-subordinate expressions turned into acquainted, brotherly ones.

[5]

It was the day after Tatsuya was hit with the surprise night shift.

The Nine School Competition kicked off as though nothing had happened.

Even counting just the direct spectators, there would be one hundred thousand total over the competition's ten days. Despite being in such an inconvenient place to get to with public transportation, an average of ten thousand people came to watch the events each day. Those viewing the broadcast were a hundred times that in number, if not more.

It may not have been as popular as some professional sports, but despite how many people had their eyes on the event, almost nobody besides those directly involved knew about the secret first act last night. The competitors all possessed top-class magic power, but they were still high school students. Nothing had come of the attempt, and it was decided it would be best not to give the students cause for anxiety.

The opening ceremonies were more about order and discipline than beauty and color. There was no need for pomp—the magic events themselves were sure to be very flashy and impressive. Also absent were the usual extended guest addresses. They moved straight into the events after they finished playing the nine schools' anthems in numerical order.

Today would be the start of a ten-day-long competition. Five days would be for the main event and five for the rookie competition, with boys and girls competing on the same days. The magic competition to host twenty events in total had finally begun.

On the first day was Speed Shooting, from the qualifiers all the way to the finals, and the qualifiers for Battle Board. The difference in schedules reflected the discrepancy between the time each event required.

"Tatsuya, the president's heat is about to begin."

"The star performer right off the bat, huh? Watanabe was in the third race, right?"

"Yes."

Tatsuya and the others had gone to the Speed Shooting stadium wanting to watch Mayumi's matches. Counting from the left, they were Shizuku, Honoka, Tatsuya, and Miyuki, not standing in the staff area in the stadium but in the general audience.

Speed Shooting involved just that: Clay pigeons would be fired into the air one hundred feet away, and the competitors would have to use magic to destroy them. Whoever destroyed more before time was up was the winner.

The event came in two varieties.

In the qualifiers, each competitor would try to get the highest score, meaning number of targets destroyed, in under five minutes. They would use all four shooting ranges simultaneously, with six heats on each of them—twenty-four people could enter in this event—and after the qualifiers, the top eight competitors would move into the quarterfinals. Twenty-four meant that if all nine schools entered three people each, there would be too many. Three of the schools, however, would only have two entrants, reflecting their weak performance from last year's competition. All the events save for Monolith Code went by the same rule.

From the quarterfinals on, the competitors would play against one another. Red and white targets, one hundred of each, would be used this time, and the competitors would try to destroy more of their color than the opponent destroyed of their own.

"Which means that in the qualifiers, you can use immense destructive power to wipe out all the targets at once, but when you get to the tournament, precise aim is the name of the game."

Shizuku nodded enthusiastically. She was the only one of their current group entered into the rookies' Speed Shooting event. "It means that normally, the magic you use changes between the qualifiers and the finals tournament, but..."

"President Saegusa is famous for using the same strategy in both the qualifiers and the tournament."

Tatsuya was about to say the same thing, but a girl sitting behind them interrupted.

"Erika?"

"Hi, Tatsuya!"

"Yo!"

"Morning."

"Good morning, Tatsuya, Miyuki, Honoka, Shizuku."

Lined up behind the group of four were Leo, Erika, Mizuki, and Mikihiko, from right to left. (Of course, they made their greetings in the order of Erika, Leo, Mikihiko, and Mizuki.) They'd been lucky enough to find four empty seats behind Tatsuya's group because they were already on some of the farthest rows up.

"Aren't there empty seats farther down?"

"Well, yeah, but then we saw all of you. And besides, you can't really tell what's going on in this event if you're too close, right?"

"I suppose."

The audience seats got higher up the farther away you were. The competitors would be shooting at targets flying very quickly through the air, so those sitting near the front rows would need the same level of visual perception the competitors had.

Despite that, the audience was jamming in as close as they could to the front...

"It's all the idiot men down there," said Erika in a disdainful, judging way, not quite seeming like she was joking.

"They don't all look like *guys* our age," responded Tatsuya wryly.

In any case, for those reasons, the front rows for this event were packed.

"You mean the girls shouting and calling her 'big sister'? Yeah, it's so sad."

"Don't be like that. It might be worth it to watch from so close up. I see her basically every day, but she looks like an entirely different person."

"Yikes! What are you gonna do, Miyuki? He's flirting with someone else!"

Erika's sarcastic remark met only dry smiles from Tatsuya and Miyuki as they both wondered what she was talking about.

"They call her the Elfin Sniper, right? The name fits her to a T," noted Honoka.

"I hear she hates being called that, so you probably shouldn't say it in front of her," warned Tatsuya, causing her to shrink down.

The boys and girls packed into the front rows were there to get a look at Mayumi, who was waiting in the first shooting range for the signal to begin.

Her long, voluminous, wavy hair sat under a headset designed to protect her ears, and her eyes were hidden behind transparent goggles. For her uniform, she wore trousers made of a stretchy fabric and a jacket that tightened at the waist and had a stand-up collar. One could mistake it for a minidress. Combined with the Speed Shooting–specific handgun-shaped device, giving her an image of a near-futuristic film heroine, you had a stunning mix of cute and elegant.

"I mean, there *are* people who make fan comics about our president, after all..." They were probably stimulated by her current outfit.

However, Mizuki's off-hand remark had been so unexpected that even Erika struggled to immediately respond. "...That's the first I've heard of that."

"…Mizuki, how exactly did you come to learn that? Don't tell me you're into *that* kind of thing. I might have to rethink our friendship." Miyuki seemed to have imagined the same thing as Erika. Her voice didn't sound like it was joking; she was maybe 10 percent serious.

"Huh?! No, I'm not interested in all that!" Of course, the one most disturbed by all this was Mizuki herself.

"It's starting." Regardless of what Mizuki was imagining as she got flustered, Tatsuya quieted her with two words.

The audience fell deathly silent.

The headsets the competitors wore meant they wouldn't be bothered by the audience making a little bit of noise, but the issue was more that it would be bad manners.

The first competitor hoisted her competition CAD, long and narrow and reminiscent of a single-shot rifle, looking sort of like a can from the right angle. Her focus and intensity created waves of tension among the silent onlookers.

The light came on, signaling her to begin. With a light gunshot, the first piece of clay soared into the air.

"It's fast…!" remarked Shizuku unconsciously, either at the speed at which the target was flying…

…or at the speed with which Mayumi's magic destroyed it.

Her device wasn't a real gun; no bullets would come out. There was no need to aim it at the target—it didn't have any sights or a scope on it in the first place.

However, she stood and held it more like one would a bow and arrow than a gun.

The clay pigeons were fired up for her one after another at irregular intervals. There would be one hundred of them shot in the span of five minutes. On average, that was one shot every three seconds. An abnormally high pace even for real target shooting. Occasionally, though, they would come out quickly and occasionally there would be ten seconds in between—and sometimes, five or six would be launched into the sky at once.

Mayumi shot down all the targets **individually**, without letting a single one go.

Her five-minute time trial was over in the blink of an eye.

"...A perfect score..." muttered Tatsuya in amazement as he watched Mayumi take off her goggles and headset and give a smile to the applauding onlookers.

"Subsonic dry ice bullets, right?" asked Miyuki as she clapped.

Tatsuya nodded with a smile. "That's right. Very good."

"...Come on, even I could tell that much..."

Erika's dissatisfied remark made Tatsuya grin drily. "I suppose you'd realize what it was if you saw it used one hundred times."

A few of their group looked down awkwardly (they probably hadn't figured it out), but Tatsuya pretended not to notice.

Honoka, on the other hand, with her honest personality, was clearly surprised. "One hundred? She didn't miss a single shot?!"

"Yeah. What's really amazing isn't how fast she repeated the magic process, but her precision. You could use all the perception-based magic you wanted, but your mind is what has to process all the information you're giving to it. Either she's had a lot of practice with Multisight, or she's a natural... She is a direct descendant of the Ten Master Clans, after all."

"Wait, the president was even using perception magic at the same time?" Mizuki was the one surprised, but this time, most of the others seemed to be as confused as she was.

"It was a long-range perception spell called Multiscope. Rather than allow you to see massless objects and information bodies, it lets you perceive physical objects from multiple angles, sort of like a visual radar giving you input from multiple sources. She makes pretty frequent use of it normally, you know?"

You didn't notice it? he asked with his eyes.

Mizuki shook her head firmly. "During school assemblies and such, she keeps watch over every nook and cranny using the spell. It's a rare skill, but... Marksmanship like that would be impossible with the naked eye, don't you think?"

"It would be," responded Shizuku immediately. She was probably watching Mayumi's time trial while thinking about when she would be getting into the shooting range herself.

"But she decelerated the movement of the air particles to make dry ice, and accelerated them to subsonic speeds, *and* used perception magic at the same time! Her perception spell was long lasting, and she had to repeat the deceleration and acceleration magic a hundred times. She's got some crazy magic power." Leo wasn't talking about the magic power used as a basis to measure one's practical skill; he was using the colloquial definition of it, referring to the stamina she needed to keep casting those spells.

It was often misunderstood; magic wasn't an activity that expended energy. Magic didn't alter events by consuming physical energy; instead it affected event change by altering information. In order to alter information, you needed to inject a magic sequence made of psions. This meant there was a limit to the number of times you could use a magic sequence with a certain scope. When Leo used the term *magic power*, though, he was referring to something closer to her ability to maintain concentration.

"Her shooting magic is a variation of Dry Blizzard, which has very good efficiency. With the president's skill at magic, she could do it a thousand times, not just a hundred."

Tatsuya's open praise of Mayumi made the other Course 1 students wear complicated expressions. The girls thought Mayumi's magic power was amazing, too, but Tatsuya was normally scathing in his assessment of magic. For him to give unconditional praise like that—they couldn't help but feel jealous.

Leo's admiration, however, lay elsewhere. "What? But even creating dry ice in this summer humidity and accelerating it to subsonic speeds takes a huge amount of energy, doesn't it? Magic is outside the law of conservation of energy, but if someone told me the burden of that kind of event changing is *small*, I wouldn't believe them right away—even if it was you!"

As they stood up to go to the Battle Board stadium, Tatsuya gave a mysterious answer. "It may be outside that law, but it's not unrelated to it.

"Magic isn't limited by conservation of energy—it's a technique to change events. But that doesn't mean the objects being targeted for those changes are also freed from that law. For example, if you accelerate an object without putting together a spell to sustain its current state, the accelerated object freezes. If you heat up a moving object without putting together a spell to sustain its movement, the object will begin to decelerate. Magic sequences **that are used by the general public** always have a state-sustaining routine to prevent undesired changes from happening, so you don't get much chance to experience it.

"Physical laws are pretty strict. Even if an **unreasonable** power like magic interferes with them, there's a recovery force that will try to make things work again. In other words, magic that takes care not to break the law of conservation of energy—a physical law—is a **natural phenomenon**, and from the magic point of view, you'll have a spell that can execute with minimal interference.

"You understand now, right? Her spell creates dry ice and accelerates it. The spell takes the kinetic energy the particles lose during the process of creating the dry ice and transforms it into solid kinetic energy, thereby deceiving natural laws. It reverses entropy, which is never something you would see in nature, but by accelerating the dry ice, it makes more thermodynamic sense than just creating it."

"...Makes me feel like we're being tricked by an opportunist."

"Remember this, Leo: The art of magic is about opportunistically tricking the world."

"So we magicians are like swindlers trying to swindle the world, huh?"

"And the stronger the magician, the more wicked the swindler."

It started off as a fairly serious conversation, but Tatsuya found himself only able to smile at Erika and Shizuku's disruptions.

◇ ◇ ◇

Battle Board was a competitive event in which you rode a spindle-shaped board six feet long and two feet wide down an artificial waterway. There was no propulsion on the boards, so the competitors used magic to reach the goal. It was against the rules to attack another player's body or their board, but any magic used on the water's surface was fine.

There was no standard to unify such waterways. The course had originally been created with naval magic training in mind, meaning magic usage was the big premise. It was nowhere near popular enough to warrant a standard.

The Battle Board event in the Nine School Competition had a course two miles long that the athletes circled three times. It contained straightaways, sharp turns, and differences in elevation at some points, like hills and steep drops.

There was one course each constructed for boys and girls, but there was no difference in difficulty.

The qualifiers would be six races, each with four people. The semifinals would be two races with three people each, the third place would be between four people, and the finals would be one-on-one.

On average, a race lasted fifteen minutes.

The maximum speed was over thirty knots—about thirty-five miles per hour. The competitors rode on just a single board, so there was nothing blocking the wind. Unlike sailing sports, where one built up speed from tailwinds, the competitors would have the wind in their face constantly. Just standing against the wind force would drain a good amount of stamina.

"It's a difficult event for girls. Honoka, have you been keeping in good shape?"

"I have! I took your advice and made sure to keep doing my endurance training, and I've been making sure to get extra sleep ever since being chosen as an athlete."

Unrelated to the Nine School Competition, not long after they met, he had had misgivings about her not having enough endurance, so he gave her advice to pursue aggressive physical training in addition to magic training. It was more of an off-handed remark in an everyday conversation, but surprisingly, she seemed to have taken it seriously.

"Honoka has a lot of muscle, too, you know."

"Stop, stop it, Miyuki! I'm not trying to be some macho woman."

Tatsuya couldn't help but laugh at the conversation with him in the middle of it.

"See... You made Tatsuya laugh at me!"

"He only laughed because you said it in a funny way."

"Not you, too, Shizuku! I guess I'm being left out again. Unlike the two of you, Tatsuya can't come to see my matches."

Honoka had suddenly started cowering; Tatsuya, at a quandary, stopped smiling. Why had she made it about him right then? "...I'm doing your adjustments for Mirage Bat, too, though."

For now, he argued the only part he could imagine this being about. However...

"But you're not doing them for Battle Board. Miyuki and Shizuku get to have you in charge for both of their events!"

...it wasn't very effective.

"...Still, I did practice with you, and helped you come up with a strategy, so I don't think I'm leaving you out at all..."

As he continued to make excuses, he grew increasingly aware that he was digging himself into a bigger hole, and finally he trailed off and stopped talking. Seeing his predicament and feeling sorry for him...

"Tatsuya, that isn't what Honoka is trying to say."

...starting with Mizuki's suggestion, given in a slight tone of voice...

"Tatsuya... I think that's a little too thickheaded, even for you."

…Miyuki…

"Ooh, it's Tatsuya's secret weakness!"

…Erika…

"He's a blockhead?"

…and Shizuku criticized him one after another.

With focus fire from the girls, Tatsuya was forced against his will to stay silent. He felt like it was kind of unfair, but obviously logic wouldn't be a good argument in this case.

He received no support from the boys, either.

Tatsuya ended up having to maintain his silence until the race's starting signal.

◇ ◇ ◇

When they finished getting the course set up and called out the competitors, Tatsuya was finally released. He'd figured out what Miyuki and the others were trying to tell him a while ago. However, understanding what they meant and being able to *deal* with that were two completely different problems. He secretly decided to be more cautious from now on, lest he say anything else that was unnecessary, as he looked over to the four people bobbing up and down at the starting line.

It was an aquatic course, so there were no lines drawn on it—there was no way to. The waterway felt a little cramped for the four people in a row, and Mari had taken up her position in the middle.

The other athletes were on one or both knees to get ready, but she was standing straight up. For the most part, it reflected the difference in their senses of balance, but depending on the viewpoint, she was kind of standing there like she was an **empress** or a **queen** being waited on by the other competitors.

"Wow, high and mighty as usual…" muttered Erika.

And you're openly hostile as usual, thought Tatsuya. He didn't say it, though—he'd just resolved not to do that a moment ago. Leo and Mizuki, sitting on either side of Erika, seemed to have ignored it, too.

The giant display hung up on a blimp in the sky gave close-ups on each of the four competitors. Mari alone had a confident smile on her face. *She definitely seems like the one to play the villain*, thought Tatsuya.

The majority of high school girls seemed to have a different opinion, though. The moment the announcer doing the introductions called Mari's name, a shrill applause shook the audience—mostly the rows in front.

Mari waved her hand in reply, causing the shrieks to grow in volume.

"...It looks like our seniors have oddly passionate fan followings."

They were several levels more wildly enthusiastic than the boys who were fans of Mayumi.

"I can understand that. Watanabe is very cool," remarked Miyuki as a complete bystander.

If she'd known that her own performance during the Nine School Competition would gain her even more zealous fans than Mayumi's male fans and Mari's female fans, she might have sympathized with the fact that Mari was using her smile to *hide* as she stared down her overenthusiastic fans. Right now, though, she acted like a complete third party.

Though Battle Board was a summertime aquatic sport, the competitors weren't wearing swimsuits. Instead, they wore wetsuits that clung tightly to their bodies, with each school's logo plastered on it, colorful and huge. Mari, with her bandana and straight, short, bob hairdo, looked like the spitting image of a knight in shining armor from little kids' picture books. Erika would have heard Miyuki, too, but she didn't object to the point.

"On your marks!" the voice came over the speakers.

Then there was the sound of a blank being fired, and they were off to the races.

"Was that a suicide bombing tactic?" murmured Erika, astonished.

Tatsuya was too astonished to actually say anything.

Right at the beginning, Fourth High's competitor had abruptly made an explosion in the water behind her. She was probably *trying* to use the big wave to propel her forward, like in surfing, and to throw the other competitors off at the same time, but...

"Oh, she's back up!"

After having made the stormy waves strong enough to throw herself off balance, what was she to do? Mari had decided to charge ahead at full speed at the start of the race, so she escaped the chaos created by Fourth High's athlete and quickly took a big lead over the others.

Her board skated along the surface of the water.

She wasn't moving the board with movement magic; she was probably moving herself and the board as a single unit. Or else she was applying the movement magic to two targets: her own physical body and the board she was on. Whichever the case, it wouldn't have been possible without clearly defining the spells' targets.

Her board gripped the water as she took a ninety-degree turn beautifully. She seemed stable, like the soles of her feet were glued to her board.

"Applying both hardening magic and multicasting movement magic..." That wasn't his analysis of magic sequences talking. Tatsuya could tell what she was doing by the way she moved over the water and how she balanced herself on the board.

"Hardening magic?" Leo asked, his sharp ears picking up the term. It was his field of expertise, so he had to be interested in it. "What's she hardening?"

"She's fixing the relative positions of her body and the board so she doesn't fall off."

Tatsuya's words didn't seem to make sense to him, and Leo gave him a confused look. Of course, Tatsuya wasn't trying to tell him he was supposed to understand from just that.

"Hardening magic isn't for increasing the hardness of objects—it's for stabilizing the relative positions of several parts in a system. You understand that, right?"

"Well, yeah, since I use it a lot."

"Watanabe is considering her body and the board to be two parts comprising a single object, and executing magic to stabilize their relative positions. And then, with herself and the board as one 'thing,' she's using movement magic. Not permanently, either. She's defining how long to sustain both the hardening and movement magic based on changes in the course, and she's arranging it well enough so that the new spells don't clash with the old ones."

Leo understood well how high-level her technique was due to his specialization in the field. "Huh..." he murmured in honest admiration.

On the other hand...

"But that's an interesting way of using it... Yes, with hardening magic, you don't have to target single structures, do you? With this, you could..." As was the habit of the genius engineer, Tatsuya began to engross himself in mad thoughts.

"Tatsuya?" Miyuki's voice pulled him out of it.

During the few moments he'd taken her eyes off her, Mari had gone behind the grandstands and out of view.

"It's nothing," answered Tatsuya evasively, looking up to the giant display. It showed Mari climbing up the ascent in the waterway, against the flow of the water.

"Acceleration magic." Judging by how she moved, she was using a spell to reverse the acceleration vector from the outside source, the water.

"And vibration magic at the same time..." Simultaneously, she used magic to create waves in the other direction, weakening the resistance the water was offering.

Words of praise naturally found their way out of Tatsuya's mouth. "That's amazing. She's multicasting three to four different types of magic at once."

It wasn't that each individual spell was all that powerful. Instead, she was combining them for fantastic effect.

Mayumi had overwhelmed the audience with her high-speed, high-precision magic bordering on the realm of pure artistry, while Mari was charming the crowds with a veritable rainbow of all sorts of different spells, always changing and adapting to what she needed in any given moment.

Neither of them was anywhere near high school level.

She reached the peak of the ascent, then jumped down the rapids. The surface of the water undulated wildly with her landing. Her magic created a big wave that pushed her own board forward, but nearly made the girl in second place do a nosedive as she came off the jump.

"She's quite a tactician…"

"No, she's just evil."

Erika insulted her upon hearing Tatsuya. Half of him agreed, so he didn't bother to argue the point. Anyway, calling a tactician "evil" was actually praise.

Mari's victory was all but assured before half a lap was even finished.

◇ ◇ ◇

The only Battle Board going on today would be the qualifiers. The fourth, fifth, and sixth qualifier races were after lunch, so instead, he decided to watch the semifinals and finals of Speed Shooting that afternoon. First, though, he split up with the others for a bit.

He was headed back to the hotel and for the high-ranking officers' room—he had a promise to keep with Kazama.

Kazama was ranked major, but because of his military service and peculiarity of the team he led, he was treated as higher than his station. Originally, this big guest room would have been used by colonels and above. As he walked in, though, Kazama was taking a room service– and tea set–enhanced break with the other executives in his battalion.

"Oh, you're here. Go on, have a seat," prompted Kazama in a frank tone to Tatsuya, who had been led here by a soldier on security detail (not one of the soldiers from this base, but Kazama's subordinate). Tatsuya visibly hesitated to place himself among the executive ranks, though.

The specialist rank Tatsuya was given referred to him being an informal soldier with the rights afforded to a real soldier by international law (there was no "special duty" officer system in the country's military at this time). He was protected as a combatant without being completely tied down to the military rank system, and would only follow the chain of command in times the entire Independent Magic Battalion was engaged in operations. Still, even without the systematic enforcement, they were his superior officers—in addition to his seniors in age. When told to sit down, he couldn't exactly say, "Okay, sure," and sit just like that.

"Tatsuya, we didn't call you here today as Specialist Tactical Magician Ryuuya Ooguro but as our friend Tatsuya Shiba. Being too reserved about it is going to put us in a bind."

"And it's too hard to talk with you standing. Could you sit down?"

Then, two of the officers at the same table again prompted him to take a seat.

"Captain Sanada, Captain Yanagi... All right, then. Please excuse me."

Their friendship transcended age. Tatsuya gave a bow and, without braving further foolishness by refusing again, took a seat across from Kazama.

The tabletop was circular. The Independent Magic Battalion believed that the purpose of round tables was to have tea on them—it was practically their motto. The table itself wasn't originally part of this room; Kazama had carried it in himself.

Tatsuya's seat was closest to the door, but the adults welcomed him into their company as a friend. "It has certainly been a long time, hasn't it? These teacups aren't too good-looking, but let's have a toast."

"Thank you very much, Second Lieutenant Fujibayashi."

The female officer working as an aide for Kazama (though her job was more like a secretary) offered him a cup, and Tatsuya accepted it on its saucer with a nod. She wasn't in military uniform today, but in a suit, so it made her "young female secretary at a big enterprise" impression abundantly more clear. The others weren't in military uniform, either; all were wearing civilian clothes, like suits and dress shirts.

"I just saw you yesterday, but I'll let Fujibayashi have her time to shine."

"Oh, you need not force yourself for my sake, Dr. Yamanaka."

"No, I wouldn't interrupt a toast to your reunion. I'm not a barbarian."

"...You just want an excuse to have your cup topped off with brandy, don't you?"

"Every auspicious occasion warrants fine drink, I say."

"Lord... For a physician, sometimes it feels like you really don't take care of yourself!"

Medical Major Yamanaka had been the doctor and first-class healing magician to answer with composure and a bit of feigned innocence to the misgivings Captain Yanagi had suggested.

All five of the others, including Kazama, shook their heads regretfully—*these* were the executives of the Independent Magic Battalion receiving Tatsuya.

"It has been a while, Captain Yanagi, Second Lieutenant Fujibayashi. Captain Sanada, thank you for yesterday." Tatsuya greeted the two he hadn't seen in some time first, then thanked Captain Sanada, with whom he had worked last month at the base.

"I'm the one who should be thanking you. With the Third Eye long-distance super-precise targeting system, I would have been up a river without you there."

"The CAD was originally made for me, after all... Dr. Yamanaka, now that I think of it, I still haven't gotten the examination results from yesterday."

"...I feel like you're treating me a little differently than everyone else, Tatsuya."

"Doctor... I'm not sure a physician who would demand someone be a human experiment to their face would engender much goodwill."

The witty retort to Yamanaka's complaint came from the lady Fujibayashi. Yamanaka theatrically turned his face away, uncooperative, causing the round table to burst into laughter.

It *had* been quite some time since he'd last seen them, but it hadn't been years or anything. Yanagi was the one he hadn't seen for the longest time at a little over half a year; Sanada and Yamanaka he'd just seen less than a month ago on his last job.

They naturally began to talk about the current situation, and the conversation moved to the Nine School Competition and the secret machinations of the criminal organization with respect to it.

The intruders last night turned out to belong to No-Head Dragon, which Tatsuya had learned on the first report he'd gotten over the phone. They hadn't yet elucidated what their goal was, however, despite questioning the men. The five here, especially Yamanaka, would easily be able to get them to spill it if they were in charge, but those *actually* in charge didn't seem to be willing to get aggressively involved at this stage.

"Still, you did some good work last night. Were you on guard already?"

"You think too much of me, Lieutenant. I was out for a walk and happened to notice them there."

"So late at night?"

"I was coming back from doing adjustments on the CADs for the competition."

Given their closeness of age, the group member that talked to Tatsuya the most naturally ended up being Second Lieutenant Fujibayashi. She'd been thoroughly trained by military service, and had vivid eyes and toxic proportions. Her looks and clothing were modest, though, and her personality equally unadorned, meaning Tatsuya found it easy to converse with her as well.

"Oh, so you *are* working on the technical staff. Do your teammates know about Silver?"

"No—for now, at least, that's a secret," answered Tatsuya to Yamanaka's question, shaking his head.

"You being the CAD engineer for a high school competition seems almost unfair. You're in two completely different leagues, aren't you?"

"Captain Sanada, Tatsuya is still a bona fide high school student, though, you know."

Sanada grinned and offered doubts that were, in a way, reasonable, and Fujibayashi, also smiling, chided him and looked back at Tatsuya.

"You won't be taking the stage yourself? You'd be fairly competitive with your Flash Cast skill, I would think. And if you needed to, you have Material Burst and Mist Dispersion."

"No—they're highly classified in the first place, and against the regulations for how deadly they are. And I can't use Material Burst without Third Eye anyway."

"But you brought Trident with you, right?"

"Yes, but that's against the rules as well because its specs are too high. Plus, Flash Cast is supposed to be a secret Yotsuba technology in the first place." Tatsuya grinned drily, denying Fujibayashi's words.

After that, Yanagi continued with a sigh. "Fujibayashi... I wonder about you sometimes. How did you manage to connect a high school competition with Material Burst? It's a tactical spell. Based on the ultimate magic, Dismantle."

"I don't think he'll have a chance to use Material Burst in the Nine School Competition, either. But in last year's competition, the heir to the Juumonji used Phalanx, and the daughter of the Saegusa used Magic Bullet Shooter, so I don't think it would be too strange for him to use Mist Dispersion."

"Fujibayashi, the Juumonji's Phalanx is classified as a defensive spell, so it's outside the lethality ranking system. The Saegusa's Magic Bullet Shooter's sales point is its flexible power setting, so its lethality is determined after the fact. Mist Dispersion, on the other hand, dismantles objects at a molecular level, so it's rank A on the lethality scale. You can't put them in the same group."

"Captain Sanada, I see you don't know that the lethality regulation at the Nine School Competition is only for events where you can affect other people. It doesn't apply to Speed Shooting and Ice Pillars Break. The pamphlet emphasized its safety quite a bit, but didn't touch on that point."

The Nine School Competition had first been held in its current form with its current rules ten years ago. The only one of their group who had actually battled in it was Fujibayashi, a championship holder from Second High.

Just before they descended into an open battle using their extensive knowledge of their individual fields of expertise, Kazama put a stop to it. "Whatever the case, he can't use magic that the military has mandated highly classified in front of such a large number of people at a competition. There's no point in arguing, is there?"

His tone was sour and slightly annoyed as he forced his way into his subordinates' argument. And then, changing completely, he spoke to Tatsuya in a voice like steel, his face the definition of expressionless. "Anyway, Tatsuya, if you *do* end up participating as a competitor at some point..."

"I understand, Major. If I'm driven to the point where I need to use Mist Dispersion, I'll give up and resign to my defeat."

One could tell the difference between a bamboo sword and a real blade even if it was sheathed. At the very least, Tatsuya hadn't misread the true meaning behind Kazama's words—that there was a merciless sword hidden deep in his calm and composed demeanor.

Kazama and Tatsuya were fellow apprentices, and there was enough between them to call them friends. But to Kazama, bonds between his fellow students and friendship didn't take precedence. If push came to shove, he would readily cast Tatsuya away. And Tatsuya thought the same about him.

"...Still, it's hard to imagine a situation in which I'd need to compete."

"Always be ready. As long as you understand."

As they smiled slightly scornfully at each other, Kazama and Tatsuya traded disillusioned glances and brought the conversation to a finish.

No one ever knew what the future held, but both of them knew that, logically speaking, Tatsuya's remark had been correct.

But deep down, neither Kazama *nor* Tatsuya had enough confidence in his own speculation.

◇ ◇ ◇

"Tatsuya, over here!"

He had returned to where the girls' Speed Shooting championship tournament would be held. The stands were already full by the time he got back from having tea with Kazama and the others. Upon looking around for the one he'd arranged to meet, Erika found him first and shouted to him.

"There are a lot of people here already for the semifinals." He pushed his way through the waves of people and sat down in the seat next to Erika.

"That's because the president is competing. The other match wasn't this crowded."

Tatsuya's words had been a nonchalant impression closer to him talking to himself, but Miyuki, who was opposite him and saving his seat, answered him faithfully.

This time, Miyuki was on the other side of Leo, while Mizuki sat behind Erika, Honoka behind Tatsuya, and Shizuku behind Miyuki.

"Honoka, can you still see?"

Tatsuya had been growing taller at an average pace since his matriculation, and he was close to six feet now. Her seat was higher up, but he still had to worry about whether or not she could see over him.

But when he turned around to ask, Honoka shook her head with a smile.

"Oh... Where's Mikihiko, by the way?"

"He said he wasn't feeling well. He went to lay down in his room." After answering Tatsuya's question, Erika used her expression to add, *What a bum.*

"It seemed like the heat was getting to him. I might have had some trouble myself if I wasn't wearing my glasses." Mizuki covered for Mikihiko.

I suppose having such sharp senses isn't always advantageous, thought Tatsuya. He was quite interested in their states of mind, too, but he decided not to think about that right now.

As soon as Mayumi appeared in the shooting range, a storm of applause went through the stands. The screens positioned here and there in the stands all displayed QUIET, PLEASE on them, and the cheering receded like a wave into the ocean. The voices disappeared, but in their place came an air that seemed even more enthusiastic.

Tatsuya started to feel a little bad for the other competitor. No matter what kind of event it was, the audience being behind the other team always came with its own pressure, but...

She was being considerate toward the girl. Mayumi released the trigger lock on her rifle CAD with a smoothness suggesting her crowd support didn't even exist, and she got ready, waiting for the sign to begin.

The beginning of the match would be displayed by a signal. The game: red and white targets, one hundred of each, would be launched in sequence into the air, and the players would compete to see how many of their own color they could destroy. For all intents and purposes, it wouldn't start until the firing machine began firing the targets. Still, there were five lights lined up horizontally from the competitors' perspective—they were the horn to announce the start.

The first light went on. Each one illuminated in turn, and when the final light activated, the bisque disks began flying into the air.

The white disks in the air danced madly.

Mayumi was to shoot down the clay pigeons painted red.

And said clay pigeons were being shot down at nearly the exact moment they jumped into the active area.

"Wow..."

Tatsuya nodded to himself at the voice of wonder he heard from behind him.

It was amazing.

It wasn't a very clever way to go about it, tactically speaking; if you shot all your own targets down first, the opponent wouldn't have to worry about accidentally shooting yours. She'd be able to attack indiscriminately. It was clever logic—but there was such overwhelming skill that it just didn't matter.

"Huh?" Honoka said in surprise, probably not meaning to. And though Shizuku didn't make a sound, he could tell she was just as surprised.

"Magic Bullet Shooter... It's faster than last year."

Tatsuya answered Miyuki's words only by nodding, not peeling his eyes from the clay swirling through the air.

Bullets of dry ice, shooting into the red clay pigeon that was flying behind the white clay pigeon **from underneath**. They weren't guided bullets. Magic like that would be too inefficient, and she wasn't prone to such whimsy. This long-range magic created the bullets of dry ice at a point where the white clay pigeon wouldn't get in the way, then sniped the red clay pigeon from there.

She wasn't creating magic bullets, but emplacements to fire them—their *shooters*, hence its name, Magic Bullet Shooter.

The magic acting on distant objects itself was extremely ordinary. Competitors like Mayumi, who used the tactic of creating bullets with magic to shoot the targets in Speed Shooting, were actually in the minority. Instead, the mainstream tactic was to apply vibration magic directly to the clay, or to apply movement magic to the clay pigeons and have them ram into other targets to destroy them both. Magic wasn't influenced by physical obstacles, so nobody really needed to use specialized skills to destroy blind targets like this.

So, then, what objectives and merits did this long-range-bullet creation and firing spell called Magic Bullet Shooter have? The key lay in the fact that it could attack from a blind spot outside the range of another person's magic.

For example, think of what would happen if both competitors used vibration magic to shoot the targets. When the red and white targets of the magic approached each other, the spells would interfere and give way to unexpectedly odd things—like the spells not going off, or making ultrasonic shock waves.

In order to manipulate objects at a distance with magic while contending with another magician, one needed to tightly restrict their target coordinates and have enough concentration to manifest stronger influence upon them.

The nature of Speed Shooting was that of an event requiring a concentration of magic power along with swift casting speed, but by sniping the targets from outside the region affected by her opponent's magic, Mayumi created a situation where she was doing the same thing as if she'd been alone.

And, of course, that went for the opponent as well. With such tactics, the match came down to pure speed and accuracy.

And when it came to speed and accuracy, Mayumi's magic power was at a very high standard even when compared to the entire world of magic.

There was no way someone on a high school student's level could compete with her.

◇ ◇ ◇

On the first day of the competition, Speed Shooting, as nearly everyone had predicted, ended with an overwhelming victory for Mayumi on the girls' side and a victory for the First High boys as well.

"Congratulations, President!"

Mayumi answered Azusa's congratulations with a smile and a nod.

"Thanks. Mari, it looks like you got to the semifinals, too." She looked to the side.

"Yep, all as planned so far." Mari, to whom she was looking, responded with a nod.

Night had already fallen, dinnertime and bathing time was over, and now all that was left was to sleep and restore their energy. The female student council members (plus the disciplinary committee chairwoman) had gathered in Mayumi's room.

Only the first day had ended, and Mayumi would be participating tomorrow, too. They wanted to leave the real celebration until after they won the whole thing, so they were just having some juice to celebrate now.

It was girls-only because of the time of day, but it wasn't a pajama party or anything, so boys being there wouldn't have been any issue. And yet, for some reason, it *was* only girls.

"It was a bit of a scare, but Hattori pulled through, too, right?" Mari said with a sigh; the boys' results hadn't been quite as attractive as they'd thought. Despite how well Speed Shooting went with both victories, the Battle Board qualifiers had been unexpectedly difficult.

"He said his CAD wasn't adjusted properly. He's been with Kinoshita ever since the match ended, redoing it," explained Azusa.

"They're not done yet," confirmed Suzune, looking at the work reports for both staff teams on a terminal.

"Kinoshita certainly isn't unskilled, but..."

"Still, he isn't exactly an expert."

Mayumi was the one to show tentative support for Kinoshita, but Mari's blunt analysis met with no argument from her; she gave a pained grin. Azusa, though, seemed to think the grade they'd given was a little too harsh.

"Umm, I don't think it's completely Kinoshita's fault. Ever since we got here, Hattori has kind of seemed a little insecure."

But even that, Mari cut down completely. "It may sound harsh, but an engineer's skill includes being able to adjust for all that."

"Well... You're right, but..."

Mari was correct. That *was* part of the engineer's job. However, wasn't the competitor partly at fault for not managing his own condition? That's what Azusa was thinking, but she couldn't say it out loud.

"Come on, Mari. Don't bully Ah-chan."

Mari and Azusa both had logic behind their words; the former from the competitor's point of view, and the latter from the engineer's. Each had its strengths and weaknesses, and both evenly applied on an emotional level. Times like this called for the leader's judgment.

"Thankfully, Hanzou is off tomorrow, so we'll just have to let him adjust it until he's satisfied... But then we'll need to put someone in for Kinoshita tomorrow."

"Kinoshita is the assistant for the girls' Cloudball. He's a sub, so I don't think it'll be a big deal if we take him out."

"You're right... We have Izumin, so it should be fine..."

"Wouldn't it also be risky to leave it to Izumi by herself? There are six Cloudball courts. There will be two matches going on at once, and if all three people win, the second round will have all three matches at the same time. You may be able to do your own adjustments, Mayumi, but someone else will need to do them for the other two at the same time. Even if there's a long interval between each round, it's easy to imagine her not having enough time. That's why we have subs, right?"

Suzune supported Mayumi's decision, but Mari displayed disapproval. That, too, was an objection based on how well she understood how important the adjustments actually were; she wasn't trying to play devil's advocate. They had to manage with a limited number of people, and that was a difficult problem in the first place.

"Why not have Ishida double as a sub for the boys?"

The girls' matches would be in the morning, and the boys' in the afternoon. Suzune's suggestion was possible in terms of scheduling, but Mayumi's reaction was negative.

"That would overwork him to be on both the morning and afternoon matches. Cloudball has the most of them in a single day, after all."

"Then why don't we put in Shiba? He's off both tomorrow and the day after."

At Suzune's substitution suggestion, Mayumi thought for a moment, then nodded. "...That would be the best option. Miyuki, can I get you to tell Tatsuya for us?"

"I will." Miyuki smiled and nodded at Mayumi's request.

She was more than happy that her brother was getting a bigger chance to shine.

◇ ◇ ◇

"...So that's why you came by so late." Siblings though they may have been, this wasn't generally the time of night young girls should be visiting rooms belonging to males. Tatsuya gestured for Miyuki to sit on the bed and sighed.

"...Am I bothering you?" Miyuki asked, her eyes wavering with unease.

"No, I'm glad you came to tell me, it's just..." There was no precedent of Tatsuya being firm after Miyuki looked at him like that. "We may be inside a hotel, but girls shouldn't be up and walking outside their room this late at night, you know? There are some unsettling things going on; someone suspicious might have gotten into the hallways."

Still, this *was* a military base. The security was stricter than even the best civilian hotels. Miyuki thought he might have been thinking a little too much about it, but she was happy he was worried about her.

"Yes, I apologize, Tatsuya."

"Don't apologize with such a smile on your face…" he complained, but his face was smiling as well. None of this turned out to be a reprimand or scolding. He was too soft on her in the first place to rebuke her very harshly. "In any case, thanks for telling me. I'll walk you back to your room."

When Tatsuya got up off his chair, Miyuki hastily stood as well and waved her arms frantically. "No, I'll be fine by myself. You were in the middle of work, weren't you? I've already intruded on your work time, so I can't make you go through any more for me…"

"I was, but this is basically for fun anyway, so you don't need to worry." Tatsuya closed up the notebook terminal to get it out of his sister's sight.

"But that was CAD programming, wasn't it?"

Miyuki wasn't well versed in hardware, but she had a degree of skill on the software end thanks to Tatsuya's influence. She'd only gotten a cursory glance and didn't understand what it was, but from the type of editor he had open and the coding format, she could tell that it was a program for an activation program.

"It doesn't have anything to do with the competition, so it doesn't matter one bit if I take a break. The program itself is pretty much a toy."

"A toy?"

"I thought up a little idea for a new close-range weapon, but it's almost completely impractical. It would probably only work for the surprise factor. Even if I finished it, it couldn't be made into a product."

"But it *is* a new spell—does that not mean something? I don't think anything you made would ever be meaningless."

"Well, I guess it's worth a few jokes, at least. Anyway, that's how it is—I wasn't rushing to do it or anything. Right now, you take **precedence** over it."

"Oh, you… Saying I'm more **precious** to you…"

Hmm? His sister put her hands to her cheeks and looked down. Tatsuya felt something was definitely out of place. It seemed like she'd altered what he'd said and took it in a strange direction. *Well, it techni-cally means the same thing, but the nuance there is what matters...*

He'd need more than a few moments to suppress his wonder-ment, but he was the first to come back to reality. "...Shall we go?"

"Yes, Tatsuya. Umm... I want you to know that I feel the same way."

"I'm sorry...?"

"You're more precious than anything to me."

"......"

Unfortunately, his sister hadn't yet returned to reality with him—at least, that's what he wanted to think at the time.

[6]

It was the second day of the Nine School Competition.

Tatsuya was in First High's tent, which was set up in the event area, wearing the blouson of his technical staff uniform. He hadn't worn the uniform since the inauguration ceremony; the only people at the opening ceremonies were the competitors.

He just couldn't seem to shake the feeling of resistance he got when he had to wear this kind of clothing—whether it was the blazer during the party or this blouson. But it was required as part of the uniform, so he knew he'd just have to get used to it.

"What's wrong? Are you mad about something?"

"No, not in particular. Why do you think that?"

He replied to Mayumi's question in a calm voice, but he couldn't quell the agitation inside him. He thought he'd kept a straight face, but apparently it was pretty easy to see.

"Hmm… A hunch?"

"Well, you can use such vague phrasing as a question, but…"

Tatsuya felt drained of strength, and not in the physical way. It seemed like he *hadn't* shown anything on his face, nor had she gotten a particularly prickly impression of him. Of course, it was even scarier—or perhaps more threatening—that she had seen into his mind like that without any reason to.

"Anyway, did you have something you needed from me?"

He put it aside for the moment—there was no point in worrying, nor was there any countermeasure if he did—and asked Mayumi, who had come to him before her match.

"No, I just came to check up on you, but... Did you memorize all the data already?"

Tatsuya had been put on girls' Cloudball duty without much warning last night, and in order to do the actual adjustments for their CADs, he had, in a big hurry, been trying to memorize the data on each competitor's psionic characteristics.

"Yes, I suppose."

"For everyone?"

"Yes, I suppose."

Tatsuya gave the same short answer a second time, and Mayumi stared at him wide-eyed. "This may sound like it's a little bit late, but... You really are amazing, Tatsuya. Isn't that like instant memory or perfect recall or something?"

"I would have preferred to get some normal magic power instead of this."

"As someone currently preparing for university exams, I find it hard to forgive such a luxurious complaint."

She'd be able to get into university on recommendation alone without even taking entrance exams, but she said so anyway—and put her hands on her hips and puffed out her cheeks, too.

"......"

"Hm? What's the matter?"

Tatsuya had put the index and middle finger of one hand to his temple and started massaging it. Mayumi looked at him askance.

"President, could it be that... You know what, never mind."

"?"

He had been about to say, "Could you be serious? I thought you were pretending," but he swallowed those words—and in any case, it was a wise decision. "...Isn't your match about to start?"

"It is. Okay, let's get out there."

"What?"

"I said, let's get out there!"

"...Yes, all right."

They weren't allowed to adjust CADs during a match, but there were some cases where readjustments had to be made right after the match ended. It was only natural he'd need to wait by the court with her instead of in the stands—well, actually, he didn't need to go with her all the way to the court, but Tatsuya caught up with Mayumi, turning back around as she walked.

"Is Miyuki in the grandstands?"

Once he got there, that was the first thing she said. "She went to watch Ice Pillars Break." The first thing Tatsuya thought about Mayumi's question was *not Why would she ask that* but *This again?*

"Oh... So you really are apart sometimes."

After Tatsuya had responded, making sure not to make such discomfort evident, Mayumi nodded very meaningfully as she walked. He started to feel a little pathetic.

"...Does it really look like we're together all the time?"

His face must have looked *really* pathetic, because Mayumi waved her hands in a fluster and showed her denial. "Oh! No, I mean, I know that isn't how it really is. She's always with us on student council work, and I know you aren't together in the classroom or during practice. I mean, well, it's more like...my imagination, that's it!"

"President... A magician's imagination is reality, you know."

Mayumi found herself forced to sweat a few beads at his glare, which had increased in humidity and pressure.

The awkwardness continued until they arrived at the courts. Tatsuya knew as much as the next guy that he couldn't keep up his morale-hindering attitude right where the matches were going to be, and after yelling to himself on the inside, he set his jaw.

But it very nearly dropped again when Mayumi removed the

knee-length cooler jacket (a heat-protected college jacket with cooling capabilities driven by thermoelectric effects) she was wearing.

"...Wait, are you going to play in that outfit?"

"Yes, why?" she said, nodding as though it were only natural.

Tatsuya felt a headache coming on. "Are you actually going to play the match in that tennis skirt?"

"Huh? Why not? Is it strange? ...Does it not look good?"

"......It looks very good on you."

"Really...? Hee-hee, thanks."

As Mayumi, in a good mood, began doing her stretches, Tatsuya looked her over again—to make sure he was really seeing what he was seeing. But no matter how many times he looked, he hadn't made a mistake.

She was in classic tennis wear: a polo shirt and a skort. Plus, they emphasized fashion over usability. She only had to bend a little bit for the hem of the skirt to pop up and expose her shorts underneath.

Cloudball involved a lot of intense movement. A shooter using compressed air would fire inelastic balls three inches in diameter, and the players would use a racket or magic to hit as many of them as they could into the opponent's court before time ran out. With one set lasting three minutes, an additional ball would be added onto the court, completely enclosed in a transparent box, every twenty seconds. At the end of it, the players would be tirelessly chasing around nine separate balls.

Normally you wore a short-sleeved shirt and shorts. Some competitors wore knee and elbow guards as well so that if they fell down they wouldn't get hurt.

If you were only going to use magic, you wouldn't need to run around and thus wouldn't need anything to dampen the impact of falling, but competitors who didn't use a racket wore clothing that could take a hit from a ball and not let them get hurt.

It was certainly not the sort of event where you could go out in such a frilly outfit with exposed arms and legs.

Anything goes for this woman, I suppose. Once he got used to the sight and thought about it, he was convinced.

"Tatsuya... You weren't thinking something rude just now, were you?"

"That would be absurd. Are you going without a racket?" He brushed the fairly sharp observation with a feigned look of earnestness and deflected the topic in a businesslike tone.

"Mmhmm. This is my usual style."

For a moment he nearly mistook her as referring to her outfit, but she was obviously talking about her "magic-only" style. "What CAD are you using?"

"This one," she said, taking a specialized CAD in the shape of a pistol out of her small bag and holding it out.

Some called it a short type, others a civilian type: Its analog for a live pistol barrel was short. (Tatsuya's CAD was a long type, called by some a cavalry type, where the barrel was longer.) CADs that took the form of smaller guns and pistols all included auxiliary aiming equipment. The "barrel" was actually an active radar for measuring magical coordinates (relative coordinates within the Idea of targeted eidos). A long barrel on a CAD indicated that it placed more emphasis on that aiming assistance. But for magicians who didn't need the aiming assistance and just wanted the activation speed of a specialized CAD, the short type was better all around; its lightness, portability, and ease of use made it convenient.

"Don't you usually use multipurpose types?"

"Yes, normally. I'm only using one thing for this, though."

She abbreviated a good portion of that, but Tatsuya correctly understood that she meant she was only going to use one type of magic during the match, which was why she chose a specialized type. "Is it movement magic? Or a reverse acceleration spell, perhaps?"

"Yep—I'm using Double Bound." Mayumi continued her elaborate stretching routine and answered Tatsuya without putting any particular emphasis on it. "Tatsuya, could you lend me a hand for a moment?"

"Sure."

Mayumi had sat down on the ground with her legs stretched out, and he lightly pushed on her back to get her more diagonal. It didn't take much for her chest to touch her legs.

"Reversing motion vector speed... Isn't it risky to go with just that? The balls aren't bouncy, so if they lose kinetic energy from the walls or floor, it may not get all the way to the other player's court."

As he felt a slightly low body temperature from his palms, Tatsuya murmured a warning into her ear from over her shoulder.

"Mmmm... Well, there is another acceleration spell in there, too, but I didn't use it last year."

She said it like it meant nothing, but there would need to be an immense power gap for her to do that. He got the real feeling once again of how ridiculously over the top Mayumi's level was.

"Okay, I'm good."

After stretching to her right and left feet four times each, Mayumi spoke and Tatsuya removed his hands. He stood back up straight and stepped back, and then she put her legs together and stuck her hand out, looking up.

He didn't immediately know what she was trying to do, but when he saw her slightly dissatisfied expression when he just stood there and watched without moving, Tatsuya finally understood her intent. He went around in front of her and took the hand she was holding up. It was small and soft. He pulled a little bit and she stood up nimbly, keeping both knees together.

"Thanks."

"You're very welcome."

Tatsuya knew right away that was an ungraceful response even for him, but Mayumi seemed happy for some reason. "Hmm! That's kind of new."

"What?" He obviously had no context to work with on that remark as he replied out of reflex.

Mayumi returned a sparkling smile. "You know, I have big brothers and little sisters, but no little brother."

"I see..."

He knew that already. Unlike the secretive Yotsuba, the Saegusa were a sociable family. They liked to invite a lot of people to their children's birthday parties, making for huge celebrations every year. Upon looking into them a little bit, it wasn't particularly difficult to learn their family makeup. If he recalled correctly, she had two older brothers and two twin younger sisters in their third year of middle school.

"Tatsuya, you don't treat me differently than others, do you?"

"I'm not trying to be rudely familiar with you, if that's what you mean..." said Tatsuya, tiptoeing around the obvious pitfall.

"That's not what I mean. You don't get all defensive or fidgety or uneasy around me, right?"

Defensive is one thing, but aren't you the one that causes the other two things? he thought, obviously not able to bring himself to say that.

"You talk to me politely for the most part, but you don't really have any restraint. One minute I'll think you're unfeeling, and then the next you're listening to my self-indulgence. I just thought maybe this is what a little brother would be like."

Tatsuya, in spite of himself, opened his eyes wide to look back at her. She was right—aside from the height difference, she had a good head on her shoulders, she was surprisingly good-looking, and showed consideration that could be a little hard to understand at times. If he'd heard someone call her a big sister, nothing would feel out of place.

But to be honest, if he had an older sister like this, he didn't think he'd have any time to rest.

"...Who knows? I only have a little sister."

"I guess you're right." She smiled at him in a way that made him wonder if she'd forgotten about the match.

Tatsuya was starting to feel uncomfortable now, so he tried to make an escape. "I'm sorry—I would like to go check on the other competitors as well, so..."

"No need for that."

His escape plan, though, ended in tragic failure thanks to the intervention of a third party.

"Oh, hello, Izumin."

"Saegusa... You just can't get over calling me that, can you?"

The female student pretended to hold her head in pain. She wore the same blouson as Tatsuya—she was Rika Izumi, a senior on the technical staff.

"Do you want me to call you Ricky instead?"

"You're doing this on purpose! Whatever, okay, Izumin is fine."

"Izumi, what did you mean by there being no need?"

Tatsuya had already learned that getting into a word game with Mayumi would last an eternity, so he completely ignored their exchange and asked about the first thing Izumi had said.

"Huh? Oh... Shiba, you can watch Saegusa's match. I've got the others."

Izumi didn't take very well to Tatsuya being part of the technical staff. It was less elitism in her case, though, and more that she had a lot of pride. She probably thought she could cover all of them even without having his help.

"I see. Thank you." He really wanted to run away, but if that's how things were going to be handled, then that was fine with him. He nodded without saying anything needless.

"Okay, I'll leave it to you," Izumi added, then left at a brisk pace.

"She's not a bad person, really..." Mayumi said as she watched her go, looking like she was going to heave a sigh. But it was no more than a soft breeze to Tatsuya, even though she'd purposely let him hear that.

Whatever Izumi's attitude was, and however Mayumi supported it, was no concern of his.

* * *

Cloudball was a ball sport similar to tennis and racquetball, but there was no serving system.

One set was three minutes, and three sets were played, with three minutes between each. (Boys played five sets in a match.)

The ball fired by compressed air at the same time as the signal for the match to begin would be added to every twenty seconds until a buzzer announced the end of the set. Until then, it would be a hectic storm of balls flying every which way.

...Normally, anyway.

The match that Tatsuya was watching happened to have a slightly different feel to it.

Mayumi's opponent was using a magic-only style like she was. As might be expected from someone participating in this event, she seemed to excel in movement magic. She was quickly swinging her own short-type pistol CAD in both hands toward the balls; maybe it was enhancing her mental image with her body movements. Any ball caught in her movement magic would change its movement direction midair before it fell to the ground on her side of the court, arcing unnaturally toward Mayumi's side—where it would bounce straight back at double the speed the moment it crossed over the net.

Every single one. Not one ball was exempt.

Mayumi held her CAD in front of her with both hands and stood in the middle of the court. She just stood there like a model for a painting. There wasn't even any wind to flutter her short skort or her hair because of the transparent walls surrounding the court.

She just stood there and her opponent couldn't get a single point.

By eye, it was maybe four inches.

That was how far from the net she ever let the opponent's balls come.

Mayumi's magic wasn't attaching any sort of precise control to the balls. She didn't try to go for blind spots; she was just hitting them back. A layman's eyes would have seen her opponent twisting and turning the balls' vectors, aiming for all sorts of different spots on the other court, and thought it was more difficult and therefore made her more skilled.

But in reality, Mayumi was the one racking up all the points.

Unilaterally—without missing a single one.

By the time the buzzer sounded to mark the end of the first set, her opponent was down on both knees, struggling to catch her breath. It was like she was crumbling to the ground, and it spoke to the despair she must have felt inside.

She never broke her pace, never disturbed her concentration, and she looked like she was using magic in a detached manner, but inside, she wasn't feeling that calm.

At least, to the extent that she unconsciously let out a long breath upon hearing the signal for the end of the set.

There was no sense that this match had been anything but one-sided. From an objective viewpoint devoid of pride, she knew her magic power was overwhelmingly superior to her opponent's. She would decide the match for certain at this rate in the next set.

Her *real* issue was the pair of eyes staring at her from outside the court.

She was used to being watched. People had been paying attention to her for as long as she could remember. Some of those eyes were purely admiring, some hid spiteful envy or carnal desires, but she was as used to them as she was to air.

But the eyes she'd felt for the past three minutes were nothing she'd ever experienced.

It wasn't on the level of someone simply watching her naked. (Though that would be a major problem, too). The gaze she felt from him—from Tatsuya—wasn't something so ordinary.

His gaze brought about an unidentifiable unease within her, like she was completely exposed, like he was seeing not only her naked skin, but everything else underneath it that made up who Mayumi

Saegusa was: the physical parts of her like her flesh, her bones, and her blood; plus her thoughts, emotions, values, tendencies, habits, preferences; the past that made her who she was today; and the talent and hard work that supported her. Everything.

This was the first time Tatsuya had watched Mayumi compete from up close. But he would have been watching all the other freshmen he was in charge of during their practice matches, and of all the ones he'd seen, none of them had complained about any anxiety.

She didn't think the younger girls would even be able to handle this sort of feeling. Which meant that either it was really all in her mind, or...that only she could have sensed it.

The three-minute break had just started. Normally, she would wipe her sweat and replenish her body moisture.

But she'd given the bag with her towel and drink in it to Tatsuya.

If she left the court, she'd have to go to where he was waiting—*lying* in wait for her.

Mayumi had to admit she was a little scared of leaving the court.

But it would look too strange to just stay on the court like this forever. Maybe she wasn't going to take a step, but then sitting down would obviously be the better option, and she needed to drink something anyway. And she would need to switch courts, too.

It would be fine if the competition officials were the only ones thinking it was strange, but with her position, she couldn't grant her fellow seniors and underclassmen who had come to cheer her on any cause for worry.

She took a deep breath and exhaled, expelling her anxiety. *Come on! Girls need guts!* She commanded her feet to go forward.

"Good work." With her towel held out for her by an underclassman, she felt a little let down. The unidentifiable choking feeling was gone, like it had never existed in the first place.

There was no doubt his pretend-earnest expression had one or two peculiarities hidden behind it; not even she could figure out what he was thinking when he had that straight face on. The younger boy made her feel both uneasy that she couldn't tell what he was thinking and oddly relieved knowing he'd never betray her.

When she'd said Tatsuya was like a little brother, she wasn't joking because she wanted to tease Tatsuya on a whim. It had certainly been a joke, but it had still partly been how she really felt.

She began to feel silly for being so scared of him and adopted a needlessly confident attitude.

"Good work? The match still isn't over. No going easy just yet!"

Tatsuya was a member of the team, but not a competitor. His role had ended before the match and would start again after it was over. During the match, he was just a spectator, so forbidding *him* from getting careless was a strange thing to do. He didn't bother to point it out, though, even though he noticed it.

"No, I believe it's over already."

Instead, he pointed out something more substantial.

"Huh?"

"Your opponent doesn't have the strength left to continue the match. Even if you started another set, it's clear she would run out of energy midway through. Their staff should know that, too. They'll forfeit the match soon."

Mayumi turned back toward the court and, sure enough, saw the other team's operations staff talking to the referees about something. Her opponent was sitting down on a bench with her arm wrapped in a medical checking device.

"She's exhausted her psions from using magic over and over. She must have made a mistake when trying to pace herself. She was a little out of her depth as your opponent, President."

"...You can tell all that just by looking?"

"If you really **look**, you could, too."

They probably hadn't heard what Tatsuya said, but right after that, the referees announced that her opponent had forfeited. Mayumi stood there dumbly, inviting a rare childish smile, but Tatsuya didn't follow suit and instead prompted her to leave. "Let's go to the tent. You should check your CAD for the next match."

"Yes, you're right. Thank you."

Tatsuya was completely in control now, but Mayumi knew refusing wouldn't get her anywhere, so she followed after him as he picked up her things and began to walk.

Cloudball had the most matches in a single day out of all the events in the Nine School Competition.

In terms of the maximum number of matches a single competitor would play, Monolith Code had the most with six, and Cloudball and Ice Pillars Break with five apiece. Monolith Code and Ice Pillars Break were held over the course of two separate days, though, so the five Cloudball matches would have to be fought through in the span of half a day.

Although the matches didn't last long, the event fundamentally required you to continuously cast magic throughout each of the three-minute sets. The burden for even one match couldn't be called light.

Therefore, in order to win through this event, it was said that the important part was how well you could hold back the exhaustion of your magic power.

With the obvious ideal being to win two sets in a row.

You wouldn't rush headlong into each and every ball during the set, either. It was set up so that you had to pace yourself well and allow for a certain number of lost points.

Competitors who could keep using magic at the same pace from start to finish like Mayumi were outside the norm, and practically breaking the rules.

Still, Mayumi wasn't just letting pride in her strength run away with her.

She had a strategy, too.

Winning two sets in a row was a must—and saying, "That's just trying to brute force it," was strictly not allowed.

She used a single type of magic that simply bounced the balls back, and it couldn't really be called suitable for this event. However, it helped stave off the exhaustion that would come from using multiple spells—and saying, "Something like that can't actually help stave off magical exhaustion," was also rejected.

In any case, for those reasons, she was in a position to go full throttle from start to finish.

However, as the second match started, strangely, she was perplexed.

She still felt on top of her game, though.

Thirty seconds passed in the first set, once again not granting her opponent a single point.

In fact, the opposite happened.

Why...?

The first match had ended with the opponent forfeiting, so she *had* gotten a longer break than usual in between matches.

But it was still a tight schedule, with five matches in half a day.

Her condition *feeling* like it was changing for the better even though it would have been actually decreasing due to tiredness was something you wouldn't normally think possible.

That could only mean that there was an *ab*normal cause for it.

The train of thought brought her to just one thing.

As the whistle indicated the end of the set...

...she decided to interrogate her lying underclassman.

"Tatsuya, you messed with the programming, didn't you?"

Completely contrary to the first match, as soon as the first set ended, she stormed straight out of the court to Tatsuya.

He couldn't hide his surprise at Mayumi's menacing look, but he sounded calm when he responded. "I didn't touch the programming. There shouldn't have been any trouble operating it; was there something in particular you were worried about?"

"You're lying!" she retorted, almost audibly sticking a finger out at Tatsuya's face before continuing, "It was clearly constructing spells more efficiently. You didn't have any time to improve the hardware, so you must have done something with the software!"

"…It was more efficient, right? Not less," he replied, confused.

Mayumi deflated like a balloon. "Well…yes."

If it had been less efficient, that would be one thing. But she finally seemed to realize how unreasonable her attitude was for complaining about it being the opposite.

"Anyway, why don't you sit down?"

Still confused, he held out a towel to Mayumi. With a slightly embarrassed and slightly sulky face, she sat down on the bench.

"It was probably more efficient because I cleaned it out."

Tatsuya sat down next to her, leaving a half-body gap between them, and purposely spoke in a pacifying tone without looking at her.

"Don't lie to me. I was right next to you. You obviously didn't disassemble it to clean it, and you didn't use a cleaner, either."

Mayumi had become somewhat obstinate as she spoke back to him. Tatsuya replied patiently. "No, not physical cleaning. I was cleaning out the garbage in the software."

A CAD's capabilities could be influenced by the user's mental state, among other things. Distrust toward the engineer would remarkably lower them. Tatsuya figured he should explain everything properly, despite not getting what he could rightly call informed consent before the fact.

"There were leftover preupdate system files cluttering up your CAD's system space, so I got rid of them. CAD operating systems are made so that sort of garbage accumulation doesn't happen often, but it isn't perfect. By eliminating such unneeded data, your CAD's efficiency will go up a bit. Of course, it isn't usually something you can tell normally, so I didn't explain before. I didn't realize your senses were *that* sharp. I apologize for my thoughtlessness."

"Oh, no, it's fine, if that's all it was," said Mayumi, waving her hands, confused at his exaggerated bow. "That just means you did your job, right? I'm sorry for doubting you like that."

Tatsuya brought his face back up to see Mayumi bowing her own in apology. *Quick to change gears*, he thought. "Let's leave it at that, then." *I guess she really can apologize honestly*, he thought as well.

"You're right."

Maybe it was because she was older than him and more flexible.

"Hey, Tatsuya?"

Still, she didn't have the flexibility to look at him from higher up.

"After this, could you teach me how to do that maintenance? The, er…garbage collection?"

It didn't make him feel bad.

"Sure. Please focus on your matches for now, though."

"Of course. Just leave it to Big Sister!"

She took a deliberately "older" attitude, and it was actually rather charming.

Mayumi went on to beat all her opponents in one-sided matches, winning every single one without losing a single point, and winning the girls' Cloudball championship.

◇ ◇ ◇

Ice Pillars Break was held on an outdoor field forty feet across and eighty feet long. It was split into halves, with twelve pillars made of ice standing at six and a half feet tall and three feet long and wide. Whoever toppled all of their opponent's pillars first was the winner.

Because of how it worked, Ice Pillars Break required an extremely intense setup phase.

Erecting hundreds of giant ice pillars in the middle of summer wasn't easy, and they couldn't have very many fields for it even despite the military's full cooperation.

Even at the Nine School Competition, they could barely create a pair of fields each for the boys and girls for a total of four, mainly due to them hitting ice-making limits. Each of these arenas would have twelve matches played in the first round and six in the second round for a total of eighteen. They were stretching the very limit of the day's schedule.

"Of course, the event consumes a ton of magic power. If they made all the matches on the same day, the competitors who had to play all five matches wouldn't last. The finals league on day two doesn't leave much room between matches, either. The fact that people say the end of Ice Pillars Break is all about guts does have some merit to it."

As Tatsuya explained as though it were a lesson, Shizuku nodded along enthusiastically.

Miyuki was here, too, but he didn't need to tell her all this anyway.

The three of them weren't in the grandstands, but in the staff seats instead.

Basically, they wanted to see Kanon's match, which was up next, from up close to really get a feel for what it was like.

Isori was the last to meet with Kanon, and they couldn't exactly be interrupted.

The other members had gone to watch the boys' Cloudball matches.

Erika went along with Sayaka, who had come to cheer for Kirihara, and Erika pulled along Mizuki, her Mikihiko, and him Leo.

When he heard about this from Miyuki, he thought, *How shy*, but as to *who* he was referring to—well, silence was golden, as the saying went.

Finally, Kanon climbed onto the stage.

Thirteen-foot-tall scaffolds were set up on either end of the field.

The competitors defend their own ice pillars and topple the enemies from there, using only magic.

It was said to be the most extreme of the magic events, as the safety restriction on magic was absent for spells affecting just the field.

"Shiba!"

Isori, who had shown Kanon onto the stage, waved Tatsuya over.

"Let's go up, too!" said Isori, inviting Tatsuya, and Miyuki and Shizuku, whom he'd brought with him.

A monitoring room for staff was located behind each of the scaffolds the competitors stood atop.

There were instruments for monitoring the competitors' condition as well as a large window that gave a direct view of the field.

"How is Chiyoda doing?"

He felt like staying silent would be rude, so he broached a harmless topic.

"She really seems into it. She's so excited we'll have to make sure she doesn't make things worse for herself tomorrow by overdoing it."

Isori answered Tatsuya's standard question with a smile.

There was no shadow of unease to be found on his face.

"I hear she won her first match in record time."

"Well, you know how she is. It would be more reassuring for those watching if she'd be a little more cautious, of course."

He answered with a pained grin, which caught Tatsuya's interest.

This morning, he'd been with Mayumi the entire time, so he hadn't seen Chiyoda's first match.

He only knew that Kanon had won it in record time.

And come to think of it, despite how short the match went, apparently a lot of her *own* pillars had been knocked over, too…

"It's starting!"

At Shizuku's murmur, Tatsuya looked to the field.

There was a rumble in the ground as the signal to begin the match came.

"Mine Spring?"

Not the bouncy sort of spring, but an "origin."

Tatsuya reflexively whispered the nickname at the sight before him.

Modern magic's selling point was in its speed and versatility, but it was used by people, so each magician had his or her own strong and weak points. As magical ability was transmitted genetically, direct blood relations would quite often, perhaps naturally, share the same strong and weak points. Yotsuba was an exception to the rule; everyone in the clan had their own special traits.

The powerful families used their shared special qualities, and were granted—or one-sidedly assigned—a nickname as a whole, apart from the nicknames individuals sometimes got.

The famous ones include Juumonji, the "Rampart." The Ichijou were called "Explosion." The Saegusa, based on the fact that they didn't lack in any family of magic, were paradoxically called "Almighty" or things of that nature. The Chiba were the "Sword Magicians." This was less about their genetic qualities than their technical skills, but still, it was applied to the family as a whole, putting it in the same category.

And the Chiyoda family was the "Mine Spring."

Its magicians excelled in vibration and long-range physical vibration magic, specifically in ground vibration spells. It didn't matter what the material was: It could be earth, stone, sand, or concrete. Whatever the ground happened to be, they could deliver powerful vibrations to that physical object. That was the effect of their special spell, Mine Origin, and they were given the nickname "Mine Spring" from the idea that they could create land mines.

After delivering an explosive vertical vibration similar to a near-field earthquake, two of the opponent's ice pillars groaned and collapsed at the same time. The opponent attempted a defense using a movement-type spell called Compulsory Stillness, which reduced movement speed to zero, but she couldn't keep up with the Mine Origin spell, which was changing targets and ripping through one

pillar after another. After five of the opponent's twelve pillars had been destroyed in sequence, she switched her tactics from defensive to offensive.

"Huh?"

"What?"

"?"

Tatsuya, Miyuki, and Shizuku all made surprised expressions, but Isori just gave a wry grin. He sighed as he watched Chiyoda's own ice pillars go down easily, and shook his head. "I don't know whether to call it impressive or lazy, but Kanon thinks she should just go all out and topple her opponents' before hers are knocked down."

"Well, I mean... Tactically speaking, she's not *wrong*."

By switching to attack, her opponent's defensive ability fell as well.

With six pillars left on Chiyoda's side, she finished knocking over all her opponent's pillars.

"Victory!"

Kanon, who had climbed down from the scaffolding, gave an elated smile and made a *V* sign.

As for who she was smiling at—it was obviously Isori.

Isori was smiling as well, though with more of a *What am I going to do with you?* feel to it.

"How can I say this..."

"They're a good couple?"

Miyuki stammered, finding it difficult to say, and Shizuku curtly expressed what she meant.

"Let's just say they understand each other."

For Tatsuya's part, he found himself forced to grin drily for a different reason than the two who had come with him. He *did* agree that they were a good couple, but seriously, they were perfect. The competitor and the supporter: Even if only one of them was up on stage, they'd won this battle through a combination of their strengths.

Still... he thought. *With such a perfect combination, can Isori really do his job when he's paired with other competitors?*

There were forty competitors, but only eight engineers. The simple average meant a single engineer would be in charge of five people. Tatsuya himself may have only had freshmen girls, but he was in charge of *six*. And with the unexpected situation that morning, it was seven.

Could he put his best foot forward with the other competitors the same as he had with this one he was so emotionally attached to?

And that went for Tatsuya himself, too. Could he really do his best work with Shizuku and Honoka as he could do with Miyuki?

"...Shiba, what's wrong?"

"Nothing, don't worry about it."

He couldn't, of course, turn to Isori and ask, "Could you be just as enthusiastic for the other competitors?" He instead responded with the safe, set phrase that meant nothing and did nothing, evading Isori's question.

◇ ◇ ◇

Triumphant at the fact that she'd won the third round, Kanon and Isori—and Tatsuya, Miyuki, and Shizuku, their companions—went back into the tent, then frowned at the unexpectedly gloomy mood inside.

"...What happened?" asked Isori to Suzune, who had, relatively speaking, maintained her ordinary calm.

When Suzune turned back to look, her face seemed more impassive than usual. "The boys' Cloudball results were disappointing, so we're recalculating the points forecast."

The Nine School Competition rankings were determined by the total number of points gained from each event. First place won fifty points, second place thirty, and third place twenty. Speed Shooting, Battle Board, and Mirage Bat awarded ten points to fourth place.

Cloudball and Ice Pillars Break didn't determine fourth through sixth place, so the three teams who lost in the third round of those events would each receive five points. Monolith Code gave one hundred points to the first place team, sixty points to second place, and forty to third, making it the most heavily weighted event in the competition. The rookie events would be calculated with half those values and added on to the total.

That was the competition's point system. If a school didn't get anyone into at least fourth place or sixth place, depending on the event, it wouldn't receive any points. But even if they couldn't win, holding second through fourth place gave a chance to get more points than the winner. Under this system, getting as many people through to the finals league or tournament in as many events as possible was the first condition for victory.

"When you say *disappointing...*"

"First round—loss. Second round—loss. Third round—loss."

The voice that answered Isori's timid question sounded almost indifferent.

"We've guaranteed our entries for next year, but we hadn't calculated this."

It may have sounded apathetic because those listening to it were in a state of shock.

They all knew that, compared to other events, the boys' Cloudball lineup was a little lacking.

But all that meant was that they didn't have the same easy, doubtless victory that the girls' Speed Shooting and Cloudball, as well as the boys' Ice Pillars Break and girls' Battle Board to come later, all had. Everyone thought they were at a high enough level to realistically aim for first place.

"It will be difficult to predict point distributions in the rookie competition, but considering our current lead, we should have a safety zone as long as we win girls' Battle Board, boys' Ice Pillars Break, Mirage Bat, and Monolith Code."

A junior on the operation staff reported the results of their calculations.

Tatsuya, listening in a detached manner, thought, *That's a bit of a high hurdle, though, isn't it?*

He was saying they had to win four of the six remaining events in the main competition, boys and girls combined.

They might have been anticipating Katsuto and Mari to win their events for sure, but those sorts of predictions ran the risk of psychological downfall should an accident happen by any chance.

Still—that was no concern of Tatsuya's. Harboring concerns about those things would have placed him above his station. Besides, there was something that was personally worrying him.

Kirihara had competed in boys' Cloudball.

He was reckless in some ways, but he had a strong sense of responsibility.

Wouldn't he be in shock right now...?

◇ ◇ ◇

He met up with Kirihara only after the day's events had ended, in the lounge just before sunset.

At first glance, he seemed the same as always.

Sayaka was sitting down next to him.

She was doing her best to act cheerfully, but her smile was plainly forced.

"Good job today, Kirihara."

"Oh, that you, Shiba?"

Tatsuya had had the option to say nothing and go past, but he had not.

"Lost after that second round. I got crushed."

That was clearly his bravado speaking, but he still seemed to be quicker to get himself back up than Tatsuya had thought. He figured athletes who went through many victories and defeats had a high resistance to losing, too, because it gave them a mental resilience. Tatsuya always lost during practice, but didn't have much experience at all in actual matches, so he couldn't understand anything more than the logic behind the process.

He stood there, unable to decide whether words of consolation were proper for the situation, and decided to just state the facts. "The luck of the draw didn't favor you. You ended up against Third High's ace in the second round; he's the favorite. Plus, you only lost three sets to two, with only eight points total between you. You were exhausted from the match with the one everyone thinks will take the whole thing, and that's why you lost in straight sets in the third round. It was essentially a forfeit due to injury."

"...You sure like getting to the point."

Tatsuya had offered a calm analysis that certainly hadn't seemed comforting, without trying to skirt the issue of his losses; Kirihara hadn't gotten mad.

"Ever think I might be, like, *depressed* about it?"

In fact, his tone and expression suggested he was amused.

"I considered it, but offering consolation is one thing I don't know how to do."

A few seconds passed in silence.

And then Kirihara suddenly burst out laughing on the sofa and bent over.

Sayaka's smile, next to him, started to look a little shaken up.

Tatsuya kept looking down at him with an expressionless face.

"Shiba... Anyone ever tell you you're funny? Anyone normal would have just made this real awkward face and pretended they didn't see me. You're the only one I could think of who'd just come up and talk to me like that!"

He had mulled over the option—pretending not to see him—but he felt sort of like passing by without a word would have been unfriendly; that had been Tatsuya's logic. But apparently it had been unwarranted anyway. *I guess I shouldn't be thinking about things that aren't like me, like how to be friendly.* Still…

"But now I feel a lot better. If you called it a forfeit because of injury, then that's probably how it really was. Guess that means I'm not a hopeless case, you know?"

…unexpectedly, that thinking had gotten him somewhere.

Leaving aside whether Kirihara really felt that way on the inside…

…and leaving aside whether this was the result Tatsuya had actually been going for.

◇ ◇ ◇

There may have been some unexpected hardships in the competition, but that didn't mean anything was different for those down on the lowest rungs. That may not have applied to those on miscellaneous affairs, but Tatsuya was still engaged as an engineer. Nobody among the First High leadership was foolish enough to risk creating any kind of obstacles to his actual work by pushing needless errands on to him.

After checking on the condition of the athletes he was in charge of in preparation for the rookie competition that would start the day after tomorrow and verifying that nothing had gone wrong with their CAD settings, his work for the day ended.

He went to the hotel's front lobby to pick up a long, narrow package addressed to him and returned to his assigned room.

It was still before dinnertime. He had a lot of free time today, so he decided to run a test on the delivery. He looked at the clock to see how much time was left before he had to be in the dining hall. It would be a little while yet before Miyuki came to pick him up, so he decided to unwrap the package and look inside.

It was the thing he'd requested a trial manufacture of from FLT's third R & D section early this morning. All of its parts were commonplace ones, and it was of simple design. Despite having been automatically manufactured purely based on the blueprints, it had been molded and assembled in half a day. He found himself in admiration at what little time it took to get here.

I just hope Ushiyama wasn't putting other things off for this... Or perhaps someone forced him to do it. Tatsuya had put the words *this is mostly for fun* in his request e-mail an annoying number of times, but... Anyway, he couldn't **truly** turn back time, so it wouldn't do him any good to worry about it now.

He removed the shipping cover made from recycled materials to reveal a thin, long, and narrow hard case with a combination lock on it. The type of case was typically used for delivering shotgun-size CADs. The dial came unlocked with the usual code.

Inside the case was a sword—one of middling length with a knuckle guard. He took it out. It was a one-handed sword, more than two feet long, with the blade itself one and a half feet long—at least, on the surface.

It didn't have a blade on it.

It hadn't been made as a switchblade; it wasn't a "sword" in the real sense of the word in the first place. It was more of a metallic reproduction of a medium-length sword rather than an actual one. Or else it was a flat bludgeon with a sword handle on it.

But of course, this was no mere club.

When he flicked the switch on the inside of the handle and let a few psions into it, a familiar sensation came back to his hand. Like Erika's baton, this was a weapon with a CAD embedded inside.

It was even narrower in usage than normal specialized CADs, and could only supply a single type of activation program. While Erika's CAD had its program-switching function intact as normal specialized types did, this was the prototype of a completely single-purpose specialized CAD, which were called integrated armament CADs.

He glanced at his distance to the wall to measure it, and then, just as he was about to begin the test, there was a knock at the door. Giving a pained grin at the "perfect" timing, he placed the prototype on his desk. She was a little earlier than she said she'd be, but he knew from the completely apparent presences outside the door that all his friends were about to intrude on him as well.

He briefly thought about putting the prototype away, but reconsidered; he didn't need to keep it a secret. Besides, this prototype was for one of those friends anyway. Thinking that it would be more interesting to have that friend do the test than him, he opened the door.

"Tatsuya, is it all right for us to come in?"

The first to open her mouth was his little sister in the front. He held the outward-opening door open as Miyuki passed, followed by Erika, who brushed closer to him than was necessary, practically touching him. After that came Honoka, Shizuku, and Mizuki, and then Leo and Mikihiko bringing up the rear.

This was less of a "ladies first" setup than a simple reflection of the power balance. But despite the twin single room's nominal extra space he used for his equipment, it was cramped with this many people in there at once. The chairs and bed weren't enough, so one of his friends sat on his desk, too—though she actually looked cool rather than untidy doing it, so he didn't say anything about it.

The one who sat on his desk, Erika, obviously noticed the sword on the desk, and was interested in it. "Tatsuya... Is this a practice sword? Like, a western kind, and not a katana?"

"No."

"Then is it a metal cane?"

"No... I don't think there are any martial artists who prefer metal canes in this country anyway."

"Martial artists these days... Then what is it?" Erika took it in her hands and looked at both sides, then noticed the trigger on the upper end of the grip and said, "...Oh! Is it a *broom*?"

"Correct. More precisely, it's an integrated armament CAD. Some people call them weapon devices. It's the combination of a CAD specialized completely in a single spell and a close-combat weapon for using the spell."

"Cool…" Erika didn't say that because integrated armament CADs were unusual, but because the "sword" was unlike any she'd ever seen before.

Erika, looking at it closely in her hands, wasn't the only one interested—Honoka and Shizuku were gazing at it in fascination as well. Miyuki, though, probably remembered their conversation last night. Her face lit up with recognition. Mizuki and Mikihiko didn't seem very interested. Maybe they were more drawn to types they were used to than new things. Tatsuya glanced at the profile of the last person, then gave a mean grin and took the prototype from Erika's hands.

"Leo!"

And he tossed it at Leo, who had looked away, uncooperative.

"Whoa! Hey, watch where you're throwing it!"

He was actually just itching to get his hands on the thing, but he had felt strangely antagonistic at the moment toward his fated enemy (?) and acted like he wasn't interested. But as he pretended to be confused, he gripped the handle like he'd been waiting for it.

Tatsuya ignored his superficial argument entirely and smiled provocatively. "Want to try it out?"

"What? Me?" For just a moment, he grinned.

Beside him, Erika made a face like she wanted to say how transparent he was, but that was something Tatsuya only caught out of the corner of his eye before he looked back at Leo. "That weapon device is a bludgeoning weapon that applies the hardening magic Watanabe used in her Battle Board races. If you replaced the blade part, it could be a slashing weapon, too. I thought it was suited to you."

"Wait, *you* made this?"

"Yeah."

"Wait a minute," interrupted Mikihiko into their conversation. He hadn't seemed very interested at first, but he had been listening carefully. "Watanabe's races were just yesterday. You made that in a day? It doesn't look to me like a hodgepodge of extra parts."

"Well, the device itself *is* a hodgepodge. The exterior is made of a common alloy; there's no special materials in here at all."

"But you couldn't have done it by hand. You didn't have time for that!"

"Well, of course not. I just drew up the blueprints and got it made automatically at a friend's workshop."

Miyuki nearly started to laugh at *a friend's workshop*, since she knew what had happened, but she always had several extra layers of skin ready to use, so she didn't actually make the blunder of letting a suspicious look to her brother get through.

"Anyway, Leo… Do you want to test it?"

Tatsuya's voice was like the whisper of Mephistopheles. He obviously had an ulterior motive, but not even knowing that made the charm irresistible.

"…All right, sure. I'll be your lab rat for this one."

"That was easy," murmured Shizuku, giving a simple voice to the impression all their friends had.

The next thing Tatsuya got out was a mirror shade–type HMD (head-mounted display) with a speaker in it.

"It's the manual." Leo, upon being offered the HMD, didn't quite understand what that meant, and a question mark appeared above his head. "The manual for the weapon devices is recorded in there, so take a look."

"Huh? Oh, right…"

After finally realizing it had images and voices recorded as a manual for the integrated armament CAD he'd been handed (or, more accurately, *thrown*), his face changed to one of understanding and he took the HMD from Tatsuya's hands.

"Isn't that a kind of virtual terminal?"

Honoka, who asked the question, wasn't the only one who felt that way. Virtual information terminals were harmful to inexperienced magicians. It was common sense, and even First High forbade students from using them.

Tatsuya, who stubbornly stuck with screen-type terminals himself, had told a friend to use the playback function in a virtual terminal, and while the HMD would restrict his eyesight and hearing, the others had their doubts.

"It's nothing so crazy, but I suppose it is similar."

"...Will it be all right?"

"Huh? Oh... You mean information terminals being harmful?"

"Y-yes."

"There's nothing to worry about in that sense. The harmfulness with virtual terminals lies in the risk of instilling falsely successful experiences. Virtually experiencing something you can actually do makes them useful tools."

"I don't exactly understand what that means..."

Honoka had always spoken politely to Tatsuya, but now it was like Miyuki's way of talking had infected her.

"Magic is a system that temporarily creates or alters reality using fictitious mental images. The experience-related functions in a virtual terminal are a technology to place you under the illusion that false mental images are real."

Tatsuya's explanation was thorough and detailed, perhaps as a reactive response to that.

"They're similar in that they both result in the perception of nonreal events as being real. On the other hand, the experiences virtual terminals can grant don't require any effort on the part of the user to alter reality. Those alterations would never fail, and that's where the risk comes in."

Tatsuya paused for a moment—even *he* felt like he was being long-winded about this. But among the faces of the friends before him, half understood and the other half didn't. He reconsidered. He must not have said enough, so he decided to continue explaining.

"There is a possibility that virtual terminal experiences can give a magician the illusion that they were able to alter reality without any effort. For those who can't use magic anyway, it wouldn't be an illusion in the first place, and experienced magicians can easily distinguish between things they can and can't do. With inexperienced magicians, though, there's the possibility that the fiction in the virtual terminal experience could mix with the reality of events they've altered through magic, leading them to mistake their own level of strength.

"Inexperienced magicians who have grown used to that virtual world in which they can alter reality without effort or risk of failure will stop thinking about why their magic—why their *real* event alterations fail. They'll lose both the ability and the desire to think about it. That's why they say virtual terminals are harmful to inexperienced students learning magic."

He paused again to look at his friends' faces. It looked like he'd explained enough, but just to be sure, he decided to wrap it all up.

"In other words, the problem is with being under the illusion that you can do things you can't. There's no issue with the virtual experience being something you can actually do. Virtual experiences like that actually have positive effects that bolster the mental image–forming process required for constructing magic sequences. The reality is that it's just difficult to pick out only the beneficial content, so from that point of view, completely banning virtual terminals is a logical choice…"

"I see… Thank you, I learned a lot!"

The way Honoka nodded seemed overly enthusiastic. Tatsuya thought that maybe he overdid it a little. What he really felt about it was that even if she felt a reliance on him, he wouldn't be able to respond to it…

◇ ◇ ◇

They decided to have the prototype device test after dinner and to borrow the indoor hand-to-hand combat training grounds outside the Nine School Competition facilities. Tatsuya didn't set it up; it was Erika's connections. Ever since coming here, she'd been making full use of her family's influential power like her life depended on it. What had happened that forced such a change in her mental state? He remembered hearing something about that at the party. Of course, he could worry all he wanted, but there was nothing he could do. Besides, he knew it wasn't something he needed to seriously worry about anyway—his own emotions were superficial to start with. Which meant it would be quite a bit more sincere to get serious and prioritize his own curiosity as an engineer instead.

After telling himself that, he admonished himself for being about to poke his nose in someone else's business.

"Leo, did you understand how to use it?"

He'd turn his focus to the test they were about to start. The thing had been created off-hand and was just a simple arrangement on an existing spell, but he was still doing a test of a new spell and a new device. If he let his mind wander, accidents would happen not to him, but to Leo.

"Yeah, pretty much... But is it really even possible?"

It referred to the predicted operation of the prototype Leo had been shown by the HMD. Probably, anyway—what else could it mean?

"That's why we're testing it—to find out."

"Right, I guess so."

The grounds were about thirty minutes' walking distance from the hotel. However, it was night right now, not daytime. And this was an army maneuvering ground in the mountains, not a city. Miyuki and Erika had both opposed the idea tenaciously, but after managing to talk them down, they'd left them in the hotel. The whole situation was still uneasy, so they asked Honoka to keep an eye on Miyuki, and Mizuki on Erika. Right now, only Tatsuya and Leo were here.

"Okay, let's get started."

"Roger that!"

For the first test, there wouldn't be any dummies set up for practice strokes (or hits, as it were). Before doing anything, they checked to make sure the integrated armament CAD's weapon portion was functional.

"Here I go!"

Leo flicked the switch on the end of the handle. There was a click as the switch depressed in his hand. Then he pushed in the trigger on the upper end of the grip with his index finger and sent psions into it.

Despite the outward impression Leo gave off, he didn't have explosive power; instead, he had excellent tenacity and stamina in terms of the psions he could supply. Of course, having that sort of endurance with his tough look was probably expected.

The CAD hadn't been adjusted for his individual use, so its spell construction assistance functions didn't do much, and the compilation process of creating the magic sequence from the activation program took more time as a result. It was about 0.6 seconds—still quite a bit faster than his grades in practice. It might have been due to this being the type of magic he excelled in, or perhaps it was thanks to the performance of the CAD and the activation program. Whichever it was—and it could have been both—it didn't matter. They weren't timing him; they were here now to observe the spell itself.

"Whoa!"

Leo's grunt was less about the spell that had activated and more because the inertia coming through his hand was more than he'd expected.

"Ha-ha, it's really floating. Cool!"

He grinned a childlike grin and swung around the "sword"—which now had less than half its blade. In tandem with his movements, the other part of the blade, which was floating in midair, arced along in front of it.

"Three, two, one..."

"Whoops!"

Leo stopped moving when he heard Tatsuya's countdown.

"...zero."

Once his countdown got to zero, the blade in the air jerked back down in front of him and returned to the piece of the sword still connected to the guard, locking in and forming a full "sword" once more.

"It worked perfectly, Tatsuya!"

Leo couldn't help giving him a thumbs-up in his enjoyment, and Tatsuya responded with the same pose.

"But how did you even come up with this? Using hardening magic to stabilize the relative positions of the separated pieces of the sword and making the blade float? I could barely believe it, and I was the one doing it! I guess hardening magic works even if they're not physically touching."

"The definition of hardening magic is to stabilize relative coordinates, after all. Once you get rid of your fixed ideas, there's no need for objects to be touching. And with the way this device works, it's more *stretching* the blade than making it float. It's just that there's a hole in the middle; the blade can only move as an extension."

"Well, that means you don't have to think about it too much. It's great—it feels the same as just swinging a real long sword."

As Leo said, this weapon device didn't have the aspect of wearing away the user's force of will to be controlled, which long-range remote weapons usually had. It would just swing around, maintaining its distance, for as long as the spell was effective and you kept moving your hand.

"By the way, how are they connected? There's no spell involved..."

"Oh, that's simple. It's electrically reactive shape memory alloy; in the moments it attaches and detaches, it runs an electrical current through it to bind and release."

Leo nodded in understanding. It was a relatively popular way of making clasps and fasteners these days.

"But that means if it's hit with a strong impact while the spell isn't active, it'll probably just pop off."

"Hey, no problem. You could just put it in a sheath while you're not using it, right?"

"I suppose. All right, want to test using it on a dummy for real? Or try changing the detachment distance?"

"Hey, Tatsuya, would there be a way to change the distance while it's on?"

"It…wouldn't be impossible, but it would be difficult. It's set up now so that you adjust the constant number of activation programs related to attaching and detaching with the switch on the butt of the handle, but you could certainly change the variables in the magic sequence, of course. But if you're trying to change the distance midway through, you'd need to overwrite the currently activated magic."

"Oh. Well, if you just make it quicker to go back to normal, you wouldn't need to change the distance in the middle, huh? I mean, you can't change the length of a real sword while you're cutting into things, anyway."

"I feel like someone like Erika could do it, though. Anyway, what do you want to do?"

"Maybe… Let's go with the dummy."

"Right."

Tatsuya used the big notebook remote control, and three human-sized straw figures came out of the ground.

"…What is this, the bronze age?"

"…Whose hobby was *this*?"

They exchanged tired glances at the anachronism in their world where biological materials that could be regenerated were commonplace.

"Well… Functionally speaking, as a striking dummy, it should be fine."

"Straw figures don't have functions! But yeah, I guess there's nothing to complain about."

Leo ran his empty left hand down his cheek and fired himself back up, then took a stance against the dummies.

He hit the switch.

One part of the blade flew into the air.

Leo swung with vigor.

The flying blade, having been given speed in response to the movement radius of his hand, struck the straw figure target.

"That really comes back to you."

It didn't seem like it had numbed him, but Leo expressed his impression while shaking his hand, holding the weapon device after it had reverted to its original medium-length (toy) sword state.

"The flying part doesn't have much mass. It compensates for the speed, but you need more physical strength because there's less momentum."

"I get it. Meaning it would be better if it was a little heavier if it was used in actual combat."

Leo nodded in understanding at the explanation, then went for another target. As Leo brought the device around again, Tatsuya thought to himself, *He's right. Even if it had a blade on it, being a little heavier would give it more effectiveness in real combat. Though this much might be perfect for using in games...*

Tatsuya had thought of Monolith Code's rules, which prohibited direct attacks. This weapon device wouldn't be breaking the rules, since the blade was floating in the air.

...Doesn't have anything to do with this, though.

He smiled drily to himself for thinking about viable ways to use it while also stating it was a toy.

[7]

Day three of the Nine School Competition.

On this third day, the finals of men's and women's Ice Pillars Break and men's and women's Battle Board would be held, leading some to call it the peak of the competition's first half.

First High's current status in the events saw two competitors in men's Ice Pillars Break and men's and women's Battle Board, with one still in women's Ice Pillars Break.

It hadn't gone quite as planned, but it was within the allowable margins of their strategy.

"Hattori will be in the first men's race, Watanabe in the second women's race, Chiyoda in the first women's match, and Juumonji in the third men's match…"

After looking at the match list, he was a little worried. Though there was a time differential in terms of starting and match times based on which event it was, he wouldn't be able to see both Hattori's and Kanon's bouts. *I guess Hattori wouldn't want me to come watch him anyway…*

Still, with Miyuki being with him on the student council, it would be a problem for her to display indifference toward his race.

"Oh, there he is. Tatsuya!"

But he didn't worry for very long—in fact, he didn't need to.

"President, did you need anything?"

"I just wanted a little help on something."

Tatsuya was then dragged away by Mayumi to the work vehicles.

◇ ◇ ◇

"Tatsuya, it's about to start!"

In the end, Tatsuya wasn't released until right before Mari's race was starting. If he wasn't there after she came by while he was working just to remind him that he *was* going to come watch her race, there was no telling what they might say about him, even though it would only be a few people.

He briefly thanked his sister and friends for saving his seat and looked over to the starting line.

He really had been just on time. Mari was already ready to go, her short bob haircut under her bandana swaying in the wind.

The semifinals would be two races with three people in each. The winners would go on to duke it out in a one-on-one final race.

As the other two competitors' faces were tense with nervousness, Mari alone wore a fearless expression as they waited for the starting signal.

The first buzzer sounded to have them get ready. The audience fell completely quiet.

A moment later, the second buzzer went off.

The race had begun.

Mari jumped ahead to first place. This time, though, unlike the qualifiers, the second-place competitor was close behind. Third place was a little bit farther back.

"She's good…!"

"Seventh Sea High as usual…"

"This is the same matchup as the finals from last year."

The surface of the water undulated fiercely, indicating the magic battle going back and forth between them. Normally, Mari being in front would be advantageous thanks to the backwash synergy, but the Seventh High competitor was riding her board skillfully to make up for her magical disadvantage. After passing the long meandering zone in front of the grandstands, they approached a sharp corner with almost no distance between them. After they went around, the crowd wouldn't be able to see them and they'd have to watch on the screens. Tatsuya glanced over at the image of the corner up on the big display.

"Mm?"

Something was a little odd there, and it caught his eye.

"What?!"

And so, mistakenly, he let the moment slip past him.

There was a scream from the audience. He hurried to look back down and saw the Seventh High competitor tumbling over.

"She went too fast?!" someone shouted.

It did look like that—her board wasn't gripping the water. She shot across the surface as if flying, and would have been on a crash course with the fence...

...if there hadn't been someone in front of her.

But Mari *was* there, having just come out of her deceleration and having begun to speed up.

Mari's body was facing the fence, but she seemed to notice the girl coming up from behind and looked over her shoulder.

The way she reacted was nothing short of incredible.

She canceled her forward acceleration then switched over to horizontal rotational acceleration. Then, using the waves bouncing back from the wall of the waterway, she turned her board around with magic and riding skills.

After that, she multicasted two spells to stop the out-of-control Seventh High competitor. Movement magic to deflect the incoming board, and a weighting/inertial dampening spell to keep the girl from being flung into the fence from the impact.

Normally, the crisis would have been averted there.

If not for the surface of the water suddenly sinking in.

It was a slight change.

But Mari had just executed a high-level technique: turning 180 degrees on her board. She was no surfing expert. She had forced herself to change stances because of those excellent spells and body manipulation, so when she suddenly lost buoyancy, she completely lost her balance.

And because of that, there was a gap in her magic execution.

She succeeded in deflecting the board trying to take her feet out from under her.

However, before her inertial dampening spell could activate, the Seventh High competitor, having lost her footing, collided with Mari.

The two of them flew entangled toward the fence.

There were several loud screams.

The race suspension flag was waved.

Tatsuya, too, stood up despite himself.

Mari had been sandwiched between the fence and the other athlete—and she didn't seem to have taken the fall well at all.

"Tatsuya!" Miyuki looked up at him, her face pale.

"I'm going. You all wait here."

Tatsuya had a lot of practice being a bodyguard—or a soldier—from a young age, so he had enough skill to do basic surgical procedures.

"All right."

Miyuki understood by his calm voice that them going would only increase the confusion. She waved their half-standing friends back down into their seats, then nodded at Tatsuya.

He began to run down the jam-packed grandstands, slipping through railings like a ghost.

◇ ◇ ◇

Her awakening wasn't what could be called swift. There was a haze in her mind; she couldn't grasp the situation.

What was she doing here...?

That question was the first thought that came to mind after she opened her eyes.

"Are you awake, Mari? Do you know who I am?"

The bad influence—and despite calling her that at such a time and only in her mind, she *still* didn't use the word *friend*—was peering down into her face. She understood what the question meant, but she didn't know why she was being asked such a thing, so she asked back quizzically,

"What are you saying, Mayumi? Why would you need to…"

…and then midway through her sentence, arrived at the answer, and to her current situation.

"This is the hospital…"

"Yes, the hospital at Susono Base. Thank goodness… It looks like your mind is working fine."

"How long was I out?"

The dull pain in the back of her head told her that she hadn't been sleeping—she'd been unconscious after failing to fall safely.

"For some of the afternoon. Oh, don't get up!"

Mari tried to sit herself up in bed, but Mayumi came around quickly and pushed her back down. She didn't use much force, but Mari only had half of her usual freedom of movement.

"You broke a few ribs. They're being held together with magic now, but they still aren't attached. I'm sure you know this, but magic is really only a temporary treatment—"

"—and I'll feel like they're healed until they're actually attached. The injury was far too heavy to recover instantly. Yeah, I got it. I know that much." Mari tiredly let her body fall back to the bed as she interrupted what Mayumi was saying, as if speaking to herself. "How long will it take until they reattach?"

"A full recovery will be one week. You'll regain normal function after a day's sleep, but just to be sure, you're not allowed to do any vigorous exercise for ten days."

"Wait! But that means…?!"

"You're out of Mirage Bat, too. I'm sorry."

"I see..."

Mari sighed and shut her eyes. It was a little while before her eyelids opened again.

"...What happened with the race?"

"Seventh High was disqualified due to the dangerous maneuver, so the finals will be Third High and Ninth High. Third place will be us and Second High. Kobayakawa seems like she's really into it, so we might be able to come away with third."

"She's more than good enough—too bad about how easily her mood changes."

"Mm. Also, Seventh High's competitor doesn't appear to have been badly hurt. You managed to protect her enough for that."

"...Doesn't help the fact that I'm badly hurt, though," said Mari, **pretending** to complain and be discouraged. Mayumi giggled inappropriately at the pretense of her attitude. Mari turned away and pretended not to notice.

"As for the boys, Hanzou is going to the finals. Murakami just barely missed out, though. Juumonji is advancing to the finals league for the men's Ice Pillars Break. Kanon is going to the finals league for the women's Ice Pillars Break, too."

"So I ended up being the only miscalculation..."

"You couldn't help it. Mari, your judgment was correct. If you didn't decelerate right there, you might have been able to just graze by the collision. And you probably would have won, too, but... Seventh High's competitor would have gotten badly injured, and that probably would have spelled the end of her career as a magician. That's how dangerous the whole thing was. Tatsuya agrees with me, too."

"...Hey, why bother bringing him up *now*?"

"Because he's the one who carried you here and stayed while you were being treated."

"What?"

"Of course, I didn't leave *everything* to him... Are you surprised?"

Mayumi smiled complacently, and Mari turned away again with a sour expression. Her relief at having woken up made Mayumi's face all the more unbearable.

"I wouldn't have let a boy see a girl changing. He made sure to wait in the hallway during treatment. But you should still thank him later. He ran straight there as fast as the relief squad did, helped get you out of the waterway, saw immediately that you had broken ribs, and even gave instructions about how to patch you up until they could get you here."

"...Who the hell *is* he?" asked Mari, eyes wide with astonishment.

Mayumi nodded deeply. "It kind of feels like he's really used to accidents and injured people and such... How are you feeling, by the way?"

"That was sudden... My head hurts a little, but it's probably just a surface injury. I'm fully aware."

"It doesn't look like there was any damage to your brain, either... Okay, maybe I should ask now."

"?"

Mari looked at her askance, and Mayumi returned her gaze with a serious look.

"What? What's going on?"

"Mari... Did you get obstructed by magic from a third party at the time?"

"...What do you mean?"

"I'm talking about when you lost your balance right before the Seventh High competitor ran into you. Did you lose your balance because an illegal magic from a third party was interfering with the water's surface?"

Mari's eyes sharpened as she understood what Mayumi was getting at. "...Yeah, I remember there being an unnatural tremor at my feet right before my board sank. But I didn't know whether it was because of magic or not, much less whether it was against any rules... Why do you think that?"

"The way the water's surface was moving when you slipped was unnatural. It had the particular discontinuity of magic-based event alteration. But at the time, neither Seventh High's nor Ninth High's competitor was using magic like that. That means the only possibility is that it was a spell from a third party. Tatsuya is of the same opinion, too. He borrowed the video from the tournament committee; he says he's going to do a wave analysis on the water's surface. That way, at least we'll know whether some unnatural phenomenon was taking place."

"I want to say I don't think a high school freshman would have enough skill to do something like that, but I'll leave that aside for the moment... I mean, I was using magic against the other competitors, too, so why bother figuring out if there was some unnatural force at work? I don't really see the point..."

"He said he was going to look into whether there was some *other* force at work and take into account the spell effects from the other racers. Isori said he'd help, too, after today's matches were over. I think we might come up with something meaningful. If you remember anything else, do mention it. This is just an issue of our—of First High's—rankings; it could affect all the magic high schools in the Nine School Competition."

"......"

Mari fell silent as she lay in bed. Mayumi told her she needed to get back soon, then left the hospital room. Now alone, Mari's eyes had only grown more serious as she stared at the ceiling.

◇ ◇ ◇

When Miyuki answered the door at the knocking, she found two of her upperclassmen there.

"Please, come in... Tatsuya, Isori and Chiyoda have come to see you."

At Miyuki's voice, Tatsuya stopped typing on his keyboard and stood up.

"Sorry for calling you out here."

"No, don't worry about it. I'm the one who said he'd help, and I can't make you bring a terminal after you've started working on it."

Tatsuya bowed lightly in apology, but Isori waved it away casually. Tatsuya nodded again, then looked at Kanon this time. "Chiyoda, congratulations on your victory."

"Thanks. Mari got mixed up in all that trouble, so I need to do good enough for both of us!"

Kanon clenched a fist; the term *ardor* fit her well, and Tatsuya found her a little hard to look at.

"Did you find anything out?"

"I did a general inspection, but it seems like we're still looking at a third party's interference. Isori, could you check to make sure?"

"Sure thing... You really do work fast, Shiba."

As Isori sat down in the chair Tatsuya pointed to, he also used his hands to express admiration.

The small desktop display (still equivalent to a twenty-inch monitor in traditional units) was split into two parts of the screen, with one showing a video and the other showing a simulated wireframe version of the video.

Isori extended the thin, metallic C-shaped object—a brain-assisted monocle viewing pointer—and placed it on his forehead with a familiar ease. Then, bringing his right eye to the monocle portion, he placed his thumb on the clicker on the bottom middle of the keyboard.

Brain assistance and viewing pointers were input support mechanisms originally made so that you didn't have to ever take your hands off the keyboard, but they had become a tool for not having to use the keyboard at all.

Still, Isori seemed to be following its original usage as a keyboard input support.

As he controlled it, the actual video and the simulation moved at the same time.

He brought the cursor over to the time bar as it got closer to the accident, and slowed down the playback.

The upper part of the simulation screen displayed all the factors affecting changes in the water's surface using numbers.

At the moment the problematic dip in the water's surface appeared, the screen displayed an entry called *unknown*, indicating that measurement errors couldn't account for this "force" in the water.

Isori stopped the video and turned around. "…This could be harder than we thought."

"What do you mean, Kei?"

"As you know, Kanon, in the Nine School Competition, there's a lot of surveillance equipment set up and many magicians excelling in anti-magic positioned all throughout each event as tournament staff. It's to prevent unfairness due to magical interference from outside. If their surveillance didn't catch this, then I'm going to guess someone created a local downburst high in the air, above where the surveillance equipment could scan, then pushed the high-pressure air bubble down to the water's surface to make it dip like that. But there's no way Watanabe wouldn't have noticed something like that, so my hypothesis has a few holes.

"But according to Shiba's analysis, the force that caused the water surface to dip originated from under the water. Any magic sequences being injected to the waterway from outside would have been caught by the surveillance equipment without a doubt. Plus, the only natural phenomenon that could have been responsible for the surface of the water descending because of something under the surface would be if the bottom of the waterway gave out—and that's impossible, too. The other possibility is that an operative was actually underwater there, I guess…but that's even more ridiculous…"

"Couldn't that just mean Shiba's analysis was wrong?"

At Kanon's unreserved remark, Miyuki's face color changed.

"No, that can't be it."

But before she could say anything, Isori rejected Kanon's doubt.

"Shiba's analysis was perfect. I can't do any more than he can with my skills, at least, and I can't find any mistakes."

Isori and Kanon both fell silent in thought.

The second hand on the clock went around almost twice before there was another knock at the door.

Miyuki asked her brother with her eyes, and after getting a nod in return, went to greet the visitors.

She came back a moment later.

Behind her were their two classmates.

"Mizuki says you called her here..."

"Sorry for bringing you two out here."

He indirectly affirmed his sister's question and turned back to face his two upperclassmen.

"Allow me to introduce you. These are my classmates, Yoshida and Shibata. As I'm sure you know by now, these are Isori and Chiyoda, juniors."

After Mikihiko and Mizuki finished their nervous introductions and Isori and Kanon their frank ones, the five of them all seemed a little confused. Tatsuya gave them all a simple answer.

"I had these two come to unravel the mystery of our little underwater operative."

Of course, that wasn't enough explanation for anyone. Tatsuya knew that from the beginning, so he continued his explanation without skipping a beat.

"We're currently investigating the possibility that Watanabe was affected by an obstacle brought about by unfair magic from a third party."

That was the explanation Mikihiko and Mizuki needed. The former frowned, and the latter was clearly surprised.

"Just before Watanabe lost her balance, there was an unnatural dip in the surface of the water. It threw off the timing of her inertial dampening spell, which resulted in them crashing into the fence. It's almost certain that the dip in the water surface came from magical interference underwater."

Mizuki's surprise still hadn't left her face.

Mikihiko, though, after hearing Tatsuya's words, had a strong glint in his eye.

"It was undetected from outside the course, and it couldn't have been done from the waterway. It's also improbable that it was a delayed-activation spell. If it had been, Kobayakawa would have noticed it in the first race."

Modern magic had the concept of delayed activation like old magic did, but it required the magic sequence to be "recorded" on the target. The target would be altered as soon as the delayed-activation spell was applied, and that alteration would then activate the next spell after a delay.

"That means we need to consider that a spell was hidden under-water by something—at least, that's mine and Isori's opinion."

He looked at the two of them for verification, and both nodded to show their understanding.

"However, it's preposterous to think that a live magician was hidden underwater at the time. As far as we know at the moment, neither mod-ern magic nor old magic has a method to cloak yourself so perfectly."

This time, Isori and Kanon nodded at Tatsuya's words.

"That means it's only logical to think that **something nonhuman** was hidden inside the waterway using the spell."

Isori and Kanon exchanged glances, doubt coming over both their faces. It was a little while before a question came in return. "...Shiba, are you thinking it could have been SB magic?"

Tatsuya nodded at Isori's words.

Magicians who used modern magic always perceived spells because of their psionic waves. But SB, short for "spiritual being," also called spirit magic, was fundamentally made from pushions, not psions. The psions that could be observed at the same time were external additions to apply direction to their "movement"—for example, the commands to use the spirits in a certain way. That was the most prominent theory at the moment.

It wasn't that magicians were unable to sense pushions—it was that they normally couldn't distinguish their states like they could with psions. As an analogy, people can feel infrared rays as a vague concept of "warmth," but we can't perceive differences in infrared wavelengths through the lenses of color and tint as we can with visible light. Energized pushions were clearly "there" for a magician. However, it was difficult to sense pushions in a state of low energy. That meant magicians of modern magic found it difficult to ferret out purposely hidden SB. Magic to use spiritual beings: If this was a time-delayed technique due to spirit magic, then it was highly likely it would have slipped through the observing tournament staff.

"Yoshida specializes in spirit magic. In addition, Shibata has a particularly high sensitivity to pushion radiation."

"So that's why you had them come here." Isori nodded again, and Tatsuya turned to Mikihiko.

"Mikihiko, I want your opinion as an expert. Given the specific condition of, say, a few hours' delay, is it possible for spirit magic to be used for a delayed-activation spell that could cause the surface of the water to dip?"

"It's possible," Mikihiko answered immediately. "With that condition, the timing of the start of the second race would be the first activation condition, and the people approaching on the surface of the water would be the second. You could command water spirits to create a wave, or even make a whirlpool. And it's possible with *shikigami* as well, not only spirits."

"Would you be able to do it?"

"It would depend on the time I had. I wouldn't be able to do it on the spot, but give me around half a month to set it up and a way to sneak into the stadium a few times, and it would be possible."

"Would you need to sneak into the stadium the night before?"

"No. As long as I understood the ley lines and terrain, I can send spirits through ley lines. The prior investigation would be for that purpose. Oh, but…"

"?"

"If you go about it like that, the spell won't have any meaningful power. Spirits borrow their strength based on their user's strength of will. I'd think that if you set it up a few hours beforehand, the most you could do is surprise an intruder, like pretending to punch someone."

"Which means…?"

"You could mess with the surface of the water, but it wouldn't make a big enough wave to make Watanabe lose her balance. Without the Seventh High racer being on a collision course with her, it would have just been a childish prank."

For whatever reason, Tatsuya nodded slowly at his explanation. "If it was a simple accident, anyway."

"Huh?" The profound suggestion obviously made Mikihiko dubious, but Tatsuya didn't answer immediately; instead he turned to look at Mizuki.

"Mizuki, during Watanabe's accident, did you see any SB activity?"

"…I had my glasses on, so no… I'm sorry."

"No, that's fine. I was the one being careless at the time, so you don't need to apologize." Tatsuya bowed in apology to Mizuki, who had hung her head, and Miyuki started to soothe her. "Back to what I was saying…"

His eyes were directed toward Mikihiko, but Isori and Kanon both knew his words were being directed toward them as well.

"I don't believe the Seventh High racer losing control was a mere accident. Look at this."

Tatsuya brought Mikihiko before the display and replayed the simulated video from the beginning. Aware of Isori and Kanon peeking at it from the side, he stopped playback a little bit before the collision.

"Normally, right here, the Seventh High racer would need to

decelerate." He started playing it back frame by frame. "But as you can see, right here, she actually accelerated even more."

"…You're right. That is unnatural."

"I get it. No magician would be chosen to compete in the Nine School Competition if they would make such a silly mistake."

Nodding to Isori and Kanon's comments, Tatsuya returned playback to normal speed. "I think someone tampered with the Seventh High racer's CAD."

An air of surprise filled the room.

"This corner is the first place in the course you need to decelerate at. If her deceleration activation program was secretly switched with an acceleration one, there would be an accident for sure on this turn. If we look at the lap times from last year's finals matchup, one could easily predict that Watanabe and the Seventh High racer would round this corner nearly on top of each other. If I had wanted to mess them up, it would have seemed like a perfect chance to have two championship contenders out of the way."

"Your logic makes sense, but… Can CADs even be tampered with? And if someone did, then when?"

"Are you saying there's a traitor on Seventh High's tech staff?"

Tatsuya shook his head slightly at Isori's and Kanon's questions. "Unfortunately, I don't have any proof. Even if I told them to show me Seventh High's CAD, they'd kick me out, and I know that. But there was a chance for it to be tampered with."

"From a traitor, right?" Kanon's guess made Tatsuya once again shake his head, this time slowly.

"I can't deny the possibility entirely, but… I think there's a high probability a spy is in the tournament committee."

The conversation stopped dead.

Even Isori, Kanon, and Mikihiko were speechless this time. Each wore similar expressions of utter disbelief.

"…But, Tatsuya, if there was a spy in the tournament committee, when and how on earth would they have tampered with the CAD? The competition CADs should be safely stored away by each school."

But the option of doubting Tatsuya didn't exist for Miyuki. She took what her brother said as concrete fact and asked for further deductions.

Tatsuya's answer in reply wasn't a direct one, but a declaration of well-known facts. "CADs *always* leave the hands of the schools one time—when they're handed over to the tournament committee for inspection."

"Oh…!" exclaimed Miyuki at the possibility she'd forgotten about. She was the only one even able to get a voice out—Isori, Kanon, Mikihiko, and Mizuki were all just standing there dumbfounded.

"I don't understand how they did it, though. That's the real problem…"

It might have been the worst-case scenario, but they couldn't let their guards down. That fact was burned deeply into Tatsuya's mind, since Miyuki was waiting to play in her matches, and he was the one in charge of her CAD's adjustments.

◇ ◇ ◇

First High's third day of the competition saw them winning men's and women's Ice Pillars Break, taking second in men's Battle Board, and third in women's Battle Board.

Third High got second place in men's and women's Ice Pillars Break and won both men's and women's Battle Board. Because of their good results, their points were even closer to First High's than yesterday.

Before the tournament began, Mari had told Tatsuya the rookie competition points wouldn't affect the overall rankings very much, but it looked as though her prediction had been untrue.

Currently, Tatsuya was doing an elaborate check of the CADs his assigned competitors would be using to prepare for the rookie competition that started tomorrow. As he worked, he received a summons from Mayumi on his terminal.

He paused his work, confused as to why she was calling him out so late at night. When he took a walk down to First High's assigned meeting room, he unexpectedly ran into Miyuki in front of the door.

"Did the president call you here, too, Miyuki?"

"Yes—and you, too, I suppose?"

Tatsuya had assumed he'd been called down to discuss the possible sabotage he'd gone over with Isori and the others as well as to think of a technical countermeasure. Miyuki wouldn't need to be here as well in that case, though.

"Well, let's go in."

"Yes."

Sometimes you had to think about things, but other times thinking would do you no good. And if it was a case of the latter, you had to act. Like the ancients said: Poor ideas are worse than none at all.

"Excuse us."

It wasn't that dense a topic—and it wasn't as if much was riding on such profound logic. It did save him some pointless worrying, at least, as he opened the door.

Inside were Mayumi, Suzune, Katsuto...and Mari, who should have still been in bed.

"Good work today. Are you finished preparing for tomorrow?"

"No, it'll take a little longer."

"Oh... I'm sorry for calling even Tatsuya away from his work." Mayumi's apologetic words clued him in to the fact that Miyuki was the main topic here. "You can sit down if you want."

The siblings took their seats next to each other as Mayumi indicated.

"I had something I wanted to talk about... Well, no, I needed to talk about. I had you come here because I have something important to discuss with the two of you." It felt like a while had gone by since she last acted this formally to them, and it felt kind of refreshing to Tatsuya. "Rin, could you give them an explanation?"

She still called her Rin, though, thought Tatsuya as he looked at Suzune.

"I believe both of you know about today's results."

It was obviously rhetorical; she wasn't expecting an answer. Tatsuya and Miyuki both nodded at the same time anyway.

"We had an accident, but our points at the end of the day are mostly as we'd calculated. However, Third High has more points than we predicted, so they have more hope to pull ahead than we thought initially."

They nodded once again to demonstrate their understanding.

"Still, we have a decent lead, so as long as we can win the rookie competition and not let ourselves fall too far behind, we'll be able to win overall by winning Monolith Code at the end. But in the worst-case scenario, if Third High gets a solid lead on us in the rookie competition, there's a possibility of them turning the tables depending on their results in the main Mirage Bat event."

This was all supposition—was she just trying to tell them to do their best in the rookie competition? They wouldn't have needed to call them down just for that, though… Tatsuya cocked his head, still with a straight face.

"The main competition gives twice the points of the rookie one. I and the rest of the operations staff have arrived at the conclusion that we need to devote our strength to the main Mirage Bat event, even if that means sacrificing something during the rookie competition."

Tatsuya's eyebrows raised just a bit. He guessed what she was getting at by the "sacrificing" bit, and it made his straight face come undone.

"Yes, that's right, Tatsuya." Mayumi sharply picked up on his slight change in expression and answered his question before he asked it. "Miyuki, we're having you compete in the main Mirage Bat event as Mari's substitute. Tatsuya will continue to be your assigned engineer, so you will now be competing on the ninth day."

Contrary to their claim at the beginning, Mayumi wasn't trying to talk anything over with them. The decision had clearly already been made, and she was just informing them.

"However, there are students among the upperclassmen who are only entered into one event. Why would I be chosen to be a substitute when it means canceling my competing in the rookie competition?"

Miyuki's voice was calm. She wasn't ecstatic about her sudden selection; instead, she asked a question based in reasonable consideration and calm calculation.

After she asked, Mari seemed surprised, and even Katsuto seemed slightly taken aback.

"Because we estimate that way will result in more points." The answer came riding in on Suzune's even calmer voice. "We had no substitutes ready for Mirage Bat. That's the main reason."

Giving additional explanation was the original competitor, Mari. "Even students representing our school would find it unfair to be asked to fly around in the air in Mirage Bat without any advance preparation. People who have already practiced it beforehand would have a better chance than them, even if they were freshmen. Plus..."

She paused, probably on purpose. Tatsuya hadn't initially thought she was this prone to theatrics.

"Tatsuya, your sister could win first place even in the main competition, couldn't she?"

And then she came in with an attack at the weak point. Her reasoning felt sly, pushy even, but Tatsuya had no reason to be modest. "She could."

"Tatsuya..."

Tatsuya spoke as though it were obvious—as though it was already a proven fact. Mari smirked, Katsuto nodded once, Mayumi's eyes widened, Suzune's eyebrows went up, and Miyuki looked down, embarrassment evident on her face.

"If she has been valued so highly, then I'll do my best for her as an engineer. You can do it, right, Miyuki?"

"Y-yes!"

Her already beautiful back burst straight up as she responded to Tatsuya in a high-pitched, excited voice—and her answer said she would gladly take on the role as substitute.

To be continued

AFTERWORD

First, I want to thank all the gentlemen and gentleladies who bought this book. This is the first time in three months I'm writing to you... I'm sure there must be those of you who just saw this today, but that is what we call a cliché (or something like it), so I'd ask you to pardon me for not going down that road.

The Irregular at Magic High School now has three volumes on the shelves, safe and sound. Episodically, this is the first part of the second chapter. I have to apologize for ending things at such a tricky place again. Still, the beginning of the fourth volume will demarcate where the freshmen (in other words, the main characters) will start really getting into the thick of things.

Next up will be the second part of the second chapter. There will be no third chapter, so you can rest easy...though in place of that, it ended up being a fairly thick book. Dengeki Bunko may allow some pretty hefty tomes, but they obviously can't keep doing it every time, so I'll be prudent starting with the next volume—or I would be, but the tough part is that I can't say that for sure.

As those of you who consider the afterword to be read after the rest of the book, you'll know that this episode mainly focuses on the competition between the high schools.

They use fictional, magical competition to decide the victors, and magical skill to compete with each other.

However, the players' skill levels aren't the only important thing—the technical skills of the staff backing them up play a great part in whether they win or lose. It is perhaps closer to motor sports than ball games and track events in this respect. It doesn't have the same sort of floridity, the same showiness that MotoGP and F1 racing have, though.

…I know it's a little late, but I feel like I might have missed out on a good chance. Maybe I'll have the next Nine School Competition have a race-like setting to it. There could be sponsored goods and ___ queens and things like that. And then my editor might be able to put together an observation tour under the pretense of collecting data. (Maybe? Probably not.)

All jokes aside, this chapter of the story was inspired by the fourth entry in a world-popular series, as I'm sure some of you have already realized. Of course, in said world-popular series, they fought individually, whereas this one is in team format. And besides, the entire way magic works is completely different, so the matches and contests don't really bear the slightest resemblance to one another.

If there was one similar thing in terms of that world-popular series…it would actually be the Qui****ch part of the rest of the series rather than its fourth installment, but in reality, I worried about how to put together such fictional competitions.

——Well, I mean, maybe the author of said series didn't have much trouble *actually* creating Qui****ch, but I sure did have trouble. And I wasn't entirely satisfied with it, so I must be hitting my limit. Each individual event doesn't have very complicated rules (at least…I don't think so), so I'd like it if you sat back and watched the students of the magic high schools casually. The main characters will all be making a big ruckus in the magic events in the next volume, Nine School Competition Arc (2). Not only will they be in the stadiums, but the main character will also be putting on a full demonstration of his antihero powers outside the stadiums as well. I would appreciate it very much if you were to stay and watch how this "nonstandard work," with all its mixed reviews, progresses.

And now, I'd like to thank everyone involved in the making of this book once again.

Mr. M, thank you very much for all the accurate advice you've given. In particular, without your advice that group field trips always had baths involved, that scene, along with its color and monochrome illustrations, would never have been created.

Ms. Ishida and Mr. Stone, once again, I have to apologize for how many things I made you do. I can't express in words how grateful I am that you patiently bore with my hard-to-understand requests and delivered such fantastic illustrations. The heroine's melty face (in Mr. M's words) in particular brought out a surprising amount of her charm.

I'd also like to thank everyone else on the staff, starting with Ms. Suenaga, the color coordinator. It's because of all of you that another volume turned out this fantastic.

Above all, my greatest thanks goes to the readers who picked up this book. Thanks to your support, it seems you'll be able to gaze upon the next chapter of the story as well.

I look forward to meeting you again next month for *Nine School Competition Arc (2)*.

Tsutomu Sato